FULCRUM

SEASON ONE

J.J. VEGA

THE GIANT COFFEE BLUNDERBUSS

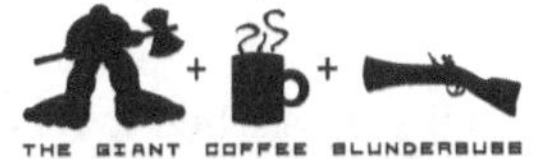

Fulcrum, J.J. Vega, The Giant Coffee Blunderbuss, the Fulcrum logo and The Giant Coffee Blunderbuss logo are trademarks of Prehensile Feathers, LLC.

ISBN 978-1-943474-03-5 (paperback)
ISBN 978-1-943474-04-2 (ebook)

Library of Congress Control Number 2022940981

Characters and events in this book are fictitious. Any similarity to real people, living or dead, is coincidental and not intended by the author.

Editing by Courtney Andersson, Elevation Editorial (elevationeditorial.com)
Cover illustration by Zoe Badini (zoebadini.artstation.com)
Book design by The Giant Coffee Blunderbuss

Published by The Giant Coffee Blunderbuss
1860 Sandy Plains Rd
Ste 204 #3030
Marietta, GA 30066
USA

Visit jjvega.com to find out about other stories by J.J. Vega

For the three other odds that keep me even:
Heather, Ender, and Zane.

Fulcrum: Season One

Contents

FULCRUM
SEASON ONE
J.J. VEGA
EPISODE ONE:
VIOLENT INTRODUCTIONS

Episode One: Violent Introductions

Contents

Welcome to Bule

"I'm gettin' too old for this shit."

That's Jack. He's fourteen years old.

Jack runs his fingers through his shaggy mop of hair as if doing so would somehow wipe away the growing sense of inevitability. It seems like every time something is about to happen, he gets a little tingling sensation in his scalp, like a colony of ants is tiptoeing around up there. The sensation radiates from the roots of a white streak that starts over his right eye. It could possibly be his imagination, but experience tells him otherwise. He's seen this story play out the exact same way too many times to second-guess his gut, or the skin on his head.

Those assholes on table five are about peaked. Cursing under his breath, he picks up another tumbler and wipes it dry. It's a constant chore keeping this place clean, but folks get really picky when it comes to the sanitation of their drinkware. They could be covered in dust and blood and chunks of who-knows-what, but if their glass has a spot on it—

"Zeke! Dry!" Jack tosses the tumbler up to the ceiling trusses, but keeps his focus locked on the trio of mercs, who appear to be as heavily armed as they are inebriated. It's only been a year since Jack took ownership of the bar, but he's been working at the place for nearly a decade. That's more than long enough to know when things are about to get really loud and really stupid, really quickly. And he knows those three sauced-up death merchants are going to be the catalyst.

The table is about as far away from Jack as it can be, but the drunken geniuses are loud enough that he can hear each angrily slurred word. So can everyone else.

"I said you're out!"

"That wasn't the deal! You can't cut me out. Me and mine got us that job."

"I won't hafta cut you out. Just cut—"

The single gunshot reverberates throughout the bar. Heads turn as the high-pitched ring drowns out the sound of a single merc at the table slumping over. For an instant, it's almost possible to see all the way through the gaping, bloody chasm in the dead man's back to the finger-sized entry point in his chest. His former compatriot sits in front of him holding the handgun, flat-faced and emotionless. He almost looks bored.

Jack starts doing the math on how much the repairs are going to cost. *About a gram of shock plus a couple liters of water to bleach away the blood stains.*

The third merc doesn't wait to have the gun turned on him. He launches to his feet and reaches up to grab the light fixture above the table. Tearing the light down, he uses it to trap the shooter's hand, then pulls his own pistol, but never gets the chance to use it. The shooter stands while stepping forward, flipping the little circular barroom table and freeing his hand. Both guns slide across the floor, out of reach.

One new light fixture. Need to reinforce the wiring harness. At least the table's still okay. As is his tendency, Jack makes up nicknames for the two mercs to use later when addressing them directly. The first one gets Shooter—obviously. The one that busted the light fixture is a bit tougher to come up with, but Jack finally decides his name is Improv.

They stand there, Shooter and Improv, hands poised over secondary weapons. Alcohol and adrenaline strain against the shackles of better judgment. Their eyes are locked on one another, attempting to anticipate whose spring will uncoil first, and whose will uncoil fastest.

Silent.

Tense.

It's as if the entire bar has just been pushed onto a landmine.

An inhuman scream pierces the silence. It comes from the ceiling trusses where Jack had thrown the tumbler, and a moment after the scream, that very same tumbler comes crashing down on the bar, shattering. It's a cue to chaos. Before the final shards of glass hit the bar and clink to the floor, the room transforms into a fighting pit.

The two mercs lunge. Shooter pulls a knife and holds it with a reverse grip. The blade extends back to his elbow. Improv opts for the spiked bat lying on the ground near the table. The knife and bat lock in a drunken stalemate, their masters exchanging hatred behind gritted teeth and coal-fired eyes. For a moment, Jack wonders about the nature of the deal that'd just gone south, but he has to put his curiosity aside as the other patrons of the bar get to their feet, too. They all pull back to a safe distance, but close enough to see the action. Bets are already being made on which merc will be left standing, and a circle of spectators forms around the two brawlers.

A couple more tables get flipped. At least two more broken glasses get added to Jack's tally.

The two break, but not cleanly. Improv lowers his bat, allowing him space to drop his elbow forward and smash it into Shooter's neck. Hard. Shooter spins from the blow, but completes the rotation and runs a mean cut across Improv's face. Dance-like, he ends on one knee and looks up, grinning.

Without waiting a beat longer, the fighters re-engage; the scent of their own blood accelerates each one's drive to drain the remaining five liters from the other.

One of these two isn't going to survive. One dead body is plenty, though. Corpse disposal is expensive, and it's not like there's a bulk discount. Jack has had enough.

A small pop echoes through the bar, followed by a percussive whir. Mid-attack, Shooter and Improv seem to lose their footing and are carried forward by their own inertia. They fall into each other, their weapons completely missing their intended targets. Then everything stops. Everything. The fighters appear to be caught in an awkward embrace, straining against their own muscles. The other bar patrons lock, frozen and motionless. It looks like a freeze frame from some kind of mercenary prom.

Arms and legs seize and shake, arguing with themselves in vain attempts to override the stasis. Eyes flit about in their sockets in alternating waves of confusion and panic as everyone comes to the realization that they no longer have control of their bodies.

Everyone, that is, except Jack.

Jack hops up on the bar and shouts up to the ceiling, "Really? Of all the times to drop a glass, you had to go an' drop it then?"

A responding scream comes from the trusswork, followed by an incomprehensible string of hoots and protesting chirps from the small capuchin monkey who swings down and lands on the bar. The majority of his body is covered in dark black fur, but from his shoulders up, his fur is solid white, like a bristly hood spray-painted over what ought to be his natural coloring.

Although the rest of him looks like any other monkey in his species, his eyes—more specifically, his pupils—are strikingly different. Instead of the circular shape common in primates, this monkey's pupils are slitted like those of a cat, but the sides of the pupils are ridged. They're like black, serrated blades against the golden amber of his irises.

After a quick scan of the bar, the capricious little four-fister grabs a shard of the broken tumbler with his tail and scrambles up around Jack's body until perched on his shoulder. The monkey swings his tail in front of Jack's face and points at the shard defiantly.

Jack examines the shard of glass. "One drop of water? That's your excuse? You got four hands and a grabby tail, Zeke! You put away glasses all the time. You're telling me that this one time, a single drop of water is all it takes to make you slip?"

Zeke answers with a barrage of chatter as he hops up and down, pointing at the rest of the broken glass on the bar. Insulted by the mere thought that he, of all the barbacks in the world, could be bested by just one unnoticed drop, he pounces on the bar and makes for a pyramid stack of recently cleaned tumblers.

Picking up the top glass, he spits on the side of it and points at the newly created wet spot. His eyes widen and brows push up melodramatically. His body language is clear: *Oh no! Look at this huuuuge drop of water! This glass is soooo slippery now!* Mockingly, he fakes losing his grip on the tumbler before very deliberately hurling it at the bar's wooden floor. A cacophony of shattered glass follows as Zeke punctuates his point by spitting on each of the pyramid tumblers before chucking them to the ground one at a time.

"Alright, alriiiiight. Maybe I gave a bad throw. I guess I was a bit distracted by those geniuses over on five." He stops and turns back to the room. "Speaking of … I'd almost forgotten."

Jack and Zeke turn their attention to the rest of the room where everyone else—still straining against themselves—are likely wondering why this kid and his marginally domesticated employee are still able to move freely. Jack raises the small remote control in his right hand.

"Subsonic paralyzers. Had an array of 'em installed beneath the floorboards three months ago after the last pack of drunken assholes wrecked my bar. You dicks have gotten the honor of being their first real test."

He'd tested them before, on himself. But this was the first use of the full array. He starts to pace back and forth on the bar top, enjoying the attention.

"It's totally sweet kit. Maybe you fringe-livin' mercs ain't come across anything like it before, though. Waves of sound—sounds you can't hear—confuse your brain to the point where it just locks your muscles 'til it can figure what the shit is going on. Exhausting as hell if you try to fight it."

Jack points to one of the needle-like kneaks inserted behind his left ear, exposed tip glowing a bright blue.

"This little guy filters out the sound for me. An' Zeke, his ear canals are too small for him to be affected at all." He plops himself on the edge of the bar and lets his feet dangle over the edge, relaxed-like. "What'd be really nice would be that instead of freezin' you up like this, I could get 'em to make you help clean up your mess. But Slim says they don't work that way. Anyhow, I'm gonna let this run a bit longer 'til I know you guys have either cooled off or you're too exhausted to do anything about being pissed off. So, let's get comfortable and—"

CRASH!

A reddish blur explodes through one of the walls and flies across the room, decimating the far end of the bar in a blast of wooden splinters and dust. That little section of the bar also happened to house the control console for this crowd control solution of Jack's. The previously frozen patrons of the bar collapse as their muscles finally relax.

Their repose doesn't last long, though.

Clearly they're not exhausted, and they most certainly haven't had enough time to cool off from the insult of being imprisoned in their own skin. All glares aim at the bar. Jack sits there, wide-eyed, as his screaming little monkey hides behind his back.

"Well, shit."

1.2

ENTER CORVA

The bar now consists of one part rubble and two parts fuck you. With the control unit for the subsonic paralyzers destroyed, the customers of Jack's bar are no longer restrained by the confusion of their own muscles. Now, they're reacquainting themselves with freedom of movement, and it appears that they're intent on exercising that freedom on Jack … violently.

Chairs are tossed aside and tables flip as the mob swarms the bar. The scene is an angry, heavily armed version of a pack of hungry three-year-olds descending on a lone cookie.

After the briefest of pauses in a shock-induced paralysis of their own, Jack and Zeke bolt in opposite directions. Zeke leaps back to the ceiling trusses and Jack rolls backward to the space behind the bar.

He lands on his knees and keeps low while searching underneath the bar top. Jack's goal is mounted right there: Plan B. That's what the old man had engraved on the stock of his double-barrel break-action shotgun. It's almost completely useless.

The barrel and firing mechanism are in perfect working order, but that's not much help without ammo. Filling shells takes time. The luxury of time isn't something Jack's had since the old man tapped out. However, that solid walnut stock is still a remarkably effective cudgel, especially if anyone attacking doesn't know how ineffective it is as a gun.

Crouched behind the bar, Jack pauses a beat and takes a breath. He closes his eyes and preps himself for what will likely be the shortest fight of his life, and probably the last. If he's lucky, maybe he'll get killed before they start tearing off his arms and legs as personal trophies.

He shakes the image from his mind and opens his eyes. *Those thoughts don't help no one.*

He looks down at the beat-up break-action shotgun in his lap, his index finger tapping the aged trigger guard. *Probably too late for bluffing.* Clinching Plan B's barrel like a club, Jack pops up from his stoop behind the bar and swings wildly, hoping for the off-chance that he'll hit one or more of his former customers as they attempt to climb over.

Whiff! Nothing.

Jack stands, perplexed. Moments ago he was absolutely sure that he was going to be literally torn apart and shown his own entrails by a vengeful mob of former customers. Now all of them—nearly a dozen capable and formidable mercenaries and fighters—lie strewn about the room like bloody, discarded laundry.

How long was I behind the bar?Couldn'ta been more than a few seconds. Jack scowls, confused by the carnage that's gifted him with a few more minutes of breathing time.

"Where is she?"

The low, grumbling voice is unsettling. It's as if the sputtering thuds of a heavy motorcycle engine had passed through a sausage grinder and got covered in tar. Jack blinks as he turns toward the voice. *Holy hell, this guy has a tiny head.*

Episode One: Violent Introductions

It's a strange thought for someone so close to being killed, but it can't be helped. The guy does have a tiny head—well, relative to the rest of him. Emerging through the detritus of the bar's newly created side entrance, this is quite possibly the largest merc to ever enter Jack's bar. Tall. Broad. And that weird thickness where you can't tell if it's muscle or fat. But despite the sheer mass of the guy, his head is strangely disproportionate, like an unshelled peanut stuck to the top of a combat-ready grapefruit.

And this guy—this peanut-domed merc—is most certainly combat-ready. His body features all manner of tune-ups and augmentations in addition to his personal arsenal of weaponry. Both his right arm and leg appear to have been bionically replaced, and he's got a chembraid woven throughout his left side, serving his body with an on-demand menu of steroids, hormones, and other "better living through chemistry" cocktails. Combine that with shoulder- and wrist-mounted cannons and blades, and Jack decides this is not someone he wants to screw around with. He's big, destructive, and worst of all, his gear probably makes him very fast despite his size.

Furthermore, the guy isn't alone. Three other mercs stalk the interior of the bar. They have more reasonable proportions, but appear no less formidable. In fact, based on where they're positioned, it's apparent that these three are the ones responsible for laying out everyone in the bar.

"Where?" Peanut repeats, impatience brimming.

"Where what?" Jack furrows his brow, genuinely confused.

"The girl. Where is she?"

Girl? Here? It's not that Jack's bar never has female patrons. Hell, nearly half of his customer base consists of women, but those grizzled messes aren't exactly the sort of ladies he'd call "girls;" he'd barely call them ladies. And as merc women, it's likely that anyone in their presence who happens to utter the word "girl" is going to get a knife through the neck. This is Bule. It's not exactly the kind of place where a girl—

Ohhhhh! Jack smiles at his sudden realization. He might not get killed today after all.

"You're in the wrong place to find a girl, sir. Maddy Shard's Red Light is on the lower side of town."

"You think you're funny?"

Oh damn. Wrong answer.

"Don't fuck with me, boy! I'm not looking for a lay, I want the bitch I just punched through the—"

The angry verbal assault on Jack's horribly wrong conclusion is interrupted by a bottle of bourbon smashing against the wall just behind Peanut, only just missing his tiny head.

Dammit, Zeke, you little jerk. Jack snaps a glare to his right. *You're gonna get us both killed.*

Only, that's not Zeke. He'd be smart enough to choose something cheaper to throw. Instead, standing among the rubble that used to be the far end of the bar, there's a woman—no, a girl; she can't be more than seventeen or eighteen years old. She's also quite a bit more attractive than the cows that typically china-shop his bar. A trickle of blood oozes from somewhere behind her hairline. Her hair itself is a dark, matted mess, knotted and choked into dreadlocks of sweat and dust with streaks of red running throughout. A tattered, dark red cloak is clasped about her neck. Its folds drape over her right shoulder and arm as she reaches for the wall, steadying herself.

For the briefest of seconds, Jack catches a flash in her eyes, like sparks from flint struck by an emerald. Though her body language says she's recovering from being knocked through a wall, her eyes betray that she's surveying the space and planning her next move.

There's barely enough time to process what happens next. She starts in a low sprint with her left hand over her hood's clasp, charging at the nearest of the three mercs in Peanut's crew, a muscle-bound thug with cybernetic eye replacements and a mean-looking rifle. In no time at all, she's up near his face, practically nose-to-nose. Her cloak flutters behind her, still catching up. Before the cloak loses momentum, she lowers her head and releases the cloak's clasp.

In that motion, the cloak's hood flips forward and over the merc's head, obscuring his vision as she escapes from underneath. Not stopping, she grabs the back of his head with one hand and pulls it forward into her other arm's elbow. There's a muffled crackle in the folds of the cloak. Something in the merc's face—probably one of his amped-up eyes—shatters under the hood. He slumps forward a bit, but there's no time to recover. The other side of his face meets the girl's knee. Likely unconscious, possibly worse, the merc flops to his back when she releases his head.

Her eyes flit down to a discarded knife. It looks like the blade Shooter was using before all this chaos started. Dropping to a crouch to pick up the weapon, she launches herself at the next merc. This one's a rough-looking woman with more scar tissue on her face and arms than skin. An array of organic hoses connect a fluid pouch in her back to couplings on her forearms.

Jack cringes. *This is going to get expensive.*

He's seen that kind of bio-rig tune-up before. Those couplings route to nozzles between the thumb and forefinger of each of the merc's hands. By flexing the muscle tissue grafted to the pouch in her back, she can pressurize the flammable fluid and direct it out of the nozzles embedded in her hands. With a flick of the strikers fused with her fingertips, this woman can instantly become a human flamethrower and lay waste to everything around her. A literal Hot Mess.

However, the fire-wielding merc never gets the chance. The brutal young girl is on Hot Mess in an instant, delivering a stiff shoulder-check. Hot Mess reels backward and the girl drops to a crouch. She spins with a leg extended, sweeping the fire merc's feet out from beneath her. Hot Mess falls and the girl stands up, raising her knife. The flamethrower merc gets a long gash through most of her left side, severing a large number of the organic hoses to her left arm.

Jack exhales, relieved that the fight with Hot Mess hasn't resulted in his bar going up in flames.

Not waiting to be put on the defensive, Peanut's third subordinate launches an attack of his own. This merc appears to be more lightly armed than his counterparts. He has a pair of pistols strapped to his back, but otherwise his only other weapons are a pair of batons, each roughly an arm's length long and as thick as a chair leg. They have a kind of shiny finish that makes them look out of place. High gloss isn't something a merc usually wants on their weapons. The merc comes in low, attempting to scissor the girl's legs with his batons. She avoids his attack with a light hop. Her descent, however, is anything but light. Instead of fully leaping clear, she stays within arm's-reach—in fact, exactly arm's reach—and drops her feet together on one of his wrists.

Blam! A small explosion erupts from where his baton hits the ground. The wooden floor is singed black.

Shit. That shiny finish on the batons isn't some fancy liquid veneer. It's a percussive gel. That stuff detonates with any kind of sharp force. The young ball of dreadlocked violence apparently already knows this from whatever fighting they did prior to entering the bar. She seizes the merc's free arm and swings it—and the baton he's still holding—to the ground near the still-recovering Hot Mess. The baton strikes the ground and the burst from the gel ignites the pool of fluid from her severed hoses.

FWOOM!

The explosion rips a hole to the bar's basement. Jack barely has enough time to duck back behind the bar and avoid the force of the blast.

Who the hell is this chick? What do they want with her? And why can't they do this shit somewhere besides my friggin' bar? Jack's mind spins with so many questions, it's difficult to tell if that's what's throwing off his equilibrium, or if it's the ringing in his ears from the blast.

He scrambles over the bar, Plan B still in hand, and stumbles over to the cavernous new hole in his floor. Holding his breath, he peeks over the edge to see the extent of the damage.

Crap. This is going to take forever to fix.

Jack raises his head from looking down the hole. Peanut and all three of his underlings lie around the perimeter, immobile, unconscious, possibly worse than that. Well, maybe "worse" isn't so bad in this case. Jack swivels around, still looking. *Where did she—*

The thought is cut short by a loud creak and a sudden crash as the flooring under Jack gives way, dropping him into the bar's basement.

1.3

Não Vão Me Pegar

Shoulda expected that.

Jack coughs up dust and does what the old man used to call the "quick check." Fingers, toes: yup, they still move. Arms, legs: nothing feels broken. Torso: he unbuttons his barkeep vest and lifts his shirt for inspection, patting his chest and abdomen; nothing sticking in or out of him that shouldn't be. Head: ears are still ringing, but there's no metallic taste in his mouth, so no concussion. And most importantly, pain: yeah … he kind of hurts all over. *Excellent! Still alive.*

Jack staggers to his feet, trying to sort out exactly where he's landed in the basement. It's not a particularly large space, but it's unevenly shaped. The basement was never really dug out in the traditional sense; a more apt description might be that the basement was created by building a bar over a hole in the ground. That hole in the ground—now reconstituted thanks to the fighting—stores the bar's inventory as well as the "business office," an old wooden desk with a floor lamp beside it. Behind the desk is a trapdoor that leads to the bar's sub-basement and Jack's living quarters.

As he regains his bearings, Jack hears it. A weak cough. It's coming from behind the desk. Peering through the streaks of light filtered by the dancing dust of the dry basement, he catches a glimpse of her foot before it slides out of view. Jack tightens his grip on Plan B and creeps toward the desk.

She laid out those three mercs like they weren'tanything.She'd rip off my face and wear it like a funny hat, no problem. He pokes his head around the desk, half ready to swing Plan B, half bracing for impact.

Nothing.

She's not there. No foot, no cough, no girl. Jack stands confused for a tic, but not much longer. He feels Plan B torn from his hand and deftly pulled across his neck in a single flowing move. A knee pushes hard into the small of his back. It takes everything in him to stay on his feet and keep the gun from crushing his throat entirely. Breathing in this position is like trying to snorkel using a drinking straw up your nose.

"Não vão me pegar. Não vão me pegar."

She mumbles the phrase, repeating it to the point that Jack can't tell if she's saying it to him or to herself. He tries to squeeze out a response, a question, a yelp, anything. But it's not happening. Plan B gets pulled tighter across his neck as the girl drags him to the back wall. He can't tell if she trips, loses balance, or just gets bored with standing, but they end up collapsing against the wall.

The girl's grip loosens before the fall, allowing Jack to land without flattening his windpipe. He pushes the old shotgun away and rolls to his side, coughing again.

Holy hell, this is getting old. If I wanted to cough like this, I'd smoke more.

Rubbing his neck, Jack looks back at the girl, slouched against the basement wall with her eyes half-open and lips silently moving to the same mantra she'd been repeating. He does the quick check for her.

Fingers, toes: she doesn't make noise or any other indication of pain when he bends them. Besides, she had a pretty good grip on Plan B when it was wrapped around his neck.

Arms, legs: she's got some weird metal bracers covering half her forearms, but aside from that and a few harmless-looking scratches, she seems fine. It doesn't look like anything's broken.

Torso: lifting her shirt, he cracks a wide, closed-mouth grin to himself. He stops abruptly when his mind flashes back to mere moments ago. This girl almost killed him, and she may very well have been unconscious for the whole thing. He releases the shirt as if it's on fire and averts his eyes. *Torso's fine.*

He moves on to check her head. Aside from the cut that she had coming into the bar, there doesn't seem to be any further damage there. Tough to check for a concussion, though.

Jack looks up to the hole between the basement and the main floor of his bar. He holds his breath, listening for any sign of movement up there. Seems quiet.

"Hey! You tasting copper?" Jack keeps his voice low. He doesn't want to instigate further violence from her, and he certainly doesn't want to call attention to their location in case anyone up in the bar survived the blast.

"Hey! Who are you?"

The girl's eyes flutter open briefly. These are not the intense, focused eyes of green fire she had when she was handing those mercs their own asses just moments ago. These eyes whisper fear. Quiet, trapped, disoriented fear.

"Hey! Hey. What's your name?"

"C-Corva."

The girl, Corva, closes her eyes and passes out completely, sliding farther down the wall.

Jack gently lowers her head to the ground so she lies flat. He stands and looks around. This isn't exactly the best place for her to take a nap. It's pretty exposed. Moving her is a risky call though, for both of them—but mostly for Jack. Some kind of restraints would be nice, but well, beggars, choosers, blah blah blah.

As quietly as he can, he grabs some of the smaller crates in his basement and arranges them around her. It's not much, but it should be enough to keep her hidden for now.

Straightening up, he looks toward the charred and splintered edges of the hole in his basement's ceiling—his bar's floor. It looks like the teeth on some traders who stumble their way into town. Not the slick schmoozy type that try to sell you a sack of sand by telling you it's "one hundred percent pure, unrefined glass." No, the really nomadic type. The ones that don't come in from the empty lands except for a few times a year. The ones with no interest in trading for dental work. They're just crazy enough to make that trade for the sack of sand and then figure out how to turn it into a window.

Jack turns his attention back to his own appearance: a little tear in his sleeve, a couple scratches in his skin. Dust, grime, and ash everywhere. He rubs his hands over his face. No permanent marks there as far as he can tell. That's a plus. Quietly as he can, he slaps the dust and ash off his clothes. Even as gentle as he's doing it, though, there's still a lot. He has to hold his breath while it settles to avoid inhaling it and going into a third fit of hacking. He waits a second and then takes a quick test breath. Air's still dusty, but not enough to make him cough.

Satisfied that he can breathe again, he rolls up his sleeves to cover the tear and smooths out the rest of his shirt as best as he can, tucking the ends back into his pants. He pulls his vest straight and re-buttons it down the front. A gift from the old man. The fabric's tough enough to resist stabs and slices, though maybe not so great against fast-moving projectiles. It's not much for protection, but it's better than nothing. At least he's got a few of his fixins in the pockets. Besides, the vest makes him look distinguished. Picking up Plan B, he makes his way over to the stairs that lead back up to the main floor.

Alright, Corva. Time to see what you're worth to these guys. It better be enough to fix my damn bar.

SURVEYING THE SCENE

Climbing the stairs back to the bar, Jack repeats to himself the advice the old man had given him.

"Go slow, Jack. Ya gotta hold off on sayin' whatcha really think. Focus on the deal. Negotiations are all about gettin' them to do what you want while thinkin' it's their idea. These days, ever'thing's negotiable. Just gotta figure the right terms."

Of course, the first thing he's got to do is make sure Peanut or one of his crew is alive. It's kind of tough to strike a deal with a corpse, especially a merc corpse. They're usually booby-trapped.

According to Slim, Bule's resident tech, mercs are sold on the booby traps as being a last attack measure, but it's primarily a means of thwarting would-be looters. To hear Slim say it, any self-respecting techsmith would take the necessary steps to prevent their gear—especially biosync weapons—from getting lifted off a body and resold in the secondaries. Not doing so is an indictment of one's professionalism and, more importantly, a potential lost sale.

Jack thinks about all the off-hours he spent in Slim's lab, chatting his ear off about gear and ideas for new kinds of kit to make. What he wouldn't give to be doing that right now. At least Slim doesn't have a pack of drunken mercs try to wreck his place of business every other week.

He reaches the top of the stairs and notices a flicker from the ceiling trusswork. *Good, Zeke is still in one piece.* The little monkey peeks his head out from behind one of the ceiling beams and looks down in Jack's direction. It's a bit dark up there, but there's still enough mid-afternoon light filtering in to make out the look of concern on Zeke's face. Jack reaches up and touches a short, red kneak among those clustered behind his left ear to record a whispered message.

"I'm alright. You stay put. Keep hidden."

When he releases the kneak, the recorded message is packaged and broadcast at an ultrasonic frequency Zeke can hear, but most people can't.

Jack remembers how he'd laughed in Slim's face when he got the kneak—it came for free as part of a bundle deal when he got the subsonic paralyzers. He smirks a bit when he remembers what he'd said. "What a lo-fi piece of crap! Anyone with a freq-extender is gonna hear that plain as day. Why would I ever put that in my 'trix?"

Of course, the port matrix behind his ear had plenty of space and Jack thinks kneaks just look damn cool, so it wasn't much of an argument. Even still, Slim had offered to install a matrix on Zeke so messages could be encrypted and transmitted digitally, but Zeke was … resistant to the idea. It took Jack a week to convince the monkey to come back within arm's length of him. In any case, low-end tech or blinky decoration, none of that matters when you want to send a message across the room to a monkey. Jack makes a mental note that if he gets through this, he'll have to apologize to Slim for this one time when the damn thing actually came in handy.

Keeping low, he edges up the last few steps to take a quick survey of the damage by peeking around the banister at the top of the stairwell. Well, he attempts a quick survey. There's a lot of damage. With the view blocked from jutting floorboards and splintered tables, it's difficult to tell which body parts are still attached to people. On the far side of the crater in the floor, charred timber still glows a dark red near the meaty splat that used to be Hot Mess. Jack winces. *Name was more accurate than I thought it'd be.*

The pungent scent of burned hair and melting sinew doesn't help, either. The odor clots the air, choking the breathable chunks into tolerable pockets where it just smells like someone has lit a meat smoker without first checking if there's a cat sleeping in there. Everywhere else in the bar, the smell is more like you've set your own upper lip on fire using gasoline and dog shit.

It's not quite the worst that the bar has ever seen, but it's close. And if Jack doesn't sort out some kind of arrangement with these mercs, it could get worse. His stomach tightens just thinking about the time and bartering it's going to take to rebuild. And Harris is for-sure going to use this as an excuse to try and take the bar away from him again.

Jack's mind starts to spin with what-ifs. What if he can't pay for repairs? What if he can? Who's he going to owe? What if he does lose the bar? Where would he live? Would he have to go back into service? He'd gotten lucky—really, dodged-a-bullet lucky—when the old man picked him. Can't count on that again. His mouth fills with the sick, watery bubble of spit that forecasts a fifty percent chance of vomit. He takes a seat a few steps from the top and lays Plan B across his lap. *Gotta let the sick wear off.*

Face buried between his own knees, he takes a deep breath. *That shit smell sure ain't helpin' anything.* He exhales slowly, trying to will the bile in his stomach to stay in its rightful place.

Jack's "please don't throw up" meditation is interrupted by the sound of mechanical scraping and whispered orders. He turns to look back up to the roof support and touches his Zeke-kneak. "How many?"

He can't see Zeke's face anymore, but the little monkey's paw sticks out from the main beam. Two fingers extend and wave in Jack's general direction. Jack faces forward and looks at Plan B. Hopefully at least one of the two is on Peanut's crew. It's not Hot Mess, that's for sure. There's a chance it's one of the customers from before all this started, but not likely. Doesn't matter. Without ammo, Plan B is going to be pretty useless, whatever the case may be.

He hears the hiss of more whispered orders and that scraping sound again. It sounds like one of them might be trapped. *That's promising.*

Jack slides Plan B off his lap and carefully props it against the stairwell wall. He pats the surface of his vest, feeling the shape of the contents in each pocket. He might have more he can barter with than just that girl. Hell, these are well-financed mercs. Maybe he can turn them into customers of his other business.

Of course, that doesn't mean he shouldn't have some kind of defense. Rolling to his stomach, he crawls up the stairwell and peeks around the top banister again. This time he's looking for something much more specific. He needs a gun, one that works. Just a plain, cheap ass gun. Nothing with anything special on it, nothing that would warrant a biometric lock or a booby trap of any sort. Should be pretty easy. Most of the mercs that come through Bule aren't in the same high-priced class as Peanut and his team.

It takes him a second, but he spots exactly what he's looking for. There's a semi-automatic rifle nestled under part of an arm. It's not more than two meters away. There's not much cover there, though.

Alright. Different tack. Give some, get some.

NEGOTIATION

Jack straightens to his full height, roughly chest-level on most folks that come into the bar, and walks up the remaining steps, exuding as much confidence as he can muster. The whispering and scraping stops, but he can already see the two people who'd been making the noise. Peanut is trapped under one of the large metal beams that used to brace part of the roof. Apparently the explosion shook that one loose.

Normally, such a little bit of roof construction wouldn't be a problem for someone with all of Peanut's gear. His rig gives him enough strength to throw that beam clear into the canyon. However, it's not the beam's weight that's causing the problem. It looks like it's punched right through his cybernetic leg and gotten itself all twisted as a result of his struggling.

The guy who's trying to get Peanut unpinned isn't much help, either. It's that last merc that the girl, Corva, attacked. Except, he's missing his batons. In fact, he's missing an entire arm. It must have been disintegrated in the explosion. A light haze of smoke still steams from the guy's left side where the heat of the blast appears to have instantly cauterized the wound.

All told, Jack figures One Side—that's Jack's new name for him—isn't doing so bad. He's alive and moving despite the unimaginable pain he must be feeling. Of course, being freshly injured and an arm short, One Side is having one hell of a time trying to get Peanut free.

"Whatchu lookin' at, boy?" Peanut's fantastic disposition doesn't seem to have suffered at all.

Jack takes a deep breath and steps forward. If he squats now, that rifle would be right within arm's reach. "It—"

He pauses to clear his throat and will his back-flipping stomach into some semblance of calm.

"It, um, looks like you could use a bit of help." Jack swallows hard and tests a smile. *Just enough to look friendly. Don't be a smarmy dick.*

"Yeah?" Technically, it's a question, but Peanut delivers it like an accusation. Jack doesn't take offense. He knows he's small. Jerks with this attitude come through the bar all the time.

"Yeah. I got some kit that can get you untangled from them pieces of my roof, no problem."

Peanut raises an eyebrow on his tiny little head and motions One Side to stop pulling at the fallen truss. "Oh? What've you got, kid?"

"Well—" Jack pulls at the collar of his vest and reaches for an interior pocket. The moment he moves, he instantly regrets it. *Shit. Too fast. Looks like you're reaching for a weapon. Dumbass.*

He sees Peanut's expression harden and One Side reaches for one of the pistols still strapped to his back. He's a little fumbly and slow, but once he gets a bead on Jack, his aim is rock steady.

Jack immediately pulls his hands back and raises them over his head. "Whoa! Whoa! We're still bein' friendly here, guys."

Slowly, he unbuttons his vest with one hand and pulls open the left side to reveal the inside. Keeping his other hand raised, he gestures, pointing with his nose. "This pocket. I just need to get somethin' outta it."

Peanut's eyes narrow, but it's not the hardened look from seconds ago. More suspicious. Curious, even. "Go ahead."

Jack doesn't move quite yet. He points his nose over to the pistol that's still trained on him. "You think you can get One Side over there to lower his piece? I'm just tryin' to help here."

The tiny-domed merc erupts in laughter. The bass in his voice jostles something uncomfortably in Jack's stomach. He keeps his friendly smile, though, and holds back his urge to retch as Peanut finishes laughing. "One Side? Great name, kid."

Jack doesn't lower his hand. He just shrugs, trying to look relaxed—well, as relaxed as anyone can look while in a killer's sights. "Barkeep habit. Lotta folks who come in here don't like volunteerin' their names. Gotta call you somethin'."

"Oh yeah? What's your name for me?"

Jack smiles bigger to try and buy time. *Shit. He had to ask.*

He tries to cycle through names that would work, names that fit without being either insulting or patronizing. *Microdome? Wallpuncher? Mech Merc? Carlos? He could be a Carlos.* None of them work. Peanut is Peanut as far as he's concerned. Even if the tiny-headed merc gives his real name, Jack's going to have a hard time using it out loud. *Fuck it. He's stuck anyway.*

Clearing his throat, he looks the deep-voiced merc in the eyes. "P-Peanut. That's your name."

The look of confused disappointment on Peanut's face is priceless. It's like he just realized there's a foul smell in the room, and that he's the source of it. "Peanut? That's the best you've got?"

Try to keep it conversational, Jack. Don't let 'em ask where the name comes from. He rolls his shoulder a bit; his arm is getting a little tired of holding his vest open this whole time. "Hey man, these things are quick an' temporary for me. Just a tool to keep track of folks. Ain't like I announce 'em every time someone walks through my door. Or my wall."

"Well maybe you oughtta put a little more thought in it before you let a name slip out. Or lie with a name that doesn't suck."

"Yeah. I'll keep that in mind." Jack tilts his head back at One Side. "So you think he can put that down? My arm's getting sore like this."

Peanut waits a beat, almost like he's pleased at Jack's discomfort and wants it to last a bit longer. Finally, he turns his attention to One Side. "Lower it, Wheps. The kid's not hiding a cannon in there."

Slowly, reluctantly, One Side—Wheps—lowers his gun. Jack allows himself to exhale and lower his arms. It's like just having the sights on him put a weight on his chest and now it's lifted, but not entirely. Wheps doesn't re-holster the pistol or put it down quite yet. He just holds on to it, tapping the barrel on the side of his leg. Jack resists the urge to glance over at the rifle near him and reassures himself it's still there on the ground, ready when he is.

Peanut looks back at Jack. "Tretch."

There's a moment where Jack just stands there, awkwardly staring at Peanut, trying to figure out what he means and failing. "What?"

"That's what you call me now. Tretch."

"Tretch?" The name tastes weird as he says it, like the guy just slapped together a bunch of tough-sounding sounds and decided to pass it off as a name. "That's your name?"

"It's better than Peanut."

If you say so. Jack narrowly avoids blurting his thoughts aloud. "So, Tretch, you wanna keep talkin' names or you want some help getting unstuck from that bit of my roof?"

"Yeah, kid, what've you got in that fancy vest of yours?"

Jack pulls his vest back open and stops to cast a glance over at Wheps. "I'm just reachin' in the pocket, yeah?"

The one-armed merc doesn't say anything, just keeps tapping the barrel of his gun against the outside of his leg.

Assured that he probably won't get shot just this moment, Jack fishes around in his vest's inside pocket. The pocket's not deep, but all the same, it takes him a second to find what he's looking for. It's a little metal cylinder, about as long as his hand and roughly the thickness of his thumb.

He pulls it out with a bit of a flourish and proceeds to unscrew the top. "As a waypoint, Bule's a bit remote, but that does get us some benefits. We get some of the more exotic merchants comin' through here. I got these from a guy trying to roll his way down-canyon. Was sayin' somethin' about pickin' through some of the abandoned mines down there."

The top of the cylinder releases with a pop and Jack pours its contents into the palm of his hand. He catches himself staring at the three irregularly-shaped beads, kind of a bluish violet color. Each has a lighter violet core that moves and undulates randomly, like little pulsing galaxies dancing within the interior of the stone-like beads.

He looks up and catches the tail end of Tretch's facial expression. Who knew a person's eyes could get so big in such a tiny head? Jack grins, snorting and just barely keeping himself from bursting into laughter. The noise is enough to snap the half-mechanical merc back to his more typical resting bitch face.

Shit. Gotta recover. Jack puts on a bit of his sales voice and answers the question before it's asked. "That's right. You're lookin' at imbued tech right here. Each of these little beads is a hollow resin casing printed way up in the bones of Old Cago. And on the inside of each—"

"Not interested." Tretch stares at Jack, right in his eyes. But it's not like he's trying to mean-mug Jack; it's more like he's actively trying to avoid looking at the beads in Jack's hand. It's alright, though. Jack is ready for this.

"Look, I know you might be a little—" He pauses, hunting for the right word. *Can't tell a hardened merc that he's scared or nervous. It's a crapshoot tryin' to figure if these are the type with egos that can't take a scuff to their candy coating.* However, the right word isn't coming.

"You're damn right I'm scared. That shit's no joke."

Well. That solves that.

"Look, kid, you can just put those things away right now. Got no interest in soulmancy."

"Naw, man. You're in a remote part of the world. We only see a raid here every other year or so. Soulmancy? Please. Always thought that was a dumb name. 'Round here, we just call 'em fixins." That's a bit of a half-truth. Jack is really the only one who calls them "fixins." And while these imbued beads did come from a crazed traveling mine-jumper, most of Jacks beads are ones he made himself.

For a half a beat or so, Jack thinks he sees Tretch raise an eyebrow in interest. *Just enough of an opening. I can totally close this.*

But for now, the deep-voiced merc still has his hard front on. "Drop the sell, kid. You do your dealin' on someone else."

"Alright, I know you're concerned. And anywhere else in the world, I would be too. Sensors are really good at tracking anyone doin' any kinda soul fixin. But you're in Bule, a small burg cut into a canyon wall." Jack extends his arm, presenting the beads like a gift. "An' although the fixins imbued in just one of these is more than enough to get you loose, the amount is so small and we're so far out, none of them sensors will ever know you used 'em."

This time, Tretch doesn't hide his raised eyebrow of interest. He casts a glance over at Wheps, who looks like he's been good to go for this ever since Jack popped the top on the cylinder. The one-armed merc even holstered his gun in its place on his back.

Tretch isn't quite ready to be reeled in, but the hook is nearly set. Jack resists smiling. Of course, it's all bullshit. Bule's last raid was just a couple months ago and sensors from either side in the war can totally sniff out even the smallest amount of imbued tech. But for one of these beads, there'll probably only be a small crew coming to town. By the time they get in, Jack will have had this deal set, his bar will be mostly fixed, and this merc and his one-armed buddy will be long gone.

The big merc with the tiny head starts to speak, offering the last little bits of resistance. Jack doesn't let him get it out, though.

"Lemme guess, the contract on your current gig says you can use all the augmentation you want, just no fixins—soulmancy. Right? No worries there either. This stuff dilutes out in twenty-four hours, longer than the travel time to the nearest other outpost or town. An' I know 'cause I tried it and tested it myself. There used to be four beads."

More bullshit. There did used to be four beads, but Jack's got no idea how long this stuff stays in the body. He used that bead a different way. Doesn't matter, though. The hook is set. Tretch is all in.

"What do you want for it?"

Jack doesn't hide his smile this time. "Twenty-five percent."

"Fuck you."

"Oh come on, man! Look at what you've done to my friggin' bar!" Jack realizes he's starting to get a little loose with his tongue. *Slow down.* He uprights one of the few chairs that hadn't been completely destroyed and eases into it. The nausea never really got the chance to subside. He takes a peek at the abandoned rifle, still slightly hidden on the ground next to him. Still within reach. That said, yakking on these guys' boots isn't going to do much good for his bargaining power.

Pausing a beat, he starts over. "Look, the girl's a bounty, right? Means you're getting' paid. And paid enough to staff a pretty badass four-deep crew. Well, one and three-quarters deep, now."

Jack nods in the direction of Wheps.

"Seems to me that I'm the one with the kit to get you out and I'm also the only one here who can deliver her to you. Since you're responsible for the damages to my bar, it's only right that some of your payday gets pointed my direction. Hell, you pay me right now, an' I'll give you a discount. No need to give me the full share of one of your dead. I'll just take twenty percent. The other five points can go to fix ol' One Side's one-handed clapping problem."

"Kid, you outta your damned mind?" Tretch squints at the pint-sized barkeep and slams his fist on the ground next to him. It's enough to make Jack's stomach lurch dangerously. Tretch's voice is a growl. "There's no deal. I could tear you apart in an instant."

"Not with that busted-ass rig of yours." Jack points at the mangled chaos of cybernetic parts dangling from Tretch's right side.

Tretch straightens his back and leans toward Jack. "Wanna find out for sure? Don't try me, boy. There is no deal. There's no choice. Just two steps: you hand over the girl and I *think* about not killing you for being annoying. That's all there is." Tretch's thick voice shows no indication of weakness, no hint that he's affected at all by his compromised state. In fact, the very sound of his voice has the same effect as a gut check on Jack's not-entirely-stable digestive system.

"Where's your leverage, ya shrunken-headed doof?" Jack is now far afield of the old man's advice he'd repeated to himself earlier. "You're having a hard time just sittin' there. Even with this imbued tech, it's gonna be trouble for you to move at all when you're out, let alone secure a prisoner like her for delivery to—"

He pauses at the realization that he's got no details on the actual bounty. But it gives him an idea. A bad one. It might be enough to push the negotiation his way, though. He leans back in his chair, casual-like. "Where would you take her? Can't be but so far. You know, I've got half a mind to cut out the middleman and just deliver her myself. Then I'll put the whole payday in my pocket. Who's the buyer? Actually, know what?"

He slips the imbued beads back into the metal cylinder and screws the top back on. "Don't you worry yourself over it. I'm sure I can find out myself in the trades."

"You little shit! I've been chasing this collar for damn near a month. Like hell I'm gonna let you steal it from me."

Jack stuffs the cylinder back into his inner vest pocket. "Hey, fair's fair. Either we deal and you stumble away happy, or we don't deal and I go on a road trip and come back to my bar very happy. 'Course, that last one is much more bothersome for me. So if it's all the same to you, I'll just take the twenty."

"Boy, you are dense. You have no idea what you're getting into here, do you? You don't even know the buyer, and you think you're just gonna mosey your way in and get paid? Ha! You haven't even asked who she is. You wanna know who's on the buy? Fine—"

"No deal." The voice floats into the conversation, barely strong enough to interrupt. Corva steps up the last stair from the basement and glowers at the three of them. Defiance fills her eyes despite the weakness in her stance.

No More Words

Aww crap. How the hell'd she get up so quickly? Jack gawks at Corva's arrival. From the corner of his eye, he can see Wheps struggling to pull his gun back out. The last thing Jack needs is for this discussion to split three separate ways. *Gotta get a lid on this 'fore I end up with no leverage at all.*

Snap decision made, Jack drops to a knee in front of his chair and snags the orphaned rifle. In one smooth motion, he raises the barrel, levels it at Wheps' head, exhales, and squeezes the trigger.

Pop!

The half-armless merc crumples like an unstrung marionette. A pink mist puffs out the back of his skull. Jack twists to aim at Tretch and whistles up to the ceiling.

Having already sorted out what Jack's up to, Zeke bounds from the ceiling holding an empty whiskey bottle by its neck. He breaks the back of the bottle as he lands on a ledge near Corva and points the remaining spires of shattered glass at her throat.

"Alright, now you have a pretty easy choice, I'd say." Jack's rifle is unwavering as he speaks. "I just bumped your margins even higher. My little twenty percent is barely a dent in your overall take. How's the deal sound now?" Jack tips his head back toward Zeke and Corva. "Girl's here. I still got the beads to get you loose. How about we make with the trade and be done? I'll even comp you a drink. There's gotta be at least one bottle that ain't busted yet."

Silence crawls by. Jack feels the rifle's weight load his arms and mind as the adrenaline subsides. He's never gotten used to seeing people get shot in the head. Stabbed, sure. Burned, no problem. Even a mean bludgeoning barely bumps the needle. But a good, clean headshot can mess with Jack for hours. It's the immediacy and invisibility of it all—way too much like witnessing someone receive the Touch. Of course, it's been some seven or eight years since the last report that the Touch was used, but it's hard to shake the image of someone's soul being forcibly ripped from them. It's even harder when, like Jack, you've seen it happen to a whole town.

"You've got a lotta sand, kid, I'll give ya that." The heavy thump of Tretch's voice shocks Jack to the present. "In other circumstances, I might be willing to take you up on your offer. Especially after all this hassle."

He tips his head over at Wheps and the smudge that was Hot Mess.

"But you've got two problems. One: this girl's worth way too much to me. You can't have twenty percent of what I'm gettin'. And two: I told you that this was never a negotiation. It was research. Needed to know the girl's location."

Tretch nods at Corva. "Hi there." He returns his attention to Jack. "That was easier than expected. And I also needed time."

"Time?" A dozen worst-case scenarios play out in Jack's mind. The barrel of his rifle dips down a bit. "Time for what?"

Tretch sneers and strains his neck to look back toward the wall through which he'd entered the bar. The act briefly exposes the base of his left ear. There's a green blinking light.

Corva takes a step forward, pressing her neck against Zeke's broken bottle. "Seu idiota! He's got a beacon kneak. You didn't check him when you started?"

"I was outnumbered!" Jack's hollow retort drops to a mumble as he kicks himself for not seeing it sooner. "'Sides, with a dome that bitty, you hardly see his ears at all."

Tretch glares at Jack. "Outnumbered is right. The second string just clocked in."

No sooner does Tretch finish his sentence than two teams of mercs storm into the bar—one through Tretch's wall entrance and the other through the main doors at the front. Backing up toward Zeke and Corva, Jack does a quick headcount—two teams, each three deep. And each of these mercs are more heavily armed and mean-looking than Tretch's first crew. *This is the second string? What the hell kinda bounty pays for backup like this?*

"How many rounds do you have left in that thing?" Corva's question is assertive, but carries with it a tone that indicates it probably won't matter anyway.

Jack winces and glances past her to Zeke. The little monkey reads the look in his eyes and lowers the whiskey bottle, dropping his head.

Corva's eyes widen in disbelief. "What? You didn't check that, either?"

"Yeah, girlie—Corva, was it? You're pretty much screwed." With that, Jack unshoulders the rifle and places it on the ground in front of him. He takes a step back with his hands raised and looks toward Tretch.

"So, how about that drink, big guy?"

A Little Social Lubrication

With his hands still raised, Jack scans across the new set of faces in his bar. Game faces. Hard faces. Not a soft or sympathetic line among them. Their jaws are set, their eyes cold. Focused. Stone sober. Professional.

Looking at their weapons and tune-ups, he does a quick tally. *Three close combat, two mid-range. One sniper. Balanced crew. Good call pullin' the snipe inside. Too tight outside to cover the exit.* He remembers the hole in the wall behind Tretch. *Both exits.*

Of course, mercs like this blow through town all the time and they all come to the bar at some point. They just tend to be more relaxed, less sober, and have a lot less "let's hurt Jack" in their eyes. This is the second time he's seen mercs with that look today. Hell, it's the second time in an hour. That must be some kind of record.

Jack turns back to Tretch, still stuck under the trusswork from the roof.

"For what it's worth, I kinda get now why twenty percent was a bit on the high side for you." He feels his stomach gurgle as he puts on a fresh smile. "But hey, bygones. Right? Nothing that can't be settled over a couple bottles of my special house cornshine. Can't get anything like it anywhere else."

Tretch shakes his head. "Kid, nomad traders don't even have this many hustles going."

"What? Naw man. I'm just trying to make things comfortable for everyone." Jack tilts his head back to address Corva. He can't see her or Zeke, but Jack's pretty sure they haven't moved since no one's shot at them yet. "Even for you. Let's see if we can't strike a deal where everyone lives." He looks around the carnage of weapons, barroom furniture, bodies, and body parts in his bar. "Everyone left, that is."

Oh yeah, and there's that giant gaping hole in the floor. Jack tries to block out his thoughts about the time and cost of repairing the place. First priority has to be on living long enough to even get that far. As Jack thinks, Corva still doesn't reply. Of course, why would she? She's been fighting these bounty mercs for who knows how long and here he is trying to sell her out for the cost of some trusswork and a whole mess of bleach.

It's no fun to be sold into someone else's keep. It wasn't for Jack. That's even knowing how lucky he was to be bought by an old man looking for a barhand in a remote canyon town. A bar's a shitty place to spend ten years growing up, but it's not as bad as most get, and this girl Corva sure isn't going to get any kind of fair treatment from these goons or whoever they're tasked with delivering her to. Maybe he can get her out of this. However, first he's got to get everyone to a table with glasses in their hands instead of guns and whatever other kinds of weapons they've got. Like the old man used to say, "Nothing lubricates a negotiation like a cuppa shine."

Arms still up, Jack cranes his neck a little farther back to address his own barhand. "Hey Zeke, you think you could check the shelves up by the ceiling? See if any bottles of the good cornshine ain't busted. I dunno 'bout glasses, but our guests look like they might be straight-from-the-bottle types. So maybe it's not a big deal."

He returns his attention to Tretch. "Your crew alright with sharing? Not sure we'll have enough bottles to—"

His voice trails off one slow word at a time as he starts to register the look on Tretch's face—on all the mercs' faces, actually. Their looks have gotten harder, more focused, and they're not paying Jack any attention at all. All eyes and guns are trained on the space behind him.

Forgetting to keep his hands up, Jack spins around. "Zeke, what the world is goin'—Oh. Oh damn."

Out Swinging

It doesn't look like much. In other contexts, it would be easy to assume that this was the start of some kind of bizarre street show. Both Zeke and Corva have their heads tilted down, eyes closed. Corva is squatting, matching Zeke's natural pose of sitting on his haunches. The air around them is electric. It's nothing anyone can see, no lights or flashes or anything ridiculous like that. But Jack can feel it. The hairs on his arms and the back of his neck stand straight out. And from the looks on their faces, everyone in Tretch's second string crew is feeling the same thing.

Slowly, Corva and Zeke rise from the squat to fully stand. It's particularly strange in Zeke's case because he's not up on his hind legs in his normal monkey way; his stance is more human-like, almost denying his own anatomy. Jack watches as Zeke rubs his thumb along the neck of the broken whiskey bottle still in his hand. Although her hands are empty, Corva's thumb makes the same movement. Reflexively, Jack slides one foot back. His body already knows that it doesn't want to be here.

Her eyes snap open. Zeke's do, too, but he drops back to his haunches, bottle just barely dangling in his hand, his face slack and confused. Corva's face is the exact opposite. That emerald fire is back. And she's grinning. It's not a "happy to be here" grin. It's scarier; one of those full-toothed smiles that has a personality of its own. Angry. Hateful. Malicious. This smile exists in its own right and her face merely transports it around.

The pit of Jack's stomach turns in on itself. For the first time today, it's got nothing to do with damage to the bar. *Don't do it, girlie. It's a bad call.*

He stares at her, trying to get the words across without saying them. If she attacks this crew, she's done for. Strangely, it doesn't seem like she cares. He's not sure she even notices him at all. He keeps his mouth shut, but he can't help but lecture her in his mind. *It don't matter how well you fought before. This is seven to one.* He catches sight of Tretch in the corner of his eye, trying to move. Trying to get unstuck. *Alright, six-and-a-half to one.* He turns his attention back to Corva.

For a fraction of a second, their eyes connect.

It's a strange experience, knowing you're *not* going to die. It's even stranger when, by all rights, you know you should probably be the first to go. This is exactly the feeling that Jack gets in that mere blink of a moment. It's hard to describe this level of assurance. It's unreal. *Maybe I did get a concussion when falling into the basement. Maybe this is all a hallucination and I'm really lying on the ground, bleeding out. Or maybe it's just that this girl's particular flavor of crazy is contagious.* Whatever it is, he knows for a fact that she isn't in any danger. And as long as he stays out of the way, neither is he.

For the mercs in Tretch's crew, the forecast is quite different.

The broken whiskey bottle slips out of Zeke's hand and drops to the ground. Before it lands, however, Corva catches it on the tip of her toe. It doesn't break or shatter, and it doesn't cut her. She moves with such precision and control, the bottle may as well be a juggling ball or kicking sack. It just balances there for a second before she flicks her ankle.

The bottle flips up and Jack can see past the spired shards of the broken end all the way through its mouth to her eye. She's already turning sideways, lifting her arm. She thrusts it out and her palm slams into the mouth of the bottle. It launches by Jack's head and across the room, a bullet with jagged glass teeth. The bottle plunges into the sniper's neck. The poor bastard never even gets a chance to raise his weapon. Blood sprays out, instantly filling the top of the bottle. The sniper collapses as his life drains into the glass funnel. It pulses out the bottle's mouth like he's a freshly tapped cask.

Jack notices that the remaining mercs' attention is now up in the ceiling. Corva's up there now. Somehow, while Jack was staring at the blood fountain that used to be a sniper, Corva must have jumped or climbed up to the ceiling trusswork. The two mid-range mercs open fire on the ceiling with their rifles while the other three pelt the roof with handgun fire.

Not a single shot hits her.

It's not like she's actively dodging them or anything. Jack's not sure if she's just that fast or there's some trick going on. She's moving unhindered, almost relaxed. It's just that she's simply not anywhere those bullets are. He's only ever seen Zeke move that comfortably up there.

Shit. Zeke!

Jack looks at the little monkey, still sitting on the end of the bar. His face holds a bewildered look. It's the same kind of look a person has when downing a glass of vodka they expected to be water. Now's not the time for Jack to worry about the emotional state of his furry employee. He bolts for the stairs leading to the basement, sweeping Zeke into his arms as he passes the bar.

He realizes too late that he's running too fast to turn down the stairs with any control. The best he can do is twist a bit at the waist and run his shoulder into the wall to change direction. The stone wall is completely unforgiving. Jack bounces off it like the steel ball in one of those vintage pinball machines. His foot slides off the edge of the top step and he drops like a rock, landing hard on his side. Pain shoots from his elbow and hip as they strike the top few steps.

Jack groans. *That sucked.* He can still move, though. Jack looks down and sees his friend still safely tucked under his arm. There's still that look of confusion, but there's no blood, bruising, or broken limbs. So at least there's that.

The gunfire stops and there's a crashing sound back in the bar area. Jack worms his way back up the stairs and peeks around the banister. One of the mid-range mercs has been thrown across the room, right into Tretch. The force was enough to get the peanut-headed merc free, but his whole cybernetic side is really busted. He can barely stand. The merc that was thrown into him isn't doing much better. He's covered in blood and his arms flop around in a particularly interesting and unnatural way, like a pair of old socks caught in a mild breeze.

Jack cranes his neck to get a better view of the front of the room. Not happening. He's just too short. He turns to head down the stairs. *Gotta put Zeke somewhere safe.* He doesn't get more than a step or two before he feels a tug on his vest.

He looks down into Zeke's strange, lizardy eyes. They don't look confused anymore, just tired. Jack takes another step down, but the monkey shakes his head. He doesn't want to go downstairs.

"What? You want to go back up there?"

Zeke nods in response.

"The fuck do you think we're gonna be able to do up there?" It's a futile question. Not just because Zeke can't speak back to him, but also because he already knows the answer. "That girl? Pretty sure she's doin' alright on her own."

Jack watches as Zeke's eyes narrow into the little monkey's best version of a scowl.

"You're gonna make life miserable for me if we do make it outta this an' we don't help, ain'tcha?"

A nod.

"Alright." Jack readjusts Zeke under his arm and heads back up the stairs. "But if we die, I'm blaming you."

He gets to the top step and feels another tug at his vest. Looking down, he sees Zeke pointing at Plan B, still propped against the wall where he'd left it.

"That? What am I going to do with—"

Before he finishes, Zeke pats Jack's vest, right where the cylinder with the imbued beads is tucked in his inner pocket.

"For serious? The old man said they ain't to be used 'cept the most dire times."

At this, Zeke sits up and tilts his head, skeptically raising an eyebrow.

"What?"

The little monkey clambers up to Jack's shoulder and uses his paws to turn Jack's head. If the wall blocking the stairwell from the bar area weren't there, Jack would be looking right around where Tretch had been stuck.

"That bit with Peanut? I was bluffing! 'Sides, I wouldn't be the one using it then." Smirking, he turns his head to look at Zeke. "But I'm glad you don't need to be carried anymore."

Zeke responds by slapping Jack in the back of the head. But there's a lightness there, a friendly touch—well, as friendly as a slap to the head can be. He wraps his tail around Jack's neck and takes a firm grip while Jack reaches over and picks up Plan B.

Ammo-less shotgun in hand, Jack takes another peek around the banister at the top of the step. Judging from the shouting and periodic bursts of gunfire, the fight is still on. Although there's no chance he can see what Corva's doing from here, he can at least check on Tretch and the merc with the broken floppy sock arms.

They're not there. At least, they're not where Jack last saw them. He does a second scan of the room to make sure they're not hiding or sneaking up on him. *Nope. Still clear. So they're either—*

A scream interrupts Jack's thoughts. Half a second later, he sees the floppy-armed merc—Boneless Joe—sail over the bar and smash into the assorted liquor bottles lined against the wall.

Jack curses under his breath. Granted, it's not a huge threat to his inventory. Most of the bottles were empty. But they're also pretty rare. Vintage pieces from before the war. The old man used to say that having them on display brought some class and history to the place. Jack had figured they'd be worth something if a collector came through the bar, so he'd kept them visible for that. Of course, that's not going to do him any good now.

Jack watches Boneless Joe try to push himself up, and fail. It doesn't matter how many on-demand amps and painkillers his chembraid must be giving him. His arms can't hold his weight. The merc twists himself to a seated position with his back against the wall and rubs his face on his knee, wiping the mix of sweat and blood from his eyes. He looks at each of his arms, lying limp and useless at his sides.

Jack holds in a snort. *What the fuck is he debatin'? He gonna think his arms into workin' again?*

Whatever he's thinking, Boneless Joe's eyes narrow with renewed resolve. He turns his head and bites into his right shoulder. It must hurt something awful; Jack can hear the merc's muffled screaming over the chaos on the other side of the bar. But Boneless Joe doesn't let go. He sinks his teeth deep into his own shoulder until blood leaks from the corners of his mouth. He jerks his head back, tearing away a small chunk of flesh.

The shattered-arm merc spits out the little bit of his shoulder and leans forward to his knee. Using his teeth, he opens a small pocket near his knee and fishes something out of it. When Boneless Joe sits straight again, Jack can finally see what the merc was after. Held between his teeth is a little glass ball. A bluish glow from the tiny pellet lights the merc's face.

Oh man. We're fucked.

Boneless Joe takes three quick breaths, like he's bracing himself to get punched in the face. Then he bites down.

Although his mouth is closed, the glow from there gets brighter as he continues chewing and crushing the pellet. Light blue tendrils lash out from his jawline, an angry, tentacled beard of light. Boneless Joe works quickly. He tilts his head to his right shoulder and spits the crushed ball into his gaping bite wound.

The glowing tendrils follow, hungrily depositing themselves into the gully of still-bleeding flesh. They retract like a spider backing into a hole. Boneless Joe's head snaps back and he screams like he's being torn in half. The veins along the entire length of his right arm get that same glow. His arm hardens and re-forms. It's no longer the loose linkage of flesh around shattered bones. It looks and works like an arm again, a freakish glowing arm double the size it ought to be.

Tretch, you tiny-skulled liar. "Got no interest in soulmancy." Yeah. Sure looks like it.

Boneless Joe swivels his head and points his eyes toward Jack. One of those eyes has changed. It's all white and glazed over. There's no pupil. Somehow, though, Jack knows the merc can see through that eye just as well as the other. Worse, Jack gets the impression that Boneless Joe knows he's been watched the whole time.

Jack ducks down, tries to hide below the top step. Immediately, he regrets it. *You know you're busted, dumbass. No use tryin' to hide. Stand back up.*

He can't make himself move, though. This merc has his own imbued tech. Beads he's brought with him. And those things are on a whole different level from the fixins Jack's made before. Way higher than the dinky little booster beads in his pocket.

The beads!

He fumbles his way to his vest pocket, slapping around to feel where that metal cylinder shifted to. But it's not there. Jack panics. Those beads might be piddly nothings, but they're the best things he's got. He feels his heart pounding in his throat as he scans the steps around him. Maybe he dropped it. Maybe—

There's a slap to the back of his head. Zeke. The little monkey leans around to face Jack and presents the small metal cylinder where Jack can see it.

"You pick-pockety sunnuvabitch." Jack smirks, taking the cylinder. "Glad one of us is thinkin' ahead."

He pops up to peek over the step. Boneless Joe isn't there anymore. *Where did—*

Jack snaps his head back and scans the ceiling. Zeke's apparently not the only one that goes up there now. Fortunately, it's all clear. No beast-armed Boneless Joe swinging from the trusswork, ready to drop down and pound Jack's head through his own chest. Of course, *not* seeing Boneless Joe up there is almost worse. He could be anywhere now.

Jack spins to look down the stairs, caught in his own paranoia. No one there, either. He lets out an unsteady breath. The air rattles and bounces out of his lungs like it's lost. He tries to swallow, but it just feels like trying to eat a mouthful of gravel.

The racket of the fight with Corva still fills up the front of the bar. Boneless Joe must have gone back into it, as the fight is going a lot longer than expected. Corva fought like a badass earlier, but the numbers are much more against her now. Plus, she's already survived an explosion, fallen through his floor, and was punched through a wall. She should be dead, or at least way easier for them to capture. Then again, someone sent ten mercs on a bounty for this girl. "Easy" doesn't seem like it was ever part of the deal.

Jack wonders if she's using any imbued tech, or if any of the other mercs have it. Doesn't matter, really. Even if Boneless Joe's the only one, there's not going to be much of the place left to rebuild if there's too much more of this fight.

He glances over at Zeke, still on his shoulder, patient and annoyed. Jack takes a deep breath. He squeezes Plan B in one hand and the metal cylinder of beads in the other. *Let's do this thing.*

Keeping low, he sprints across the short gap between the bar and the stairs. He slides to a stop not far from where Boneless Joe had been sitting. Broken glass is everywhere. Squatting, he faces the underside of the bar. It's a bit dirty, but still mostly organized and intact. His eyes land on a pair of backpacks nestled in an open compartment. Gitfo packs. The old man used to say it's the gear you need when the only option left is to get the fuck out.

Not yet. Can't go anywhere if I'm dead. 'Sides, maybe it's not so bad.

A gun goes off, two shots. One bullet ricochets off the back wall and up into the ceiling. The other punches a hole through the bar, missing Jack by no more than a hand width. It smacks into the rock wall behind him. A small explosion of dirt and newly formed pebbles sprinkles Jack's back.

He allows himself to exhale, reminding himself that it was a stray bullet. It wasn't aimed at him. Still, it left a pretty big honking hole. Just a little bit to the right and there'd be a matching crater in his own chest. He shakes the thought from his mind and leans over to look through.

"Fuuuuuuck me."

1.9

MISFIRE

It's chaos. The bar is a wreck. Broken tables and chairs. Broken bodies. Orphaned weapons. Spent shell casings. Blood pools around collapsed bodies, mixing with alcohol from shattered glasses. Corva is taking on three mercs at once. It's Boneless Joe and two of the remaining close-range mercs. They can't touch her. It doesn't matter if it's a fist, a knife, or a bullet. They simply don't connect. She's not where they are. And she's enjoying it.

She spins and ducks, jumps and dodges. All the while, she grabs broken chair legs, knives, pieces of glass, even a disembodied foot—anything she can improvise as a weapon. She uses them and discards them as easily as she picks them up. And she's fast. Man, is she fast. Especially her arms. There's something like an afterimage of each arm as it moves. Jack can't so much see her arms as much as catch glimpses of where they were.

Thing is, she's not really connecting with any of the three mercs herself. It's difficult for Jack to tell if she's wearing down or if she's just toying with them. As fast as she is, she *should* be having more of an impact on them. That smile of hers is disorienting.

He shuffles to the side a bit. *Need to see who else is around.*

None of the other mercs seem to be in or near the fight and there's no sign of Tretch. Of course, the hole doesn't give Jack the best view of the room. His head drops. He's going to have to prairie dog his head above the bar to get a better view. It's not like the bar itself is offering much in the way of protection, but there's definitely a certain advantage in the fact that no one knows he's there. Well, no one except for maybe Boneless Joe.

Jack pauses. Maybe there's another way.

He turns and looks over at Zeke. "Say, you don't think you could—"

The monkey doesn't even turn his head to acknowledge Jack. He doesn't let the question finish, either. His tail covers Jack's mouth as he just stares forward and delivers another slap to the back of Jack's head.

Jack sighs and pulls Zeke's tail from over his mouth. "Figured not." Keeping an eye on the action through the hole in his bar, he rests Plan B's barrel on his shoulder, then raises the metal cylinder to eye level. "But I ain't pokin' my head up there without bein' armed."

Jack reaches into the inner breast pocket of his vest and pulls out a small rectangular case. It's got his last cigarette for the day. He rolled it in the morning so he wouldn't have to think about it come closing time. Of course, the case also has additional rolling papers in it for those days when one smoke isn't enough. He puts the case on the floor in front of him. At the same time, he hands the metal cylinder up to Zeke.

He takes Plan B off his shoulder and cracks open the break-action shotgun. With Plan B balanced on his knee, he pops open his smoke case and slips out one of the spare papers. He reaches up with his free hand. No words need to be said. Zeke gives the cylinder back to Jack. The top is already off. "Thanks, Zeke."

Jack pours one of the beads into the center of his rolling paper. He hands the cylinder back to Zeke and starts wrapping the paper around the bead, forming it into a more evenly round shape. He jams the wrapped bead in one of Plan B's twin barrels and checks to make sure it's a snug fit. The last thing he needs is to have a bead slide out right when he needs it.

Quickly, he pulls another rolling paper and goes through the process of wrapping a second bead for the other barrel.

With the beads loaded, Jack snaps Plan B shut. *This better friggin' work.* The last time they tried this, the results were, well, unimpressive.

He closes his smoke case and takes the cylinder back from Zeke. Stuffing them back in his vest, he takes another peek through the bullet hole. Now it's two to one. The third merc that had been in the fight lies crumpled on the floor. A splattery mix of blood and hair decorates a fresh head-sized crater in the wall above the body. Now it's just Corva against Boneless Joe and one other merc, a mean bitch with a face tattoo and a chembraid. Strike that, it's two chembraids, each bound to one side of her body. Of course, as much as Jack likes chembraids, it's the face tattoo that holds his attention the most. Half her face is painted to look like a skull. *That must've hurt something awful.*

There's a popping sound from the rear of the room, out of view from Jack's improvised peephole. *One more still in the fight. Tretch?*

The projectile shot at Corva is much larger than a bullet. It's like a bola, but with a fine metal cable connecting the two weights. She catches the middle of the cable and the weights spin around her arm, clanking against her forearm bracer. They must be a lot heavier than they look, because her arm drops like a rock, dragging her down to one knee.

She struggles against the weight; her wrist is pinned to the ground. However, she can't focus on that for long. Boneless Joe and Facepaint are already on top of her. Facepaint goes to work with kicks to Corva's midsection. Boneless Joe starts dropping down his oversized arm like a hammer.

But the fight isn't out of this girl yet. A mule kick sends Boneless Joe flying. He crashes through a table at the front of the room. Facepaint gets her legs swept out from under her. She lands hard on her back. Air rushes from her lungs and Jack can see Facepaint making that same fish face everyone makes when the wind gets knocked out of them.

Corva's back on her feet. With great effort, she's managed to use her free arm to help lift her weighted arm from the ground. The wire from the bola slides down her bracer and digs into her skin. The weights knock against each other as she steps over to Facepaint.

She doesn't pause, doesn't hesitate, doesn't even take a breath. She just rolls her hand into a fist and lets that weighted arm drop right into the merc's tattooed head. There's a meaty crunching sound, like dropping a sack of rocks on a melon. Facepaint's legs kick up in an uncontrolled, flailing last twitch.

Corva stands back up. She uses her knee to push away the crushed mess that used to be Facepaint's head. Blood drips from her face and arms. And that smile. It's still there, bigger even, like she's constantly on the verge of laughing. She pauses a beat to look at the back of the room.

Jack tries to get a better angle of the back from his squat behind the bar, but it's no good. He can't see anything. Can't tell if she's staring someone else down or just looking. She turns her head and looks at the bar. At Jack.

1.10

FIRE

"Shit!" Jack jumps back, slamming the back of his head unto the underside of the bar. Immediately, he clamps one hand over his own mouth to hold in a scream. The other hand shoots up to the back of his head and tries to rub the sting away. *She saw me. Saw us. How'd—*

He pauses, suddenly realizing that Zeke is no longer on his shoulder. If he had been, he would've hit the bottom of the bar even harder than Jack's head did. But he isn't there. He must have jumped clear before she turned their way. Jack scans the area behind the bar and finally spots the little monkey curled in a ball, trembling by the gitfo packs.

Jack frowns, adjusting his grip on Plan B. *Ain't like him to be more spooked than me.*

He chances another look through the hole in his bar. Sure, everyone might know he's there, but that's no reason to give up the little protection he's got.

She's not even looking at him anymore. Her attention is at the front of the room, on Boneless Joe. The big-armed merc is still dragging himself out of the pieces of broken table. There's a broken piece of something—a chair leg?—sticking all the way through one side of his abdomen. He probably shouldn't be able to move at all. He stumbles forward, almost falling, but catches himself. The palm of his monstrous right arm slaps the floor and supports the bulk of his weight in a kind of modified three-point stance. His smaller, normal-sized arm flops at his side, completely useless.

There's a thudding crack as Corva gets the metal bola unwrapped from her arm. The weighted balls settle on the floor, resting in the cracked dent made when they fell. She rubs her wrist; her face still holds that hungry grin.

There's another pop from the back of the room. This time, though, she's not fast enough. A new bola flies in. Its wire connects with the back of her neck and the weights spin around, choking off her air flow. She immediately drops to her knees, pulled down from the weight. Her face turns red as she claws at the thin wire wrapped around her throat. There's almost no sound, just a few week croaking noises as she tries to squeeze air into her lungs.

Jack relaxes and turns around, putting his back to the scene. He lays Plan B across his lap. He's just got to wait now. No use trying to negotiate for anything. Best to just let them collect their bounty and get out of town. He shakes his head, thinking about the carnage on the other side of the bar. Fixing this mess is going to be stupidly expensive. And these mercs clearly have no interest in compensating him for his trouble. He turns his head to give those gitfo packs a good long look.

Instead of seeing the packs, however, he just sees Zeke. The little monkey is right up in his face. He's frowning, serious, way different from the trembling ball of fur from mere moments ago. He pushes Plan B toward Jack.

"What? You want me to stick my neck out *now*?" Jack hisses the words, trying to keep his voice low.

Zeke pushes the shotgun again, nodding his head toward the other side of the bar. His hands go up to his neck, mimicking Corva's struggle for air.

"Help her? You outta your damned mind? She's the whole reason the bar—our bar—is a wreck. The old man would never—"

Jack's head is turned sideways by a smack to his face.

He snaps his head back and stares hard into Zeke's eyes. Zeke holds steady and glares right back. Jack's shoulders drop. He knows he's lost.

"Alright. You're right. The old man would stick his neck out." He opens his mouth and works his jaw from side to side. "Fuckin' hell, Zeke. One of these days I'm gonna figure out how something your size hits so hard."

Jack sighs, taking hold of Plan B. "I loaded it. May as well use it. 'Course, there's no guarantee that this'll shoot right at all. Don't blame me if nothing works."

Zeke eyes soften and he puts his paw on Jack's chest. It's a reassuring gesture. Not helpful at all, but it's reassuring all the same.

"You're welcome." Jack smiles as Zeke nods and then climbs up to his perch on Jack's shoulder.

One more deep breath, and Jack springs to his feet, spinning to face the room. Plan B's stock is nestled against his shoulder, ready. He has to move fast; Corva's not going to last long with that wire on her throat.

He's got no idea who's at the back of the room, so he swings the barrel around, landing his sights on Boneless Joe. *Known quantities first.* The words echo in his mind. It's one of the many little catchy expressions the old man would repeat to Jack. With a quick exhale, he pulls the trigger.

Click.

That's the only sound that comes from Plan B. Nothing else. No boom, no burst of energy, no kick. Nothing.

Jack sees Boneless Joe's face over the shotgun's sight, grinning, knowing. Jack's shoulders drop. "Son of a—"

56

Fizzle and Pop

Nothing happens. Granted, he's never tried to shoot Plan B with an imbued bead as ammo. Maybe he just has to wait a second for it to work.

Maybe he loaded the bead in too far and the firing pin couldn't reach it. Maybe he used too much rolling paper and that stopped the bead from getting ruptured. Maybe Plan B works fine and the bead is a dud. Or maybe—

Maybe nothing. It doesn't matter at this point. Jack feels Zeke shift uneasily on his shoulder. It doesn't matter that Plan B was supposed to erupt with a shot of energy. It didn't happen, and it's not going to happen.

Besides, there's not really any time to wait or check. Boneless Joe turns and stares at Jack along the sight of the old shotgun. He apparently heard the empty click, too.

Boneless Joe punches his massive, imbued beast fist into the ground and squares his shoulders to face Jack. At this point, that arm is nearly the same size as the rest of Boneless Joe's body. The veins in his arm pulse with a subtle blue glow. His other arm, still shattered, still useless, swings as he shifts his weight. If it hurts, the merc doesn't show any evidence of it affecting him.

What is it with these crazy mercs and smiling while they fight?

Jack thinks he hears Boneless Joe growling at him. However, there's another sound that's got more of his attention. The wheezing and gasping from Corva has gotten slower. Weaker. Jack risks a glance over at her. She's leaning forward, still clawing at the fine cable wrapped around her neck. The weights from the bola hang between her and the ground. If he doesn't act soon, this whole valiant effort is going to be for nothing.

Stupid girl. If she'd just lie down, it'd take off the pressure from those weights. But Jack knows that's not going to happen. This girl, Corva, nearly choked him out while she was barely conscious. She isn't the type to willingly lie down for anyone. His neck is still sore.

Jack returns his gaze down Plan B's barrel. Boneless Joe is still staring back, face now completely serious. He lowers his weight, ready to launch.

It's now or never. Jack swings Plan B around and puts Corva in his sight. He uses his thumb to shove over the barrel selector and takes a deep breath. *This better work.*

The experience after squeezing Plan B's trigger is very different this time. There's no empty click. In fact, there doesn't seem to be any sound at all. The shot comes from the barrel almost instantaneously. It slams into Corva broadside, a glowing blue fist of light. Her body slides across the floor and doesn't stop until it collides with the wall. The weights of the bola come to a rest on the ground next to her.

All of Plan B feels like it's vibrating in Jack's hands. Or are his hands just shaking? And shouldn't his ears be ringing or something? The silence from the shot seems like it's still going on. *Am I deaf?*

Imbued tech always has side effects, especially when used in a way outside of the original design. Jack wonders if this silence is the side effect of these beads. Definitely something he should've thought to test when he made them. Of course, how would he know he'd be trying to direct the energy of these things out the barrel of a shotgun?

They're supposed to be strength enhancers, and not even good ones. Either way, he'll need to record this in his logs and talk it over with Lyia … if he survives.

Jack feels Zeke climb on top of his head and leap back up to the ceiling trusswork. His hearing might be shot, but at least he can still feel. Well, except for perhaps his other shoulder—the one Zeke wasn't on, the one securing Plan B's butt—that shoulder is completely numb. On the upside, half of his hand on that same arm is tingling, like he's been sitting on it for hours and just now pulled it free. So at least there's that. A tingling feeling is better than no feeling.

Still, Zeke just ran away. That's not helpful. Granted, shooting Corva probably wasn't exactly what the little monkey meant when he suggested that Jack help her. Jack looks up to the ceiling, but it's tough to see anything among the twisted knot of shadows. *Probably escaped out the ceiling hatch. Coward monkey.*

He lets Plan B's butt slip from his shoulder as he brings his view back to Boneless Joe. The gun is pretty useless now. Besides, there's no telling what kind of damage his makeshift imbued ammo has inflicted on the barrel and firing assembly. It's likely he'll have more reliability with wads of paper and a drinking straw.

Jack can feel himself talking. Can't actually hear the words he's saying, though. Hopefully, it should sound something like, "There. She's dead. Now you've got no reason to be here."

Judging from the confused look on Boneless Joe's face, it hasn't come out like that at all. There is a response, though. Jack can hear it. Sort of. It's just not from Boneless Joe. The beast-armed merc turns to the back of the room. The sound is kind of like listening to a conversation underwater. But from the way the deep sound rattles Jack's gut, there's no mistaking the speaker.

It's Tretch. And he's pissed.

The words start clearing up a bit as Jack follows Boneless Joe's gaze. Tretch is standing just a meter or two away from where he'd been stuck under that ceiling truss. His gear is still busted all to hell. *How'd he get there? I just looked back that way a few seconds ago. He wasn't there. No way he can move that fast. Can he?*

Jack puts the thought aside and tries to concentrate on interpreting the garbled noise that he's hearing come from Tretch's mouth. It's a pretty hopeless endeavor. On the upside, it looks like the tiny-headed merc leader isn't actually addressing Jack. He's ranting at Boneless Joe.

It's like he doesn't even care that Jack's there.

The rumbling from Tretch's voice stops, and there's a moment of silence. No, not silence. Jack sees that Boneless Joe is responding just as emphatically. His voice just doesn't have the same stomach-churning weight as Tretch's.

Then, all of the sound comes rushing back in. It's a sharp contrast with the near total deafness from moments ago. Jack winces as Boneless Joe's voice thunders in his ears.

"… should be thanking me! Bitch woulda killed us all!"

"The contract had two hard stips: a live collar and no soulmancy. You've gone and fucked up on both of them."

"Hey, I didn't shoot her. The kid did that!"

The two mercs each swivel to face Jack. *Oh hell.*

He should be saying something right now. Some kind of rebuttal. Some string of words that convinces these two that they no longer have any interest in being here. He doesn't have any of that. He's just got a busted shotgun and an uneasy stomach. Nervous droplets of sweat sprout at his hairline.

All those hours and years of instruction from the old man have left him here, frozen, on the verge of puking like a sick cat. *What would the right words be for this situation, old man?*

Tretch takes a step toward Jack. The wreckage of his cybernetic parts drags along with him. He doesn't seem to notice. "You just earned yourself a giant debt, boy."

Jack stares back at Tretch. Any leverage he had at the start of all of this is now completely spent. Corva's down, maybe dead. Plan B's busted. Any other working weapon is well out of reach. Zeke's up hiding in the ceiling somewhere, or gone altogether.

Episode One: Violent Introductions

All in all, Jack realizes that he's painted himself into a pretty shitty corner. His mind fills with words, all of them exactly wrong. Everything he wants to say will just put him in a deeper hole. Even worse, he can feel himself caring less and less how deep that hole gets.

"Hey! You listening? You're going to spend the rest of your life as my bitch, paying me back for this."

Fuck it. The wrong words are better than none at all. Jack tilts his head and looks back at Tretch. He gives himself a smile. Why not? Everyone else was doing it. "Aw … did the big ol' bounty hunter pay all his dead merc buddies in advance? Genius move there, bud. Dumbass."

The look on Tretch's face is priceless. He was obviously expecting a completely different kind of response from Jack. But there's something else in his expression, something just below the surface of his hard veneer. Could it be?

"Oh shit! You did, didn't you? You *did* pay all these corpses in advance!" Jack can't contain his laughter. "The only thing that would be funnier would be if you took credit to pay 'em."

Tretch is uncharacteristically silent.

Jack blinks at the realization and slaps his hands on the bar, erupting in a new burst of howls and cackles. "Oh man! You're so screwed. Who'd you borrow from? The Fiends? One of the northern cartels?" He wipes a tear from the corner of his eye, still giggling. There are a few bottles and glasses nearby. They're all that's available for any last-ditch effort. And they're all just out of reach. "Least now I know why you couldn't spare splitting any of the payday with me."

Tretch mumbles something and Jack notices Boneless Joe shift his weight forward a bit. Jack tries to slow his breathing. Fun time is over. He keeps his attention focused on Tretch. *If I'm gonna bite it, may as well be sure they do it quick.*

"Hey. Before your friend here jumps me, I gotta ask. What's with the tiny head? That thing is *so* small compared to the rest of you. That a side effect of the 'roids in your chembraid or has it always been that small?" He leans forward across the bar. "I mean, I guess it's no wonder you make such shitty business deals. You just don't know any better." Jack brings his hand up and looks at Tretch between the tips of his thumb and forefinger, as if measuring. "Not enough capacity."

Suddenly, Tretch smiles. "I know what you're doing. Unlike some others in my crew, I'm not a victim of low impulse control." He nods his head to Boneless Joe.

The giant-armed merc grunts in response and keeps edging closer to Jack.

Tretch lunges forward and is at the bar in just two large steps. He snatches Jack up by the front of his shirt. Jack has no time to react. Despite all the damage done to Tretch's body, the tiny-skulled bounty hunter is still plenty fast. He lifts Jack off the ground, bringing him nose-to-nose.

"You think I'm just going to kill you in anger? No, little boy. I told you. You're gonna be my bitch. I've got costs to recoup. I'm going to rent you out as a piñata. People will pay good money to beat the shit out of you. Just gotta prime the pump by letting you talk for a few seconds."

Jack grimaces as his legs drag across the edge of the bar. Some of the larger shards of a shattered tumbler are almost within reach. "Yeah? 'Good money'? How much do you think I can get for a five-minute session?"

Tretch's laugh shakes the entirety of Jack's body. "Five minutes? No. They're gonna beat on you for days. I'll see to it that you don't die and you don't black out. You'll feel everything."

"Yeah, I'm not sure there's much in that for me. It's a gracious offer n' all, but I think I'll pass. Now, if you would—"

There's a crash at the front door, followed by the *fwitp* sound of compressed air escaping from a dart gun. Jack turns his head just in time to see Boneless Joe take a dart in his gigantic imbued arm. Tretch pivots his head to look, too.

With the small opportunity afforded by this distraction, Jack lifts his arms and lets gravity take over. He slips free of his shirt and vest, landing sideways with a thud on the top of the bar. Scrambling, he grabs the largest shard of the broken tumbler and rolls off the surface. The floor behind the bar is solid and unforgiving. Jack thumps to the ground on his chest. The fall doesn't knock the wind from him, but it hurts something awful.

There's no time to think about the pain, though. Tretch could be reaching over the bar to get him. Jack rolls over and raises the broken glass to defend. But Tretch isn't looking at him.

The big bounty hunter's small head is still twisted to face the front door. "And who the happy hell are—"

A deep thud shakes the room. Tretch is gone, replaced by a heavy rush of air. Jack hears Tretch's body crash into the debris at the back of the room.

A second deep thud. Another corresponding crash at the back.

Confused, Jack frowns until he hears Boneless Joe's grumbly voice, pained and cursing. He must have been the second crash.

There's a bunch of indistinct clatter at the back. A third thud rattles from the front door, but this time there's no crash.

A new voice breaks through from the front of the room. "Shit. I missed. You three, track them. Make sure they leave town. They can trail up or fall down, I don't care as long as they're off my wall. And pick up Gorm on the way. I'm sure he's got a couple goodies in his shop to use."

Footsteps lead to the back of the bar and out the hole in the side. Not everyone has left, though. The voice that gave those orders is still in the bar. "Hey Jackie! You back there?"

The voice is unmistakable. Jack knows exactly who it is. *Fucking Harris.*

SECURITY

Jack pulls himself up and clambers to his feet. Bits of dirt and little pieces of broken glass stick to his chest and arms. The air is thick and he's covered in sweat and wasted alcohol. None of this is going to brush off easily.

There's a low whistle from the front door. Harris slings his air cannon to his back and swaggers up to the bar. For a guy his size, he gracefully manages the minor gymnastics to step over—and not on or through—the litter of various bodies and limbs. "You've got yourself a merry little mess here, Jackie."

"Good to know your eyes still work, Hairless."

Harris pauses while picking up an overturned barstool. He turns his head and snorts in disgust. Jack resists smiling. It's almost too easy to get a rise out of the balding chief of Bule's militia. Harris is quick to regain his composure, though. He rights the stool, but doesn't sit on it. "While I'm being so observant, your bird cage is showing. Again."

Jack looks down at his shirtless chest, wet and dirty. He is rather scrawny. The only notable definition in his upper body comes from his ribs. That's not necessarily a disadvantage, though. He lifts his face back to Harris. "Stupid mercs always grab at the collar. Never think a small guy can slip out."

Under the bar is a stack of rags Jack normally uses for drying glasses. He reaches down and grabs one. It does a slightly better job clearing the mess from his body than just using his bare hands. "You happen to see where my shirt went when you hit him with that cannon of yours?"

"Nope."

The silence after Harris's answer is as awkward as it is intentional. *Asshole.* Jack tilts his head to the gaping hole in his wall where the guards in Harris's militia chased after Tretch and Boneless Joe. "Took your goon squad long enough to get here."

"Could've been here sooner if you'd use the kneak we gave you months ago." Harris strolls around the barroom, nudging bodies and weapons with his boot. "I wouldn't need to try to speak Monkey."

That's where Zeke went? Thanks for the vote of confidence. Jack tries to hide his look of disappointment before Harris notices. "Zeke had to go and get you? The sound of that damn explosion wasn't enough to scramble your asses together?"

Harris raises an eyebrow, smirking. "Couldn't be sure. Crazy stuff happens in bars all the time. You let us tap in with our surveillance kneak we gave you and we'd be able to respond faster."

"Bullshit. The old man said no when he was around. I'm gonna say no. Customers here don't need no extra eyes on 'em. I pay the dues just like everyone else on this wall. Least you could do is offer my place the same protection."

"Jackie—"

"It's Jack, Hairless."

Harris stops kicking around the bar and focuses his attention on Jack. "Right. Jack. Old Man Vardin was from a different time. Let the old ways pass with that old man. You know how important it is to have a good, functioning bar in a burg like ours. It's a necessary destination in a gray haven. Just like the Red Light."

"Yeah. And Maddy Shard don't use your damn peekaboo kneaks, either. Try again."

"She's also got her own security detail. You've got an antique shotgun."

Jack looks away. The burly balding bastard has a point. The bar has never had good on-site security. Since so much business happens at the bar, mercs are usually pretty good about keeping themselves in line. Crowd control gadgets like the sonic paralyzers were for dealing with the few occasions where troublemakers got out of control. They did a reasonably decent job, though the paralyzers were supposed to be an improvement on the previous gadgets.

No doubt, though, incidents of merc stupidity have been up since the old man died.

Harris continues, "Look, Jack. You're a smart kid—a smart guy. We want you to be successful with this place. But if it ever gets to be too much for you, we—"

The entire surface of Jack's face instantly feels hot. "You sunnuvabitch. Don'tchu fuckin' threaten me. You ain't gettin' my bar. I don't care how much you delay bringing out the goon squad when shit goes down. It ain't happening."

A groan sounds from the wall behind Harris. He spins around, unslinging his air cannon and aiming it in a single fluid motion. It doesn't take more than a second and the balding militia chief is ready to pull the trigger.

The problem, though, is that the groan is coming from Corva.

"No!"

Without thinking, Jack vaults over the bar and reaches Harris with just enough time to push down on the back of the air cannon. The barrel swings up as Harris pulls the trigger, sending a blast of air up at the bar's ceiling, safely clear of Corva. The recoil from the cannon, however, sends Jack's hands straight back into him. He's not sure what hurts worse, the instantly swelling welt on his cheek, or the humiliation at the fact that he's just punched himself in the face.

He trips backward, flopping across a pair of dead bodies.

Harris turns his head back toward Jack. "What the world was that all about? Seriously, that could've messed you up in a bad way."

Jack takes a moment to look at Harris and then look over at Corva, still lying against the wall. Still unconscious. Still alive.

"She's—"

He pauses, clearing his throat, and starts again.

"That's my new security detail. Just hired her today."

J.J. VEGA
FULCRUM
SEASON ONE
EPISODE TWO:
BACK TO NORMALISH

EPISODE TWO: BACK TO NORMALISH

CONTENTS

2.1

Corva

"You're going to need these." The old woman's raspy voice hissed as she jammed fist-sized bags of seed into the young girl's hands. "Don't let them get wet. And never, never let anyone know how much you've got!"

"I don't understand, Avó. How will I pay, then?"

It was ten years ago and that girl didn't know anything about anything. If she thought about it, it would be hard for her to imagine how she managed to survive the first week after that day. But the old woman was patient with her. Always patient. Avó wasn't the old woman's name; it's what children in Fareburne called all of the elder women. However, this particular older woman was more than that to the young girl; she was like a grandmother to her.

The woman had paused a moment, gripping the girl's hand in her wrinkled, earth-worn palm. The girl couldn't help but notice how much smaller and softer her own hand was.

"Before you get into a town, take out a small amount and stow the rest. You don't use more than that little bit while in the town. Dear word, you're not ready for this." She went back to frantically stuffing a sack with gear, mumbling. "She's not ready."

And the girl had stood there. Dumb. Watching her elder work. Trying to keep track of where the old woman put each item, and failing. It didn't matter much; the girl didn't know what half of those items were. The woman probably didn't, either. She was on autopilot, grabbing through teary blindness at anything that might be remotely useful.

"Will I see you again?"

The girl's question was simple enough, but it stopped the elder in her tracks. Her hands were trembling.

"Me? No. I'll be gone soon enough."

"But what about the others. What if I—"

"You see anyone you think you recognize, you run, child! Do you understand? They aren't those people anymore. They aren't people at all. You stay out of sight and you run. The Shadowfold has come to Fareburne. The Umbrati and Karui won't be far behind. The others— our people—they are gone. You're all that's left."

"*We're* all that's left." The girl reached out and placed her hand on the older woman's arm, trying to console her, but not really knowing how to do it, or why.

The old woman smiled faintly, knowingly. She turned her head to the door and then nodded. "For a little while longer."

Her hands had stopped trembling and returned to diligently stuffing the sack. Her renewed calm triggered panic in the girl, a sudden realization.

"What will I have people call me? I've not yet earned a name."

The old woman stopped again. This time she made it a point to looked at the young girl. "You can use my name. Have them call you Corva."

2.2

STATIC

Corva wakes, eyelids thick and heavy. The remnant smell of coffee tinges the air. There's a strange sound, kind of like gurgling static. She shakes the fog from her head and notices her arm, outstretched forward and upward. At the end of her arm, she holds the throat of a flailing boy.

That boy!

This self-serving little snot was going to leave her flapping in the wind with Tretch and his ilk. And then after that, he shot her.

She squeezes harder. That gurgling static sound transforms into gasps and wheezing. She's distantly aware of another noise. Screaming?

There's a popping sound followed by something that sounds like the wind, and she's suddenly no longer able to move.

A moment later, everything goes black.

74

2.3

REVIEW

Jack holds his throat, still coughing.

Holy hell, that chick's got a grip. And she hadn't even fully come to.

"You weren't concentrating." The voice behind him is soft and melodic, a voice not fit for the harshness of this world. Lyia. Still, the rasp of frustration rings in her words. "How can you expect to do this at all if I'm not here? You can't only feed her once a day when I'm on a break. Using soulmancy for healing only goes so far. She needs food to regain strength."

Jack tests clearing his throat before speaking. It's tender, but he can get words out. "I know. I know. Stop treating me like I've never done this before."

"Then stop acting like it." Lyia's voice loses a bit of its edge. "I've got to ask again. Is it even worth it to keep trying to tend to her?"

"I told Harris that she's my new bouncer. I throw her out and he'll take the bar." Still rubbing his throat, Jack turns to face Lyia. Despite his discomfort, he can't help but smile at her. Of all the people in the world, she's the only one who really *gets* him. She's also known him longer than anyone else. "Why can't I just flip on the subsonic paralyzer and pour the broth down her throat?"

He was able to scavenge one of the remaining subsonic paralyzers from the array mounted under the bar's floor. Wiring it to work independently was a bit tricky, but it was worth it. Didn't even need Slim's help. Now, with it placed under her cot, he fires it up any time he needs to get close.

Lyia shakes her head. "That piece of tech you shoved under her isn't going to help for that. The swallow reflex isn't like breathing or your heart pumping. You'll drown her."

"Well, whattya want me to do, then? Every now and then, her eyes open and she starts blindly lashing out. This go-round, her eyes didn't even open first."

Lyia reaches out and pulls Jack's hand down from his neck to inspect where they'd had to pry Corva's fingers away. "You'll be fine. Won't even bruise. You just need to practice more." She narrows her eyes to a scowl. "Real practice. Not making those imbued beads of yours. And not that business you were doing with Vardin."

Jack eyes Lyia. "You know about that?"

"Of course I know about it, Jackspin! Vardin deteriorating over the course of a year. You always looking like you're tired. It wasn't hard to figure out."

Jackspin. Usually she just calls him Pin or Pinny. No one else gets to call him that; Lyia is the only one who has earned that right. But she didn't this time. She used his full name.

He lets her finish looking at his neck. Her fingers are soft and kind. They feel nice. But ... "Stop mothering me. I've basically backed off on that kinda training since V bit it." He notices her wince. "Sorry, since he passed. Anyway, what's the big deal with the beads? What's the matter if I make a few nits by selling a fixin or two?"

She squeezes his neck before letting go. "Those beads can be tracked! You know that. Do you really want another raid coming to Bule?"

"We've handled raids before. They're never all that big a deal. 'Sides, I put up the same shielding we've got here when I make the beads. They're fine to make."

"I'm not talking about making them. I'm talking about when someone uses them. Your soul has a fingerprint. Anything you make can be traced back to you. That's how they found the Shadowfold and—" She stops, scowl slowly fading. Her hand drifts to her forehead and she runs her fingers through the vibrant blue streak of hair that starts there. She's not going to finish that sentence. It's probably for the best anyway. Jack's well-versed in that particular story. It ends as badly as it starts. A series of mercies—exterminations—of large townships by a community of well-meaning mages. The wrath of retribution for that act. Two survivors, children, on the run afterward. Lyia pivots the topic. "And so what if I was 'mothering' you? I was almost your age when you were born."

"Not even! You were barely ten."

"And I was still taller than you are now." Lyia jabs Jack on the shoulder. Her scowl is entirely gone, replaced with a big grin of her own.

"Shut up."

Jack knows she's just ribbing him, trying to change the topic. Still, he isn't overly fond of being reminded of the difference in their ages, or their heights.

He turns his back to her and looks down at the girl lying in the cot. "I still don't get it. Why can't I just tie her to the damn cot?"

"She's a person, Pinny, not your prisoner. Besides, if you'd just practice more, you wouldn't need rope."

Jack's face spreads into a devious smile. "They use ropes over where you work."

Lyia lets out an exasperated sigh. It's one of those sighs that says a whole conversation at once. *Don't pick on me.It doesn't matter that I picked on you.Yes, I know I work at the Red Light.No, that sort of stuff doesn't happen on my floor.Cut it out.I'm not in the mood to deal with your dirty fourteen-year-old boy brain.*

Jack gets the hint and looks up at Zeke, who is peeking down through the trapdoor into Jack's living quarters beneath the bar's basement. "This'd be a lot easier if you came down and helped! You're the whole reason she's here."

The monkey isn't even looking at him. All of Zeke's attention is on Corva. Neither Jack nor Zeke have slept much in the three days since the incident with the bounty mercs. It's not just tending to Corva, but they've also been cleaning up the bar. Zeke's face reflects what Jack feels all over.

Lyia lowers her voice. "How's he doing? You sure it's okay to have him here? From what you told me, everything went crazy after they got close to each other."

"Zeke's fine. That's about the closest he'll let himself get to her, anyway. He's tired, though. We spent the better part of yesterday trying to get most of the bodies—and body parts—outta the bar. Zeke's job was to help make sure we didn't accidentally set off any of the booby traps on the custom gear. It's slow work. The smell didn't help."

Neither did Harris or anyone else in his militia. Yeah, they made sure Tretch and Boneless Joe left town, but body disposal is apparently outside of their job description. So much for the importance of a "good, functioning bar."

That said, Slim was able to help with one of his gadgets. The portable incinerator rig wasn't quite large enough for a full body, or even half of one, really. But it got the job done.

Lyia releases another sigh. "Look. I need to get back. I'll get her neck re-dressed for you. She's only had half of the broth, though. You need to make sure she finishes the other half before the end of the hour. Use what we've practiced."

"But—"

"No. No tech. She's healing well—remarkably well, actually. But she's still weak and short on nutrients. Probably was low before she got here. You need to get her to drink without fighting her." She rests a hand on his shoulder. Soft. Warm. "I know you have the focus to do this."

Jack shakes his head. "Beads are different. They ain't got any moving parts. With people—"

"How long does it take you to make a bead?"

Jack purses his lips. He knows how the rest of this conversation goes. Knows that he's going to lose the argument. "Around a half hour or so."

Lyia nods. She knows, too. "If you can concentrate and focus on a bead for that long, I'm sure you can focus on her for the much shorter time it takes to drink some broth."

His shoulders drop. He knew it was coming. That doesn't make her any less correct. "Yeah. I get it."

"Good. I've got to go now." She stops and makes sure that he's looking her in the face. One hundred percent compassion. "There's some extra meat in that sack I brought the broth in."

"Thanks, Lyia."

And with that, she turns and makes her way up the ladder and out of the bar.

Jack lets out a long breath and turns his attention to Zeke. "How about you nest up and get some rest? I'll take care of this. We've got more work to do in a bit."

Zeke's attention is still mostly on Corva, but he nods all the same. A few seconds later, his face is no longer filling the opening of the trapdoor.

Shaking his head, Jack focuses his thoughts back on the bar. With the help of a few other folks around town, Jack should be able to start serving drinks again in a day or so. Of course, the bar's seating capacity is substantially reduced now. Most of the barstools survived, but he's down to only two tables and a handful of chairs to go around them.

The sooner he can get the doors open, the sooner he can afford more proper repairs. The planks he's got crisscrossed over the holes in the floor and wall don't do much for the place's aesthetics.

Jack fishes out the jerky that Lyia mentioned and sits on his bedroll opposite Corva. He tears at the meat with his teeth and chews while he thinks. He leans back against the wall, staring at the strange girl asleep in what used to be the old man's cot. Jack is still not entirely sure exactly what happened that day she showed up. Yeah, he was there, but there are so many questions.

He reaches up to his ear and activates his playback kneak. Memories are one thing, but recorded video has no bias, even when your own eyes are the cameras. Playback is an absolute must when dealing in trades and barters where the closest thing you get to a contract is some trader's word and maybe a handshake.

Of course, in this instance, the playback isn't helping very much. Jack has run the video countless times and he still can't sort it out. This girl, Corva—she survived being punched through a wall, an explosion, being strangled with a weighted bola, and getting shot with a blast from an imbued bead. Any one of those things could kill a normal person.

She should be on the brink, if alive at all. How is it that she could absolutely decimate nearly every one of those mercs? She'd moved as if possessed. And so fast! Even on the playback, there are afterimages of her arms that make it look like she's got an extra set.

And now, she's unconscious. Been in and out of it for three days, sleeping like she'd been shot from a cannon into a wall of fists. But she's mostly healed. The swelling and cuts on her hands were basically gone after the first day. The bruising around her ribs looked to be cleared up yesterday. Just about the only visible damage left on her are the cuts in her neck from the wire on that bola. Sure, Lyia's skills at healing with soulmancy are helping, but this girl's body is knitting itself together much faster than it ought to.

Finishing the stick of jerky, Jack shakes his head. *Not gonna make any more sense 'til she fully comes to.*

He casts a glance at the remaining portion of broth next to the cot and presses his head against the wall behind him. *Who knows? Maybe she'll stick around.*

EPISODE TWO: BACK TO NORMALISH

Rising, he steps over to the cot and picks up the broth with one hand. His other hand is free. He focuses on the palm of that hand, feeling warmth flow into it as he extends that hand over Corva's belly. *Also, it wouldn't hurt to have a guard dog for a bit.*

2.4

FIELD OF BOOM

Corva finds herself on an open plain, inspecting her surroundings.

I haven't been here before. Have I?

Rolling grasslands engulf the gravel path where she stands, nothing like the dusty sage and cacti that pepper the land outside of Bule, and even less like the jungle of her youth. The sky is the strange, sunless, ruddy orange-pink that makes it difficult to tell if the day is coming or going.

Tracing up the path, she notices a diminutive figure standing silhouetted on a chunk of granite that protrudes above the sweet-smelling grass. It's not a person. Not a full-sized one, at least. Too small. An animal of some sort? It could be a sculpture, forged in wrought iron, a tangible shadow given presence by the bizarre light. Or, wait, no, it's moving; beckoning that Corva come closer. Perplexed, she takes a wary step toward the shadowy summoner.

And then another.

And another.

After covering half the distance between them, the figure becomes more defined and takes on more dimension. The silhouette effect isn't just from the lighting. Starting just below its head, a furry black shroud—or maybe a coat—covers the thing, which is definitely not a person. People don't have tails or night shine in their eyes. The little animal signals to her more urgently.

What's the hurry? There's no one around.

Corva stops and looks to her left and right.

Something certainly doesn't feel right. Is the sun setting? Feels like it's getting darker.

Turning back toward the little beast, she notices that it's gesturing even more frantically and pointing?—yes, pointing up in the air. Looking up, dread creeps up Corva's spine. Two enormous swarms billow up from the horizon and charge at one another, mottling the sky.

The swarms loom closer and the flying creatures in each become more distinct. They appear to be flying bundles of dynamite, fuses already ignited. In one swarm, they have leathery bat-like wings while in the other, they sport wings that are much more akin to birds of prey, like hawks or eagles. The clouds twist about one another in a serpentine concert of opposition. They're not after her. It's a dogfight of flying dragons and she's merely collateral damage caught below.

Corva turns to the tailed creature that had been signaling to her, only, it's no longer there.

No doubt it scurried off to hide.

She's left to fend for herself among the flying explosive bundles that are already detonating in the sky above her.

As she watches, explosions get closer and closer.

GET OUT

Corva's eyes snap open to pain pulsing through her body. Her hands, her ribs, her legs. If it doesn't outright hurt, it aches. Her head throbs. When she sits up, it feels as if it's doubled in size and weight. Her neck is wrapped in bandages. She runs her fingertips across it. It's a solid dressing; it's not choking her, but it's also not something that will just slip off at the slightest movement. She'll have to cut it off when she gets out of here, wherever "here" is.

Am I in a different dream? Have I been captured? Who's holding me? What—

She stops. She's getting out of control, getting ahead of herself. *Se acalma. Take stock.*

She looks around the room. It's dimly lit with a cord of light wrapping the stone walls. A cheap woven rug covers most of the ground in front of her cot. There's an opening to another room on her left and, on the opposite side, a metal ladder reaches up to a small trapdoor in the ceiling.

Across the room from her, asleep on the floor, is that boy. That little opportunistic jerk. *He's the one that—*

Memories hit Corva like muzzle flashes, bursting images one after another. They feel as if they're her memories, but everything is kind of detached and dreamlike. Was it really her slicing and shooting and striking all those people? She rubs her eyes with the palms of her hands. Now's not the time for this.

She pulls back the thin, tattered blanket and swings her feet around to the floor. Corva shivers a bit and looks down at herself. *Where are my clothes?*

Her undergarments are still in place, but she's got cloth bandages wrapped around her midsection and parts of each leg. She scans the room again. She spots her metal arm bracers and remnants of her travel gear on the floor next to the cot, but there's no sign of her clothes.

She cuts a suspicious glance at the boy asleep on his bedroll. She should wake him up. Slap him around. Make him tell her what's going on.

Corva stands up a bit too fast. Overwhelmed with the onslaught of light-headedness, she drops to her knees. She waits a beat and takes a deep breath while her head clears.

It only takes a few seconds for her eyes to focus again. That's when she notices the small medkit lying on the ground near the boy's head. There's medication, ointments, and the same type of bandages that she has wrapped around her wounds.

He shot me. Why take care of me after?

Her mind flails in a sea of questions. She doesn't need answers, though. She needs to get out. She grabs her arm bracers and puts them on before collecting the rest of her small pile of things. Gingerly, she stands. No light-headedness this time. Grabbing the blanket from the cot, she wraps it around her shoulders as she approaches the door on the far side of the room. She'll find new clothes later.

The handle to the door is cool to the touch. As quietly as she can, she turns it, testing it.

Great! It's not locked.

She cringes as the door creaks open and takes a quick look back at the sleeping boy. So far, he hasn't moved at all or given any sign that he's waking. Corva turns back and peeks through the doorway.

Crap. A toilet.

She stares at the toilet for a moment, tempted to make use of it. The sight of the modest little room makes her realize just how much she really has to go. *How long was I out?*

But she can't risk it. First priority is leaving.

The trapdoor has got to be the way out. She creeps back across the room and up the ladder, careful not to wake the boy. Pushing open the trapdoor, she recognizes the old desk in front of her. It's the only thing she recognizes, though. Her last memories of this desk are only in flashes. It was much dirtier, surrounded with busted crates and the smell of burned timber. Everything is a lot cleaner now.

The important thing is that now she knows where she is. It's the storeroom under that bar. Good. One question answered. The kid must live here.

Corva looks back down the ladder at him and the medkit by his head. *He's still a jerk.*

She closes the trapdoor and sneaks up the stairway leading to ground level. As she comes to the top step, she can see that the place has been patched up, though there's still a lot of work to be done before it's serviceable. A draft of desert cold competes with moonlight to squeeze through the boards that block a gaping hole in the side of the bar.

She'd gone through that hole in the wall; created it with her body. That's her last solid memory before a patchwork of foggy images. She'd been slipping the same pack of bounty hunters for weeks, but they'd cornered her on the narrow canyon path to this town. There was no choice but to fight. She never expected to survive.

Corva takes a moment to glance back down at herself again. She should look and feel a lot more battered than she does. She'd been caught in a few fights in the ten years since Fareburne, but never against bounty hunters like those. She'd certainly never been punched through a wall before.

Through the filtered light, Corva notices the silhouette of a small figure perched upon the bar. It turns and looks at her, eyes glowing, reflecting dim light from some unknown source. The silhouette raises its hand with an indication to stop moving. The little creature's tail lifts and twitches with a bit of nervous energy.

"You!" For some reason, Corva's mind swings to the smell of sweetgrass and explosions. A dream or a memory or a memory of a dream. She can't quite put her finger on it.

"His name is Zeke." The voice comes from behind her. "I'm Jack."

Corva watches as the strange little monkey swings over her and lands on Jack's shoulder. It peeks around at her from behind his head. She takes a step toward him. "What are you?"

"Me?" Jack is incredulous. "I should be asking you that. I'm not the one who went all batshit crazy and killed almost everyone in my bar."

"I wasn't talking to you." Images from memories and dreams bombard Corva's mind to the point where it's difficult to tell which is which. She looks at Zeke, or at least tries to look at him as he skulks behind Jack. "I know you. I don't know how or why, but I know you."

Zeke pokes his head out at this, curiosity apparently getting the better of his caution.

"What do you mean, you 'know' Zeke? He's been a part of this bar for decades. Got photos of him with the old man from when the place opened. And as far as I can tell, you ain't never stepped foot in here 'til a few days ago." Jack squints at the girl. "How about we cut to the chase and you tell me why you're a bounty worth at least nine mercs?"

Corva can't be distracted by that. Not now. *This monkey, how do I know him? Why am I drawn to him?* She leans in to see him better.

Jack continues, "Hey! I'm owed some answers here. The least you could do is—"

Episode Two: Back to Normalish

Corva won't be derailed. She takes a step closer, reaching out to Zeke. Everything goes dark. An overwhelming shot of energy courses over her body. It's like an arena full of people are all screaming at her at the same time.

Then, she feels herself collapse.

2.6

A Proposition

Corva awakens in the cot, again. Her memories are still a flashing foggy mess, but she's got a better sense of which memories are from dreams and which ones are from real events. At least, she thinks she does.

Sitting up slowly, she notes that the room is brighter than before. The boy, Jack, sits atop his bedroll, mug in hand and a fresh bandage over his right eye. He grabs a second mug from the ground next to him and points it at her.

"Coffee?"

Corva nods and watches as Jack pours half of the contents of his own mug into the one he'd offered her. He notices the tinge of revulsion in her face and smiles. "It's fresh. I haven't drank any yet. Just sat down, in fact. Weren't sure how long it'd be 'til you came to. If I'd known, I would've brewed more."

He reaches forward and offers her the coffee. She hesitates a moment, inspecting the mug without touching it. Curls of steam twirl up from the dark liquid, carrying the bold, pungent aroma toward her.

It smells fresh at least. And it's hot. Two marks in favor.

She accepts the mug with both hands. It's warm to the touch, comforting. She takes a sip. Hot, but not scalding. Hot enough to hurt him pretty badly if she splashes it in his face, though. Is he stupid or is he trying to get her trust? Still, she finds herself enjoying the drink's flavor. It's been a while since she's had a coffee with this much care put into it. Coffee isn't exactly easy to come by. Most of the time, it's from dirty old bags that'd been stored for way too long. This doesn't taste like that. No tinge of mildew. No aftertaste of dust.

She stares into the mug, trying to decide between finishing it and smashing it over his head. She knows where she is now. Getting out would be easy.

She glances up and sees Jack's grin grow wider. He looks up to the top of the ladder. "Ha! I told you she'd like it!" He pulls his gaze back down to her. "Zeke here was convinced you'd splash me with the coffee and bolt. He don't know how good my coffee is. Ain't no one in the world who'd waste that deliciousness."

Corva resists the urge to toss her coffee in the kid's face out of spite. There's something else that has her interest instead. Or better stated, someone else. She looks up the ladder and sees the monkey hanging from the top rung. Zeke. He studies her with his strange, almost reptilian eyes. She returns the monkey's intrusive stare with one of her own.

"Bule's a shithole." Jack's voice scrapes against the awkward silence. "The ground sucks for growin' anything. It's a pain in the ass to get in or outta town. An' the mineral shafts around us were picked dry ages ago. 'Bout the only thing this place has going for it is the fact that it's a shithole. Neither side in the war wants to waste their time on this chunk of rock."

Jack looks to Corva. She doesn't give him the pleasure of a reaction, just keeps her focus on Zeke. He continues.

"Look, I got a little testy. But I got questions. An' from the looks of things, you got some of your own. You'll have more hunters gunnin' for ya, but it'll be a while—weeks, maybe more. You've been here four days and no one's come knockin'. Damn near everyone who saw you in my bar is dead and word travels slow around these parts, 'specially with the limp you gave that Tretch guy. They'll think you moved on 'cause, well, Bule's a shithole. 'Sides, it ain't like I showed you any loyalty in the fight."

"You shot me."

Corva keeps her eyes on Zeke. She can't get a good read on his behavior. His facial expressions and the way that he looks at her; he's not like any monkey she's seen before. But he's there, hanging upside down by a couple paws and his tail. He's definitely a monkey.

Jack slurps his coffee. He's clearly flustered. "What else was I supposed to do? You were chokin' yourself out by trying to keep standing. If I hadn't shot you, you wouldn't be sittin' all cozy on that there cot, that's for sure."

She nurses her own coffee, thinking, trying to remember. That whole block of time is too jumbled to make sense of it. He could tell her that she'd spent the whole time singing road songs and discussing the challenges in procuring high quality coffee beans. She wouldn't be able to confirm or refute it. The only thing she's sure of is that all of this has something to do with that monkey.

Jack doesn't stop. "So I've got a deal for you. I'm opening the bar tomorrow. The place is beat all to hell and I'd say it's mostly your fault. I'm gonna need help. At the same time, you've got this giant bounty on you. There's probably no chance I'll ever collect on it, what with the fact that you've nearly killed me in your sleep more than once. I couldn't take you in if I wanted to. And just guessing, but I'd say it's probably either the Sheeps or the Goats that's after ya."

He pauses with an expectant smile. He's waiting for something. A question from her. He's probably done this setup a thousand times. Say obtuse names that he's made up, then wait for the question so he can brag about how clever he is. She's not taking the bait. She just keeps staring at Zeke.

Jack clears his throat. "Sheeps an' Goats, them's my names for 'em. You probably call them the Karui and Umbrati or Light and Dark or whatever. I think Sheeps an' Goats fits 'em better."

They are clever names. However, there's a war going on. A real war. Forces greater than humanity are vying for control, for ownership over this whole plane of existence. How sheltered is this boy—this whole town—that he's able to trivialize it with cute names over coffee? Has she actually found such a place? Or is this naming thing just a coping mechanism he has? So many questions.

She decides not to react to his customized naming at all. Her view remains locked on the little monkey hanging from the ladder. If there are answers, that's who has them. She hears Jack take another drink from his mug before starting anew.

"And you've got this … this thing with Zeke. He's freaked out more than usual and I got a pretty good idea that you've got no clue what happens when you get near him." He leans in and points to the bandaged wound over his eye. "I'll give you a hint. This wasn't here yesterday. An' it didn't get there by itself."

Corva notes the bandage from the corner of her eye. It's not large, but it's already starting to soak through with blood from the wound beneath it. *I caused that?* More questions.

Jack takes a long draw of his coffee and puts the mug on the ground next to him. He slouches back against the wall, comfortable. Despite that, the demeanor in his face is a lot more businesslike. All of his attention is on Corva. She wonders if he's practiced this whole thing. If she's really been unconscious for as long as he says, he's certainly had the time. He probably imagined that she'd be more responsive, that her focus wouldn't be fixed on Zeke.

Jack clears his throat again.

"So here's the deal. Although you did beat the hell outta my bar, you did save mine and Zeke's asses. An' although I *did* shoot you, I saved your ass, too. I figure we each owe each other a bit. So I'll finish patching you up and help you lie low for a spell."

"I'm doing alright." She doesn't look at him. The monkey is the only thing she cares about right now.

"You're doing alright? Yeah, sure. Keep telling yourself that, Miss Attack-and-Black-Out. You have any idea how hard it was to get your zonked-out ass down that ladder without re-injuring you? Twice? 'I'm doing alright.' Please. You're tough, but you ain't that tough."

Corva takes a moment to glance up from Zeke to the trapdoor above the ladder. How *did* he get her down here?

Jack sits upright, legs crossed, hands pressing down on his knees. She catches him take a quick glance up at Zeke before he starts again. "But you do heal up quick. No doubt. At this rate, you'll probably be back up to spec in a day or two. So here's the real pitch. Zeke and I will help you figure out what's goin' on between you two. See if we can figure out what it is, and if you can control it. Zeke seems to think it's possible. For that, though, you've gotta work my bar; serve drinks, wash dishes, and show the occasional mean drunk out the door. How's that sound?"

Corva tilts her head, eyes still trained on Zeke. If she's really been here for four days, that's longer than she's stayed anywhere in a long time. She could risk a little longer. Besides, leaving wouldn't get her any answers.

She takes another slow sip of her coffee and finally turns away from Zeke to face the young dealmaking jerk on the other side of the room.

"Are meals included with this deal of yours?"

The Cost of Repairs

"I dunno, man. It'll take a bit. You got yourself a lot of damage here." Slim drapes his lanky body over the bar and props himself up on his forearm. He looks at the tattoo on that arm and begins making a series of taps and gestures on it. "I mean, your floor's about fixed, so reinstalling the array won't be a problem. But the control unit is hosed. I'll need time to print out new parts for that. My guess? You're lookin' at about … fifty thousand nits."

"Fifty?" Jack stops pouring Slim's drink well below full. "That's almost as much as the cost to install those things the first time! No way, man. I risked enough just bein' a guinea pig for your new tech."

"But it worked, didn't it?" Slim stops tapping on his tattoo and turns his narrow, shaved head to look around the barroom. His grin is huge. "I would've loved to have been here when the subsonics fired up; seen the whole room froze up in person."

"I shared the playback with you. You saw what it looked like. And yeah, it worked. *At first.* Aside from maybe tightening down the deadzone behind the bar, the problem wasn't while it was on. The problem was what happened when the array shut off. People weren't calm. They were pissed."

Slim swivels around slowly and looks Jack in the eye. The smile is gone. He's not using his wheeling-and-dealing face. This is his more sincere side, or his best attempt at one.

Here it comes, Slim's version of a pep talk. "I saw your playback. Heard it, too. Well, the clip that you wanted to show at least. In any case, you probably shouldn't have been standing up here on the bar, gloating." He snags the partially full drink and pours it down his throat before continuing, "It wasn't the kit that pissed them off. It was you."

Jack grabs the glass from Slim's hand and turns away. *You're startin' to sound like the old man, Slim.* He pours the second half of Slim's drink, careful to account for the amount he'd already poured. "Yeah, well, all the same, fifty is too high a price. I ain't payin' that much to be an experiment, not twice."

The thin-framed maker goes back to tapping his tattoo. "Look. I tell you what. We can redistribute the array pieces you have left and probably get about the same coverage. The only thing that actually needs to be made fresh is the control unit. How about I only charge you the cost for that and my time to do the install?"

"How much?"

"Twenty-five."

"Ten."

Slim squints at Jack. It's difficult to tell if he's seriously considering the counteroffer. "Alright. Ten thousand nits, plus first dibs on a bottle from your next batch of shine."

Jack does some quick math in his head. There's a lot of demand for his cornshine. Even outsiders come to the bar asking for it. A whole bottle goes a long way, even though it's just a portion of the overall batch size. He peers at Slim and slides over the second half of the drink. "You sure you don't just want a bottle from inventory?"

"Nah. Gotta be fresh."

"Slim, man. You ain't gonna try to burn it for fuel again, are ya?" Jack points to Slim's shaven head, where singed tips of hair pepper the left side. "You lost quite a bit last time around."

The lanky maker smiles in earnest. "Progress don't come without risk, little man."

Jack sighs. "Alright, ten plus a first bottle. But if you're gonna waste perfectly good drinking shine, I wanna tack on one more little project for you."

He pulls a cloth-wrapped bundle from under the bar and sets it in front of Slim. The maker's eyes light up, curiosity piqued. He tries to pull up a corner of the cloth to see what's inside, but Jack slaps his hand away.

Slim doesn't take his eyes off the bundle. "That the old man's gun?"

"Nah. I can handle repairin' that myself. This is something else. I want you to get the traps off and get 'em functional again. Thought you might find it fun."

"Traps are tough to work around, little man. But"—Slim picks up the bundle and tucks it under his arm before continuing—"you do know how I like a challenge. You've got yourself a deal."

Not waiting for a response, Slim swallows the second half of his drink in a single gulp and heads for the exit.

"Hey! You gonna pay for that?"

The skinny maker waves his tattooed arm back at Jack as he heads out the door. "Down payment!"

ABANDONED TO THE FLIES

Jack drops his head to the bar, arms dangling at his sides, and lets out a long exhale. Slim's a good buddy and Jack got a good deal on the repair, but even ten thousand trade units is steep. And it's going to hurt worse if business doesn't pick up. He rolls the weight of his head so his cheek rests on the surface of the bar. He's got a great view of how dreadfully empty the place is.

It's not like he's expecting a big fanfare or a rush or anything. However, today is the bar's reopening, and it's not like there's another bar in this town.

"So what's the name of this place?" Corva's voice sends a jolt through Jack. He jerks his head off the bar and glares at her.

"Holy hell! You 'bout scared the crap outta me." He squints. "How long've you been standing there?"

"Long enough to see you rolling your head on the bar. You taking a nap or is that some kind of special cleaning technique?" She smiles, full-toothed and genuine. It's not an ugly smile, but all the same, it pisses off Jack. It's smug, knowing.

"I wasn't napping." Reflexively, Jack grabs a rag and wipes down the oily smear on the bar where he'd planted his face. "And it doesn't need a name. It's just the bar."

"But you could call it something else, though. Right? Like Jack's Place? Or The Hole in the Wall? Or The Hole in the Floor?"

Jack squints at Corva before answering. Did she really just suggest naming the place after the hole—holes—she made? "Why would I call it that? It's just 'the bar.' Most gray havens aren't big enough to have more than one, an' Bule ain't no different. Coming up with a cute name only serves to annoy the thirsty pass-throughs who just want to know where the damn bar is."

"But 'bar' means so many different things in English. Ooh, how about calling it a saloon?"

Jack can feel his irritation coming to a peak. If he were the old man, his eye would be twitching right now. "What're you gettin' at?"

"I'm just thinking that it seems kind of dead in here. Maybe a bit better presentation could help."

"It's just 'the bar.' Days are usually slower than nights."

She crosses her arms and eyes him suspiciously. "I get 'slower,' but this is barren. Empty as a desert. Entregue às moscas."

"Entr—I got no idea what you just said." Jack tries a couple more times to sound out the words, contorting his face in a vain effort to replicate Corva's accent.

"It means 'abandoned to the flies,' idiota!" Corva gestures to all the empty seats. "No one is here."

"So … what? You think I shoulda put up a big ol' banner or something? 'Grand reopening!' Something like that?"

"No, I—"

"Bars are high-traffic places. Most burgs ain't got more n' one. Bule's the same. People want a drink, they come here." He gives one more angry wipe to the bar and turns away, mumbling, "Don't need no giant sign to tell 'em about the only watering hole in town."

He turns his attention upward to the ceiling trusswork. "Zeke! I'm on my last rag. You usin' the rest to build a nest up there?"

"Hey." Corva's voice is softer now. It doesn't have the ragged tinge of sarcasm that he's gotten used to hearing from her. "Hey. Calm down. I was just trying to say that maybe there's a reason it's so dead in here."

"Reason?" Jack tilts his head back to her and raises an eyebrow.

"Yeah. A reason. You've been so wrapped up in fixing the place, you haven't been out and around town."

"Hell, you've only been awake for about a day. What do you know?" He pauses. She did spend part of the morning getting a few supplies while he went through the last few bits of prepping for the reopen. "Wait. What do you know?"

"Not a lot. The swap shop guy—Garth? Corn? Norm?"

"Gorm."

"Yeah. Gorm. He seems to think that this place is going to come under new management some time soon."

Jack's eyes widen and he feels his face flush hot. He squares his shoulders and faces her directly. She's got his full attention. "That sunnuvabitch."

"Who? Gorm? He seemed pretty harmless. A big guy, sure, but—"

"No. Harris. Gorm is part of Bule's security militia. Kinda their armorer. I funded a good part of the repair by trading him all those spent shell casings from the guns that got shot at you. He'll repack and resell 'em." Jack pauses a moment to silently congratulate himself. He got a really good deal on those casings. "But Harris, Harris runs the militia. That bald fuck has been angling to take over the bar ever since the old man died."

"Old man?"

"Old Man V. The dude who used to own this bar. An' me, actually. Got me for workin' as a barhand when I was four. He died about a year back. The bar got left to me. Friggin' Hairless wasn't a big fan of that arrangement. Been trying to sappotach me ever since."

"Sappotach? You mean 'sabotage'?"

Jack pauses to glare at Corva. "Yeah. Sabotage. That's what I said." It's not enough that this girl could beat him senseless with hardly a thought, she's got to correct how he speaks with her funny accent, too?

If his tough-guy glare has any effect on Corva, she isn't showing it. Her mind was apparently stuck on another thought. "Why fight to keep the place? Why stay at all? You're free to go and do whatever you want."

One name jumps to his mind. Lyia. She's his "why." *The* why. This chick doesn't need to know that, though. "I got my reasons." He turns back to look up at the ceiling. "Zeke! Get on down here."

"You sure you want to do that? If he gets too close, I might have another … episode."

Jack doesn't look at her when responding, "He was able to hang from the ladder in my room without anything happening. I figure that as long as he's at the other end of the bar from you, you'll be fine."

"I'm not worried about me." She steps to the side, just within his field of vision. She's pointing at the scabbed-over cut over his eyebrow. "By the way, that's healing up nicely and everything, but are you sure you shouldn't keep that thing covered?"

"Nah. It'll gimme cred with the customers." Jack frowns and scratches his head. There's no movement in the spots where Zeke usually likes to sit.

It's possible that the little monkey slipped out through the roof. He's been spending more time up there since Corva's fight a few days ago. It's hard to tell what he's been doing up there, though. He's certainly not tending to the roof garden. There's ladder access to the lookout scope, but Jack dismisses the thought. That would be pretty paranoid, even for Zeke. *Probably napping. He best be around when some real customers come in.*

Corva's voice breaks through his thoughts. "You'll get cred? By letting them know that someone else knocked you around?"

He lowers his head. This girl certainly has a way of striking a nerve. "Ain't the damage in the bar enough to say that? This just means I didn't puss out an' hide in a corner somewhere."

"But that cut on your face happened after the fight."

Jack feels his face bend into a bitter smirk as he turns back toward her. "You just gotta be right all the time, don'tcha?"

Corva opens her mouth to respond, but is cut off by the sound of the front entrance swinging open. Two men step across the threshold with all the joy of someone who's been slapped in the mouth. Sure, one of them is smiling, but it's one of those unhinged sneers that gives the impression that the person wearing it has but a fingernail's grasp on reality.

Jack's heart drops into his stomach as his scalp starts to tingle. Of course his first customers for the day are outsiders looking for trouble.

FIGHT OR FLIGHT

The two new "customers" to the bar set off every alarm in Corva's mind. Every nerve in her body tells her to run. To get out of there. To escape and evade, the same as she's been doing ever since Avó helped her escape Fareburne. She's not a fighter. Not like this kid, Jack, seems to think. She doesn't even fully remember the fight he keeps telling her about. All she has are flashes. The only reason she fought in the first place was because that small-headed bounty hunter and his team had her cornered.

Remembering Tretch, she gives a second look to these two new arrivals. They can't be after her, can they? No. Their gear is more like that of scavengers, road mercs. These are the kinds of mercs who spend the bulk of their time looting corpses and raiding nomad camps. They're tough, but they're no bounty hunters.

Then why won't they stop looking at me?

"Gentlemen!" Jack claps his hands together. The sound snaps Corva out of her thoughts and echoes through the empty bar. Jack doesn't seem to notice. "What can I offer you?"

The road mercs completely ignore Jack as they cross from the front door. They spread out a few paces from each other and approach her spot at the bar.

They're not blocking the door, though. She could make a run for it. Get out of the bar and just keep going. Her travel pack is stashed just outside of town. She'd made it a point to take a detour during her supply run to check on it. Amazingly, even after four days, the pack was still there, undisturbed.

She almost brought the thing back to the bar with her, but the advice Avó gave—"Take what you need, stow the rest"—has become an ingrained habit after all these years. It's a good thing, too. From the look of these mercs, hitting the road again might be her best option.

However, she doesn't move. Sure, part of it is fear, but her questions are really what have a lock on her. The two road mercs close in, surrounding her from a few steps away. Were those flashes of memories real? Maybe this Jack kid is right. Maybe she can fight. Maybe—

The mercs attack. Now's not the time to get lost in thought. She's vaguely aware of Jack yelling something at the mercs, but she can't be distracted by that. She has to focus. The first merc to charge is the thinner one, the one with the smile that doesn't fit the sadness and anger in his eyes. Cackling like a wild dog, he rushes in. His head is down and his arms are spread wide, like a child pretending to be a bird.

He's fast, but Corva manages to sidestep out of reach—and crash right into the chest of the other merc. He's about the same size as the merc with the weird smile, but thicker, hairier, more deliberate. His big, meaty hands lock on her upper arms and squeeze. A wave of panic rolls up Corva's spine as he looks down at her. She can't move at all, can barely struggle.

He grunts through his nose, almost as if disappointed. The hot air rolls out from his nostrils, washing her face in a sick odor that smells like smoke and old shoes. She coughs, but before she can turn away, the hairy merc swings his head forward. His forehead collides with hers, just above her eyebrows.

Corva's vision blurs and she feels her body go limp.

2.10

A Fluke

What in the world just happened?

Jack blinks, trying to make sense of the scene before him. Corva's body sags, held up only by the hairy merc's sausage hands. Something's not right. This is not the same brutal expert fighter from a few days ago. That girl would've torn these two apart with hardly any effort. Downed by a diversion trap and a head-butt? Ridiculous. Even Jack saw that one coming.

Maybe she's not fully recovered. Perhaps she's got some kind of internal damage that can't be seen. *Nah. Lyia woulda noticed somethin' like that when she checked.*

Then what is it? Is she only an unstoppable killer when Zeke is near? *Speaking of which, where did that little monkey run off to?* He's supposed to be here, helping with the reopening. It's not like him to run off like that.

A voice from the front of the bar interrupts Jack's train of thought. "Whoo. Wow, Jackie. That's some security detail you've got there. Really impressive."

Harris. Shoulda guessed. Jack focuses his attention on continuing to wipe the same clean spot on the bar top. "Mornin', Hairless. These two sandpounders belong to you, I take it?"

The smug bastard smiles and tilts his head. With his beak-like nose, his pose makes him look a bit like a curious bird. "Belong? No, kid. Freelancers. Can't do a proper security audit using anyone you know."

"Security audit?"

"Just a routine check of your security, Jackie-Boy. Gotta make sure this place is suitable for being reopened. With what went down a few days ago, we can't be too careful." The militia chief strolls up to the bar, hands clasped behind his back like some kind of official inspector.

He's not. He's just some old bald dude. An old bald dude who runs the gang that defends Bule.

Jack feels his ears heat up. He squeezes the rag in his hand, trying to keep his cool. "'Suitable for being reopened'? Bullshit. You ain't never done a security check like this before. You're trying to shank me down. Well it ain't happenin'. You're not gettin' this bar, not ever." He points his nose over to the two mercs, the hairy one still holding Corva. "An' if these two ain't paying customers, they gotta go."

Harris leans on the bar with a single elbow. "First of all, it's 'shake me down.' Secondly, who's gonna make 'em? Your bouncer looks to be down for the count." He pauses, and a tinge of fear raises the small hairs on the back of Jack's neck. Harris is right. Without Slim's gadgets or Corva's ability to fight—well, the fighting ability he thought she had—he's basically flapping in the wind.

Smiling, the bald militia chief rotates his face toward his "freelancers." He keeps his eyes on Jack, though. "You two can fuck off. See Gorm at the swap shop to get your payment."

Sausage Hands releases Corva's arms and she crumples to the floor, her eyes half-open and dazed. Together, the freelance mercs mosey their way out the front door with a strut that Jack would find funny if he weren't so pissed.

Jack doesn't wait for them to get out. He hops the bar and sets to work on getting Corva's discombobulated mess of limbs unfolded so she can lay flat. Taking the rag he'd been using to wipe the bar, he rolls it into a makeshift pillow and jams it under her head.

A cold compress for her forehead would probably be a good idea. There's a second rag on the other side of the bar, the last clean one he's got until Zeke comes back. He could wrap that around some ice or something. He stands, looking for the rag.

Harris is right in front of him, blocking his view. "Look, Jackie. It's no secret that I think it's a mistake to let you run this place. But I've made peace with it. I really have. I'm not asking for much. Just let the militia install peepers in the main bar area. It's the best thing for the whole town."

"It's Jack, Hairless. And you're in my way." He steps around Harris and clambers up a nearby barstool. Leaning over the bar, he gropes around. That other rag is hanging right around there somewhere. *Ah-ha! Got it.*

"I told you—" He leans a bit farther over the bar and scoops a handful of ice in the rag. "I told you last time. I don't need your creepy little spy cams."

With the rag wrapped around the ice, Jack hops back to the floor and kneels at Corva's side. He rests the makeshift ice pack on Corva's head and glares up at Harris.

"A bar's reputation is built on trust and discretion." It feels weird to hear the old man's words coming out in his voice. But truth is truth. Doesn't matter who says it. "Your 'peepers' would shut this place down an' you know it."

"Jackie—"

Jack hardens his glare at Harris.

"Sorry. Jack. Look around. Your place is basically shut down already." He points down at Corva. "And your 'security detail' just got bested by a pair of half-wit road mercs. You're on a tightrope and I'm the closest thing you've got to a net."

"Why don't you just—"

There's a clatter up in the ceiling trusswork. Half a second later, Zeke swings down and lands on the bar top. Breathing heavily, he looks down at Jack, his eyes wide, emphatic.

Jack can feel his back teeth grinding as he speaks. "Where in the world have you been? You're supposed to be helping me with the reopening. You're—"

There's suddenly a hard, crushing pain in Jack's arm. He looks down and sees Corva's hand clenched around his wrist. Her eyes are wide open, deep green, defiant, and dangerous.

She stares at Jack, almost through him. "They're almost here."

Confused, Jack looks up from her, searching Zeke's and Harris's faces for answers. "Who's almost here?"

Harris shrugs. No help there. However, Zeke bounces on the bar. He alternates between pointing up to the ceiling and the front door of the bar.

"Dammit, Zeke. How is it that you know what she's talkin' about? This would be so much easier if you could talk." Jack tries to stand, but Corva's grip on his wrist isn't letting him go anywhere.

She pulls his arm, yanking him down closer to her, nose-to-nose. She's still staring through him as she whispers, but her words are absolutely clear.

"It's a raid."

Jack bolts upright as far as her viselike grip on his arm will allow. "A raid?"

This soon? Both sides in the war have raid parties that regularly scan for folks using soulmancy, even in imbued tech. He and Lyia were super careful when healing Corva, so that couldn't be it. There wasn't *that* much imbued tech used in the bar fight a couple days ago, was there? The beads used in Plan B were piddly little boosters. Jack never even bothered to tell Harris that he used them—well, one of them.

Just how powerful was the imbued tech that Boneless Joe used?

Jack tilts his head up to Harris. "There's no raid comin', right? You'd get notice on your comm from the lookout, wouldn't ya?"

Harris turns away and taps the comm kneak behind his ear. He speaks under his breath, so Jack can't really make out what he's saying. In the meantime, Zeke hops down from the bar to Jack's shoulder. Between the onslaught of chirps and the pulling of Jack's hair and ear, it's clear that he wants them to get out. Now.

The militia chief turns back around. "Lookout says that there isn't much going on." He points at Zeke. "They just said that this guy was sitting up there with them and suddenly started freaking out. Almost wrecked the place trying to get them to look in the scope. And when they did a scan with the scope, there wasn't anything to be seen."

Jack twists his neck to look at Zeke on his shoulder. The little monkey isn't letting up. Hopping. Pulling. Pointing. It's not like him to get this bent out of shape over nothing. Jack looks back to Harris. "Much as I hate to say it, your crew at the lookout is wrong. Zeke's got a sense for this kind of thing. We should make our way to the siege caves. Gimme a hand with her?"

Harris scoffs. "You want me to trust a concussed girl and your bar pet over the crew I trained myself? Who's spouting bullshit now? The scopes at that lookout give us a full view of the area around this town. We've been scanning hard ever since your snafu. That big-armed one was leaking a lot of juice from that tech he was using. If my crew sees anything, you'll hear the raid sirens going and I'll get immediate notification."

He puts a hand up to his ear. "Do you hear that? No siren. And my comms? Completely silent." He lowers his hand, uncharacteristically sincere. "Look, we know they're coming. Just not right n—" He stops and his facial expression completely transforms to a wrinkled look of concern.

He taps his comm kneak. "What? Are you sure? You just said— how far off? Yes." Harris pauses to cast a suspicious scowl at Jack and Zeke. "Of course you trigger the siren, dammit!"

Bule's raid siren echoes across the canyon. Its sound pierces every nook and cranny. Jack can feel it reverberating in his chest. He exchanges a look with Zeke, then turns back to Harris.

Jack lifts his free hand and cups his ear. "Hey Hairless, do you hear somethin'? It might be a siren."

2.11

RAID COMING

The world is a foggy, muddled mess. Corva blinks her eyes a few times. It's so hard to focus. The middle of her forehead is cold, and it aches. Despite knowing that she's lying still on her back, her body feels like it's slinging between passing out and throwing up. What in the world made her think it would be a good idea to work at a bar in an isolated gray haven?

An image flashes in her mind. At least, she thinks it's in her mind. It's his face. Zeke. The monkey. The edges of her vision sharpen and she can see a bit more clearly. It's not an image in her mind. Zeke is really there. He peers down at her, concern filling his slit eyes. But it's brief. A moment later he's turned away from her, pawing Jack's shoulder and ear.

Why is the boy leaning over her? He isn't paying attention to Zeke. He's not looking at her, either.

"So you gonna gimme a hand here, or what?" Jack is holding a cold, wet rag on her forehead, but he's talking to that older guy he keeps calling "Hairless." His voice registers in her mind like there's a wall of water between them.

The balding older man shakes his head. "Sorry kid. Got protocols. You're not the only one living in this burg." He spins on his heel and takes long, quick steps to the front door. "Make your way over to the north siege caves. We'll talk later about how you brought this on the town with your failure to manage this bar."

Corva can feel Jack's arm tense and tighten in her hand. She's holding his other wrist, and hard. She's the reason he's leaned over her. He's unable to sit fully upright. She must've pulled him down.

She looks to his face. Anger. Hairless's comment appears to have really affected him. His eyes are closed and his ears are bright red. She can feel his heartbeat through her grip on his wrist. It's fast, as if he's currently sprinting full-out across a field. His lips are moving, but no words are coming out. *Is he talking to himself?*

And then, just like that, his arm is slack. Relaxed. Even though she knows that his heart is still racing, she'd swear he almost looks calm.

His eyes open and he shouts to the front door, just as the bald man is nearly out. "Hey, Hairless! The raid party. They the Sheeps or the Goats?"

"Umbrati. Not that it matters. Get to the caves."

Despite Zeke's insistent prodding, Jack waits a few seconds after Hairless is gone before looking back down at her. His pupils are tiny, constricted dots in a circle of gray. "We should go. Can you stand?"

"Yeah. I think so." She releases his wrist and props herself on her elbows as he takes the rag off her head. She waits a beat. The watery fog over her vision and hearing clears a bit more. She pushes herself up to a sitting position and leans back against the bottom of the bar. "What's a siege cave?"

"Side benefit of putting a town on the side of a canyon is that you can burrow into the rock for protection. The way I hear it, the caves were the first things they built when they made Bule. Expanded some mines that'd gone dry and built out from there."

"How far away are they?"

"Not far. Maybe ten minutes if we hurry. Depends on how fast you can walk." He pauses. A look of confusion bunches up his brow.

"What?"

He hesitates a bit, like he's trying to choose his words carefully. "What's your game? You coulda beat those two guys, no problem. Why didn't you?"

She looks away. Being a bouncer for the bar was part of their deal. It's the part that she knew she couldn't live up to then. And she knows she can't live up to it now either, regardless of what he—or her spotty memory—says. Sure, she'd gotten a bit of combat training with the other kids in Fareburne, and years of living on the road have hardened her. But evasion is her talent, not confrontation.

"I'm no fighter. I couldn't beat them."

"Bullshit. I've got playback that shows otherwise. If you had any tech on you, I could get you to see that."

"Look. I don't care what you or your little neats say—"

"Kneaks."

"What?"

"They're called 'kneaks.' With a 'K' … two of 'em actually. Kirsch Neural-Enhancing Aug—"

"Whatever. Point is, I know what I am and what I'm not. I'm not a fighter. I'm good at avoiding, escaping, and hiding. Not engaging."

Jack stares at her for a moment. A constipated stillness fills the air between them. Even Zeke briefly pauses his hopping and pawing at Jack's shoulder. The boy lowers his head to one side, away from both her and Zeke. "Augmentation Kit."

"Puta que pariu! Are you even listening to me at all?" *What's wrong with this kid?*

He blinks, his mind returning from wherever his compulsion to finish his thought took it. "What? Yeah, I'm listenin'. Look, you're wrong. I seen what I seen. You're just gonna hafta believe me until I can get a screen to show you the playback."

He twists his neck over to look at Zeke, who's resuming his nervous gesticulations on Jack's shoulder. The raid siren continues to blare, an annoying screech adding anxiety to their every word. "But right now, we've gotta get movin'. Ain't smart to be here at the bar during a raid, 'specially since them Goats are probably trackin' the imbued tech that was used here."

He rises to his feet and pauses to tug on the bottom of his vest. As he smooths the vest with the flat of his hand, it lingers a moment over the left side. He gives that spot a quick pat before he reaches out, offering his hand. Corva reaches past his hand and grabs at his elbow to pull herself up. The poor kid has to brace himself against a barstool to prevent himself from collapsing—and her with him. Fortunately, although her head swims a bit, her feet are steady, stable.

She looks to Zeke and Jack. Zeke. The little monkey is almost close enough that she could touch him. There are secrets behind those strangely slitted eyes. She'd just need to reach out and—

There's a slap on the top of her hand and she realizes that she really *is* reaching past Jack's face to Zeke.

Jack scowls. "None of that now. Don't need you goin' all freak out, then black out on me. Not here. Not now. Got enough problems with this raid. Don't need the extra worry of dragging your unconscious ass across Upper Bule. And that'd be after bandaging whatever damage you end up doing to me."

Zeke lets out an insistent chirp and pushes again on Jack's shoulder. Jack doesn't look at him, and instead keeps his eyes focused on Corva. "Zeke, I swear if you push on me one more time, I'm gonna stop trading for that dried fruit you like so much. You'll be back to eatin' potatoes and toast."

The monkey's eyes push incredibly wide before narrowing to a bitter squint. He drops back to his haunches and rests his arms on his knees. His gaze darts back and forth between Jack and Corva, impatient. Petulant. That said, he's not jumping or pawing on Jack anymore.

Jack is still staring at her. "You ready?"

SEE THEM RUN

Motherfuckers better keep that door open. Jack leads Corva along the dog-legged alleys and corridors on the way to Upper Bule's north siege cave. They wasted a lot of time getting out of the bar. He watches Zeke ahead of him. The furry little beast bounds from one rocky wall to another, swinging and sliding along bits of piping and conduit that run along the narrow paths between buildings.

Show-off. Jack looks up. Pockets of sky peek down at them through the chaotic nest of stone and metal that make up this rock city. *This would go a lot faster if we could take the roofs.*

That's not possible, though. He glances over his shoulder at Corva. She's keeping up pretty well, but her coordination is off. A mere shadow of the spinning ball of fury he's watched and rewatched on his playback. She'd need to be a lot more sure-footed to work across Bule's rooftops without falling.

What's she on about? "Not a fighter"? He shakes his head. Something isn't right. How could she not know her own abilities? It doesn't make sense. Maybe she hit her head and she just can't remember. Of course, it's possible that she's lying. But getting her bell rung by that road merc is one tough-assed way to sell a lie. *Also, fuck Harris an' his bullshit "security audit." I got your number, you bald bastard.*

He straightens his head just in time to see a wall in front of him. His feet don't have enough traction to stop him. The best he can do is turn his shoulder as he slides into it. The wall is unyielding. His arm grinds into its rough surface before he bounces off it, landing as gracefully as a cow falling from a tightrope.

"You okay?"

Corva stands over him, back straight, head on a swivel. *Has she been in a raid before? Of course she has. Everyone has.* Still, there's something off about how she carries herself. She's intense, alert. Anxious.

It's not like everyone is super casual during a raid, but these are fairly routine things. Sirens go off and folks either hole up in personal bunkers or work their way to the protection of the caves. Most go to the caves. Personal bunkers might be cozy, but if they're breached, you're done. It doesn't matter how tough you are. At least in the cave, you've got other folks as backup. Well-armed backup.

"Hey! Are you alright?"

She's looking down at him now. Jack pushes himself back to his feet, slapping dust and grit from his clothes. His shoulder is a bit sore, but otherwise he's fine. "Yeah. I'm good."

"You even know where you're going?"

Of all the— Jack's chin shoots up as if spring-loaded. Back straight, he whirls around to face Corva. "Yes, I know where I'm going! This is *my* damn town, girlie."

She takes a step back. "Sorry, I didn't mean—"

"We got three more turns and a short run of steps to the doors. Zeke's probably already there." He pivots back in the direction of the path, careful this time to avoid running into anything. He doesn't look back, just starts jogging again. He turns to yell over his shoulder, "See if you can't keep up."

His ears are hot. *Of course I know where we're goin'. Wouldn'ta even run into that wall if I weren't looking back to make sure you were okay.*

They round the last corner and slide to a stop at the base of the wide steps up to the siege cave. Harris is at the top. He and two members of the Bule militia are guiding the last stragglers through the little sliver of space left between the large bay doors closing in front of the cave.

Jack spins around, scanning the buildings that line the edge of the little courtyard. "Where's Zeke?"

Corva steps up next to him. "Maybe he's already inside."

"No. Zeke wouldn't do that. He'd wait. Make sure we get in." He gives a harder look at the empty kiosks and darkened windows. "Somethin' ain't right."

She tugs on his arm. "Well, let's get up the stairs at least. Maybe your militia friend up there has seen him."

He jerks his arm back. "Harris is *not* my friend."

"Whatever. We've got to get out of the open. We're too exposed here."

Jack squints, and the words come out of his mouth before he can even think about it. His bullshit meter is pinging at nine. "'Too exposed?' Funny way to talk for someone who ain't a fighter."

THIS IS NOT THE WAY

"You really wanna hash this out here? Now?" Corva looks around. They shouldn't be wasting their time here. She isn't a fighter, but that doesn't mean she hasn't seen her fair share of raids. They're not anything to take lightly. Her mind flashes back to the attack on Fareburne. Sure, that was ten years ago, but it's not like much has changed since then. Doesn't matter if the raid is Umbrati, Karui, or other people. When a raid comes, you run and hide. She knows that better than most.

That said, folks in this town seem to be on the same page. Even though nearly everyone here is heavily armed, they've all piled into the security of their caves. Even the militia. She sees two guards duck behind the closing siege doors. The only one left up there is that Harris guy.

And then there's this kid, Jack. Unarmed. Standing out here without cover. Looking for a monkey. Trying to argue with her about whether or not she's skilled at fighting. *How in the world are you not dead?*

Uncharacteristically, he hasn't spoken. The little brat is actually considering an answer to her question! She snaps her fingers in front of his face to get his attention. "Hey! It was rhetorical. The answer is no. You don't want to hash that out here and now. Not if you have any sense."

She grabs his arm and starts dragging him to the steps. "Come on. We've got to get in the cave before your *not*-friend closes the door on us."

He doesn't pull his arm away this time, but he's still dragging his feet. "What about Zeke?"

The question gives her a moment of pause. Only for a moment, though. She can't put her finger on why, but she knows that Zeke is near. "Something tells me that your monkey is pretty good at taking care of himself. Even if he's not already in the cave, I'm sure he'll be fine. Neither side of the war has any interest in pets."

That makes Jack yank his arm back. "Zeke ain't no pet! He's— he's family. An' he's the ..."

Jack's words trail off and his eyes focus somewhere behind her, farther up the stairs. All of the color drains from his face.

Corva doesn't need to turn around. She already knows what's standing there. An eerie collision of clicking and growling fills her ears, like a small group of people trying to clear their throats at the same time. Nothing else makes a sound like that.

It's an Umbrati grunt.

The thing is close. She can feel its body heat on the back of her neck. The putrid smell of it overwhelms her senses. She can even taste it. Her eyes start to water, and she can barely breathe. Every attempt to inhale gets caught in her throat.

Choking, only one word repeats in her mind. *Escape.*

She ducks as low as possible while remaining on her feet and charges at Jack. There's a crashing sound behind her, but she ignores it. She sticks her arm out and hooks it around Jack's waist, pulling him with her.

Jack keeps trying to say something. Corva isn't sure if it's shock or the fact that she may have knocked the wind out of him, but there's only one sound coming from his mouth.

"Fffffffff—"

They make it a few paces before she spins around to face their attacker.

This creature is grotesque. There are signs that it used to be a person. A man, perhaps. But the tattered scraps of clothing are the only hints remaining of its former life. Maybe it once had a smooth, even complexion and a regularly proportioned body. Now the grunt's dark green skin looks like it's been stretched over its gaunt frame and elongated limbs. A dark, greasy mane of hair extends down its back to its waist and a mottled layer of dirt, grime, and dried blood covers it from head to toe.

The thing looks like it spends its off-hours just standing in a room of exploding pigeons.

Crouching in a pile of rubble at the base of the steps, the grunt rotates its head to face them. The metal plate riveted over its mouth would be bothersome enough, but … its eyes. One of the empty sockets is surrounded by deep scars, evidence that at some point in the past, the grunt had clawed the eye out on its own. The second eyeball is still in place, but it doesn't function as an eye at all. It doesn't even move. The gray, glassy orb is skewered into the socket with a nail jammed through the grunt's temple. A glint from the tip of the nail reflects from within the empty hole where the other eye once was.

Still clicking and growling, the grunt raises from its crouch. The creature's abnormally long arms remain on the ground, but even so, it towers two or three heads taller than Corva. The thing extracts its arms from the pile of rubble. One arm is noticeably heavier than the other. As the dust and pebbles roll off, it's easy to see why. The hand on the heavy arm looks like it's been replaced with a weighted metal ball of some sort. The opposite arm moves more freely, not burdened by a weight. However, the free forearm is a veritable pincushion of spikes and long knives that have been stabbed through, all the way to their hilts.

The grunt stalks toward them on all fours, shoulders raising and lowering with each step like a big cat.

Corva slides a foot back and keeps Jack behind her. Desperate, she scans the tiny courtyard for options. There has to be something, anything they can use to protect themselves or get away.

Nope.

Their best choice is to turn around and make for the narrow alley they'd used to get here. Not wanting to telegraph her plan, she takes a sidelong glance at the alley. There's a small cart that they'll need to run around, but other than that, the route is clear. She cuts an eye over at Jack, still behind her. He's not paying attention to her at all. His eyes are glued on the grunt.

He doesn't look afraid, though. More like he's coming up with his own strategy. One hand is wrapped tightly around the bottom of his vest.

What's he holding there?

It doesn't matter. There's no time to clue him in on her plan. She reaches back and grabs his free wrist. He'll just have to improvise and keep up.

Now or never. The grunt lowers its upper body, ready to pounce. Corva waits a beat, letting the thing commit to its attack. The second it bolts forward at them, she spins, springing toward the alley. She yanks on Jack's arm and feels it pop out of socket as he struggles to turn and follow. He screams out in pain, but he doesn't stop moving. He's right there with her.

There's a smashing sound behind them as the grunt collides with a street vendor's cart and shelving. The cacophony continues as it tries to untangle itself. But she keeps her attention in front of them. They're almost back to the alley.

Almost.

She hears a familiar clicking, throat-clearing noise. However, it's not behind them, where she expects it. It's somewhere up ahead. They're a mere two or three steps away from the alley when a second grunt rounds the corner, blocking their exit.

Corva and Jack skid to a stop, sliding just out of the grunt's reach.

"Filho de uma puta."

AIR SUPPORT

Don't pass out. Jack swallows hard and grabs his arm. The pain is causing the edges of his vision to blur. The feeling of floaty light-headedness alternates with waves of agony radiating from his shoulder. At least Corva isn't holding his arm anymore. Downside: now there are two grunts.

This second one is smaller than Eye Kabob, but no less sick and mean-looking. This one might've been a woman before being conscripted by the Goats. A person. Not any more, though. Now it's got the markings of a Goat grunt. Dark green skin, stretched arms and legs, a steel plate covering its mouth, and no eyes.

Compared to Eye Kabob, this grunt has less body hair, and its eye sockets don't have the drama of scars and self-skewering. The eye holes on this one seem to have been scooped out much more cleanly. Likewise, its arms don't appear to have the same extreme modifications. No spikes or replaced hands, just a whole mess of chains wrapped around its stretched-out forearms.

Still, that doesn't mean Scoops here is any less dangerous than Eye Kabob. Jack silently curses. Nothing's going right. He should've left the cylinder with the imbued tech back at the bar. It's useless here and would only draw in more grunts from the raid party. Even stupider, they left the bar without any real weapons. Also, Zeke is missing. And apparently Corva doesn't know how to be the vicious ball of violence that he knows she can be.

What's up with that? She shows up an' fights with more skill than any merc I ever seen. Then she heals up faster than anyone ever ought to be able to. But she can't remember any of that? How does—

"Get down!"

Harris's voice echoes across the canyon, cutting Jack's thoughts short. Jack doesn't even look back. He drops to a squat immediately and covers his head with his arms. Well, his one good arm, at least. The other one is over his head, too, but it isn't so much covering him as it is just serving as an obstruction for whatever may fall on him. Glancing up, he sees that Corva is still standing.

"G'down, girlie!" He reaches up to her wrist with his good arm and tries to pull her down. Even as blasts from Harris's air cannon slam into Eye Kabob and the ground around them, she's not budging. Bits of rock and a healthy helping of dust rains down on them. She doesn't even shift her weight. *Damn it. Of all the times to let fear get the best of ya.*

Jack preps himself to jump and push her over, but he never gets a chance to act. He's preempted by a familiar high-pitched scream. *Zeke!*

The little flash of fur skids into view and hops on Jack's back. Still chirping and screaming, Zeke climbs up Jack's arm and pries his grip from Corva's wrist. Jack lets go despite the mountain of questions piling up in his mind. Patting Jack's forearm as if thanking him for letting go, Zeke slides down to Jack's shoulder.

Scowling, Jack turns his head to Zeke. "What in the world was that all abou—Oh."

As Jack finishes twisting to look at Zeke, he catches a glimpse up at Corva's face. She's still standing there, not moving. But something's changed. The green in her eyes dances as she focuses on Scoops. Her smile is as unsettling as it is wide.

"Not a Fighter"

This feeling is unreal. Corva has complete control of her body, but she's moving in ways that she's never moved before. Technical maneuvers that require years of practice and training. Training that wasn't available in Fareburne or any town she's passed through since. But it's fluid for her; she hardly has to think. She has muscle memory for techniques she's never done. In three steps, she's already slipped behind the grunt with the cleanly scooped eye sockets.

From this angle, she can see the other grunt, the one with the skewered eye. It's being battered by bursts of air as that militia chief rushes down the stairs to them. Jack is still cowered in a squat, covering his head and neck as best as he can. Zeke sits on his shoulder, staring at her.

He nods, as if giving her permission.

Immediately, she steps on the back of the grunt's leg and launches herself up. She's eye level with the back of the grunt's head, and still has plenty of upward momentum. Without thinking, she reaches out and grabs on, one hand on each side of the thing's head, then lets the inertia swing her body all the way around like she's the spinning part of one of those noise makers that kids play with. However, only one sound comes from the grunt: *Crack!*

She's back on the ground, standing in front of the grunt. But she's still looking at the back of its head. Its face is pointing completely the wrong way. She releases the head, allowing it to flop uselessly to one side on the grunt's slumping shoulders. Its body follows suit and crumples to the ground.

Corva takes a moment to look down. The thing is lying on its belly, but its empty eye sockets stare straight up. Her foot nudges the grunt's head, almost playing with it. Its neck is broken, and the head rolls around like a ball on a string.

She did that.

Well, sort of. Her body did the moves, but she doesn't feel like she can really take credit for them. She's not even sure that she's the one in the driver's seat. Even now, her foot is still toying with the grunt corpse's head. And despite her misgivings with this whole situation, she can feel her mouth forming the shape of a smirk. An amused, contemptuous smirk. That's not exactly her go-to facial expression at a time like this.

There's a scream behind her. Not Zeke. Not Jack. It's the militia chief, Harris.

She glances over her shoulder. Even though his air cannon did a lot of damage, he's apparently still having trouble with the skewer-eyed grunt. Pieces of the air cannon lie scattered at his feet. It was likely smashed by the heavy ball the grunt has for a left hand.

Harris is doing his best to fend off the grunt with a shock baton, but the thing has his leg held down with its bladed pincushion of a right arm. It leans its weight on Harris's leg. The sound of Harris's knee bending the wrong way is drowned out by the balding militia chief's own screaming as he repeatedly stabs at the grunt with his shock baton.

Of course, every time his baton makes contact with the grunt, Harris has a bit of hiccup in his screaming. The jolt from the baton must be traveling through the grunt to where it's leaning on the man's knee. However, that doesn't seem to stop him, or the grunt for that matter. The skewer-eyed creature lifts its other arm, ready to drop its weighted ball of a hand down on Harris.

Corva turns to look away. She can't help him, and she'd rather be trying to find an escape than see the contents of some stranger's skull. But her body isn't responding. It tenses. It wants to engage. No. It's *going* to engage. There's a moment of resistance—fractions of a second—as she fights to regain control of herself. It doesn't work.

At first she thinks she's turning away, but its only to reach down and grab the dead grunt's hand. She twists until there's a slight mechanical click and she feels the hand come loose. She gives a little tug and the hand pulls free. The chain that's wrapped around the dead grunt's forearm connects to the back of the wrist.

Corva doesn't have time to wonder how she knew that would happen. She spins back to Harris, dragging the hand-connected chain behind her. With a single leap, she launches herself over Jack and Zeke, toward the grunt that's attacking Harris. She shoots through the narrow space between Harris and the grunt, pulling the chain taut just in time to block the grunt's weighted arm from smashing Harris's face into a sticky goo.

The grunt tries to push down against the chain, but Corva's already on the next phase of her attack. Still holding the chain, she runs to a spot behind the grunt and stomps her foot on the metal links. The chain jerks the grunt's weighted arm back into its chest, rocking the grunt backward, toward Corva. It's not a heavy strike, but it's enough to make the grunt lift its blade-pierced arm and adjust its center of gravity, giving Harris just enough space to drag his mangled leg free and worm himself clear.

Not waiting for the grunt to turn and face her, Corva leaps on its back and wraps the remaining length of chain around the thing's neck. She can hear it choking, gasping for air behind the steel plate over its mouth. But lack of airflow isn't enough to take the fight out of this thing. It reaches up at her with its bladed and spiked arm, swinging violently.

She easily dodges the arm each time. The whole while, she keeps the chain tight around the grunt's neck. Although the grunt seems to be swinging its arm haphazardly, there's a certain rhythm to it. She can feel herself anticipating it, getting its timing. Getting comfortable. *Ready. Set. Go.*

She lets go of the chain with both hands and reaches up at the pincushion arm just as it's beginning its downswing. She snags its thumb in one hand and a few fingers in the other. Letting her weight drop, she adds her momentum to that of the already fast-moving arm. There's a tearing sound just as it hyperextends and she uses that as a cue. With as much strength as she can muster, she pushes the pierced arm forward. One of the longer spikes is lined up perfectly. It gouges a hole right in the base of the grunt's neck.

There's a squealing sound from the grunt, and then it stops moving. Corva, still holding onto the grunt's hand, pulls herself up and places the base of her palm on the flat side of the spike that's been buried into the back of the grunt's head. She gives a single hard push, and it's enough to cause the whole creature to fall forward. Hand still on the base of the spike, she rides the grunt to the ground. Just as it hits, she drops all of her weight into her hand. The spike jams the rest of the way through the grunt's arm and burrows the tip further into the back of its head. The scraping of metal on rock beneath the grunt is the final punctuation on the creature's death.

Corva hops off the grunt's back and on to firm ground. She lifts her hands and looks at them. Heavy, but there's no resistance. Her body is listening to her again. The giant smirk she's been trying to fight has dissolved into a look of shock and confusion that more accurately reflects how she's feeling. She's got no words.

Harris sits on the ground a few meters in front of her. Wincing and holding his knee, he gives her an appreciative nod. She stares at him blankly, not quite able to cobble together an adequate response. Suddenly light-headed, she turns to look at Jack and Zeke. *Is this what they saw of me in that bar fight?*

She doesn't get a chance to ask them the question. She doesn't even get to see their faces. Her legs suddenly lose the ability to keep her upright. As her knees buckle and she collapses to the ground, everything goes dark again.

A Bad Time to Negotiate

Still covering his head, Jack peeks out between his arms. Corva's lying facedown on the ground. Spent. Dead? Ignoring the pain in his shoulder, Jack scrambles over and checks her pulse. He breathes a sigh of relief. *Good. Not dead.*

The same can not be said for Eye Kabob and Scoops. They're both clearly never getting up again. He looks back down at Corva. *"Not a fighter."* *Yeah. My ass.*

He feels movement around his neck and catches a glimpse of Zeke leaning down from his shoulder to look at Corva. The sight of the curious monkey reminds him that he's got something to be pissed off about. "What the shit, Zeke? Since when did you start abandoning me during a raid? Dick move, man."

"Afraid that's my fault." Harris is on his feet, limping over to them. "I think he came to let us know you guys were on the way. Raised a helluva stink when we started to close the main doors on the cave. Little bastard did all sorts of things to slow us down from closing them all the way. When that didn't work, he took to jumping up and slapping each of us one at a time. Had me pissed off enough to chase him to the stairs. That's when I saw you two."

The thought of Zeke slapping Harris in the mouth instantly melts Jack's anger with the monkey. He grins, casting a quick sidelong glance at his four-handed buddy. "That sounds like Zeke."

He looks down at Harris's leg. His knee is already wrapped in a stretchy fabric with a series of stiff ridges that run vertically around it. Jack nods at the knee wrap. "That Slim's handiwork?"

The militia chief snorts and follows Jack's line of sight to his leg. "It's a tactical brace. And no. It's not one of your tinkerer's broken toys. New tech from up north. Normal use adds strength to the joints. Augmentation. Gorm traded for a set of 'em a couple weeks back." He runs his hands along the brace's ridges. "Didn't expect to need this secondary feature so soon."

Harris looks up the steps, back toward the siege cave. "We've gotta go. Lookout said six grunts in the raid." He does a quick survey of the courtyard. The look on his face is that of someone who doesn't believe what he's seeing, but has resigned to accept it. "Who the hell takes on an Umbrati grunt with their bare hands?"

"Two." Jack's grin is only getting bigger.

"What?"

"Two grunts. She took out two of them Goat grunts."

"Yeah." Harris shakes his head as if doing so would suddenly rattle the world into making sense. "Yeah. Well, we're gonna catch hell if we're still out in the open when the other four find out. Time to go."

Jack squats down next to Corva, who is still mostly unconscious. Zeke hops off his shoulder and sniffs the air around them, keeping a lookout. Jack looks up at Harris. "You gonna help me with her this time?"

Harris gives another head shake and finally manages to pull himself out of his daze. With a pained look on his face, he squats on the other side of Corva.

Jack points at Harris's knee. "You gonna be alright?"

"Yeah. The brace is great for gettin' you moving, but it doesn't do much of anything for the pain. I'll be fine. Let's just get to the cave. One. Two. Three!"

With effort, the two of them hoist Corva up so her arms hang over their shoulders. Of course, at his height, Jack can't help lift her but so much. Fortunately, she's not completely unresponsive. Besides, the last few days gave him a lot of practice with moving her around while incapacitated.

The trio shuffles their way up the steps to the siege cave. Zeke leads the way, pausing every few steps to wait for them and nervously scan the area.

Jack cuts an eye over at Harris and notices that the balding man is staring at him. It's a look that says either he's in a lot of pain or he's heavy in thought. Could be both. Jack points his face forward and focuses on getting to the cave entrance.

They get to the top of the steps and Harris reaches for his comm kneak. "I got 'em, Denny. Let us in."

There's a series of clanking noises from the smaller steel vault door next to the main entrance to the cave. A second later, the door cracks open.

As they drag through the last dozen or so paces to the door, Jack looks back across Corva's shoulders at Harris. The militia chief still has that look of mental constipation on his face. Jack takes a deep breath and mentally repeats more negotiation advice Old Man V. gave him. *Go slow. A distracted mark is an easy mark.*

"Hey, Harris."

"Now isn't the time, Jackie."

Shit. Maybe he isn't as distracted as I thought. Regardless, Jack pushes the point. "Way I see it, there ain't no better time than now. You seen what she can do. Two grunts! With her bare hands, man! We got a town full of mercs and there ain't a single one of 'em who ever even tried that. They're all hiding in the cave."

"They're smart. She's unpredictable. And unconscious."

Jack glances at Corva, her head hanging forward, bobbing with each shuffling step they take.

"Look. Sure, she's a bit rough around the edges. But she can obviously handle herself. Between her and the kit repairs I'm gettin' from Slim, that should be enough to keep the bar crowd under control."

Harris lets out an audible sigh. "Jack, this last blowup—literally—at your bar was the third one since you started running it. And the worst one, too. Bule exists for two reasons. It's—"

"Yeah. Discretion and trust. I know. Ain't like I just got here."

"A bar massacre with imbued tech isn't discreet. Raids aren't discreet."

"An' spy cams in a bar don't build trust. We've had this back 'n forth before."

They make it to the heavy vault door, and the people inside push it just wide enough for them to slide through. Jack decides it's time for his final plea.

"Look, Harris. Just gimme a trial run—an honest one. No surprise audits or any other bullshit. If we can't control the bar, then you can put your peepers in. How's that sound?"

"A month."

Jack gawks at Harris. The balding older man answered way too fast. Was he expecting this? "What?"

Finally in the cave, the vault door closes behind them. Jack and Harris sit Corva on the ground and lean her against the wall. Zeke hops up and reclaims his perch on Jack's shoulder. Once he's sure that Corva won't slump to the side and hurt herself, Jack stands up and spins to face Harris.

The militia chief straightens, stretching his back. He accepts a rag from one of the folks near the door and mops the sweat and grime from his head. He's talking to them like Jack isn't even there. "No, I'm good. This brace kicked in right when it needed to. Air cannon's a total loss, though. Wore it out blowin' those metal-faced bastards back to Hell."

With great effort, Jack keeps his mouth shut. *Let him take credit. Treat it like a favor. Besides—* He glances down at Corva. *The bar don't need any more special attention.*

Harris sends the people near them on their way and turns back to Jack, getting right in his face. He speaks fast, just loud enough that only Jack can hear him. "You have a month, Jack. A month with no serious incidents like this last one. And we're past the peepers discussion now. You lose control of your place even once in that month and you're done. Town'll reclaim it."

"What? You can't do that!" Jack tries to keep his voice down, matching Harris, but it squeaks and cracks on the last word. Fortunately, it doesn't seem that anyone else is paying any attention to them.

"Not me, Jackie. The town. I'm not the only one tired of cleaning up after the shit that's been leaking out of Vardin's bar since you took over."

"But—"

"Or, the town could just reclaim the bar now. I'm sure there's enough people from the board here in the cave to make a vote."

Jack's shoulders slump. This is not the way this was supposed to go. "No. No need for a vote. You've got a deal. One month."

Harris smiles, the smug bastard. "Good luck, Jackie."

"Fuck you, Hairless."

2.17

Death

I fucking hate telepathy.

Thegn cranes his pale, gaunt frame over a massive table, staring at his maps. His open fingers, old and deceptively frail-looking, stretch one of the maps so it lays flat. He spits at the ground. *Yeah, yeah. I know you can all hear me. So what? For fuck's sake, when's the last time I heard actual words from a voice that wasn't my own?*

Looking up, he scowls at the Karui technician entering the room. Being blind and mute, the Karui can only effectively communicate by way of telepathy, but Thegn is too annoyed—and too drunk—to care. He's barely heard even his own voice in the last few weeks; communicating with one in the Karui hive is a poor substitute.

Part of the problem is you don't use words. You push the whole idea, fully baked, into my head. You know how annoying it is to have your questions answered before—

See? That's exactly what I mean! Fuck efficiency! It'd be nice to get a complete thought assembled before you yank it out of my skull.

Aiming his face in Thegn's direction, the technician adjusts his grip on a cylindrical metal container about the height and diameter of an adult chicken. The technician tilts his cleanly shaven head inquisitively. His eyes and mouth are covered in their ceremonial bandages, so any cues from facial expressions are impossible for Thegn to see. Of course, it's not like there's much to see under the bandages. All conscripts to the Karui are first enlisted among the legions of the hive. And all members of the hive undergo purification—a removal of hair, eyes, tongue, and memories. The Umbrati have a similar induction process for their new recruits, but they don't use sugary terms like "purification."

Over a hundred and fifty years, and still no clear winner in the war. Not that I expected anything else.

Thegn takes a step away from his maps and straightens his back. His old bones creak in about half a dozen different places, but there's thankfully no stiffness as he reaches his full towering height. Walking past the newly arrived subordinate, he reaches for his jug. He takes a deep swig and wipes his mouth with the back of his opposite hand. It's an ineffective gesture; a good portion of the overflow already found its way along his short, scraggly beard and is now dripping on his shirt. He lowers himself into his chair and stares out across the length of his dank subterranean room.

The only surviving member of the original Four, Thegn, the Reaper, was there when the war between the Karui and Umbrati started. Technically speaking, he helped start it.

What a fucking wreck that turned out to be.

He takes another pull from the jug and glares at the technician. *No, not yet. I'm in the middle of a memory here. Every time you interrupt, I'm going to take another dr—.*

Gulp.

You made me do that.

Thegn attempts to punctuate the point by taking yet another deep draft but finds only a couple drops left in his jug.

"Fine. But I'm talking out loud. What have you got?" He faintly smiles at the sound as his scratchy voice echoes across the chamber. The smile doesn't last long.

"Wait. What? *All* of them? We contracted three teams of hunters for this! Should've been more than enough." Thegn stands, perhaps a bit too abruptly, and lurches his way to the glass wall on the opposite side of the room. "Let me see the playback."

The Karui technician dutifully sets the canister on Thegn's table and proceeds to unscrew its lid. A plume of fog pours from the container as its lid is removed, revealing a head preserved in a cryogenic bath.

"You said he checked in at a desert post? Which one? Not the number! That doesn't mean anything to me. Use its name or the name of something near—thank you. So he reported at the desert post just north of canyon country." *Stupid bastard. He should've known better than to report in with nothing more than information and an injury.*

Thegn looks back at the head resting in the canister. *Your head is much easier to transport than that large body you had ... especially a skull as small as yours. Hey—*

"Hey!" He reaches out and stops the technician from putting the canister on his table. "Not there! I've still got stains on my maps from the last time. Use the stand." Thegn points to the metal stand at his right. "I put it there for a reason."

Complying, the technician sets the canister on its proper location. With his hands free, he holds them a bit above the face of the small-headed bounty hunter. The technician's hands pulse light blue, and the muscles in the disembodied head begin to twitch and seize rapidly. Slowly, the twitching synchronizes with the pulsing glow of the Karui tech's hands. Eventually, the seizing stops and the head comes to rest.

The technician splays his fingers. The eyelids of the small preserved head snap open as consciousness is forced back behind them. The headless bounty hunter's eyes dart about, frantically trying to figure out what's going on.

Poor dope. Seeing your mouth move, I can practically hear the screams you'd make if you still had lungs. I hear that being decapitated feels like being suffocated on air. What an odd feeling that must be.

The cold, logical brutality of the Karui—the Force of Light—ceased to bother Thegn ages ago. It no longer strikes him as hypocrisy, just merely ironic.

Take this situation as an example. The Karui at that post could have easily healed this bounty hunter when he checked in. But failure, coupled with his wounds, made knowledge his only valuable commodity. Since playback kneaks use the brain for storage, the obvious solution was to remove the hunter's head, preserve it, and transport it to base for analysis. Sure, they could have just downloaded the images from his playback to a data sphere, but kneak downloads aren't as reliable as what the Karui term "primary origination" data. Makes perfect sense.

Keeping one glowing hand above the bodiless head, the Karui technician reaches behind the hunter's left ear and activates the playback kneak. Returning his hand above the silently screaming face, the technician leans back. On the glass wall before Thegn, moving images materialize from an amorphous cloud, like ink dripped into a glass of water.

The bounty hunter's life flashes before Thegn's eyes. *I have to hand it to humans. They continue to innovate in even the most dire of circumstances. This was so much harder to do before they invented these "kneak" devices. And nearly impossible to do with a corpse.*

The images from the hunter's kneak play in reverse. Though there are gaps missing, it tells a definite story. Decapitation, a fruitless argument with the mute Karui field soldiers, a slow trek through the desert, huddling by a fire next to the corpse of a bounty hunter with an enlarged arm, being dragged out of a canyon by that same hunter, a bar fight—

"Wait! This block. Run it forward in real time from here."

Thegn watches the carnage unfold on the glass wall. It seems that this particular bounty hunter got hurt early and spent a good portion of this fight hiding. And then Thegn sees it—sees *her.*

"Stop! Track backward slowly until—there! They *did* find her."

Thegn walks up to the wall and reaches toward the blurry image of a dreadlocked girl with empty green eyes, blood floating in the air around her, a slight smile on her face. This is her. The only known survivor of the Fareburne massacre. The Karui believe that with that much soulmantic energy being poured into a single town, any survivor would be a valuable addition to the hive. But this face. This face doesn't quite belong to the girl they've been looking for. It isn't hers. It belongs to a memory.

Durga?

Thegn catches himself and halts his mind before any further thoughts escape. He lingers a moment with his hand on the wall and glances back at the purified technician. No expression. No reaction. If the hive noticed any of that last thought, this technician isn't indicating one way or the other.

"Wait a moment. There's no way she should be this powerful." *What happened?*

"Push back to the start of the fight and see—What do you mean you can't? Head trauma?" *Shit.*

Thegn glares at the head before pulling his long, bony middle finger back and delivering a solid flick right between the bodiless bounty hunter's eyes. "Stupid tough guy merc. Wear a fucking helmet!"

The bounty hunter's face scowls in pain and confusion. Thegn turns back to the glass wall and addresses the Karui technician. "Alright, just take it to as early in the fight as you can."

The glass wall shows images of bodies—and body parts—flying through the air in reverse. Blurred flashes of the violent girl show in spurts. Then, the images get less distinct. They become a blurred haze. It's like trying to read while someone blows in your eyes.

"Crap. We're not getting anywhere with this. Push before the fight. What town are they in? Yeah, I know it's a canyon town. Need to be more specific than that. Those things are warts on a giant axe wound in the ground. They're everywhere. I just need—"

An idea comes to mind. His own idea. Not one jammed into his skull by the hive. He looks in the canister, past the horrified eyes of the disembodied head. "Wait a minute."

He knocks the technician's hand away and wraps his fingers around the head in the canister. Yanking the head out, he turns it to look at the jack matrix behind its left ear; the array of pore-sized receptacles that kneaks can plug into.

The hunters we hired for this are supposed to wear beacon kneaks. Where's—

"Damaged, you assume? Well in all you're assuming, did you think that maybe the broadcast coords for that kneak might also be saved in his gray matter? Head trauma, right. You didn't look. Well, go look. With what's left of that data and the vid from this playback, you can piece together where she is. Let me know when you have something. I've got preparations to make."

Thegn dumps the head back in its canister and walks toward the chamber's entrance. He stops and faces the room. "Caffiel! Where the fuck are you? Get out here. We've got work to do."

A squeak sounds, and a large albino rat crawls up from behind the chair Thegn was sitting in earlier. It perches itself atop the chair's back and casts an incredulous glare at Thegn with eyes that are distinctly non-rat-like. They still show the expected albino red, but unlike typical rat eyes, these are slitted and lizard-like.

Thegn returns the glare with a hiss through his teeth. "Get your furry ass over here."

Caffiel squeaks in affirmation and scurries across the floor, up Thegn's leg, and around to his shoulder. Turning to the door, he pulls up the hood from his cloak. A pair of enormous black wings grow from his back.

"It's time to ready my scythe."

FULCRUM
SEASON ONE
J.J. VEGA
EPISODE THREE:
NO TIME LIKE THE PRESENT

149

EPISODE THREE: NO TIME LIKE THE PRESENT

CONTENTS

3.1

JACK

"But, V, why? I just don't get it. Fighting is—"

"Jack, I gotta say you're askin' the right questions, kiddo. Just in the wrong order."

The old man paced around Jack, shuffling on the dirty stone floor. He adjusted the placement of the boy's feet, his arms, even his back. The gnarled surface of the old man's cane lifted an elbow, touched behind Jack's knee, and tapped the side of the kid's foot. Jack did as he was told.

Vardin was a gruff old bastard and this was about as nice as he got, partly because neither he nor Jack really knew what they were doing, and partly because he said Jack had a "lack of discipline." He probably wasn't far off on that.

"I still don't get why we're goin' through this. Lyia says that this ain't something I should know. She said the Shadowfold got taken out because they were fightin' folks like this. Said it don't matter what their reasons were."

The old man kept nudging Jack's stance into place, referring to the worn pages of an old notebook. Apparently he traded an awful lot to get his hands on that thing. "Your girl and I don't agree on much, but she's right. That's exactly why your people got it from all sides. But their way don't hafta be your way. They figured they were saving humanity."

Vardin snorted at that last comment.

Jack held his posture, but confusion riddled his face. "That don't make any sense. How're you gonna save people by fightin' them and killin' them? Escaping seems like a better option."

"The way they figured, they *were* helping folks escape. Permanently. It's why they called what they did 'mercies' instead of callin' them what they were. Mass murders." He stepped back to check Jack's pose. "Relax your shoulders."

"Yeah, fine. But then why am I learning this stuff?"

"The thing they got wrong is that you can't escape *for* people, kiddo. You can only defend them. Escaping is their decision, however they choose to do it." He checked the notebook and nodded roughly, mostly to himself. "But, even if their philosophy was fucked, their way of fighting was unmatched."

He was right. The soulmancers in the Shadowfold had been damn near unstoppable. And not just because of techniques like the Touch. It took both the Sheeps and the Goats attacking the Fold at the same time to finally take them out. That was probably the only time each side in the war came close to working together instead of tearing the world apart trying to destroy each other.

Vardin continued. "You an' your girl Lyia come from that same stock. You two have a talent for this in your blood. Ol' Maddy has got Lyia leaning into hers. I figure I should help you find yours. And besides, I ain't gonna be here to save your scrawny loudmouthed ass all the time. You're gonna need ways to defend yourself."

Jack couldn't help but roll his eyes at that. Vardin was older than dirt and he'd been talking about "not being around" for as long as Jack had known him. Together, they'd built that little training space in Cliff City, hauling down all kinds of heavy gear into that room. Vardin said the room was originally something called a "kiva", but he didn't know how the room was originally used. Apparently no one did. The whole of Cliff City had been abandoned well before the war even started. Even before proper civilization. The only memory that survived all that time was the name for the place. Looking at the worn and gray features of the aging barkeep, Jack thought Vardin was old enough to have actually seen it when it was originally constructed. That said, when he and Vardin built out that room for training, the old guy was always picking up Jack's slack. Always quit after Jack. The man may have still had all his hair, but he was way into the gray. Despite that, he never even seemed to get tired. The joke was on Jack, though. Vardin died about a year later.

"Alright, sure. But why does the bottom arm need to be so close to the body? This doesn't feel natural at all."

Vardin paused mid-stride in his loop around Jack and tilted the notebook so it could be seen better in the light. "No idea. That's just what's in these illustrations. Might be something you need to ask Lyia about."

"You could ask her. I still think you should show that notebook to her. I betcha she could help."

The old man let out a long sigh and resumed circling, his cane clicking on the ground. "It says here that 'the shield posture is fundamental to nearly every other advanced posture, defensive and offensive. It's not comfortable because you're not supposed to hold it for long. Your discomfort is your strength. If you're uncomfortable where you are, your mind and body are more willing to accept change. Fighting, like life, is defined by change.'" He paused to tap Jack's shoulders. Poked the other knee. "Basically, if you're comfortable, you're vulnerable."

Jack let out his own snort of frustration. Old Man Vardin had been good to Jack. Treated the boy a quite a bit better than just about anyone else in Bule, except maybe Lyia. It always bothered Jack how they never quite saw eye to eye. Vardin refused to include her in those practice sessions. Jack knew better than to press on that issue, though. He adjusted his weight to fix his stance like the old man wanted and kept staring forward. "But that still don't answer the question. Why wouldn't both of my arms be the same distance from my body?"

Finally finished circling, Vardin stood in front of Jack, wrinkled hands resting on the handle of his cane, notebook held by its spine. "When you fight with soulmancy, you ain't always gonna be fightin' mercs with tech or weapons. With this kinda fightin', you need to be prepared to battle with and for your very soul."

Jack couldn't take it. Too many riddles. Too much mystery. Not enough straight answers. He dropped his arms to his sides and gawked at the aging barkeep.

"What does that even mean? What you're saying doesn't make—"

Jack should've seen it coming. Vardin's foot had slid back ever so slightly and his arms were raised before Jack even had a chance to understand what the old guy was doing. In fact, if Jack thinks back on it, he'd have to admit that Vardin probably held himself in the shield posture for a full second, waiting for Jack's brain to catch up. It was the exact same pose Jack had just been holding moments prior, but better. More correct. Resolute.

An instant later, Jack felt a pressure—a draw, both a push and a pull downward. But it wasn't like anything was actually in contact with his body. The pressure came from deep inside. It was everywhere and nowhere all at once. Intense and forceful. Demanding.

Next thing Jack knew, he was on the ground. His hands and knees barely kept him from lying on his belly. He wheezed and gasped as everything at the edge of his vision started to darken. It was all he could do to keep from blacking out.

And then the feeling was gone.

No draw of energy. No pressure. Things were back to normal, but Jack felt light and airy. Light, airy, and exhausted beyond anything. He looked up and was greeted by Vardin's grin. He'd already lowered his hands back to their rightful home atop his cane.

They gray-haired barkeep tilted his head, eyebrows raised. "Is that a good enough answer?"

"Yeah. I guess."

Episode Three: No Time Like the Present

In honesty, no. That wasn't the answer Jack had asked for, but it was the answer he needed. Of course, like with any good answer, this one brought even more questions. Jack rocked back to sit on his knees and collect his thoughts along with his breath.

He must have sat there a while, because the next thing Jack knew, Vardin was sitting next to him with a hot cup of coffee. The old man wasn't looking at Jack. Just staring at the same wall.

He placed the cup on the ground in front of Jack. "Drink."

The boy took the cup and sipped it. Bitter. The way the old man liked it. At the time, Jack's tendency was still to put in whatever kind of sweetness he could when he made coffee. Jack was pretty out of it, though, because he was well into his third pull before he realized that this wasn't one of the crap mugs from the bar. This one was polished steel. Jack was drinking from Vardin's personal kit.

Jack's surprise must have been plastered all over his face when he looked at the old guy. Vardin's mouth went from the already uncharacteristic grin to full-on toothy smile. Way weird. "Looks like the caffeine has finally started to kick in."

His smile faded as his gaze shifted away from Jack, looking a million klicks beyond the windowless training kiva. Vardin did that staring thing a lot near the end of those practice sessions. Jack never did get that. They'd spent weeks building out that room during off-hours. Fixing the old masonry. Rebuilding its roof. Putting up shielding. And now that they were using it, all of the old guy's focus was always someplace else by the end of a session. Jack wasn't ready for this one to end just yet, though. Not when he felt he was so close to understanding.

"You didn't tell me you were practicing on your own."

"There's a lot I don't tell you, kiddo. But I can't teach you unless I know a thing or two myself. That said, I don't have your talent. You get this down and your version will be on a whole 'nother level."

That move he did had dropped Jack to his knees in an instant. What the hell would a stronger version feel like? The boy sat in silence, his brain spinning. It was exciting to think about. And scary as shit.

Jack took a couple more sips of coffee before speaking again, wincing each time at the bitter flavor. "So, what you just did … was that offense or defense?"

Vardin kept looking straight ahead. His voice was distant as he said, "The notes say even though it's called a shield posture, you are a sword as well as a shield. You can attack and you can defend. But, who do you attack? Who do you defend? And why? You gotta know the answers to these questions—not by rote, you hafta truly feel the answers. Your own answers. That's the only time you're really gonna get it."

He let out a long sigh and rested his hand on the top of Jack's head. In that moment, he suddenly seemed so much older. Worn. Weary. It was probably around that time that he had actually started trying to learn the Touch on his own. Learning it so he could teach Jack. Even though Jack called him "Old Man V," he never really thought of Vardin as actually being old until that last year.

They sat there for a bit, silent and thoughtful. Not at all normal for either of them.

Jack found that his finger was tapping on the side of his cup, a bit of an involuntary tic of Vardin's that Jack had picked up. "There's no straight answers for any of this shit, is there?"

The slightest hint of a smirk leaked onto the old man's gnarled face, like he'd just remembered a funny joke. He pushed on Jack's head to help himself back up to his feet. "Ask your questions. Asking leads to answers. But those answers hafta be yours. Too many folks rely on the answers of others."

Helping Jack stand too, Vardin looked into the boy's eyes, deep and piercing. "The questions should never stop. Never. Even if you think you've found the answer, keep asking. If your answer is the right one, questions will only reinforce it as being that way."

TRAINING

"Alright! Let's try that again." Jack and Zeke look down at Corva through a hole in the floor.

Fidgeting, Corva sits on the stone floor of her "training room"—more like a pit, or a dungeon. Jack said the room is called a "keefa" or "cave-a" or something. Whatever it's called, it's dark and suffocatingly thick-aired. About the only thing it's got going for it is that its location is even more remote than Bule.

It's part of a canyonside cluster of ancient stone buildings that Jack calls Cliff City. It's not that far from Bule, not much more than a klick farther along the canyon. Maybe it's a few hundred meters deeper below the lip. But that's the straight shot to get there. Without being able to fly, straight shots to this place don't seem to exist.

They've been coming here every night since the raid and Jack has yet to take her on a path that isn't packed with switchbacks, blind turns, and ledges barely wider than a grown man's foot. It's actually pretty remarkable how well he knows these cliffs. Even in the dark, he's a sure-footed guide. More than once, he prevented her from taking a step that would cause her to plummet to the bottom of the canyon.

Still, it's a hassle. And all for this dark, musty hole in the ground. It's not like she's used to an easy lifestyle of class and luxury. She's been on the road long enough to consider running water a top-tier feature. And decent lighting. The only light source they've got here is the illumination cord from Jack's room under the bar. Only once have they ever made a fire, and that was the first night. They'd forgotten to bring any source of light at all that night. It took them forever to find enough burnable material for a fire. They were only able to train for about half an hour that time. Since then, they've been better prepared, and able to go for much longer.

On the nights that they train through to dawn—like this one—the cool light of the cord is touched by accents of orange when the early morning sun rays stumble their way through the tunnels and corridors of Cliff City. However, there's never enough time to take full advantage of the daylight. They have to rest up and prep the bar for the next evening's pack of drunken merc jerks.

Frustration brimming, Corva sits on the stone floor and taps her metal forearm bracers with a finger-length carpenter's nail. She purposefully avoids looking up at Jack and Zeke through the hole in the ceiling a few meters up. "I still don't see why we have to do it this way. Why couldn't we do this back at the bar? There's plenty of space in the basement if we move around some of those boxes."

Jack sighs, exasperated. "I told you, Harris is watching the bar like a damn hawk. We still got another two weeks left in his stupid one-month 'probation period.' Ain't gonna risk losing the place on account of you goin' all DestructaBilly in one of these little training sessions. Least down here it don't matter so much if you can't control your fits."

Fits. That's what Jack has taken to calling her "fighting mode." The kid sure likes to put names on things.

She tilts her head up so she can see Jack and Zeke. "But it takes so long to get here. We lose so much time just in transit."

"Look, you're still trying to lie low. Ain't no one come lookin' for you. And since Harris took credit for killin' those grunts during the raid, no one else in town knows about the fits. Or the bounty on your head. How long do you think that's gonna last if you start going an' wrecking the place on the regular?"

"Oh, come on. I'm not that destructive."

"Really? I thought you said you can remember what goes on durin' a fit now."

"It's more complicated than that." What he said is true, though. When it's happening, she's fully aware of what her body is doing. Memories after are a bit patchy, a bit dreamlike—especially considering the kinds of dreams she's been having recently. But it's easy enough to piece together what she's done. The problem is that she's a passenger. No control.

"Everything's always complicated with you. Like your bounty. You're the only person I ever met who don't know who's after 'em, or why. I still think you're feedin' me bullshit on that."

She looks back down to the ground. "Little bit of both, actually."

"What's that?" Jack's voice cracks. Corva can't tell if it's a mixture of excitement and incredulity, like he can't believe he guessed something right, or just his voice cracking.

"I don't exactly know who set the bounty. But I've got a pretty good idea why someone would." She lowers her voice to just over a whisper. "Fareburne." Some leftover Shadowfold mage could be trying to tie up loose ends. Of course, all of the soulmancers from the Shadowfold were supposed to have been taken out, but that hasn't stopped Corva from living a life of looking over her shoulder. She escaped Fareburne. Who's to say someone didn't escape when the Shadowfold was attacked?

"Look, if you're just going to sit down there and mumble to yourself, let's just get back to training. The sun'll be up soon."

So it really was just his voice cracking.

Corva shakes her mind free of the past and focuses back on training. "Yeah. Training. What's next?"

"Well, take a good look at the wall in front of you. Remember that?"

Corva raises her head and scans across the wall. "The shiny bit right there?"

"Look closer."

Jack points to a small cluster of circles glimmering in the light of the illumination cord. They look like coins glued to the wall.

She squints. "Those circle things?"

"It's not just shiny. An' those little circles? They're nail heads for the exact kinda nail you got in your hand. Notice how they're drilled all the way in the rock. They got that way because you *threw* them. You're gettin' stronger."

Her eyes widen. She does remember. Images flash in her mind. She sees her hand grabbing nails one at a time and flinging them at the wall. Still, it's all in a patchy fog. It doesn't feel like those are her memories.

"Oh, and this is my favorite part." Jack leans into the hole. Almost his entire upper body hangs upside down. He points a couple paces to the right of the shining cluster of burrowed nails.

"Have a look at this little crater in the wall. See the indentation at the center? That's from your friggin' fist!" Jack continues to hang upside down while wildly gesticulating with each word. He looks a bit like a wet shirt on a clothesline, flapping in the wind. "You did all that shit. And no sign of damage to your hands."

Corva looks away from the wall, inspecting her hands, alternately opening and closing them. If she punched that wall, her punching hand should be swollen to the size of her head. The bones within, a shattered mess. But both of her hands look just fine. Barely a scratch. Not even so much as a bruise.

Jack continues his diatribe, still hanging the upper half of his body into the room. "We've been over all this before. You gotta lie low. That means you train outside of Bule. We figured out how to trigger your fits pretty easy. Get Zeke close enough to you and, boom, you're set off. But you got shit control and you tend to pass out after. Good news is that you've been wakin' up faster afterward. If we can get you to have a fit when I ain't afraid of being killed—"

"Anyone ever tell you that you talk too much?"

"No one that matters."

"Asshole. Fine. Let's just do this thing, then." She stands, slapping the dust off her pants. *Asshole?* She's not a huge fan of the fact that she's starting to pick up some of his ways of speaking. Clearing the thought from her mind, she looks up to Jack and Zeke. "How far did we get last time?"

Jack wriggles his way back up so he's no longer half hanging into the room. He points down the length of rope hanging into Corva's training room. "We had Zeke down to the fourth mark. That's obviously too close. And the third mark wasn't close enough. I figure Zeke needs to climb down to the third mark. Then he can creep forward a bit at a time."

"Didn't we try that already? I don't think it's the way to go. These … episodes—"

"Fits."

"Yeah. Anyhow, they feel pretty all-or-nothing. I don't think there's a sweet spot that Zeke has to be from me where I'll suddenly have more control. Besides, there's only like a single hand-length between the marks on that rope of yours. If distance were the key, Zeke would have to maintain that distance the whole time I'm triggered. That doesn't feel right. I don't think that's quite how it works."

"Yeah, yeah. And the rope sways when Zeke is on it, too. It ain't exactly a perfect way to go about it. You gotta better idea, girlie?"

Silence. She doesn't have a better idea yet. But there's something else. Disrespect. "I told you not to call me that, Jack. I have a name."

"Yeah, maybe you do. But it's a shit name. What the hell kinda name is 'Corva,' anyway? Sounds like half a cough."

Avó's face flashes in Corva's mind. She clinches her fist around the nail in her hand. Tight. She can feel her fingertips digging into her palm. "It was a gift. A personal one. That's the last time you disparage it, *child*. I don't make fun of your stupid streak of dyed hair. The least you could do is respect my name."

Jack reflexively runs his fingers through the curly mop on his head, right through the white streak that starts over his right eye. "Bitch, you don't know me. Don't know anything about me. This ain't dye."

"Oh yeah? Then what is it? Some kind of birth defect?"

"It's what happens when Death misses his mark."

"Death?"

Corva feels her eyes widen. It's like she's lost her breath for a moment. Death? The last of the Four?

She turns her head away from Jack and stares at the metal bracers on her forearms. "Death doesn't miss."

"Yeah, well, there was a lotta killing going on that day. S'pose it's easy to get sloppy and lose track. Only two of us got out."

Her full attention spins back up to Jack. The story was familiar. "You survived one of the Shadowfold massacres?"

Jack's head tilts the same way he always does before saying something smug or sarcastic. "Yeah. Something like that." He stares at her for a second before turning his gaze away and shrugging. "We all gotta be survivors from somewhere, don't we?"

Corva's mind flashes back to her last moments with Avó. "Yeah. I suppose we do."

There's a bit of silence after that. Jack must notice the awkwardness in the pause because he starts filling that void with words. The kid isn't the smoothest of talkers, but what he lacks in finesse, he makes up for in volume. As he talks, his tone changes and he gets a strange look in his eyes, a weird combination of wistfulness and something else, perhaps nostalgia.

"My memory of the thing is pretty spotty. I was only five years old then. The first wave was like a normal raid, just larger in scale. We holed up an' hid ourselves in as dark a spot as possible. Away from any vid or drones or ..." He stops himself from finishing, caught in his memories. He shakes his head before continuing, "Hell, I think we even avoided all other people, just in case."

"We? There were other survivors?" What she wouldn't give to have even just one other person from Fareburne with her.

Jack doesn't seem to notice her change in expression. He continues right along, "Yeah. We. Weren't you listening? I said two of us got out. Lyia an' me. Pretty sure we were the only two, though. Lyia's the one who helped you recover after the bar fight. Brought the meds and gear."

"That wasn't you?"

"Some of it was. But—" His face twists into a disgusted look. "She also helped clean you up when you pissed yourself—you *were* unconscious for three days. You were pretty out of it, though, so you might not remember her."

He smiles and his eyes seem to lose focus. "But if you were awake, you'd remember. She's pretty hard to forget. 'Course, she's only been by the bar once or twice since then. Ol' Maddy Shard has had her pretty busy the last month or so."

"Maddy Shard?" Corva knows that name. Jack's mentioned that name before. Not fondly, though. *Which shop does—*

Suddenly, Corva knows exactly the business that Maddy Shard runs. "Lyia works at the brothel?"

Jack gives Corva a look like she's suddenly sprouted a second head. "The Red Light. And yeah, she works there. After the—" He pauses, like he's searching for a word. "Well, after the thing, we got picked up and carted off to an exchange. Maddy Shard got Lyia an' me in a bundle auction. Soon as we got to Bule, the dirty skank traded me off to Old Man V."

His smile returns at this. "Maddy couldn't get rid of me fast enough, apparently. Seems I was more than she could handle." He shrugs and turns his head to look at Zeke. "I been at the bar ever since."

"Having a weepy five-year-old stomping around the halls and crying all the time probably isn't great for her kind of business, either." Corva can't help but smile a bit at the thought of Jack interrupting the—*ahem*—business that happens at a place like that.

Jack's smile, however, completely disappears. It's replaced with a hard stare in her direction. Uncharacteristically serious. "What do you mean, 'weepy'? Why would I be crying?"

Something about what she said really got to the kid. She tries to smooth things over. "Oh, nothing. Just you said you were five and you just lost everyone you knew. I assumed that you'd be upset."

He turns his face away from both her and Zeke, back in the general direction of Bule. "I didn't lose everyone."

His voice is quiet and his sentences are short. Very un-Jack. It takes Corva a few seconds to realize that he's talking about the fact that Lyia survived, too. In any case, the attempt at smoothing doesn't appear to have taken hold. Maybe explaining herself a bit more will help.

"Hey, I'm sure that Lyia is great. But she's not family, right? Didn't you have a mother and father in your town? Siblings, maybe? Losing any one of those would make anyone sad. You lost them all and you were still a young child. I was eight when the Shadowfold took Fareburne. It makes sense that—"

"Fareburne? You're from Fareburne?" Jack's eyes widen, but it's difficult to tell what emotion is causing that.

"Yeah. Fareburne was my town. Like you said, we're all survivors. It actually feels really good to talk about this with someone who can relate. Weird that you said Death was part of what happened to your town. I don't remember hearing about him being part of—"

"You need to stop."

Corva feels herself blink in surprise. "What? I was just saying that a little trauma would make sense for a situation like that. I get it. Even though Lyia survived, too, I can't imagine it'd be enough to make up the difference."

"I said you need to stop. You're talkin' about stuff you don't know nothing about, girlie."

Alright, now he's being a jerk on purpose. "It's Corva, Jack, get it right. I'm just trying to have a conversation with you. For someone who thinks he's so mature, you sure are acting like a child."

"Child? Child? Fuck you, Corva. You ain't that much older than me. You don't get to call me that. In fact—"

He raises his eyebrows and springs to his feet. The idea pushing up his brows seems to have continued pushing until he's standing with the rope in his hand. "You know what? I think it's time for a break. A little time for reflectin'. Zeke an' me will just go. We'll get some rest and get started for the day. Let you think things over a spell, and then you can find your own damn way out."

With that, Jack yanks at the rope and brings it all the way up out of the hole he was looking through.

"Wait. You're taking the rope, too?"

"Yeah. It's my rope. See how you like things without my help."

Corva grits her teeth. He really is going to leave her. "You go ahead and do that. When I get out, I'll be sure to wake you up before I start beating on you."

"Whatever. Zeke, let's go."

SANDWICH?

Jack takes a few steps away from the kiva entrance and squats by the pack of overnight supplies he brought. He shoves around snacks and water containers, mumbling angrily, "Stupid bitch. Call *me* a child? Can you believe she called me that, Zeke?"

Of course, the age thing shouldn't bother him. And deep down, it really doesn't. Not all that much, at least. He knows he's young. Harris won't let him forget it. It's not even the disrespect. You get used to that when dealing with mercs and merchants all the time. It's the other things she said. She's from Fareburne. The Fold—the folks who were apparently his people—murdered everyone she knew.

He raises his hand to run it through his hair again, but stops himself. Zeke never responded. Not even a chirp. Back at the entrance to the kiva—the repurposed training room—Zeke hasn't moved.

"Zeke? Hey! What're you still doin' over there? I said let's go."

Zeke looks up at Jack and tilts his head to the side, pointing into the hole.

"Yeah, I am gonna leave her down there. Stop messin' around and come on. What do you want from me? She's got the light cord. And she's smart. She'll figure a way out." He digs in the pack until he finds a cloth-wrapped packet of food. "I'll leave her some breakfast from the pack. She'll be fine."

Zeke closes his eyes and puffs out an exasperated breath. He rises to stand on his hind legs, but he doesn't come to Jack. He just stands there, eyes closed, his back remarkably straight for a monkey. Unnaturally straight, actually. A moment later, Zeke drops back to his haunches and stares at Jack with his odd slitted eyes. He points to the kiva entrance again.

"Shit's sake, Zeke, what's got you in a twist?" Jack tosses Corva's breakfast back on the bag and rises from his squat. "Fine. I'll look in the stupid hole at the stupid girl."

Jack doesn't get more than a step back in Zeke's direction before Corva pops up from the hole.

Holy hell. She jumped it?

He doesn't get a chance to think much more than that. She's on him in an instant. Her forearm shoves against his chest, pinning him between her metal bracer and the tunnel wall. The tip of her carpenter's nail rests a hair's width from the center of his throat.

"What's that you were saying about leaving?"

"Shit shit shit! No. Wait. Jokin'. Sa-um—saaaaandwich?"

Jack knits his brow, confused by his own stammering. The words come out panicked and crackled. It sounds like he can't tell if he's offering Corva a sandwich or asking for one himself. His hands are down at his sides, uselessly trembling, not offering any form of defense. Nor are they pointing at the cloth-wrapped meal sitting on top of his pack. His mind spins, hopelessly trying to figure a way out of being killed by this merciless killer of a girl.

By chance, his wild-eyed gaze returns to her face. In the flurry of panicked fumbling, a single rational thought squeezes to the front of his mind. *Something's different. She's different.*

Episode Three: No Time Like the Present

Corva's fiery emerald eyes still have the wrathful glint that Jack's gotten used to seeing during her fits. Only now, she doesn't have that bloodthirsty smile. Sure, she's still smiling and it's kind of creepy, but it's not *that* smile.

Also, he's not dead.

That carpenter's nail in her hand is touching his throat, but it's not in his throat. Her arm bracer digs into his chest, but he hasn't been crushed like that crater down in the kiva. She might actually be in control. Awake.

Jack tests the waters. "You're—you're talking!"

Corva's grin widens. "Took you long enough." She takes a step back, releasing him from the wall. "My, you're slow. You should've seen the look on your face. 'Suh suh suh—sandwich?' Ha! What does that even mean?"

"Oh fuck off. It's the best I could come up with. I thought you were gonna kill me."

Jack rubs his shoulder where he'd struck the wall. *Fingers, toes, arms, legs, torso, head … pain. Alright. Still alive.*

"But, wait." His eyes narrow as he looks at Corva. "How did you—how are you doing it? I pulled the rope. Hell, you didn't even need the rope to get out."

"I'm not sure. I was angry you left. Wanted to get out as quick as possible. Mostly to beat the mess out of you. Then I felt it—well, him. Zeke. I knew exactly where he was without even looking up. I still know where he is. And I feel, um …"

"What? Stronger? Faster?"

"Yeah, those things. And like throwing up. I don't know. I still can't—"

Corva's eyes roll back and she collapses into Jack. The nail clinks across the stone floor. Caught by surprise—and not at all capable of managing the difference in their body sizes—he rolls her off him and tries to lower her to the ground as gently as possible. She lands on her side with a thud.

Jack stands straight for a moment, but it doesn't last. He slouches back against the wall, and the aftermath of his adrenaline dump starts to set in.

"Fuuuck that was close."

He takes a few minutes to slow his breathing and regain something that resembles good composure. Zeke quietly sits near Jack and Corva, as if keeping vigil. Jack looks down at Corva, crumpled on the floor at his feet. Her pose kind of looks like a reenactment of the fossilized skeletons he sometimes sees when exploring the canyon. *Ooh … that can't be comfortable.*

Squatting down, he rolls Corva to her back and straightens all her limbs so she looks just a little bit less like a discarded ragdoll. He reaches back to the pack and moves the sandwich aside so he can pull out the jacket he'd brought for the chilly hike back to Bule. Wadding the jacket into a flattened bundle, he places it under her head.

Of course, her head won't sit straight. *Friggin' girl is disagreeable even in her sleep.*

He spends a full minute trying to center her head on his makeshift pillow, but it keeps rolling to one side or the other. Eventually, he gives up. Flopping back to sit against the wall, Jack notices that Zeke has been watching him. A hint of a smile stretches across his little primate face.

"What? Don't look at me like that. We're here later than usual and the sun's gotten higher. The walk back'll be hot an' I don't wanna carry more weight than I have to. Figured that if the jacket was under her head, it wouldn't get blown away by the wind."

Zeke raises an eyebrow, skepticism oozing from his entire posture.

"Cut it out. Whatever it is you're thinkin', you're wrong. I'm just— no. Not gonna argue with you about this. We've been at this since we closed last night. S'almost eight now. Only got a couple hours before we need to be up in Bule to catch the morning drunks. You do whatever you want." Jack leans his head back and closes his eyes. "I'm takin' a nap."

Only he doesn't. Not really. *She's from Fareburne.*

3.4

TIMES PAST

Where in the world am I now?

The more Corva realizes that she's dreaming, the less she has control over her actions in the dream. It's kind of the opposite of how things have been going with her fits.

There she goes again, using one of Jack's words. Fits. This is the longest she's spent time anywhere since Fareburne. Maybe she's been in Bule too long.

That said, little by little, the more she's remained in one place and trained, the more she's gaining control over herself when she's in that state. But in these dreams, it's the other way around. She's a spectator in her own skin. At least, she thinks this is her skin. She's certainly never worn clothes like this.

For one thing, her midsection is almost entirely exposed, front and back. A length of silk wraps her chest and shoulders before crossing down to wrap her waist. It's like a scarf that's making believe it's a sleeveless shirt and a belt at the same time. The loose, baggy pants she's wearing have a similar identity crisis; from a distance, they could be mistaken as an ankle-length skirt.

Sure, the clothes are comfortable and she's deceptively mobile in them, but the patterned silk is way more refined than anything she's ever come close to, let alone worn. And this getup exposes an awful lot of her skin, which she notes is a lot lighter than she's used to, like she hasn't been in the sun for weeks. In any case, this outfit doesn't offer nearly as much protection from the elements as she would like.

And in these dreams, everything is so big. Impossibly big. She can't reach things she normally could. Even running or walking from place to place takes more steps than she'd normally need. It's like she's been dropped into a world for people twice her size.

Corva feels along the outside of her left calf. *Good, at least I still have a knife.*

She's been having this dream—or variations of it—ever since coming to Bule. All of them start differently and she feels like she's playing the part of a different person in each one.

However, they all end the same.

As best as she can tell in this one, she's been following Zeke. Only one other time has he appeared to her in a dream. Just like that one, he doesn't respond when she tries to talk to him.

But where is that little hand-footed beast now?

Corva studies the enormous, cavern-like room in which she's found herself. With a curved ceiling that arches into the walls, it's got a dank subterranean feel. Despite shoddy lighting from a few rows of flickering bars of light overhead, there aren't an abundance of hiding places where Zeke could be.

The most obvious place would be in the wide fissure that runs the length of the room and extends into tunnels on each end. Looking into the creek-like concrete trench, Corva notices there are steel rails running along the bottom.

An underground train route? Those aren't supposed to be active anymore. Avó said they collapsed early in the war when the mega cities got hit. This is pretty close to how I imagined they'd look, though.

Corva stops herself.

Idiota! Of course it's like you'd imagine. You're dreaming!

Getting back to the business of figuring out where Zeke is, she hops down into the trench and looks in each direction. *Well, fifty-fifty shot at this. Let's see what's to the left.*

Corva pivots on the balls of her feet and bolts to her right.

Wait, what? Left! I want to go left!

She strains her mind, vainly grasping for dominance over her own limbs. In previous dreams, she's been able to regain control by sheer determination, but her willpower simply isn't enough this time. She's riding shotgun in her own mind. Even worse, she's got no idea who's driving.

Sprinting down the trench, she reaches the tunnel entrance and plunges into the gloom. Her body doesn't hesitate at all. It moves with a confidence, an assertiveness that she's not used to. In the darkness of the tunnel, the air is still and silent. There's hardly an echo for each brief pat of her bare feet on the dusty concrete floor. She marvels at the fact that she hasn't tripped or fallen or even slowed her dash along the train tracks.

A dim flickering dot shows ahead of Corva and quickly expands, revealing the next stop in the subterranean train route. Suddenly, she's no longer running; she's sliding on her feet to a stop nearly twenty meters from the opening. Corva tries to look around but feels her eyes focusing on the ground near the mouth of the tunnel.

I can't even control my own eyes? Really? Isn't there a—

Her thoughts are cut short when she realizes what her eyes are focusing on. There's a small furry creature standing right at the center of the tunnel entrance. It's backlit, so she can't catch any details, but the thing seems to be about the right size.

Zeke?

She feels her left arm descend and withdraw the long knife strapped to her calf.

Wait. What?

She resumes her sprint, faster than before, knife arm rising in front of her as she nears the opening.

No! Don't kill him! I need him!

Her body doesn't slow down.

Corva tenses her mind. *Gotta stop this.* She can feel her limbs moving, but nothing changes. *Try smaller muscles. Maybe the knife?* She focuses all of her energy on her left hand, repeatedly visualizing each finger unwrapping from the knife handle. *Come onnnn … open up, you little bastards.*

Ting!

Hearing the knife clang on the ground, Corva realizes that her eyelids are clinched shut and she's no longer running. She's forced herself back into the driver's seat. Opening her eyes, it's apparent that she regained control just in time. She's within spitting distance of Zeke.

However, it's not Zeke.

A large white rat—one of the largest she's ever seen—sits balanced upright on its haunches, staring at her through slitted red eyes. This strange rodent doesn't appear to be phased in the least that she is two steps away from slicing it in half. Instead, the rat shoots right toward Corva, scurrying between her legs to the space behind her.

Tracking the rat, she spins about. However, there's no follow-through for her spin. She stops herself mid-movement, mind and body locking tight as horror washes over her like a swarm of ants. She can't see the rat anymore. There's something blocking her view. Someone. The same person that shows at the end of all these dreams.

The Reaper.

He towers over her, menacing despite the thinness of his frame. Corva can see the rat's head peek over his shoulder.

Death's enormous black wings spread to more than twice his already imposing height as he hunches over, bringing his hooded face within inches of hers.

"Durga." A single word. A name. The most he's ever said in a dream. The sound of his voice seeps from the gloomy void of his hood. Somehow, though, that sound has a volume and weight that echoes across the chamber.

Although the hood shadows most of his features, Corva can see his beard move again. It's as if he's opening his mouth to say something, then closes it before any more words manage to escape. All that remains is silence. Each ticking second drags behind it the gravity of eons.

"Forgive me." There's regret in the old Reaper's voice. Genuine regret.

Forgive him? For what?

Death lurches up to his full height. From the corner of her eye, she sees his scythe arcing toward her head. In an instant, she can feel each sinewy filament of muscle in her neck tear at the scythe's jagged edge, every crackle in the bones of her spine, and the cold metal from the flat side of the blade rubbing against the exposed surfaces on either side of the cut. Pain erupts with the blood.

3.5

SANDWICH

Corva lurches upright, screaming and flailing her arms.

Eyes wide and shaky, she snaps her hands to her throat, applying pressure to a wound that doesn't exist. She doesn't feel any cut or slice or even an abrasion. She pulls her hands down and stares at them. No blood.

Double-checking, she touches her neck and looks at her hands again. Still clean.

Slowly, she regains composure. Leaning forward with her elbows on her knees, she relaxes her shoulders and exhales in relief. She shakes her head, vainly trying to rattle away the fear that sticks to her like a wet rag. She's in a cold sweat and can feel her lungs desperately trying to slow down. Her whole chest cavity aches like her heart has been trying to punch its way out.

I'll never get used to dying.

Even as the words sound in her head, she feels her face knit into a scowl. What an odd thing to think. Who *would* get used to that? And she didn't think "in a dream." The thought came out with a conviction that she didn't expect. It's almost like she really has been killed by Death in every one of these dreams. But that can't be right, can it?

Resolving to focus on the present, she looks around and realizes she's still on the tunnel floor in Cliff City. Jack's bundled jacket rests where her head had been. A small cloth bundle lies next to it. She grabs the bundle and unwraps the folds.

A sandwich.

She doesn't wait for her stomach to finish growling. She takes three bites before even starting to chew. Meat and cheese. Gulping down the food in her mouth, she takes her next bite more slowly. Briefly, she smiles at Jack's awkward sentiment. Perhaps the kid isn't so bad. Then, suddenly, she comes to a fresh realization.

She looks around and notice that the light in Cliff City isn't the red-orange mix of dawn. It's fully in to morning, and there's no one around.

Filho da puta. That jerk did end up leaving me here alone.

Morning Meditation

Jack stands at the top of the narrow series of switchbacks that lead up from Cliff City. Well, he's not so much standing as he is leaning against the cliff wall in an attempt to catch his breath.

"Much as I go down there, you'd think I wouldn't still get winded from the climb up." He looks over to Zeke, perched on his shoulder, oblivious—or indifferent—to Jack's insufficient lung capacity. "You ain't helping, either. Maybe I need to cut back on the free rides."

That gets Zeke's attention. He squints at Jack and blows a curt razz. Reaching into Jack's shirt pocket, the monkey pulls out the only remaining cigarette from the set Jack rolled before they descended to Cliff City last night. He shakes the cigarette in Jack's face with a full-bodied rebuke that says, *No, no, this is your problem!*

Jack shifts his view from the cigarette to Zeke and back to the cigarette. "How thoughtful. Thanks."

He snatches the cigarette from Zeke and pops the end into his mouth. Zeke reaches to grab it away, but Jack already has his lighter brandished and flipped open. A quick thumb-flick from Jack and a low, wide flame erupts right in the path of Zeke's outstretched hand.

Zeke retracts. Victorious, Jack smirks and brings the lighter's flame to the tip of his hand-rolled tobacco envelope. He closes his eyes and takes a long, slow drag from the cigarette. Exhaling, he looks back at Zeke. "See? I'm already taking deeper breaths."

Zeke buries his face in his hands, but Jack interrupts this display of frustration.

"Still, we made pretty good time. Got plenty to make it across town before it's time to open the bar. Actually—" Jack glances up to the sky and cracks out a sheepish smirk. "We've got enough to make a little detour."

Hearing this, Zeke looks up at Jack's stupid smile and rolls his eyes. He knows exactly what Jack's planning. Jack is going to see her; Lyia. Perhaps "see" is too strong of a word. He's really just going to watch her from a distance while trying to avoid being seen himself. With good reason, though. The last time he got caught snooping around Maddy Shard's, he almost left without a pulse.

Jack's known Lyia his whole life, and he's worshiped her for nearly as long. The only surviving members of the Fold. No one except the old man and Maddy Shard knows that, though. As far as anyone else knows, they're actually survivors of the string of massacres that the Shadowfold used to inflict. Mercies. That's what the people in the Fold used to call it when they organized an attack on a town. Jack was too young to be involved with any mercies, but he had started his training. Had the Fold not fallen, he would eventually have been expected to participate. To use the Touch on whole townships. Towns like Fareburne.

Fareburne. Corva is from there. And she survived. Jack hasn't heard of anyone ever surviving a mercy. An extermination. If the Shadowfold was anything, it was thorough. Granted, from what he can remember, Fareburne was the largest mercy that had ever been attempted. It makes sense that someone would fall through the cracks. That doesn't make Jack feel any better though. The term "mercy" never made sense to Jack. Lyia had tried to explain it once, but it never took. Never sat right with him. How could killing off a whole town of people be considered a mercy? It's a mass murder. It wasn't a "mercy" when everyone else in the Fold was killed. When Death made his mark on them. How was what they did to others any different?

It's no wonder the Fold got attacked from all sides. Survivor? Jack doesn't feel like a survivor. He didn't survive anything. Lyia saved him. Kept him from dying.

Old Man V told Jack to think of the fall of the Fold as his birthday. He was already four years old at the time, but that was the event that marked the start of his current life.

All told, it hasn't been a horrible life. Jack served his time as the old man's barhand, cleaning and maintaining the bar. Tough work, sure, but it beat working at the Red Light. Lyia hadn't been as lucky. When Maddy Shard figured out that Lyia was the one that saved him from being marked, there was no way the old bat was going to let Lyia go. Healers are too rare, too useful, and too valuable to trade away.

Jack's contract expired within a few years. Lyia took quite a bit longer to pay off her bond. Jack never could quite figure out the math behind that one. The old man said it had something to do with the costs involved in training a healer. Whatever. Probably Maddy is just better at haggling. In any case, even though both of them were in the clear, they stuck around in their respective roles. Lyia originally wanted to skip town, but Jack had convinced her to stay. It's not like they had anywhere better to go.

With Zeke still on his shoulder, Jack navigates his way along the long cascade of steps that connect Lower Bule to Upper Bule. He stops part of the way up, ducking behind the short stone wall along the stairs. Zeke lets out an exasperated snort and hops off the wall to sit next to Jack on the steps.

Maddy Shard's Red Light is on the lower side of town. From this spot, Jack can safely peek over the wall at the whole of Lower Bule unobstructed. The area is a whole mess of stonework buildings so tightly packed that a person could almost get from one end to the other just by leaping rooftops. Granted, a lot of them are only stonework on the outside, a façade for blending in with the cliff. Materials inside each building, like Maddy's Red Light, tend to be higher-grade stuff. Of course, he can't see inside any of the buildings. Maddy and most of the folks in Lower Bule are adamant about ensuring their businesses' privacy. Only eyes backed by a sufficiently high number of nits get the privilege of pulling back the curtain.

Jack isn't interested in what's going on inside, though—not this time. Instead, he fixes his stare on the roof. Waiting. *Almost ten. Should just be startin' her day.*

As if on cue, the roof access on the Red Light swings open and Lyia steps through. Her attire is markedly without glamour—cotton sweats and a white t-shirt—but Jack's pupils dilate all the same. He mentally traces the silhouette of the body that gives form to those clothes and follows it as she moves out to the roof. He lets the image sear into his mind before moving up to her face and the kindest eyes to ever paint their amber warmth upon him.

He knows that she's not overwhelmingly attractive. Not by conventional standards. Certainly not by Red Light standards. None of that matters to him, though. She's the girl of his dreams. Of his memories. Of his future. It seems like everyone these days has survived *some* kind of massive attack. But the fall of the Shadowfold belongs to Jack and Lyia. It's theirs. And they made it through that together.

Her eyes are closed now, wrapped by the warmth of her dark, almost reddish skin. From his roost on the stair, Jack watches as she turns her head toward the canyon wind, allowing it to sweep the strands of straight onyx locks from her face and snap in the air behind her. The distinctive blue streak that starts at her forehead flaps and flows along with the rest of her hair. Jack knows that under the blue dye, that streak of hair is just as white as the one that starts in the same place on his own head. A mark of their shared history.

Jack has every step in Lyia's morning rooftop ritual memorized. At the start of each day, she steps out on the roof and stands for a minute. She allows the sun and wind to wash off sleep and short-term memory. In her right hand, she carries her morning meditation: one cigarette, one match.

EPISODE THREE: NO TIME LIKE THE PRESENT

She steps behind the door to the roof, treating it as a makeshift wind shield while she lights her cigarette. Cigarette glowing, she steps out from the door's protection and closes it behind her. This is her moment alone. In the exposed, open air of the world, she has her personal bubble of solitude.

As Lyia slumps against the door, enjoying the first luxurious pulls from her morning smoke, Jack coordinates the last remaining puffs from his. Quenched by their surreptitiously shared moment, he spins around and sits on the stairway, leaning against the stumpy stone wall. A contented grin stretches across the full width of his face, if only for a few seconds.

A voice penetrates his calm. "You've got good taste, kid, I'll give you that. But she is waaaaaay out of your price range."

"Fuck you, Corva."

3.7

En Route

Thegn thunders over the battered remains of a highway road, his gnarled hands on handlebars. Black exhaust pours out of the back of his ride as he thumps his way along. He knows he's playing out a cliché—or at least, it would be a cliché if this were an earlier time. Death crossing the land on his pale fire-breathing steed.

He couldn't care less, though. The continued rumble of the old motorcycle's engine is just loud enough to mask the persistent buzzing sound in his mind. His connection to the Karui hive. He's a long way from the closest nexus, so he's out of range from their pervasive means of telepathic communication. At this distance, they can't read his mind the same instant way they can when they're nearby. Still, though, there's that buzz in his brain. A constant hum that reminds him the connection is still there.

He exhales deeply and lets the droning pulse of the motor and wind roar over his mind as the road rolls under him. It's the most calm he's felt in a while.

Do you really think it's her again?

"Fuck!" The unexpected voice in his head breaks Thegn from his reverie, causing him to swerve. If he was in a state of calm before, he's at the far opposite side of the spectrum now.

He fixes his course and glances down at the white rat sitting in the saddlebag to his left. Caffiel. His only companion over the years. The one who has been with him the longest, even through this current hundred-and-fifty-year debacle. *Annoying know-it-all rodent.*

The rat continues, the voice in Thegn's mind clear over the growling motor. It's Thegn's voice, but the rat's words. **I mean, it's been quite some time since you last dispatched her. You seemed hopeful that last time would be, well, the last time.**

Thegn keeps his eyes straight ahead. "You do realize that I might've laid this bike down from that, right? I cut the wheel too hard and you'd be a road stain."

You're avoiding the question.

"I'm not avoiding anything. You interrupted me." Thegn pulses the throttle to punctuate his point.

How exactly did I interrupt you? You weren't saying anything.

"It's my head. I was here first."

If he could sigh telepathically, that's what Caffiel would be doing right now. Thegn focuses on the road, but reflexively smiles. The mental picture of the rat trying to reach its forehead with its tiny arms and pinch its brow is just too good.

Fine. I know how much you dislike telepathy as a means of communication. However, I'm not exactly within your field of view, so visual cues aren't a viable option.

"You could just quietly enjoy the ride."

We've been on the road for hours. And it's not like I have enough space in this sack to do something that might occupy that time.

"You are the sleep sigil. Sloth incarnate. Your waking hours are few and far between."

And I very much prefer to be productive in those hours. So. Back to my question. Do you really think it's her?

"Again."

Pardon?

"You asked if it was really her again."

There's the briefest of pauses before the rat responds, **I'll not be dragged into a semantic debate, young one.**

Young one. Caffiel likes to remind him of the difference in their ages, despite their respective appearances. Thegn looks at his aged, spindly fingers wrapped around each handle of the bike. His arms, pallid and scarred, have been pickled in the vinegar of time. He has certainly put this body through its paces, but there is still more to be done.

He revs the motor before he responds. "Yes. It's her."

The silence between them feels louder and says more than the chugging engine of the bike as they push forward down the road. He had found her again. Fairly late in this generation, though. There's only been a few times where he's allowed her to get this old. The others are harmless, easy to manage. They're easy to bend to submission. But not her. Not Durga.

"Do you think that—"

Thegn's words are cut short as the minor buzzing in his head suddenly explodes and envelops all of his senses. He's vaguely aware of his body riding along on the motorcycle, but there's nothing he can do to control it. He's stuck in a mental void. Words from Caffiel echo far away, like in a deep chasm.

The buzzing increases. Insistent. Demanding. The Karui hive. Thegn may be out of reach of any members of the hive or a nexus, but they can still communicate with him across that distance. However, since he's not fully part of the hive, there are trade-offs.

Motherfucker! I told you to give me a warning before reaching out to me this way. Ping my comm.

The response from the hive doesn't have a voice. Not like how it is with Caffiel. For the hive, the buzz simply gets louder, and Thegn suddenly understands its meaning.

Well, you should've pinged more than once. Motorcycles are loud.

Yes, I'm on a motorcycle. Why do you think I'm so pissed off? My consciousness can't be in two places at the same time. This long-distance telepathy has me frozen on that bike. Not exactly safe.

The buzz's response—the hive's response—is impatient. Displeased.

I'll take whatever risks I damn well please. That's part of our deal.

Look, do you want to get to the point? The highway in this area is straight, but—

The hive cuts off his thought. They want her. Another of the Four to bolster their ranks. A weapon to carve their path to victory.

You can't control her.

They convey that they can, and they will. One way or another. Just like they control him.

It's a bad move. It's better to kill her, as we've done before. Better for everyone. Thegn has more thoughts on the matter, but he can't think them. Not now, when they can hear. He made that mistake before when he recognized her and said her name.

I'm retracing the path of that merc's head. There's another outpost town just south of here; that may be where his team fought her.

It's not certain she's been triggered yet. I won't know until I face her directly. Then—

Stop interrupting! I don't care if you know my answer without me thinking the sentence. Yes, I can still defeat her.

The drone of the hive pushes to the edges of his mind. Prodding. Searching. Testing.

I'll get you your fucking weapon. Are we done?

Episode Three: No Time Like the Present

The answer comes in the form of a quick release of the buzzing and humming in his brain, soon replaced by the bellow of the motorcycle engine, the feeling of wind in his face, and the sensation of Caffiel digging claws into his shoulder and screaming in his mind.

Thegn!

A chunk of the road is missing, replaced by dirt, scrub brush, and a ten-inch drop. Thegn manages the drop reasonably well, but the other side of the hole is too close. Thegn and Caffiel are launched from the bike's saddle. He watches as the motorcycle somersaults beneath them as he feels a sharp, burning sensation at his shoulder blades. His wings have emerged. He glides down to the road on the other side of the hole and continues to walk as his wings fold up behind him.

That outpost town isn't far from here. He has a job to do. *Fuck the hive.*

They did their long-distance thing on you again, didn't they? From his perch on Thegn's shoulder, Caffiel looks back at the wreckage behind them. **You lose so many bikes that way.**

"Stay the fuck out of my head, Caffiel."

3.8

Hubris

"You know what? No, I'm done. No more." Jack spits the words in anger and frustration, then turns and boils his way up the stone steps toward Upper Bule.

Zeke starts to scamper along the steps to follow him, but stops. Hesitates. He looks back at Corva.

She stares up at the bottom of Jack's feet as he leaves. "So you're saying I have the day off?"

Jack stops mid-step. His fists clench until his knuckles are white. For a moment, they flush with color as he relaxes ever so much. It doesn't last long, though. A moment later, they're fully flexed, solid white, and shaking. He mumbles something that Corva can't quite make out.

"What was that? You talking to yourself again?" She raises the pitch of her voice at the end of the question. *He knows I'm just ribbing him, right?*

"Do whatever you want. I don't care." The words are still delivered quietly, but with each word carrying the weight of a restrained scream.

Gobsmacked, Corva watches Jack run the rest of the way up the stairs. Hoping to read some hint or insight, she looks over to Zeke, who is still standing on the stairway's boundary wall. Instead of answers, she's given a blank gaze that reeks of disapproval.

"Don't look at me like that. How was I supposed to know that was gonna set him off?" She plops down on the step and tries to digest what just happened. It started innocently enough—she'd caught Jack peeping on a whore. *So I hit him with a friendly jab or two. Nothing too serious. After all, without bickering, we might not speak to each other at all. Besides, that hooker's gotta have at least ten years on him.*

"Screw him. Don't need to waste energy on an infant who gets all bent from shape over some piranha. About time I moved on anyway. Pretty much got what I needed."

Corva cuts an eye over to Zeke.

"I have to say, it's nice to be able to sit this distance from you without passing out. I still have that shaky feeling—feels like my bones are humming under my skin—but I guess I'm getting used to it. Almost like I can maybe control it."

She twists on her step to face Zeke more directly. "So, what do you think? Want to ditch this hole and come with me? You obviously don't belong here any more than I do."

Zeke blinks. His face shows a bit of surprise at the question. He looks up along the steps, but Jack is already well out of sight.

Corva continues, "Oh, we can bring Jack along, too. He's upset, but you know how he is. He'll get over it. The kid cooks a mean meal and knows the area around here pretty well. He'd be a good guia for us. Of course, asking is really only a formality. You and I both know I can take you both whenever I want. I would just prefer that you come along willingly."

That gets Zeke's attention. Corva smiles when he finally looks back at her. Though monkeys can't exactly look skeptical, the folds of his brows give the closest reproduction of that expression.

"What? You know it's true. After all, I—"

Corva doesn't get a chance to finish her sentence. Zeke springs from his spot on the stair into the air over Corva. He doesn't stop until he connects with the sheer stone wall behind her. As each of his paws touches the smooth surface, his body compresses. For a fraction of a second, he looks a bit like a furry barnacle stuck to the rock wall.

In an instant, he uncoils and launches from the wall. He hits Corva's back with a lot more force than she expects from something his size. She's thrown off-balance and takes a step forward, bending at the waist.

Zeke uses her body's momentum to swing around her shoulders. He looks her in the eye as he swings by her face. His lizard-like eyes pierce to her core. It feels like the moment lasts ten times longer than it really does, but she still doesn't have any time to react.

Before she knows it, he's grabbing her dreadlocks. The follow-through of his continued swing pulls her upright again. An instant later, she can feel the weight of his little body squatting on her head. He leans over so she can see his face again.

You assume too much, Corva.

"What the fuck?"

Corva lurches backward as if doing so would somehow put distance between her and the monkey sitting on her head. Zeke stays up there, like he's been glued in place. Although upside down in front of her, he never breaks eye contact. She stumbles back on her heels and avoids falling by catching herself against the flat rock wall behind her.

However, that does little to settle her internal disorientation. In her gut, she knows that Zeke just spoke to her. However, his mouth hadn't moved; he really didn't even have a voice. In fact, focusing back on that moment, she hadn't heard anything at all. It was more like the idea spontaneously materialized in her mind and its echoes generated the words. Stranger still, if she really thinks about it, she can only imagine hearing the sentence in her own voice, but not the way she'd say it. Befuddled, she hunts in Zeke's slitted pupils for some semblance of an answer.

I never wanted to do this. I've stalled and put it off as much as I could. But seeing that you and Jack won't let this go, now I see I should've done so much sooner.

"What—what are you talking about? Get off my head. Get out of my head!" Corva reaches up to pull Zeke off. However, before she can get to him, he speaks in her head again.

You assume your abilities are enhanced by my proximity. This is only half true. You caught me off guard that first time when you came into the bar, and again in the kiva a few hours ago. But I have a will of my own.

"Those fighting skills, that … that power. It's you?" She speaks aloud, despite hearing his half of the conversation in her mind. Could he read her thoughts?

The skills are yours. Dormant, but yours. As for the power … the bar fight? The grunts during the raid? You only had strength to defeat them—to survive—by my consent. My control of the flow.

Still unsettled by how his thoughts instantly pop and echo in her mind with her own voice, Corva straightens her back and closes her eyes. He must be right about the closeness thing. He's sitting directly on top of her head and there's barely any of the hum in her bones that she normally feels this close.

A barrage of questions bubble up, like an air pocket opening in the watery depths of her mind. But there's one thing he said—he thought—that sticks out.

"Dormant?"

All these years, I've managed to avoid all of you and each of your incarnations. And you. I've seen you fight. Same bloodlust as always. You haven't changed. What makes you think I'd change for you over all the others?

He's not answering any of her questions, only giving her more. Questions laced with a thin hope. Avó's face appears in her mind. "Others? There are other survivors from Fareburne?"

From Fareburne? No. From everything I've heard, that annihilation was regretfully thorough and complete. You're the first survivor I've ever heard of from that ... event.

Zeke's face stretches into a look of—well, it's difficult for Corva to read. But it appears like his mind wandered off for a moment. The look dissolves as quickly as it came, replaced with a mask of renewed seriousness. **No. Not Fareburne. I'm talking about where you *really* come from.**

"I don't get it. If you're not talking about Fareburne, then what 'others'? I've traveled a lot of places in the last ten years, but Fareburne is where I'm from."

Amazing. You truly don't even know who you are.

"Who the hell are you to tell me who I am?" Corva can feel her face warming. She's upset. Indignant.

Maybe it's for the best that you don't know. Maybe that's why you've managed to survive for so long.

Then it occurs to her. The reason she's upset. She's not bothered because he's making assumptions about her. It's because he does know something, and he's not telling her.

"Fine. You're so smart, why don't you—"

She never gets a chance to finish her sentence. Still looking at Corva upside down, Zeke reaches out and places a finger at the center of her forehead. The moment the tip of his finger touches her skin, Corva's head snaps back like she's been shot. Zeke leaps clear to avoid being flung from her head. He lands at the ground near her feet as she crumples to her knees.

In those few seconds, she is overwhelmed with a surge of sensory memory. It blasts across her in fast-forward, nearly impossible for her to keep up. Her mind was a canal lock and Zeke just opened the gate holding back a tsunami. Lifetimes of images, sounds, smells, and feelings wash over her mind while her soul is tossed in the undertow.

How many lifetimes? Six? Seven? A dozen? Physically, she's different in every one, but they all tell the same story. Fighting. Battles. Mayhem. And each ends the same, an apology and the violent edge of a scythe. *The* scythe. The blade of A Velha Barba, the Old Beard. Death.

Those aren't dreams she's been having.

She's not Corva. Not really.

"Who—*what* are you?" The words dribble out with labored exhalations, barely coherent.

Zeke turns away from her and gazes out as midmorning sunlight prances over the rooftops of Lower Bule.

One thing at a time, child. Let this bit soak in first.

3.9

Impulse

Stomping his way across Upper Bule, Jack still seethes. "Stupid bitch. What the hell does she know? And Zeke! That dick stayed with her! Whatever. They can have each other. Make little dreadlocked, lizard-monkey babies."

He speaks loudly to himself as he trudges along the pathways and conduits on his way to the bar. "Corva don't know nothin'. No sense of what Lyia n' me got."

The walls echo his voice as he tromps along. "So tired of this bullshit." His face twists into an expression intended to mock, well, everyone. "'You got no chance with Lyia, Jack. You can't run the bar, Jack. You can't stop the mercies, Jack. You can't save the Fold, Jack. You couldn't have saved the old man, Jack.'"

Jack squeezes his eyes shut as he walks, cutting off the tears before they get a chance to run down his face. "You ain't no help to no one."

He rubs his eyes with the back of his arm. The wet patches on his arm feel chilled despite the warming morning air. When his eyes open back, he can see clean smears in his arm among a thin layer of dust and grime.

"Fuck all ya'll. I'm tired of being told what I can't do."

He pauses at the unpainted steel door at the entrance of Gorm's swap shop. It's unmarked and uninviting, but Jack knows the door isn't locked and the shop's open. At almost 11 a.m., it's early by Bule time, but the big guy's swap shop is always open. Mercs blow in and out of town at all hours of the day and it makes no sense to let that potential business slip away. Staying open also prevents break-ins at those odd hours.

Jack used to try to convince Old Man V to keep the bar open like that, but the old man never went for it. He had some pretty old-fashioned opinions about the necessity of sleep. Something about him being too old and Jack being too young to handle a chembraid, let alone the on-the-fly mix of uppers and downers it would deliver. The old man had promised they'd look into it after Jack hit eighteen years, but he went and died a year ago. Five years too early.

Speaking of not sleeping, Jack catches a glimpse of himself in the door. The reflection is distorted by the scratches and stains on the door, but even with that, he can tell he's looking pretty rough. Barely an hour of sleep, a full night of training with Corva, and round-tripping Cliff City will do that to you.

Combine his current appearance with the unfiltered exchange he's having with himself, Jack's the very picture of madness in miniature. It's not uncommon to catch an unkempt person mumbling and clomping along in an aimless patrol around town. However, it's far less common for that to be someone everyone knows, like Jack.

Static from the talkbox just to the side of the steel door snaps Jack out of his daze. "Heya Jackie. You have another long night getting roughed up at the Red Light?"

"Kiss my ass, Gorm."

A hiss of laughter rattles out of the rusty comm. "Hey, you're the one tripping the prox on my door. You comin' in to get something? Or are you just goin' to block the way so no one else can come in?"

Jack looks back his distorted reflection in the door. Disheveled. Tired. Pissed.

He looks to his left and right along the corridor. No one else around. He shakes his head. *What's it matter? I'm grown. I can do what I want.*

A couple long steps and he's right next to the talkbox, his hand on the door handle.

"What's the price on a chembraid like the one you got, Gorm?"

3.10

MISTAKES, REGRETS

Keeping vigil over Corva, Zeke holds his post at her feet. A stupefied shock casts a dull, glazed shadow over the trapped forest-shimmer that normally bounces within her eyes. She remains crumpled and slouched against the stair wall. She hasn't blinked.

Without checking her pulse, anyone passing might think she's dead. This is Bule, though; Corva would sooner be looted and cleared off the steps as a corpse than checked and administered first aid. Knowing this, Zeke holds fast. She may not have changed much over the course of all her lifetimes, but that's no reason to make her life harder than it's going to be.

Still, his impatience and unease mounts. He needs to get to the bar and look after Jack. The boy can handle himself pretty well, but he exhibits an incredible talent for getting himself planted in the center of all manner of untenable situations. It almost always starts the second he opens his mouth and vomits his unfiltered thoughts on exactly the wrong people. And for the last hundred and fifty years, *everyone* has been the wrong people.

Vardin put a lot of effort into coaching Jack, and it certainly wasn't in vain. Zeke can almost hear glimmers of his old friend in Jack's voice during his attempts to hustle and negotiate. Shaking his head, Zeke silently curses the frailty of the human form. Although Vardin lived far longer than most people in this age, his passing was still far too early.

Since the old barkeep's death, there hadn't been much of a counterweight to Jack's braggadocio and inexperience. Even the best among the miscreants of this town are hardly model examples of decency. Zeke is nothing more than a monkey to Jack, and as a long-rotted carcass, Vardin has—unsurprisingly—become an ineffective mentor.

Zeke looks back at Corva. Physically, she's not much older than Jack. But as her true self, there's experience there in spades. He shakes the thought out of his mind. What's he thinking? Even in the times that she's worked beyond her natural impetuous bloodlust, she's been cold, verging on heartless. In those times, people are mere numbers, subjects bent to her own brutal mathematics. Prolonged exposure to that kind of ruthlessness would shrivel even the largest heart.

Her body recovers quickly. She'll snap out of this state soon enough, but it will take much longer for her mind to fully absorb everything he's shared with her. Years. Decades, perhaps, if she lives long enough.

He curses to himself again, this time at his own hubris. He'd allowed himself to be goaded into showing too much. Really, he never should have let Jack tend her wounds. She would have died on her own and it would've ended there, at least for another generation.

Unfortunately, that's not what happened. Instead, she's learned that she can be activated and now she's had a peek into her own past. All because of him.

He shakes out the series of what-ifs, should-haves, and could-haves. That's not doing any good now. There's responsibility in sharing truth. He can't open a door and expect her to walk through it alone. But that's etiquette. There's no contract. He's not strictly obligated to go with her. Besides, Zeke promised his old friend that he'd look after Jack, and there's no recanting that.

Episode Three: No Time Like the Present

Decision made, Zeke snorts an affirmation to himself. When Corva recovers, she'll need to decide her next move on her own. If she sticks around, he can help. In the meantime, there's a fourteen-year-old bartender whose mouth is probably already getting him into a heap of trouble.

3.11

Old Beard

Jack pours another shot of shine for his only customer. This is an even slower start to the morning than anticipated. It's coming up on noon and so far he's only seen one of his first call regulars stagger in.

But Wall-Eyed Clyde didn't even stick around for a drink. Dude made it two steps in, stopped, and took a long stare at the guy already drinking shots at the bar. A moment later, Clyde was out the door.

Thinking back on it, Jack frowns. It's not like Clyde to pass on his morning dose of dog hair. Of course, that guy's been around the circuit a few times. Gotten close to packing it in more than once during some pretty major-league battles, if you believe his stories. Left him a bit shaky and unpredictable. Prone to erratic behavior. Especially if things are different from what he expects.

Maybe Clyde was thrown off by Jack's new chembraid. It's only visible up near Jack's neck and down his left forearm. The rest of the flat braid of cables and wires is hidden under his shirt, but the whole twisted thing itches something fierce. The annoyance of that alone is enough to keep him awake. Knowing that, he could have passed on paying Gorm a thousand nits and just gotten Zeke to stab him in the arm with a fork every two minutes.

Oh yeah. He winces. Zeke's not here. It's been a couple hours already and neither that double-timing little monkey nor Corva have made it back to the bar yet. Normally he'd be a bit concerned, but he's still pretty pissed off.

On the upside, there is at least one good customer. And a new one at that. The guy is a pretty scraggly old mess, even by Bule standards. However, he was waiting when Jack showed at the bar, raring for his first call fix. Even better, the man's two-drink down payment was made with a fist-sized bar of rock salt. That's more than enough to run a tab for the rest of the day.

Inspecting the dark, angular block, Jack raises an eyebrow. It's not that strange for out-of-towners to make payments in all manner of raw materials. Since every township has its own independently grown monetary system, commodities like minerals and grain are de facto exchange currencies. He should probably clue in Corva on that fact, if he lets her stick around.

The thing is, though, that most folks stop at the Exchange when they get into town and swap goods for trade units—nits. That's not a mandatory thing, of course. A bunch of other towns don't have an organized setup like that, so a lot of traders and mercs aren't used to it. Many will simply skip the Exchange and try to deal direct. Most shop owners in Bule end up sending these people back to the Exchange to get nits for payment.

This stuff is special, though. When an outsider usually tries to pay in salt, it's usually solar salt or salt refined by boiling seawater. Rock salt, however, has to be mined. With the war going on, it's tough for any individual person to find a claim, let alone mine it. Drilling and explosions attract attention, and attention is rarely a good thing. Just about every salt mine worth digging has been confiscated by either the Karui or the Umbrati. So if a person pays in rock, it means they've probably done work—merc work—for one side or the other. Possibly both.

Jack cheats a glance at the old-timer, venturing a quick once-over. He's seen old people before. They're rare, but some people do manage to survive that long. Hell, Old Man V was well into the gray before he finally bit it.

However, this grizzled fossil of a man looks to have been kicking around well beyond his expiration date. There's no possible way he contracts in the war. Maybe when he was younger … Jack risks a second look.

Was this guy ever younger? The man has wrinkles cut into his wrinkles. His skin hangs from his bones and sinew like a slice of ham draped over a clothesline, and his gnarled white beard more closely resembles a choked system of tree roots than hair.

Maybe he's an old miner who's been picking at rock underground for years and finally managed to crack off a chunk that's worth something. Or perhaps he's some senile elder from a passing group of trade nomads. He wandered off, stumbled over the body of a merc who actually works the war, and found the rock salt while looting. Or what if—

"You're staring, boy. If you've a question, you should get around to asking it." The wrinkled man leans forward. One of his eyes is open comically large while the other is barely open at a squint.

Jack clears his throat and looks away, remembering his lessons. *Go slow. Think first. Think second. Then think about speaking. Then keep your mouth shut until you've thought one more time.*

"Hey! 'S fucking rude to ignore the only customer in the room."

Jack looks up, pacing himself. *Ol' Wrinkles must've pre-gamed and got here already sauced.* "Um, no … no. Just lookin' at this rock and wonderin' if I gotta be worried about anyone who might show up with an eye for their 'misplaced' property."

"Oh, that." The old man curls his body back over the bar, a buzzard hunched over the carcass of his destitute shot glass. "No need to worry about that. It was mine. Got plenty more. I've also got an empty cup."

Alright, so the senile trade nomad theory is out. Wrinkles must be a miner. Jack spreads his arms wide on the bar and leans his weight forward so he can speak more directly at the hunched-over old man. Sure, there's no one else in the bar, but folks like to feel like they're getting an inside secret, especially when they're being sold to.

"What'll you have this round? Whiskey? I got some of the best salvage barrels from a sacked mill town. Stored right, and aged well. Tequila? It's hard as shit to find blue agave, but I got a source that grows and distills her own. I'm the only place she ships to this far north. Or I can give you another hit of our house cornshine. It's set some folks blind, but that shouldn't hurt if you're gonna mole your way underground for more salt."

Wrinkles doesn't even raise his head when he replies. "You sure talk a lot more than you pour. I'll let you know if I want different."

It takes Jack a second to fully register Wrinkles's terse answer. He doesn't let that stop him, though. If Old Man V taught him anything, it's good customer service in the face of assholery. "Cornshine it is! Good choice. Made with the best trade grain, plus a spike from my own hybrid. Grow it right up on the roof."

Jack watches Wrinkles launch the contents of his glass to the back of his throat. *Floppy-armed old coot sure ain't slowin' down. Not my problem, though. His tab is paid up.*

Still holding his glass, Wrinkles signals a need for another refill by tapping the side of his glass with a bony forefinger. The nail on that finger is long and looks like it's been sharpened. Freckles and liver spots cover the full span of his hand and forearm. He doesn't set the glass down for Jack to pour the refill. Instead he holds it hovering out over the bar, hand surprisingly steady. Innumerable scars trace the length of his forearm.

He raises his gaze to meet Jack's and shakes his glass expectantly. "You think I'm a miner? What gives you that idea?"

Jack struggles to make the pour at such an awkward height. "Uh, well, you just—alright, hold on."

He uprights his bottle of shine and plunks it on the bar. "If you want me to serve this drink, ya gotta put the glass down. Have a little friggin' patience. I ain't gonna get pulled away to pour for someone else right now. And it's not like—thank you."

Even with the glass lowered, Wrinkles keeps his focus on Jack's face. "You didn't answer my question."

"Yeah, well, you were being a d—"

Jack! Slow down! Think.

"D-um, difficult. Distracting." Jack finally manages to pour another shot of shine in the old man's glass. "Couldn't concentrate on talking while serving at that angle. You mighta took notice, I ain't all that tall."

Wrinkles nods and swipes up his glass. "Yup. Noticed."

"Anyhow, how'd I know you're a miner? You squared up in rock. No way you got that as merc pay. I figure you got a little private claim somewhere up-canyon and you're hand-diggin' it."

"What gives you the idea that I'm from farther up the canyon?"

"You got no hair, old man! Gettin' close to Sheep country up there."

"Sheep country?"

"Yeah, Sheeps. Karui, lightheads, cloth faces … you know. Them things in the hive don't got any hair on 'em. Probably best not to stand out too much. Though your disguise needs some work. That ratty-assed beard of yours makes it kinda obvious that you ain't one of 'em. Whattya do? Wrap a scarf around your mouth?"

Jack pauses a moment and gives Wrinkles a long look. It could be that the chembraid is making him extra sensitive, but there's something off about the old guy. Something weird. He's different from most of the heavy drinkers that find their way to the bar. At the same time, there's something familiar about him. Uncomfortably familiar. Like walking a path and seeing two nearly identical natural rock formations a klick apart. Enough to make you wonder if you walked a loop even though you know you've walked a straight line.

He gives his head a little twist, clearing away the thought. "But maybe that's not why you're hairless—tryin' to hide out in Sheep country. Maybe you're just old. Either way, I know you're not comin' from down-canyon. Been all over that way. If there's a claim out that side, I'd know about it."

"Well that's valuable information." The ancient drunk leans his head back and empties his glass. "You got a knack for guessing, kid, I'll say that much. But you got me all wrong. See, I have been underground my fair share. Thing is, though, I'm no miner. I'm a hunter. Tracking myself a pretty big payday right now, actually."

"Ha! What? I call bullshit, Grandpa. You're a pile of bones shoved in a wrinkly deflated old balloon. That cornshine's startin' to make you think all sideways." Jack pauses. He may have gotten a bit ahead of himself. Probably would be best to try and correct course. "If, you know, you'll pardon me for being a bit frank."

"Believe what you want, Frank, but facts are facts. I can—"

"My name ain't Frank. It's—"

"I know that's not your name, Frank. And as rude as you are, I don't care to know what you call yourself. Now, if you don't mind, I was in the middle of saying something. I was saying that I can prove I've been in the hunting game for a while."

"Oh yeah? How's that?" Jack pauses a beat. "And my name is Jack."

"Sure thing, Frank." Wrinkles turns his squint toward the top of Jack's head. "I noticed you've got a bit of premature aging going on."

The white streak in Jack's mop of hair. He's used to people staring at it. Talking about it. "Yeah. My mom was part skunk. If you want, I can prove it to ya by shittin' in your drink."

The laugh that comes out of Wrinkles's throat sounds like something between a squeaky door and an uncontrolled series of coughs. The old coot's face stretches in a way that shows it's not used to smiling. "That's a good one, kid. I like it. It's funny." Just as fast as it came, though, the smile is gone. "It also distracts folks from asking what it really came from."

For a fraction of a second, Jack reflexively eyes the corner of the bar where the gitfo bags sit. He's not sure why, but he suddenly has the strong feeling that he shouldn't be here right now. It's a ridiculous urge, though. He knows it. Just an old man telling old man stories. He pulls his focus back to his wrinkled customer. "What it really came from? Whattya mean?"

"That streak of yours. Mind if I have a guess at a few things?"

This should be interesting. Maybe the old guy came from a traveling circus group. "Alright, Old-Timer. Shoot."

"That whole area where the hair grows white. I'm guessing it feels numb most of the time, but there's no real scar there—not on the skin at least."

"Sure." A little specific, but not too difficult a guess.

"Except it isn't always numb, is it? Sometimes it burns a bit. Aches even." Wrinkles leans back. "Like right now."

Jack feels his stomach jump to his throat. Things are striking a bit close to home. He's got no response for Wrinkles. He just stands there, gawking.

"There's only a couple ways you could get that streak in your hair. My guess? That's Death's Mark. I'm thinking you're one of the few people who got the mark, but didn't get what comes after it." The crusty old man pulls on his beard, reflecting. "In all my years, I think I've only come across three people like you."

Jack clears his throat and finally finds his voice again. "How do you—"

Nope. Wrong question. Start over, Jack. "So you think you have a knack for telling the origin of a scar. How in the world does that prove you're a hunter?"

"Because of those three people like you, two of them are ones I've tracked."

"What happened to the third?"

"Someone else got that one." Wrinkles chews a bit on part of his upper lip, bitterly staring off into the distance. Suddenly, though, his demeanor changes. "But enough nostalgia! Give my glass a reload."

Pleased to have a change of focus, Jack dutifully pours some more cornshine in Wrinkles's glass. The whole time, the old guy looks around the bar, particularly the areas with patchwork repairs.

Wrinkles grabs the glass and swings it around, abstractly pointing at the entirety of the bar. "Looks like this place has seen better days."

"It's functional." Jack's gaze follows everything Wrinkles points at with his glass. "We'll have everything all the way back to normal in no time."

The thick hairs on Wrinkles's eyebrows push up. "Is that so, Frank?"

Jack ignores the incorrect name and keeps talking. "Yeah. Aside from repairs, the bar's got pretty low overhead, no competition, and a steady stream of customers. It's a good business to be in."

Wrinkles turns and sits forward in his stool to give Jack his full attention. "Speaking of customers. I was wondering if you might be able to help me out."

Jack smiles. "See, now you're convincing me that you're a bounty hunter. Every hunter that enters this bar looking for someone eventually gets to the 'speaking of customers' lead-in. Took you long enough to get there. You shoulda started with that."

The hairs on Wrinkles's beard seem to bristle more as his face scrunches up to show mild frustration. "I'm on the hunt. A live capture."

Wrinkles stops for a moment and stares, like he's daring Jack to interrupt. It takes some effort, but Jack manages to keep his mouth shut for the time being. Old Man V would be proud.

Seemingly satisfied by Jack's monumental act of self-restraint, Wrinkles continues, "I'm tracking a girl—a bit older than you—she blew through this area about a month ago or so. Hear she actually made a stop at this bar."

Jack blinks. It feels like all of the air has suddenly been sucked from the room. "Oh? What's she look like?"

"Knotty hair. Green eyes. Dark skin. No tech." Wrinkles keeps staring at Jack. It feels like he's digesting Jack's every action.

EPISODE THREE: NO TIME LIKE THE PRESENT

Sooner than I'd thought … but this guy?

Pouring the man another shot, Jack feels the muscles in the back of his throat start to flex. He may have doubts about how effective Wrinkles might be as a bounty hunter, but nobody lives that long without some kind of advantage. Maybe it's the sleep deprivation talking, or maybe the chembraid isn't keeping him sharp; Gorm did say it may take a little while to tune. Of course, it could also be the years of paranoia, but something is definitely askew.

Play it safe. Play it stupid. He's played poker before. Never won much, but he's definitely bluffed his way outta losing at least once. "No tech? Really? Who is she? Some rich guy's runaway concubine?"

"Can't say. There's rumor that she's a survivor from Fareburne. Don't really care. She's on my list, so I'm hunting her down."

Fareburne? The back of Jack's throat feels like it's instantly dried up. That's specific. And it's not information that could be found in the trades. Jack had looked up Corva's bounty to figure out who might be after her. The report there was really thin. Where was Wrinkles getting his information?

Suddenly aware that he's not said a word since Wrinkles mentioned Fareburne, Jack clears his throat. He needs to find out more about what the old vulture wants with Corva.

"You don't care? That's the town that got wiped by them Shadowfold fuckers. They took out whole towns without setting foot in them. I'd certainly care. Anyone who survived that ain't someone I'd want to mess with. For a live capture, I'd care an awful lot. I'd 'care' a bullet right into her head." Jack pauses a bit. This whole thing about Fareburne and the Fold has gotten him more twisted up than he'd like. "But anyway, ain't no one looking like that been through here. You sure you got the sand to take on someone like that?"

The old man ignores Jack and reaches into the folds of his cloak. "Here, maybe this'll help your memory."

Wrinkles pulls a leather glove from his cloak. Well, not a full glove. When he puts it on, the thin bleached skin of it only covers the old man's first two fingers and his thumb. A data sphere sits at a junction near the base of the thumb, and from it runs three wide, flat metal strips, each one tracing along the back of a finger or thumb.

He smiles at Jack. A crooked, toothy grin. "I hate wearing this thing. Feels gross."

With that, he uses his newly gloved hand to reach out and steal the bottle of cornshine from Jack's hands. He finishes off what little remains in the bottle before Jack even comes to the realization that his hands are empty.

Leaving no time to react, Wrinkles holds the bottle in front of Jack's face. The surface of the bottle glows a soft blue in the space between the ancient bounty hunter's thumb and fingers. In that illuminated space, a faint image begins to coalesce. A short sequence of images, actually.

It's Corva, in the bar. Jack recognizes the chaos from the bar fight just over a month ago. But it's from an angle he doesn't recognize. Someone else's viewpoint. Whatever the view, though, she's ruining everyone and everything in her path.

The wrinkly bounty hunter brings his face up next to the bottle. He's close enough that the only thing Jack can smell is Wrinkles's aura-like haze of alcohol. The old codger still has that grin smeared across his face. "This is the girl I'm hunting. You saying that *isn't* your bar getting all beat to shit in there? Sure looks like this place to me."

Jack's stomach twists into itself and his skin tightens like a shirt shrunken in the wash. This is almost the same sick feeling he had when trying to negotiate that day. The picture of Corva isn't what has him fazed. It's obvious that Wrinkles has been talking about Corva. The problem is this old coot has—and is using—imbued tech.

It's not just the imbued tech, though. It's the nonchalance with how he's using it. Like it's perfectly natural. No different than putting on shoes in the morning. That's just not done. Without first doing some pretty heavy-duty preparations, any kind of soulmancy can be easily traced. That's the whole reason Old Man V put up the shielding down in Cliff City and why he and Lyia did the same when healing Corva. People don't just go shining their fixins all over the place. Not unless they've got something big to back it up.

Jack thinks about the raid that came after the bar fight. That whole mess was for some pretty minor imbued tech. A couple infused beads. This thing that Wrinkles has on his hand is on another level altogether. It's not just some simple bead with imbued power. This thing is playing back memories on glass.

That's not something just anyone can do. Only the Karui have that ability. In fact, that glove probably isn't even leather. It can only be skin peeled from some low-level conscript in the Karui hive. And here this wrinkly old bastard is shaking it in Jack's face.

As he watches the sequence of memories dancing on the bottle, the situation becomes abundantly clear. These are Tretch's memories. That peanut-headed merc brought this whole mess to Jack's door. Well, not exactly his door. It was through his wall, actually. In any case, even after skipping town, that dick is still causing trouble for Jack. At least now there's no wondering where that tiny-skulled bounty hunter ran off to.

It also clears up the question of who Tretch was working for. The Karui. They're the ones with the live-capture bounty out on Corva. Despite his appearance—and his age—Wrinkles *is* under contract, and Corva is his target. That the Karui want her alive means only one thing: conscription.

It's a lot of effort for one person, though. What's so special about being a survivor from Fareburne?

A wave of nausea rolls over Jack; he can feel a sick heat emanating from behind his eyelids as he tries to blink as calmly as possible. *Don't matter where she's from or which side this guy's huntin' her for, no one deserves to be pulled in the war 'gainst their will.*

Jack sticks to his plan of playing it stupid. He peeks around the bottle and looks at Wrinkles.

"Oh, that bitch? Yeah, I know who you're talkin' about. Wrecked my bar something stupid while doin' the same to a whole buncha your kind. Hunters." He pauses, looking at the wrinkled, bony old man in front of him. "Well ... the younger, stronger, more heavily armed sort."

Reminding himself to slow down and think, he takes a deep breath in. Big mistake. It could be nerves or his body getting accustomed to the juice from the chembraid, but most likely it's the overwhelming miasma of booze wafting off Wrinkles. Whatever the cause, a wave of sickness rolls over Jack. His mouth instantly fills with saliva. *Aw, crap. Which is it gonna be? Words or stomach?*

He tries for the former. "She skipped town not long after she kicked the—"

Nope. Spit glands turn into firehoses as Jack clamps his mouth shut and covers it with his fist. He sprints to the end of the bar and buries his face in a spittoon as the contents of his gut cascade out. He'd hoped that putting his face deeper inside would dampen the sound of his retching, but the old brass pot resonates with every little grunt and groan. The putrid smell of old, expended tobacco juice and other assorted trash only amplifies his spasms to a sequence of post-release dry heaves.

Jack pulls his face upward a bit, just enough to feel the cooler air outside the spittoon flow across the misty beads of sweat on his face. Keeping his head down, he reaches up, blindly pawing for a towel that should be hanging at the end of the bar. After a few fruitless pats, he finally grabs hold of the gritty, sweat-starched cloth and yanks it from the hook. He bunches the stained rag over his face, wiping away the sweat and breathing through it as a makeshift filter.

Real smooth, dumbass.

"Anxiety, Frank?" The sound of Wrinkles's voice crackles on the other side of the rag. But it doesn't come from his seat back at the bar. It's much closer, like the old buzzard is still somehow close despite the distance Jack's traveled to the side of the bar.

What the shit?

Jack's eyes snap open and he topples backward from his squat. The decrepit old man arches over the edge of the bar like the most menacing of wilted flowers. His head hangs above Jack with the same amused, closed-lip smile that a child given a frog and a magnifying glass on a bright day might have.

Jack regains his composure and drags himself up to a kneel. "My name still ain't Frank. An' no. I'm not anxious. Least, I wasn't before. Think you could get back on your side of the bar, Gramps? You're freakin' me out." He leans over and spits the last of his excess saliva into the spittoon. "Just had too good a time last night. Guess I don't recover as fast as I used to."

The ancient bounty hunter retracts to his stool, then removes his skin glove and places it back into the depths of his cloak.

Jack stands up, dusting himself off with the towel. "As I was saying, that chick skipped town after she wrecked my bar. That was about a month ago. Took me this long to get the place put back together. You find her, you tell her she owes me damages."

He stops, noticing the bottle that Wrinkles emptied and used as a makeshift playback screen. "And your tab only covered that bottle of shine. You want more, you'll need to pay more."

Wrinkles doesn't even look at the bottle. His gaze never leaves Jack. "You're a remarkably poor liar, Frank, you know that?"

Jack tries to stammer out a protest, but he's cut off before any coherent syllables cross his lips.

"Don't take it that way, kid. There was a brief span of time in history when that was an admirable trait. A man like you was trusted because he couldn't help but speak to the truth of things. Of course, that time has long passed. What used to be honored—celebrated, even— is now a liability."

"I—I got no idea what you're talkin' about. Girl's gone. Been gone. Ain't comin' back." For the briefest of moments, Jack feels a touch of relief. That last part is true. Probably. After how he blew up at her on the steps between Lower and Upper Bule, he wouldn't be surprised if she never comes back. She *is* gone. Hopefully, for her sake, she stays that way.

"Then where did she go? She's got no trail after showing up here. Scent is hot here and cold everywhere else. Do you even know who it is you think you're protecting? I'm doing you a favor, boy. You've got no idea what kind of danger you're really in."

"From this girl you're talkin' about? Or from you? Don't matter much in either case. She ain't here and the only danger I got from you is the chance you might black out and lie on my floor until closing time."

The aged hunter bolts to his feet, stretching to his full height before lurching forward and pressing his hands against the edge of the bar. Tilting his head to the side, he continues to stare at Jack. The smile from earlier is gone, replaced with a grim stone-faced glare. Wrinkles closes his eyes and breathes a heavy, liquor-filled sigh before reopening them. "Let's try this a different way. How familiar are you with the way the war started?"

"Really? What is it with old fuckers and tellin' stories on how things used to be? I got no patience for history lessons, Grandpa. 'Specially for something that's known."

"Yeah? Tell me what it is you think you know."

"Look, I ain't playin' this game. You can help the Sheeps and Goats fight their war. I've got my bar. Keep a low profile, make some cash offa you saps, and tend to my own. Your girl bounced. She ain't here." He tilts his head toward the door at the front of the bar. "You're a hunter. Go fetch."

Just as Jack finishes, the door to his bar swings open. Hard. A pop echoes through the bar as the door claps against its frame. Corva steps across the threshold and stumbles in, showing all the grace of a duck with a brick strapped to its head.

Wrinkles grins at Jack. His rotting teeth emanate their own biosphere, along with the smell that accompanies it. "Not playing a game, you say, Frank?"

J.J. VEGA
FULCRUM
SEASON ONE
EPISODE FOUR:
DEATH COMES FOR YOU

Episode Four: Death Comes for You

Contents

4.1

Meet Death

Jack's shoulders drop. Not only is the jig up, but Corva doesn't look to be in fighting shape at all. *Has she been drinking? I mean, why not? Seems like everyone else in the room is drunk. Speaking of everyone else—*

He cranes his neck to look around Corva, but fails to find his four-handed compatriot. *Where in the world is Zeke?*

"You? Y—You!" Though her movements are unsteady, Corva's head loses its wobble. Her attention is focused in Jack's direction. Why would she be saying that to him? Today's not a day for guessing. Best to ask.

"Who? Me? You know me. Why are you even here? I thought I was clear when I said—"

Corva's head turns ever so slightly. Now it's absolutely clear that she's talking to Jack now. That means it's equally clear that she wasn't talking to him before. "No, not you. Him! Why's *he* here? Do you even know who this is? And I had to come back. Zeke said—"

221

Corva doesn't get a chance to finish her sentence. In an instant, she's lifted from her feet and pinned against the wall by her neck. Gnarled, spindly fingers wrap her throat as the ancient bearded bounty hunter touches noses with her. She chokes. For a moment Jack can't tell if it's from the pressure on her windpipe or the heated rot wafting from Wrinkles's open mouth.

"It's rude to talk about a person like he's not even here." Wrinkles's voice seems darker, deeper than it was before. There's still a bit of a slur there, but his tone is a lot more serious than it had been.

He's also not paying any attention to Jack at all.

Jack takes this opportunity to dive behind the bar. Plan B. With all their after-hours time dedicated to training, there hadn't been time to give the beat-up old shotgun a proper repair. He did at least get the barrels cleaned out and the firing mechanism mostly functional. He's also got the less damaged barrel preloaded with his last fixin bead. The gun isn't fit for loading with real shot, but since going for it is a desperation move anyway, may as well have it ready with something. Should be enough. Hopefully.

As Jack gets Plan B off its mount under the bar, he hears Wrinkles's voice, still turned away from him, still close to Corva. "Hello, Durga."

What the fuck is a Durga?

Still frowning, Jack spins to take aim at Wrinkles. If the last time he shot this was any indicator, the blast from the bead is pretty wide. He's going to need to get Corva clear. Also, it wouldn't hurt to be closer.

He takes the handful of steps needed to close the distance, trying to keep his feet light as possible. Taking a step to the side, he can see Corva's face around Wrinkles's shoulder. Her eyes are closed as weak gasping sounds squeak out of her mouth. She's clawing at the wiry, bony hand wrapped around her throat, but her struggles are fruitless. She may as well be attacking a statue of the wrinkled jerk. A putrid statue with an eye-watering stench pulsing from his, well, everything. It's like a rancid mix of hard liquor, garlic, and horse shit.

Corva keeps grappling with the old man's arm, but Jack can tell her strength is draining; a few more seconds and she'll probably black out.

Jack raises Plan B and levels it at the old man's head. "Hey Wrinkles! Ya mind taking your hand off my waitstaff?"

His shout goes unanswered. The aged hunter keeps his attention on Corva. This isn't going to work if he can't get Wrinkles's attention.

"Hey! Who's bein' rude now?"

Wrinkles lets out an annoyed sigh and turns to face his young distraction. He's still got Corva pinned against the wall, though. He stares at Jack over the twin barrels of Plan B as if daring him to shoot.

Keep him distracted. Jack purposefully avoids glancing at Corva to check on her. He keeps his full attention focused on Wrinkles. "Yeah, this woulda been a lot easier if I had a pump-action. More dramatic, too. You'da heard that sweet *chunk-chuck* sound and turned around immediately ... and I could still be behind the bar. Sadly, Old Man V had a preference for the break-action sort. Upside, though, is he taught me how to use this thing. I'm damn good. And I'm pretty sure I can't miss from here."

The grizzled old hunter's eyebrows push up, deepening the creases in his brow. There's the faintest hint of a smirk growing from the corner of his mouth.

Got his attention. Now what? Amusement isn't exactly the reaction that Jack was hoping to get, but at least it's something. Best to keep talking. "I got no want for messin' my bar again. How 'bout we cut this dance right here?"

"Ha!" It doesn't even qualify as a full laugh. More like a cough pitifully disguised as a laugh. "Frank, Frank. You don't seem to understand the situa—"

The lower half of Corva's body cuts off Jack's view of Wrinkles. Her feet scissor around his face. There's not a lot of strength in her movement, but it grants her enough leverage to twist against his thumb and torque her way out from his grasp. She drops to the ground, awkwardly landing on her shoulder as she coughs and wheezes, gulping air into her lungs.

Jack takes this opportunity to pull the trigger, but before the hammer drops, Wrinkles wraps his bony fingers around the double barrels and pushes them away from him. The blast from the bead launches across the bar and crashes into the wall.

The sound is deafening, but there's hardly any change in the old man's expression. His movements are deft and deliberate, but they're done with the same casual, almost bored demeanor a person might have while taking out the trash.

Still, there's power in his moves. Jack remembers that the last time he shot one of these beads, the kick knocked him back a few feet and slammed him into the wall behind the bar. Wrinkles is still holding on to Plan B and Jack didn't feel any kick at all this time.

Seeing Jack's eyes widen, Wrinkles gives a full grin and releases Plan B's barrels. He takes a step back, but not like he's trying to get away. It's more like he's making space, a bigger cage to include Jack.

Don't matter, space is space. The step back creates just enough room for Jack to slip himself between Wrinkles and Corva. Though the ammunition in Plan B is all spent, he keeps the gun trained on Wrinkles's face. May as well try to keep playing it brave. "So—"

Jack's voice cracks. Talk about shit timing. Sure he's scared out of his wits, but his voice doesn't have to sound like it right when he's trying to put up a strong front. Wrinkles is still standing there, though. That amused grin is still stretching his beard wide across his face. Jack clears his throat and tries again. "So, how's about we start this whole thing over?"

He looks up at the wrinkled hunter. The old man is a lot more imposing at his full height. No longer the slurring vulture craned over a shot glass, he looks down on Jack. Haughty. Superior. It's a dramatic contrast with the drunkard from mere moments ago.

Unfazed and caught up in his own diatribe, Jack doesn't flinch. "Since you're all concerned with rudeness and manners, let's do this formal-like. Start with introductions. I'm Jack. This is my bar. I'd like to avoid payin' for repairs … again."

He cocks his head up, pointing at Corva with the back of his skull. "This is Corva. She's a pain in my ass. Your turn, Old-Timer."

Corva, wide-eyed, hisses a whisper up from behind Jack. "You don't know who this is? I thought you said you survived Death's Mark."

"Shut up!" Jack tries to whisper back, but with his cracking voice and the fact that, well … he's Jack, there's no subtlety in his delivery. "You're not even supposed to be here. Where's Zeke? And what do you mean before when you said that he said something to you? Zeke's a—"

Something clicks in Jack's mind. He starts connecting the dots between what Corva just said and the familiarity Wrinkles seemed to have with Death's Mark.

"Death?" Jack turns, momentarily taking his attention off of Wrinkles. "What? Really? This guy?"

"Yes! Death! You know, Death. The Reaper. Old Beard. The Collector. Death! He's been collecting recruits for the Karui since the war started. How did you survive his mark without knowing what he looks like?"

"It's complicated. He doesn't—" Jack, still skeptical, turns back to the old man.

"Jack!" Corva's warning is too late.

Before Jack is able to get his eyes back on Wrinkles, the ancient bounty hunter places the palm of his hand at the tip of Plan B's barrels and shoves downward, stripping the shotgun from Jack's hands. The gun goes vertical as the barrels drive into the ground near Jack's feet and embed themselves in the wooden floorboards. Plan B is no longer a gun. It's not even a club. It's a signpost. A short signpost. The back of Plan B's stock only reaches up to Jack's chest.

Wrinkles places his hand on Plan B's butt, as if he's casually waiting for Jack's slack-jawed surprise to register. "You're gonna let bugs fly in there if you keep that thing open like that."

Jack has nothing. No response at all. He snaps his mouth shut like he's been given an order. Wrinkles treats this almost as a signal. He spreads a gigantic decayed-tooth grin and delivers a hard push forward with the hand that's resting on Plan B. His fist and Plan B's stock jam against Jack's chest. The torque tears up the floorboard, splintering as Jack slams against the wall.

Plan B is as ruined as the floorboards, barrels bent and stock cracked. For a fleeting moment as Wrinkles tosses the remains of the gun to the side, Jack wonders if Harris is going to use those messed up planks as a final excuse to take the bar. He doesn't dwell on it, though. The giant blooming pain in his chest is a much higher concern.

The old vulture looks down at Jack, tilting his head to the side. "How the fuck have you managed to live this long? You embarrass me. You'd think someone who survived my mark would have more sense."

Jack opens his mouth a few times, trying to reply. Unfortunately, it's hard to deliver any kind of snide quip or retort with the wind forced from his lungs. The feeling that his spine has been punched from the front isn't helping matters, either. The best he can manage is to look up at Wrinkles and glare for a few seconds.

This is Death. The one responsible for the streak in his hair. For the extermination of the Fold. Everyone he and Lyia knew in their previous life. Yeah, it was the last wave of a series of attacks from both the Karui and the Umbrati. But the Mark of Death had been the finishing touch. The thing that ended everything and ultimately sent him to this shithole town.

Repressed bitterness has a way of revealing itself at the most unexpected of times. Jack feels heat raising in his face and his vision blurs from the tears collecting in his eyes. His fists clinch so hard, he can feel his fingernails digging into the palms of his hands.

The old hunter gives a single knowing nod. "You've finally put it together. Good." He straightens his back before sweeping to a low bow. His face is level with Jack and Corva as he addresses them. "Thegn Nateusch, here to collect."

Jack coughs. The sudden flex jolts a wave of renewed pain over his body, forcing him to double over. However, the cough affords him a trickle of air, and he manages to finally choke out a response. "How about I just keep calling you Wrinkles?"

The bearded Reaper ignores Jack's gibe and, still in his bow, turns his face toward Corva. "The boy doesn't recognize me because a person doesn't have to see my face to be administered the mark. Much like"—his face swings around to look at Jack with his crooked-toothed smile on full display—"the Touch."

Jack's eyes widen and he risks a glance at Corva. Her face is a strange mixture of fear and confusion. He can't say anything. Breathing hurts, and all the questions he's got are jammed somewhere in his throat.

Thegn's face—no, Wrinkles's face—lifts knowingly, like the old bag of bones can guess the words that are piling over each other to get out of Jack's mouth. "Of course I'd recognize my own handiwork. I know exactly where you received that streak in your hair."

No. No. No! The only people in Bule who know Jack's from the Shadowfold are Lyia and Maddy Shard. Corva's from Fareburne. This is not how she should find out that his people were the ones who killed everyone she knew.

Still with that annoying look on his face, the bearded Reaper suddenly rises up from his bow. "But, we'll have to settle up later. I'm not here for you. Like I said before—"

He looks over to Corva as she raises herself to a knee, pointing at her with his sharpened fingernail. "You're my target."

Corva's voice is tense, a whisper through her teeth. "No way. No way I'll let you recruit me. I'd rather die than fight your war."

"Good. This will be quick, then. The Karui want you alive. I never said I do."

Wrinkles takes that sharp nail on his forefinger and runs it along his opposite scar-covered forearm, slicing deep into his own leathery flesh. Blood drains from the cut quickly, but in a weird, almost controlled way. It's certainly not spurting like he'd hit an artery, but it's also not pouring out in a way that Jack expects.

Closing his eyes, Wrinkles swings his arm to the side. Blood continues to drain from his arm and flow to his palm, coalescing and growing into a twisted, contorted shape. In an instant, the shape extends in both directions to form a gnarled pole that's nearly

Wrinkles's full height. At the bottom, a knotted bloody ball forms; a counterweight. From the top, the blade of the Reaper's scythe stretches and arcs outward.

When Wrinkles opens his eyes, he turns his attention to Jack. "Close your eyes, kid. Not sure your dainty little stomach can handle what's coming to her."

"Sunnuvabitch." Jack frantically scans the room for something—anything—that could be used for defense. Plan B's out, but that was kind of a one-trick pony anyway. *Really shouldn't have sold all those merc guns. Way to go, dumbass.* They could hide behind the bar, but this is Death. *Friggin' Death! How do you hide from Death?*

Apparently he'd done it before. But he was five years old then. It was a fluke. An oversight. It's not like he'd avoided the mark on purpose back then.

Jack turns to look at Corva. *Maybe she has an idea, or—*

Nope. Nothing. Corva isn't there. There's just an empty spot on the ground and the front door to the bar, still swinging shut.

RUNNING

Corva sprints along Bule's stone pathways and tunnels, chaotically zigzagging between buildings and skittering by anyone in her way. She can feel her heart beating in her teeth.

Merda! Shit! Where in the world is Zeke? He said he'd only be a minute.

Said. It still feels weird—crazy, even—that she can hold a real conversation with a monkey. Yeah, only she can "hear" him, but it is real and she needs his help *now*. With every turn she makes, every cut in and out of an alleyway, she scans the ground and walls for any trace of the little monkey.

Sure, she escaped the bar. Escaped Death. But it doesn't matter how serpentine her path is or how far she runs. He will find her. Death. Thegn. Thegn will kill her. He'll do it the same way he's done in every one of her dreams. They're not dreams. They're prophecies. Or they will be if she can't get Zeke's help. Unfortunately, the little monkey is nowhere to be found. Each empty turn through this cliffside town amplifies her despair.

She needs to hide.

There's a narrow pass between two buildings up ahead of her. In the pass, there's a little connecting bridge between the buildings and beneath that bridge is a little space—a drainage duct—not much bigger than her body. She drops to her belly and slides backward into the space. The whole time, she focuses on the direction she came.

Mouth dry, she gulps hard to force her heart back down into her chest. Her hands shake as if they're buzzing, but there's something pecking at her mind like a jay on an acorn.

Thegn. His words back at the bar. But it's not Thegn that's bothering her. It's Jack. His face when Thegn mentioned the Touch.

Jack's face had been full of fear. Not from having Death at his door. Not from the Touch itself. But from her. He was looking at her and seemed scared out of his mind. Why would that be?

She squeezes her eyes shut and buries her forehead into the ground. It doesn't help that her head is still throbbing from her interaction on the stairs with Zeke.

Caralho! It feels like my brain is jumping on the back of my eyes. What is going on? It's too much. I'm talking to a monkey. I have some kind of natural gift for fighting. Death wants to kill me in my dreams and in real life. My only friend in years—

Corva lifts her face from the dirt. Her head no longer hurts, and a sense of peace settles upon her. It's as if she's been tucked in under a blanket of calm. She can't move. She doesn't want to. Her face becomes a placid mask as a large white rat ambles into the drainage pass. It turns to face her.

She looks at the rodent and smiles, her eyes slowly glazing over. "Hello Senhor Rato. I think I had a dream about you once. A tunnel and a knife and—"

Her eyes close and the dark tranquility envelops her mind.

4.3

PROPER

"So, uh … ain'tcha gonna follow her?" Jack shifts, uneasily pulling himself back to his feet and leaning back against the wall near the front of his bar. It's unsettling to see this scarred-up old sack of a man casually plopping himself back on his barstool, scythe still in hand. Of course, he's Death. Why wouldn't he be casual?

He pauses at the thought. All this time and he'd never thought to find out what the Reaper, Thegn Nateusch, looks like. The person who'd killed everyone he and Lyia used to know. Who nearly killed him. Now the bony, wrinkly assassin is sitting in his bar, drinking Jack's shine, and—strangely, come to think of it—not actually killing anyone. He's returned to his craning, hunched posture. But no matter how much like "Wrinkles" he looks like, Jack can't unknow his real name.

Of course, that doesn't stop him from using the made-up name out loud. He tries speaking again. "Hey Wrinkles, you know she's not coming back, right?"

Thegn doesn't respond. He just uses his free hand to fiddle with his empty shot glass.

231

In the lull, Jack risks trying to stand up. *Maybe I ca—*

The scythe cuts across Jack's vision, the dull back edge of the blade slamming into the wall between him and the door. The wall cracks as the blade punches into it. Jack's eyes trace up the length of the handle all the way back to Death's hand.

"Holy shit! The handle—er, shaft—pole? Well, whatever you call it, that thing stretches?"

"Boy, you have an absolute crap notion of what good customer service is." Not looking at Jack, Thegn taps the rim of his glass. "You learn that from your old man, too?"

Jack stops himself. Throwing insults at Death is probably unwise. Also—*Bah, bullshit. No one speaks bad about the old man.* "What the hell do you know, you wrinkly old fuck?"

The head of the scythe retracts toward Thegn, but only far enough to dislodge itself from the wall. With a nonchalant flick of his wrist, he sweeps the blade at Jack, slapping him with the broad side of it. It's a slight move for Thegn, but Jack is knocked off-balance.

Careening toward the bar, Jack raises his arms mid-flight and braces for impact. But before he strikes the bar, he feels the back of his shirt and vest get caught with Thegn's free hand.

The Reaper lifts Jack by his shirt the same way someone might hold a dog by the scruff of his neck. They're face-to-face and the smell is making Jack's eyes water. *Why the hell is this grizzled old fuck givin' me the stink study? So what if I dodged his stupid mark.*

"It's a snath."

Jack's face scrunches in confusion. "What?"

"The 'handle-shaft-pole' of a scythe. It's called a snath. If you're going to talk about a weapon, you should know the proper names for its parts."

The creases in Jack's face just get deeper. Nothing this guy is saying makes sense. "What's your game, Grandpa? I thought Corva was your payday. Why would you wanna kill her? An' if you wanna kill her, why're you still sittin' here at my bar, holdin' me a foot off the ground, tryin' to school me on naming farm equipment?"

Thegn doesn't respond at all. He's just got a distant stare, like he's not even looking at Jack anymore.

Jack stares back, hard. *Ain't no way I'm survivin' this anyway. No reason to hold back.* All his lessons on minding his tongue can't do anything to help him now. May as well spit out what he's really thinking.

"Whatcha starin' at, Wrinkles? Damn creepy old bastard. What's your problem? Trying to remember what it's like to not have your skin slap itself when the wind blows? Look, we're done here. Girl's gone. Your chunk of rock salt is barely gonna cover the damages you've done here. Either put me down or kill me, but it's time you got the fuck outta my bar."

Thegn exhales through his nose like an annoyed horse and … does nothing. He's definitely not studying Jack's face anymore. It's more like he's looking through Jack, through the bar, and over the horizon at something a million miles away.

Still, Jack waits for a response, hanging there like a fart in an elevator. His armpits are getting sore from the way Thegn has him held. His shirt and vest are bunched up there and holding all of his weight, cutting off circulation to his arms. His fingertips start to tingle as his arms begin to go numb.

Seconds drag by, and Jack has no answer from the old man. *The hell?* "Yo, Wrinkles! This 'living statue' thing is boring. What happened? You nod off? I said it's time for you to get."

Nothing.

Jack twists his head back and looks at how Thegn has him held. Fortunately, the old vulture only has him by the shirt and vest. The chembraid isn't caught in his grip at all. Tearing that out would hurt more than he wants to think about. Not to mention the fact that it would be a waste of all those nits he paid for it.

For a moment, he reaches up to Thegn's arm, but thinks better of making contact lest he pull the old man out of his million-mile stare. Instead, Jack reaches for his shirt's collar and pulls it wider. However, he can't just slip out of the shirt. Either his arms are too numb to raise any higher, or something is caught somewhere.

But maybe if I just swing—

Taking care not to touch Thegn, Jack sweeps his feet forward as hard as he can while pushing his shoulders back as far as possible. No dice. But there's a little give.

A little more.

He swings his feet forward again, harder this time, and pulls on his collar with all the strength his numb arms can muster. Right as his feet reach eye level, he hears a slight tearing sound in his shirt.

His head and shoulders slip free as he flips upside down. A fraction of a second later, Jack thumps to the ground, headfirst.

4.4

ON PAUSE

Fucking telepathy. I told you, you can't pull this long-distance shit on me. Holds me up. You wrecked my ride last time. I had to walk for—

Not your problem? I'm not part of your accursed hive. If I bite it mid-fight, it's over. There's no carbon copy around to fill these shoes. That's what you get for yanking out your tongues. You—

Bullshit! Fuck purity of thought. Use a damn comm. I'm in the middle of—

Yes, I know I have everything under control here. Kid couldn't be a threat to anything but my patience. He's got an interesting history, though.

No. I don't think I will. Not yet. It's pretty rare that anyone escapes the mark. Even more rare that I get to speak with any of them. I'll have to come back later to have a little chat with him.

What? How many? Where's Caf—

Stop interrupting before I'm done. You already got me held up. Show some courtesy and let me finish a fucking thought.

Does Caffiel have the girl?

He what? That wasn't part of the plan.

Of course I can still track her. I know how she thinks.

The horde is going to complicate things. How far away are they? Yeah, I know you won't get here in time. I'll handle it.

And don't fuckin' Pull on me again until I contact you. Can't afford you holding me up if I've got to fight a whole legion from the horde on my own.

* * *

Thegn blinks, but holds still for a few slow breaths. He's been doing this for ages. The Karui may be able to do a Pull and get into his head at a distance, but they don't need to know how quickly his consciousness returns after they let go. A fun little loophole in the hive's abilities. Their telepresence may allow them to see action really well, but they can't get in his head over such a distance without holding him up.

Exhaling, the Reaper leers at the empty shirt and vest in his hand. The kid barkeep lies on the ground in front of him, unconscious.

"Idiot."

Dropping the shirt, he strides to the front door, mumbling to himself. "That fucking rat. You had one job."

4.5

CORVA

"Corva."

Her voice shook when she tested the name, standing in front of a dirty bathroom mirror. It was the first time she'd ever said it out loud. Her new name. As children in Fareburne, they never received names. The elders told them this was because they had to earn it. To earn their place in the bairro. The name was to be their rite into adulthood. The more Corva thought back on it, though, the more she believed that was just a glossy coating. Children are weak. They die easily. It's easier to manage the loss when you haven't taken the time to name it.

But Corva suddenly had a name. A gift from Avó. Her name.

She'd actually never known Avó's real name. The old woman was always just "Avó" to her. How much more could Corva have learned from her, learned about her? Corva could feel the rims of her eyelids start to ache. She'd been crying all day and now was out of tears. All she had left were bloodshot eyes and a cavern of loss deep in her chest.

Corva was still in the bathroom, toothbrush in hand. She couldn't remember if she'd brushed her teeth. She'd been running all through the prior evening and into most of the next day. She'd found this abandoned outpost about an hour prior and couldn't bring herself to keep going. She had to stop. Had to grieve.

The bathroom was not functional in the least, but it'd been abandoned long enough that the smell was no worse than the rest of the place. She stood at the sink below the mirror, mostly out of habit. Some semblance of normalcy. Normalcy that she'd never know again.

The assault—the massacre—had happened so fast. The township had survived many raids before. The Umbrati. The Karui. Nomadic gangs. Neighboring villages, jealous of Fareburne's growth. This, however. This was like nothing the town had experienced before. Systematic. Complete. Scores of people had fallen over dead before anyone even heard the first drone.

The Shadowfold.

They attacked from a distance using their cursed magical atrocities. The Touch was their tool of choice. A bastardization of Death's Mark, a technique from the last of the Four, mutated and refined by people into a weapon even more ruthless and efficient. Corva shuddered just thinking about it. The Touch could be used remotely, channeled through vid to the intended target. The only reason anyone in Fareburne knew anything about it was because the Shadowfold posted footage of an attack on the satmesh. Images of those horrors were their way of recruiting more soulmancers to their cult.

The children of Fareburne were shown those vids as something the Fareburne council called an "Emergency Preparedness Protocol." It was absolutely worthless. Horrifying as the vids were, nothing could've prepared them for what happened. On the vid, it never seemed like much. A drone would show up and a person would collapse, dead. Sometimes, their heads would snap back, like they'd been hit in the face by an invisible bat. Even when the Shadowfold's field mages came in to finish off anyone they missed, it hadn't seemed like much on the vid. Their movements weren't large or showy. They were slight and specific. Just two fingers placed on a person or live vid of that person.

Corva never saw any of them when they came to Fareburne, though. She stayed under cover. Dodged the sounds of drones. Avoided reflective surfaces like the mirror she was in front of in this abandoned bathroom. She ran. She kept out of view. Even as the cluster of mages came through the North Gate, she lowered her head and ran. The mage's black cloaks were mere flashes in her periphery. She never really saw any of them. But she hated them all.

Unfortunately, the hatred didn't last. It was overshadowed by her feeling of isolation. Of loneliness. Corva had nothing. No one. She had a toothbrush and a name. The hastily stuffed backpack didn't even register in her mind. She might've still been wearing it. She'd been on autopilot for about thirty-six hours, in a hyper-aware dream state where her only focus was on running and hiding. That automatic mode was wearing off and reality was crashing in.

She looked at herself in the grimy, cracked mirror, but all she could see were the faces of her family. Her friends. Her Avó.

"Corva."

Her vision turned watery. As it turned out, she still had tears to give.

4.6

PERSPECTIVE

The black saturates her brain, a tide of nothing that washes over less than that. A fog of soot smears across thoughts, memories, and personality. A blanket of emptiness.

Corva!

Her eyes roll forward, draped in a lethargic bliss. It takes an epoch to reopen her eyelids and blink without feeling a heaviness pull them shut. She can feel individual granules of dust slide off her face as she stares through the blurry shapes before her.

Corva!

That does it. Consciousness shocks through her like a giant flicking her forehead. The formerly blurry shapes snap into focus. It's that rat, but it isn't alone. The solid white rodent is twisting and writhing, trying to get a comparably sized capuchin monkey off it's back.

"Zeke?"

His face scrunches and his eyebrows knit. **Have you been holding conversations with other monkeys?**

Apparently this is not the time for stupid questions.

The rat takes Zeke's distracted moment to arc its head back and snap its jaws. Zeke leans back, dodging easily, but the shift in his center of gravity allows the rat to buck and squirm out from beneath him. Zeke snags the rat's tail and wrestles it back into the open. Corva squints through the dust at the flurry of paws, teeth, and fur.

Run, Corva! Get Jack.

She scrambles out from under the bridge and hops to her feet. With her gaze fixed in the direction of the bar, she takes a step, but hesitates. The Reaper is there. She glances down at the roiling scuffle at her feet. It appeared so much bigger moments ago when she was still on the ground.

It seems stupid to run away from a fight between two animals no taller than her knee. Especially stupid if she's running from that right back to the same place she just fled. Right back to Death. And she'd be going without Zeke for help. Again.

Mind made, Corva reaches down and grabs the two fighting animals, one in each hand. A shock bolts through her, making it feel like her skin is vibrating. She knows this feeling. With difficulty, she muscles through the initial impact and accompanying nausea. She looks at the rat in her left hand.

"I know you. You're with him. With Thegn." There's a familiarity with the name as she speaks it, almost tastes it. She looks at Zeke, his face a flurry of emotions. "You two, you and this rat, are the same."

The rat writhes in her grip, twisting far enough to bite the meaty part of her hand between her thumb and forefinger. She screams and her fingers snap open reflexively, but the rat doesn't let go. It hangs there with its putrid yellow incisors buried in her palm. Looking close enough, it almost looks like the albino rodent is smiling.

When she opened her fingers, she also released Zeke from her opposite hand. He grabs her wrist and darts up to her shoulder as she reaches with her free hand to pry the rat loose.

Before she can get to it, though, the rat opens its mouth and drops to the ground. Zeke jumps down and gives chase, but loses the rat as it snakes into a small drainpipe.

EPISODE FOUR: DEATH COMES FOR YOU

Corva grabs her hand and winces while inspecting the rip in her palm. It hurts something awful, but the bleeding is pretty light. She clenches her jaw against the pain and uses her good hand to squeeze at the base of her palm. Working her way toward the punctures, she milks the blood from her hand to clean out the wound as best as she can.

Having given up on chasing the rat, Zeke leaps back up to her shoulder. **The Reaper is here. Caffiel is never far from him.**

"Caffiel? That the rat's name?" Corva kneels to pack her wound with dust and sand. Its sticks to her hand, hungrily soaking up the blood. "What the hell happened when I touched you two?"

I have much to explain to you, to share. But it seems I'm losing the time to do so. Zeke's voice continues to reverberate in her mind. Insistent. **How is it that you came to know the Reaper's name? I've never shared that with you.**

She looks over to the slit-pupiled monkey.

"He introduced himself. Seu caxias. He's at the bar. Where were you? I needed your help."

I told you at the stairs that I had to check on something. You were pretty incapacitated, though, so I could see why you—wait. He arcs over so she can see more of his face, which has a mixture of panic and disapproval. **You left Jack at the bar? With Thegn?**

Corva stares at the monkey. "I couldn't stay there. He was there for me. Death came to collect. I did what I do best. I ran." She punches the ground with her injured fist. It stings, but she can handle it. "If you'd been with me, you would've seen the thing you were checking on yourself. Maybe I wouldn't have run."

He wasn't what I was checking on. We need to get Jack away from Thegn. Away from this town.

Zeke returns his attention up the alleyway, back toward the bar. Corva stands up and looks in the same direction.

"I can't go back. He'll kill me. Again."

There are worse things than dying, child. Worse things than Death, even. And they're almost here.

JACK

"So when were you gonna let me have a go with the nanobots?" Jack busied himself with setting all of Slim's tools in even rows while the lanky maker kept his face buried in his work. His latest project. A new line of defense he wanted to test out in Jack's bar.

It was only a couple months ago, before Corva had arrived. Slim still had his long, oily mop of hair, no singes or shaving. Back then, Jack was spending most of his free time at Slim's place, helping in his shop. Jack's personal training sessions in Cliff City had dropped to happening only a couple times a week. In those sessions, he'd only made a handful of beads, let alone tried anything more interesting. In fact, Jack had held off on doing the "interesting" stuff after the old man passed for … well, for a lot of reasons.

In any case, Slim's assortment of half-working tools and gadgets were a welcome distraction. Slim was good to Jack. Treated the boy a lot like Vardin did. Like Jack was worth his time.

"Nanos ain't ready yet, little man." Slim spoke without lifting his head. He was always like that. Kept focus no matter what else is going on. "Pass me the iron, will ya?"

Jack grabbed the soldering iron and handed it over to Slim, careful to keep the hot end pointed away from both of them. "Whattya mean they're not ready? They fly. The controller works. You even tested their lifting capacity."

"They got a flaw. Keep overheating."

"So? Group 'em together and make 'em a space heater."

"They explode when they get too hot. Here." The bony techsmith handed back the soldering iron, face still buried in his work.

"Oh."

They kept silence for a while after that. Slim working on his project, Jack passing him tools when he needed them. It was a good way to work. Focused. Calm. Life could've been way different if Slim had bought Jack off Maddy Shard instead of Old Man V. Of course, Slim probably wouldn't have trained Jack in fixins like the old man did. Slim likes his tech too much to look into imbuing it. Jack even offered to try making some imbued tech with Slim a couple times, but the maker refused outright, saying something about not being able to trust anything he couldn't take a screwdriver to.

Still, that didn't stop Jack from continuing to ask.

"Whattya think about puttin' a fixin on this? With the right draw, we could bind their feet in place so the sound bit don't have to work as hard. I've pretty much got push-pull figured out. Would be a cinch to get it to work through tech."

Slim smiled while he kept working. "Subsonics don't work like that, little man. They're a glorified speaker set to just the right tone. It's just sound, so they work the same no matter what. Just need to get enough of them in the array to get full coverage."

"But how do I stop myself from gettin' froze?"

"I made you a kneak to filter out the tone. The paralyzing effect won't work on you as long as you've got it in."

"Oh yeah? I need you to make a tweak to my matrix ports anyway. Kneaks have been fallin' out on me if I get jostled too much."

"Sure thing. I'll have a look once I get done with this. Actually"—Slim finished tightening a screw on one device's enclosure—"you wanna give it at test?"

"For sure!"

Slim didn't need to hear more than that and he didn't offer any kind of warning. He just turned the device in Jack's direction and flipped a switch on its control unit.

The effect was as immediate as it was shitty. It felt like Jack's whole body was shaking at its core. Not trembles, like from being cold or afraid, but it was like every part of Jack wanted to go everywhere at the same time. He could feel himself starting to panic, but it was weird. His body wasn't able to do any of the normal things that happen when panicked. Or if it was, Jack couldn't tell. He just knew he wanted to do anything else but just stand there, and his body wasn't listening.

Slim flipped off the control switch and Jack crumpled to the ground. The techsmith had a bucket under Jack's face before the first heave of vomit found its way past Jack's teeth. When Jack looked up at him, Slim already had a rag ready. Slim had that kind of strange duplicity. He'd sucker punch you one second, but he'd have exactly what was necessary for recovery the next.

Jack's whole body ached. It was like that time Old Man V had him billy goat his way to Cliff City and back as fast as possible with jugs of water in each hand. Jack was sore for a week after that. The boy could tell this was going to leave him the same way.

"How'd that feel, Jack, my man?" Slim's smile stretched from ear to ear on his goofy smudged face.

Jack spit the last of the bile into the bucket before answering, "I thought you meant you wanted me to test that filter kneak."

"I did. But how're you going to know the filter works without knowing how it feels when it don't?"

"Still kind of a dick move, man."

Slim let out a breath and ran his fingers through his greasy strings of hair. "Yeah. I guess you're right. I've been testing this thing on myself so long, I kinda forgot how it feels on the first go."

Jack blinked. "Wait. You tested this thing on yourself?"

"Yup." Slim leaned back, relaxed-like, clearly pleased with himself.

"But how'd you turn it off if you couldn't move?"

Slim let out a chuckle as he recalled the memory. "That took quite a bit of time to figure out. I nearly passed out that first time."

Jack pushed the bucket away and sat on the floor as Slim spoke. When Jack looked back up at the maker, it was obvious Slim had already moved on. The techsmith was tapping some notes in his forearm tattoo. Jack wasn't going to let this go just yet.

"Well?"

Slim blinked and looked back at Jack. "Well what?"

"Well how'd you figure out how to turn off the thing? If you were able to move, that seems like a pretty big hole in the design."

"Oh, that. Yeah." The techsmith lowered his arm and put his attention back on Jack. "Involuntary movement."

He said it as if that was the whole explanation and all that Jack needed to know. No way. "What kinda movement?"

"Involuntary."

"I don't get it."

There was a flicker of disappointment in Slim's eyes before he continued. Jack couldn't tell if Slim was disappointed in him for not understanding or just annoyed at needing to say more. In either case, the techsmith masked it pretty well and recovered before he went on, "Did you notice that when you were paralyzed, you didn't die? You could still breathe. Your heart didn't stop. I think I even saw you blink."

No, Jack hadn't noticed. But it was true. Jack's heart was beating and his lungs were pumping.

Slim didn't wait for the boy to respond. He seemed to know Jack was starting to catch on. "See, the tone from the subsonics only works on voluntary movements, the movements you explicitly think about doing before you do them. It don't affect muscles you don't think about moving."

"So, what? You stopped thinking and you could move?"

"Ha!" For some reason, what Jack said seemed to have amused Slim. "No, kiddo. Well, not exactly. I had to short-circuit my brain a bit."

"You electrocuted yourself?" Jack's forehead creased heavily. This was hard. Nothing Slim was saying made any sense.

"What? No. Look. Think of it like a trade. Subsonics don't let me move what I wanna move, but they let the things that move on their own keep goin'. So I figured that if I force myself to not do one of those involuntary things, maybe that'd buy me a second to move the parts I want."

"You willed your heart to stop? That's the kind of thing Lyia can do. I thought you didn't like fixins. Also, that ain't safe."

"No. It isn't. It's also not what I did." The lanky maker leaned in close to Jack, like he was ready to tell him a secret. "Why stop your heart when you can just hold your breath?"

Jack blinked at Slim, feeling really dumb for missing something so obvious. "And that worked?"

"I'm here, ain't I?"

"Do ya think I could do that?"

Slim's smile couldn't have gotten get bigger. "Only one way to find out, little man." He paused. "But we may want to clean out that bucket first."

4.8

Time to Go

"Jack. Jack! Get your butt up. We gotta move. Where'd the old man go?"

So many words all at once. His eyelids crack open to see Corva leaning over him, yelling. Zeke is standing on her shoulder and looking back toward the door.

Jack sits up and rubs the back of his head. It hurts something fierce, like it'd been rolled down a hill in a sack full of hammers. "What're you talkin' about? Old Man V's been dead over a year."

"What?" Corva scrunches her face in a look of confusion that's about as ugly as his head is in pain. "Not him. Thegn. Where is he? And why aren't you wearing a shirt?"

The memory of his graceless attempt at escape flashes to the front of his mind. He feels his cheeks and ears heat up from the embarrassment. Best to let the words fly. It won't stop him from feeling like a dumbass, but at least they'll be talking about something else.

"Ol' Wrinkles? Fuck if I know. He was real nonchalant about you bolting—thanks for that, by the way. Helluva team attitude. Anyhow, he sat here just chillin' out, telling me to pour him another shot. All of the sudden, he's all tranced, starin' off in space. Ya ask me, dude ain't all there."

Corva glances over at Zeke before her next question. "So you're okay? He didn't do anything to you? Why were you unconscious?"

"I'm fine. Just got knocked out."

He's not fine. He's tired. His head hurts. The chembraid is sore and itches. He feels fucking useless and ignored. So what if Zeke and Corva came back? It's a pity play. He really is just a screwup kid.

Jack grabs his shirt and vest from the ground next to him and sluggishly fiddles with separating them so he can put them back on. Meanwhile, he mentally tests some of the neurolink commands Gorm gave him to control the chembraid. He doesn't need much. Just needs to will the thing into serving up some painkillers and a pinch of go-go to clear the fog over his brain.

Corva hasn't said anything about his chembraid. Without his shirt on, the whole extent of the augmentation is fully visible, twisting around his arm, chest, and back, kind of like a giant cybernetic leech. Zeke's not even looking at him. Jack would've expected at least some kind of screeching monkey reprimand.

Finally, he manages to extract the shirt from the vest. There's a tear at the collar, so there's no way the shirt is going to lay right, but at least he'll have some kind of covering. It sucks to pull the shirt back on, though. Between the chembraid's microneedles and the feeling of an invisible knife in the back of his head, Jack's body protests every little movement. *Those painkillers sure are takin' their sweet-ass time to work.*

"Alright. We've got to go." Corva grabs the vest and puts her hand out, ready to help him stand.

Jack yanks the vest away from her. "I've got it. Don't need help from you. Got no time for bitches who bail. You got no notion of who your friends are." He tries to stand on his own. *Fingers, toes: check. Arms, le—* The pain in his head cuts in and punches him in the base of the skull. He drops to a knee and tries to stabilize.

Corva hoists Jack up to his toes, bringing them face-to-face. "Look here, you stubborn little jerk off. I'm here, aren't I? I wouldn't even be here to save your sorry tail if it weren't for Zeke. I'd be long gone."

Her face twists up, like she's holding a frog in her mouth. Then the dam breaks loose. "And friends? What would you know about friends? You're a kid serving drinks in a hole in the ground at a town that's in a literal hole in the ground. You've got no friends. You run a watering hole for drunk mercs. You live with a monkey and you're stalking a whore. Your mentor—who used to own you as property, by the way— is a long rotting corpse. I'm the closest thing you've got to a friend and I barely know you. Barely even like you. But I'm here. And we've got no time for arguing nonsense. It's time to go."

About halfway through Corva's tirade, Jack turns his head away. His face is hot. Surely it's entirely red now, all the way back to the kneak receptacles behind his ears. Not that she'll notice. His shoulders slump forward, chest deflated. His hands hang in front of him, twisting the fabric of his vest. All the words he wants to say hammer against the back of his teeth. He can barely contain them.

He feels her hand on his shoulder. "Hey! Did you hear me? It's time to—"

"I ain't leaving."

Jack raises his head. His eyes are watery, but he couldn't care less. He pushes back his shoulders and crosses his arms, vest still clutched in his right hand.

Corva turns to her shoulder to check with Zeke. He's no longer watching the front door. His gaze is fixed on Jack. He breaks his stare for a moment to exchange a glance with Corva. Rolling her eyes, she lowers to a knee so she's looking slightly upward toward Jack's face.

"Jack. Jack, look. I—I'm sorry. I crossed a line there. But you can be upset at me later. Zeke says it's not safe here anymore. He—"

Corva might be saying something after that, but Jack isn't paying attention. *Zeke said?* Surely he misheard something. How hard did he hit his head? He squints, trying to refocus on what she's saying.

"Bule's on the map now. He went to the lookout at the top of the ridge. Said he saw them coming. A thousand, at least."

"Bullshit. Zeke can't talk."

Corva gives Jack the same kind of look a person has when they try to run somewhere but find that they're tethered back to where they started. "What?"

"You're a shit liar. Harris put you up to this? Want me to leave the bar in a wreck like it is so he can do another one of his 'surprise' inspections?" Jack shakes his head like he's been told a bad joke. "'Zeke says.' Ha. You and Hairless need to have a better story if you wanna take over my bar."

The look on Corva's face fluctuates between anger and confusion. "What are you talking about? There might not even be a bar after this. A raid is coming. A big one. Zeke says it's bigger than the one that took out Fewkestown a few years back."

Jack feels his eyes widen as he looks over to Zeke. The monkey nods slowly. If Jack was masking his surprise before, that mask is totally gone now. Zeke can talk? How else would Corva know about Fewkestown? Jack uncrosses his arms, leaning in slightly. "What color did the last rung of the ladder to the lookout used to be?"

"What?" There she goes again with that ugly scowl of confusion. "Why in the world does that matter? We're wasting time."

"It matters. It's how I can tell you're lyin' about talking to Zeke. I can't trust you for shit. Anyone could know about what happened to Fewkestown just by askin' around. So I'm not leavin' until—"

"It was pink, alright?" Corva twists her head away from Jack to look at Zeke. "Pink?"

Jack opens his mouth to speak, but he's got nothing. She got it right.

Still looking at Zeke, Corva keeps talking, "Yeah, pink. Apparently it broke a couple years back and Harris somehow convinced Vardin that you were the one that needed to fix it. So as your own personal fuck you to both of them, you cut up an old pink plastic broomstick and used that to replace the rung. It took Harris another seven months to paint it over" She pauses, smiling despite herself. "Huh. That is pretty funny."

Jack doesn't know how long he sits and gawks at Zeke and Corva, but however long it's been, it's long enough that Corva is looking at Jack with the same sympathetic impatience as someone with an old dog who constantly wants to lie down and sleep in the middle of a walk. Apparently, though, she can talk to Zeke. Somehow. She did it just now. Right in front of him. Got the color right and gave the history of it.

But, best to find out how she does it later. If she can talk to Zeke, then she's also telling the truth about what he saw at the lookout.

Jack puts his attention on Zeke. "Sheeps or Goats?"

Corva tilts her head, obstructing Jack's view of his furry compatriot. "What?"

"The swarm of baddies up on the ridge. I was asking Zeke if they're Sheeps or Goats. So which is it?"

"It's the Umbrati again. Goats. But a lot more than last time. Guess Thegn—"

"Wrinkles."

"Yeah, Wrinkles, whatever. Guess he caught word somehow and skipped out. Even Death can't fight off all of hell."

"They here for him?"

"Gotta be. Could be retaliation for the raid, but Zeke doesn't think that's likely. Not with a horde this big. They're either coming for him or they're coming for me. But *Wrinkles* doesn't personally stick out his own neck all that often. Seems most likely that they're capitalizing on him being here. Since we killed all the grunts in the raid, Zeke doesn't think the Umbrati know about me. Probably."

Jack squints at Corva. "I don't know about you." He looks back at Zeke. "And apparently I don't know shit about you, either. Why ain't you ever talked to me?"

Corva shoves her face between him and Zeke again. "It doesn't quite work like that. But we're wasting time. We need to get out of here."

"Why? You said the Goats're after Wrinkles."

"You think he's gonna go with them easily? A fight between them is going to slide this whole burg to the bottom of the canyon. Even if he escapes them, his presence here pushes Bule front-and-center onto the map. They'll interrogate everyone and conscript anyone who doesn't take a deal." She pauses, as if suddenly understanding her own words. "Puta merda. Death and misery really do follow that man."

"Misery follows him. Technically speaking, Death is following you." Jack pauses; this probably isn't the right time to be nitpicking semantics. He's got to think about the folks in town. It's a shithole, but it's his shithole. And Lyia, Slim, even Maddy Shard—they're his shithole people.

He turns to the bar; his comm kneak is sitting by the wash station. "I gotta burst a broadcast. Let Harris know. Folks gotta prep."

"Zeke said he already did from the lookout."

"Oh? They didn't ignore him this time?"

"Yeah. Seems your balding friend and his militia learned their lesson from the raid. Town's on alert. Saw so on the way here. Some are skipping out. Most are locking down. Fools. The three of us, we're taking the smart option. We're skipping. You got a go-bag?"

We? The frown on Jack's face deepens. "Why all three of us? Zeke an' I can just hunker down in the siege caves until it blows over."

"Aren't you paying attention? One *thousand* grunts in this raid. At least. There's no 'blowing over'! Anyone who thinks that is a moron."

Jack looks from Zeke to Corva and back to Zeke. He's starting to get it, to notice—to really understand for the first time—the sense of urgency in their faces. This is serious. *And here I am, thinkin' in slow motion.* "Yeah. Gitfo bags are behind the bar. Gotta beat the dust off 'em, but they should be stocked."

He continues over to behind the bar, though not for his comm kneak now. The packs are there, still partially buried behind some boxes and empty bottles. He shoves the clutter out of the way to dig them out, but stops for a moment. Just looks at them, dirty black canvas packs. It's hard to believe he actually has to use them.

Old Man V had made him check and repack these things every week for as long as he'd worked there. He'd make sure the travel gear was in working order and verify that there's enough non-perishables and tradeables to last a good while on the road without resupply. When the old man died, though, the check and repack ritual was one of the first things Jack stopped doing. He hadn't even taken the time to consolidate them into a single bag. It was a dumb practice, anyway.

Jack shakes the memory from his mind and immediately regrets it. Pain stabs the back of his head from where he landed on it. *Holy shit, that hurts.* Standing slowly, he grabs the two packs and heads back to Corva, tossing her the old man's one. "That's a dead man's bag, but the kit should still be good. Been a while since I last checked. And, oh— almost forgot."

He steps back to the bar and grabs the brick of rock salt that Thegn paid with, as well as a small bag of seed that someone traded the day before. He stuffs the rock in his gitfo bag on his way back to Corva. The bag of seed goes in her hand. "We'll need these. Try not to let them get wet."

She stands there, still, stupidly gawking at him.

"Hey! You get bonked on the head too? Stuff that seed and let's go." Jack pulls his gitfo bag onto his back and turns to head for the door. He knows the urgency of the moment, but he can't help but take his time.

The bar—*his* bar—deserves one last look over. He knows every inch of the place. He grew up here. Played, worked, and schemed in every corner. He's repaired or replaced just about every non-rock surface. There are still some stash holes and secret nooks that he never got around to finishing. Now he never will.

Ain't no use dwellin'. What's done is done. Blinking away his tears, he jams his chin to his chest and marches to the door. "Need to drop by Slim's on the way out. He n' I been working on something that might come in handy. Got a destination in mind? Probably best to go down-canyon. I know a buncha places to hole up that way."

As he talks, Jack peeks back over his shoulder at Corva. She's not moving. Looking harder, he notices that she's set her pack on the ground, bag of seed resting on top of it. He stops and spins back to her. "Fuck's sake, girl! I thought you said we gotta go."

Zeke leaps from her shoulder up into the ceiling trusswork. Corva squares up, her weight shifting so she's balanced on the balls of her feet. "Can't now. He's back."

As if on cue, the entrance to the bar swings open with such violence that it tears off its hinges and spins uncontrollably into a nearby set of tables and chairs. The Reaper's silhouette engulfs the gaping hole where the door once was, scythe drawn and cloak billowing. But he's only there for a fraction of a second. Before Jack can even think to duck or move or do anything, really, Thegn is already past him and slicing his scythe at Corva.

Corva is ready this time. Poised. She hops in a sidestep, just barely dodging the swinging blade. The palm of her hand slaps down on the flat side of the scythe. That's enough to redirect the blade and Thegn as his momentum carries him by her.

The old, bearded hunter looks back at her with a glint in his eyes and the faintest of grins. His rotted teeth peek from behind his thin lips for a fraction of a second. A moment later, the gnarled ball at the bottom of the scythe's handle—sorry, the snath—extends, like a fist aimed for Corva's head.

Whatever that part of the scythe is called, she's faster than it. She ducks under the ball like a boxer slipping a jab. Instead of dodging away, she steps in closer to the scythe, closer to Thegn. The extended snath rides on her shoulder.

These are the moves of "fighter" Corva. Except the expression on her face is cold, mean. Not the typical manic smile that Jack's used to seeing when she gets this way. She reflects none of Thegn's earlier amusement, no matter how slight. She's all business.

With a pivot of her back foot, she now has the snath across both shoulders and the back of her neck. Grabbing the scythe with her hands, it looks like she has just enough leverage to disrupt the wrinkly bastard's balance.

But Thegn holds fast. A quick yank and he retracts the bottom of the scythe. Corva is jerked off-balance, even closer to him. However, instead of trying to stop, she steps with the pull and launches herself at the Reaper.

Nothing connects. Not a knee, a fist, or a foot. Thegn evades her rush and steps back, creating distance between them.

Back near the front of the bar, Jack hasn't moved; hasn't had time to. He stands there, mouth agape. Wide-eyed. This is a fight between Corva and Death.

She's fighting Death!

But it doesn't matter how incredibly cool it is to see someone stand up to a legend. To trade blows. There's no way she can win. This is Death. No one wins against the Reaper. Even if he's a scrawny old man with skin that looks like undercooked bacon. Jack had escaped when he was a kid. He certainly hadn't won.

Shit. Gotta do something. She ain't dead yet, but ol' Wrinkles has that weed whacker. Need to make it even.

He looks over at the remains of Plan B, barrel buried into the floor, and hope deflates a bit as he remembers how easily he'd been disarmed.

Frantically, he scans the rest of the bar. The air feels hot and electric. *There's gotta be somethin'.*

His eyes come to a rest on the gitfo pack he'd given Corva. *Maybe there's something in there.*

Forgetting that he's still wearing his own pack, he sprints over to hers. He curses himself on the way for not keeping up with the routine of checking the bag. He can barely remember what's in it.

Before Jack can get to the bag, however, Zeke drops from the ceiling and lands in front of him. He raises his little monkey finger to his lips in the universal "shh" sign.

"Zeke! What're you doin'? Shouldn't you be helpin' her?"

Jack's words pierce the air and echo through the bar. Only now does Jack realize that despite the intensity of the fight between Corva and Thegn, they've been overwhelmingly, amazingly quiet. Zeke's head and shoulders slump. So much for "shhh."

Zeke turns and focuses his slit pupils on the fighters. Jack follows the monkey's gaze and sees that his outburst has actually interrupted the fight. Both Thegn and Corva are looking toward him. But they're not paying any attention to Jack. All eyes are on Zeke.

Recognition floods Thegn's face as it compresses and knots, every wrinkle folding over itself in hatred and fury.

"It's *you!*"

4.9

SAVE THE DAY

"What? You know this saggy old bastard?" Jack glares as Zeke. "Why the fuck does every new person in the bar know you?"

There's no time for any kind of response. Thegn is on Zeke in a blur, seizing the monkey in his bony grip. Corva tries to help, but doesn't make it more than a single step. The head of the old Reaper's scythe extends toward her at breakneck speed. She catches the rib of the blade in her hands, but it keeps pushing. The force of it pushes her back and pins her against the wall.

Jack edges closer to one of his barstools. *Wrinkles don't think I'm worth payin' attention to. Mayhaps I can take a swing on him.*

Thegn brings Zeke closer to his face and leers at him like a starving man might eye a turkey leg. "Smells like you've been in a fight with my rat."

He turns back to Corva. "Things are starting to make sense. You've gone and found yourself one of the sigils. But it doesn't look like you've broken him yet." He starts to squeeze Zeke. "And you won't get a chance to."

261

Now! Jack grabs the barstool and lifts it to swing at the Reaper's head. He never gets the chance, though. Still squeezing Zeke, Thegn turns and lowers his gaze on Jack.

"You think I don't see you, boy?"

The old man slides his foot behind Corva's gitfo bag, still sitting on the ground. The next thing Jack knows, the pack is in the air, launched right at him. It's too fast to dodge, to duck, to do anything. The bag hits him square in the chest and sends him flying backward into the bar.

Jack feels all of the air escape from his lungs. He wheezes, attempting to coerce them to inflate. No good. The wind has been knocked right out of him. He shoves the pack off himself and leans forward. With great effort, he's finally able to suck in half a breath of air. It doesn't help much. A fit of coughs, gasps, and dry heaves rewards him for his troubles. He lurches forward on all fours, like he's vomiting air.

Painful as it is, it doesn't take too long to get back to something that somewhat resembles breathing. He lifts his head and turns his eyes —bloodshot and teary—back to Thegn.

The fight has moved on without him. Apparently Jack's stupid, stupid failure to sucker punch Death with a barstool had provided enough of a distraction to let Corva wrench her way free from the scythe. Now she's in close on the Reaper, dodging his attacks and attempting to land her own. And she's fast. Ever so fast. Jack is reminded of the first day she crashed into his bar. She moves at a brutal, frenzied pace, but not without grace. Getting hit by her must be like being punched by the sunset.

But Zeke is still in Thegn's hand. The wrinkled old Reaper hasn't loosened his grip at all. Zeke's little body—normally active and expressive—flops about limply as the fight progresses. Contrasted with Corva, Zeke is nothing like he was that first day she showed up.

Jack pauses as fragments of a memory squeeze their way to the front of his mind, coalescing into the seed of an idea. *Like the first day!*

He hauls himself back to his feet and heads to the most recently repaired section of the bar. With each step, he lets out a string of coughs and wheezes. Yet he still somehow manages to stumble over and drag himself onto the bar.

Now that he has a full view behind the bar, he can see the old control unit for the subsonic paralyzers. It's still not fully repaired. The thing sits there silently, almost as if it's staring back at him. Mocking him.

Jack swings his feet over the bar and lowers himself to the raised floor. He picks up the busted control unit and gives it a hard look. *Slim said the array could be activated manually through this thing. Probably shoulda asked him to be more specific.*

It's a plain box, not much bigger than Jack's hand, with two cables coming from it. One is for power and the other runs down through the floorboards and branches to each of the paralyzer units in the array underneath. Other than that, though, it's just a nondescript black box with a couple glowing lights. Jack picks it up and looks closer. There's not an obvious button on it anywhere. *Slim! You an' your friggin' "simple" designs.*

Desperate, he scans around for the device's remote. *Maybe Slim was wrong. Maybe that part ain't busted. Maybe the remote will work.* He spins around to look behind himself, stupidly forgetting that he's still holding on to the control unit. The two cables tear from the back of the box and drop to the ground.

"Shit!"

He bends down and picks up the cable ends, inspecting them. The connectors are a little bent, but otherwise don't seem any worse for wear. Carefully, he plugs them back into the control unit, first the array cable and then the power cable. *Please don't be fucked. Please don't be fucked.*

The moment that he inserts the power connector, there's the pop and familiar whirring sound as the subsonic paralyzers suddenly cycle up. Jack stares at the little box in disbelief. His eyes widen as the realization hits him. "Yeah! That's how ya do it, ya little asshole of a box! We win!"

Jack pauses after his shouts of celebration, realizing that the sounds of Corva and Thegn fighting have stopped, replaced by the pulsing hum of the paralyzer array. *Right. Gotta check.*

He sneaks a look over the bar at where he last saw them fighting. They're not there. Well, not quite. They're still in the bar, just not in the same place. And the interior of the bar itself, it's not the same place either. It's an absolute wreck. Tables are torn in half, chairs look as if they've spontaneously exploded, and every surface is cut, scratched, or shredded. It's as if a tornado of chainsaws was let loose in the bar. Jack's shoulders drop as he surveys the small-scale demolition. Maybe Harris is right about his inability to keep the bar from being trashed. "Seems I can't do anything in this place without destroying it. Can't even leave!"

He looks over toward the front of the room at Corva and Thegn. They're caught mid-fight, unable to move. He can see their bodies shake as their muscles seize in waves. Zeke is still clutched in Thegn's hand.

That's right! Zeke!

Jack stands up and works his way along the bar's back. Almost able to breathe normally, he moves quickly, ignoring the pain in his head and chest. A few steps in, he's going at a pretty good clip. *Get the bags, get Zeke, get the girl, get the fuck out.*

He reaches the end of the bar and grabs the edge of it to let his momentum swing him around. However, the moment he crosses the threshold from behind the bar, a wave of sound hits him, followed by a wave of regret. He's stepped out of the deadzone behind the bar. A hum fills his head, cycling in waves. The pulsing tone vibrates his skull, as if his brain has suddenly transformed into the world's loudest purring cat.

He tries to look down. No dice. He's got no control over any of the major muscle groups in his body. What's worse, he's off-balance from swinging around the bar's end and he can't move any of his limbs to catch himself.

Episode Four: Death Comes for You

His face and shoulder slam into the ground, and he slides a bit along the well-worn floorboards. He can see Corva's face, partially obscured behind her raised arm. She must have been dodging or blocking something. She can't move much, but with what little expression she can manage, the message is clear: *Jack, you monumental fuckup.*

And she's right. As he stops skidding along the floor, something slides right into his field of view. An innocuous little needle-shaped electronic rod with a blue tip rests on the ground in front of him. The filter kneak that pairs with the paralyzer array. It must've popped out when he fell from Thegn's grip earlier. Normally when he wakes up, he goes through his inventory of kneaks and makes sure they're all jacked in correctly. Of course, normally he also avoids dropping himself on his own head.

Dumbass.

4.10

Breathe and Touch

Filho de—

Corva's heart sinks as she watches Jack faceplant and slide across the floor. *Way to think ahead, genius. You're sure to be a big help that way.*

The use of his paralyzing speaker system was a good idea. When they last spoke about the array, there were apparently a few steps left in repairing the array's control unit. That he got the thing up and running on the fly like this is impressive. His execution of that idea, however, is much less impressive.

She focuses her attention back on Thegn as the pulsing reverberations of the paralyzer array continue to roar in her head. The old Reaper appears to be struggling with the effects of the sound as well, though he seems to be making some headway against it. Ever so slowly, and with substantial effort, he's straightening his posture and trying to level his scythe toward her. It comes in jerks and fits, but he's making progress. Apparently his way of extending the scythe operates under the same constraints as the rest of his body. Even still, the scythe continues to extend, bringing its blade closer and closer to her.

She looks at his scythe, the black blade forged of his blood. It has a gloss on it that makes it look like it's still liquid. She knows better. In this fight alone, she's blocked and parried that thing enough to know how solid it really is, regardless of how much it shines. *Can't let him use that on Zeke. Not on any of us.*

The vague images from her dreams—no, memories—of prior lives flit through her mind. She's crossed paths with Thegn over and over again. His scythe. His cloak. His stupid beard. They always fight. She still doesn't know why. All she knows is that she's never won. And here she is, fighting him all over again.

Only, something's off. Something's different from those memories. In all those fractured images, those fragmented feelings, she was alone. Isolated. Even if there were others around her, they weren't with her and she wasn't fighting for them. It's always been like that for her. Even in Fareburne where she had friends and family, she was still alone. Her only meaningful connection there was Avó.

But something has changed. She doesn't have that feeling of isolation now. Granted, it's not like she's put down roots in this rock town, but her connection to Zeke is undeniable. Maybe even stronger than what she had with Avó. And even Jack has managed to weasel his way into meaning something to her. The little brother she never wanted. He helped her when he didn't have to and since then, that awkward little schemer has grown on her.

She's not just fighting for herself anymore. She doesn't have to and she doesn't want to. Corva isn't alone. And she doesn't have to lose again.

She rolls her eyes to her other arm, down to her hand. *Move, damn you.*

Summoning all her strength and willpower, Corva fights against her own muscles. If Thegn can do it, she can, too. She tries to manually overpower the pulsing waves that echo through her skull. Her efforts are rewarded with no movement in her arm at all. All her straining yields nothing more than a groan, to which her body reacts violently. She finds herself deep in a fit of gasps and coughing that causes her to violently double over.

Episode Four: Death Comes for You

Damn! This is absolutely useless.

She pauses, bent over and unable to straighten back to being upright. *Wait a minute. I moved!* Sure, she only coughed herself into a horribly vulnerable position. At this point, she's only able to see the floorboards under her feet. She has no view of Thegn, Zeke, or Jack.

But she moved. If she did it once, she can do it again. Maybe this time she can do it with a bit more control. She has to do something fast, though. The scythe's blade has already started to creep into her peripheral vision.

She concentrates on her feet. If she can get closer to Thegn, she can attack and save Zeke. The poor little monkey is still stuck in the Reaper's hand. No doubt that Thegn is trying to squeeze the life out of him. She forces the thought out and puts her whole mind on her feet. At this point, even getting them to twitch on command would be a minor victory. But it's the same as before. No matter how much willpower she exerts, her body only responds with pain and resistance.

She's close to passing out—or is that the scythe that's darkening the corners of her vision? *One last push.* That's all she has left in the tank.

Corva takes a deep breath for her final effort, and immediately a wave of convulsions crack their way across her body, fiercely flexing and relaxing in rapid succession. The pain is unimaginable, like being a pincushion for every blade, needle, and pointy stick ever created. Corva's lungs scream fire and her vision starts to blur. However, she can feel a slackening in the resistance of her muscles. It's ever so slight, but there's a sliver of control there that's available for her to seize.

And then it's gone.

What happened? For a fraction of a second, it almost felt as if she might be able to move, if only a bit and with an incredible amount of pain. Now her muscles shake under a weight of resistance just as they had before. She has to try again. But what had she done to get that feeling?

There was the straining in force of will she'd tried to exert, but that had been an entirely fruitless effort. This last push, she hadn't even had the chance to get to try straining. The pain kicked in the moment that she took that deep breath while preparing to—

The breath! Somehow it has something to do with her breathing. Or maybe not breathing. Whatever it is, she has to make it work now. The blade of the scythe has passed her head. Thegn is going to rotate it and try to pull the edge across the back of her neck.

She's got to make a big movement of some sort. A little foot shuffle isn't going to cut it. Actually, maybe that's exactly what she should do. If she can pull one foot in far enough, it should throw her off-balance and cause her to fall. Good. She has a plan. Now she just has to make it work.

With that, Corva tightens her lips and tries to pull in a deep breath.

Just as before, fits of pain immediately roll over her. But she's expecting it this time. She holds her breath, waiting for the feeling, that thin crack of control that she can force her effort into.

And there it is! The second she feels the slightest bit of control, she focuses all of her effort on moving her front foot. It moves surprisingly easily, though with absolutely no authority over its placement. Her foot swings toward its instep with enough force to lift it off the ground, as if an invisible opponent had just swept it to the side.

She drops to the ground with a thud, body still half-curled from her coughing episode earlier. The pain of her impact with the ground blooms across her arm and shoulder. However, she's out of the way of the scythe and she has a clear view of everyone else in the bar.

Thegn hasn't changed position all that much. His back is straighter and his head is pointed more clearly at the space in front of the scythe where Corva's head used to be. Zeke is still held in his hand, limp and unconscious.

Jack, however, is not at all in the position he used to be. Somehow, he's managed to crawl his way over to being within an arm's length of Thegn's legs. He's moving in a kind of staccato rhythm to get there, but it's faster and smoother than either she or Thegn have managed. If it were possible for Corva to shake her head in disbelief right now, she would. But of course Jack would've practiced trying to move with the paralyzers turned on.

The pain he must be in has to be immense. Sweat rolls off his face as he reaches out to Thegn. Only he's not looking at Thegn. He's looking at Corva. And it's not pain that's showing on his face. It's something else. Guilt?

He breaks the rhythm of his movement to lock eyes with Corva, his watering, hers confused. She sees him using tremendous effort to mouth the words, "I'm sorry."

And then he places two fingers on Thegn's foot.

4.11

WITNESS

Jack can't move, but his stomach shoots to the top of his throat the same way it would if a trapdoor had opened beneath him. Corva can hardly move, but the expression on her face is a clear progression from confusion to surprise to horror, ultimately ending in anger. He just used the Touch—well, a variation of it, as best as he could know from that beat-up old notebook the old man used in his training. If she didn't know before, then there's no question now who Jack's people were. The Shadowfold. The people responsible for wiping out entire towns. Towns like Fareburne.

He may have been doing it from an awkward position, there on the floor, half trapped by the subsonic paralyzers, holding his breath in spurts so he could move, but the movements for the Touch are direct, distinct, and without fanfare. If she'd witnessed any of the Shadowfold forgivers—those were the ones who actually went into the towns during a mercy—she'd recognize the distinctive application of two fingers on a person or a live image of that person. From the look on her face, there's no doubt that she's put it all together.

But he had to do it. How else were they going to stop Death? The bony jerk already had Zeke. He was going to cut Corva's head off with that blade of his. What choice did Jack have?

Still, something's not quite right. If Jack had performed the Touch correctly, Thegn would be a crumpled mess now, dead. Instead, the old wrinkly bastard tripped over Jack and careened across the floor. He hears Thegn crash to the ground. Hopefully the fall didn't injure Zeke any further. Jack can't see either of them, but he knows they're not dead. He can feel it. Something broke in the Reaper, but Jack's variation of the Touch didn't force the life out of him like it should've.

Maybe he did it wrong. It's not like Jack's had a lot of practice with the technique. Old Man V only ever walked him through the steps on dandelions and flowering cacti that they brought into the training kiva in Cliff City. Said it was too cruel to test it on rodents or even insects and it was certainly too dangerous to try out in the open, without soulmantic shielding.

Maybe he did it right, though. This is Death they're dealing with, after all. Techniques that destroy normal people might only be a minor inconvenience for the last of the Four. Maybe—

The skin and skull at his hairline starts to ache. No, not ache. It feels like a hot iron is being held up to his head. Something definitely didn't work right. It can't have. Even on those small walkthroughs with plants, he'd never felt anything like this.

Jack grimaces at his pain; he can barely even cough. It doesn't help that Thegn's leg had swung out after he got hit with the Touch. The wrinkled old man's foot had collided hard with Jack as he flew back, and all Jack can feel there now is the increased blood flow pumping to where foot had met chest. It also doesn't help that he still can't move. The subsonics are shaking him to his core, and he can feel exhaustion seeping into his muscles. Using that breath-holding trick took a lot out of him.

If he could get rid of just one of those sources of agony, he'd at least be able to move. To get up. To talk to Corva. Explain to her that even though he was born into the Shadowfold, he didn't have anything to do with Fareburne. With the death of everyone she knew.

Episode Four: Death Comes for You

He looks at her face from his spot there on the floor. Her face is usually never hard to read, but right now, the emotions mixing in her eyes compete for control of the rest of her face. He wouldn't blame her if she felt betrayed. That's how he'd feel. Maybe he deserves all this hurt.

The searing pain at his hairline seems to agree.

STALEMATE

Corva stares at Jack's pained face. *What just happened? Merda.*

It's strange enough that Jack has apparently found a way to resist his paralyzer array and move more easily than either her or Thegn. However, the way he placed his fingers on Thegn—and the immediate violent reaction afterward—it's too much to be a mere coincidence. Granted, it's not like she saw it clearly while cowering and running in her escape from Fareburne. But it's unmistakably the same technique.

Where in the world did Jack learn the Touch?

Sure, she's aware that he's been practicing soulmancy. She's seen him on a couple evenings, huddled in a corner under a bit of soulmantic shielding, making those little imbued beads that he sells on the side. But the Touch is a technique on an entirely different level. Was he even alive when the Shadowfold hit Fareburne?

Whatever. She lets air escape from her mouth. She needs to focus. *We've got bigger problems right now.*

The Old Beard is down for now and his scythe has become a pile of ash, but all three of them are still stuck in Jack's ridiculous sound trap. If Zeke was right, there's a horde of Umbrati grunts about to descend on Bule. The cliffside town is difficult to get to and mildly fortified, but once the horde makes it in … well, it's not going to be pretty. At the end of the day, it doesn't matter why the horde is invading. The horde sees anyone with significant skill or training as either a threat or an asset. That fact paints a giant target on people like Jack and her—whatever she is. They've got to bolt. Now.

She shifts her eyes to Zeke, who is lying at the base of the bar. He'd popped free from Thegn's hand when the old Reaper hit the ground, but he hasn't moved since he landed there. *Is he—*

A wave of relief washes over her. He's not dead. Corva isn't sure how she knows it, but she does. She's got to get him awake, though. He's the only one in the room that isn't affected by the subsonics. He could turn off the array and they could get out of there.

If she were closer, she could turn the array off herself. That relax-and-move thing worked for the most part, but it was exhausting. *Can I work across the whole room that way?* Her arms and legs feel spent just from the effort of the movement she made. A movement that would've nearly gotten her killed if it weren't for Jack. No way she'll make it across the room.

Maybe she could somehow signal Jack to take care of it. He seemed to move so easily when he reached Thegn. Looking at him now, though, he looks utterly spent. His eyes are half-open as he lays fully prone on the floor. Nope. Jack's not an option, either. She needs Zeke.

But she can't reach him. Not physically and not through her mind. She doesn't even know how she would. So far, she's just spoken to Zeke directly and he responds in her head. The mental communication thing was a one-way street from him to her. But now she can't speak. She tries, but the best she can manage is a noise like a bawling child trying to squeeze words out between crying and wheezing for air.

Zeke can reach my mind. Why can't I reach his? She thinks back to when Zeke caused her to collapse on the stairs up from Lower Bule. It was just earlier this same day, but it feels like ages ago. He'd said something. Something about flow. She'd had a hard time paying attention at the time; the realization that he was in her mind had been enough to overwhelm her and put her into shock.

But that word. Flow.

Him talking to her on the stairs. Him channeling energy to her in Cliff City. Her pulling energy from him in the fight at the bar. It was all flowing in one direction. Every time, she's been on the downstream side of things.

What was it Avó used to say? *A water drop cannot flow upstream, but with time, it can still find the top of a mountain.* The old woman's proverb didn't make sense then and it barely makes sense now, but it keeps repeating in Corva's mind. Something about the way Zeke phrases things reminds her of Avó. Cryptic and cautious. Speaking in riddles and metaphors. Neither of them seem capable of just giving straight answers. They treat facts like prized weapons. Weapons you're not allowed to train with until they think you're ready to handle them.

To flames with all of you. How are your secrets helping you now? Avó, you're dead. Zeke, you're not faring much better. "Can't flow upstream." Bah!

You know what bothers me about the Four? All your minds have always been so noisy.

What? Corva darts her eyes around her limited field of view. *Who said that?* The voice sounded like her own, but not at all the way she speaks. It's almost the same way she hears Zeke speak to her. However, this certainly isn't Zeke. The delivery and cadence are different. And it's definitely not Jack. Weariness and fatigue are still carved into his face.

It's amusing to watch you try to figure this out. But we're all short on time here.

She catches some movement in her peripheral vision, down near her feet. The rat! It's that same large white rat that tranced her back in the ditch. Back before Zeke chased it off. Now, it ambles around her feet, stops, and turns to face her.

You'll have to forgive me for being a bit talkative. The rat tilts its head in the direction of Thegn. **That young man absolutely abhors any form of mental communication. It's been so long since I've been able to speak at length with anyone. Of course, you Four are the only ones who can hear us. Unfortunately, he keeps killing you and the others before I can even begin to have a decent conversation with any of you. Really, he acts like he has no consideration for my feelings at all. So frustrating.**

Corva stares at the rat, confusion wrinkling her face. Her mind reels, trying to keep up. Everything he says is accompanied by images. No, they're memories—sights, sounds, even smells and feelings. They flow by her mind, bombarding her as he speaks. Not *her* memories, though. They're like a full-sensory series of visual aides, reinforcing and buttressing his words in her own inner voice. All she has is more questions.

But look at me, I'm going on and on. The rat rears up to sit on its haunches, freeing his forepaws to move as he pushes his words into her mind. He leans forward in what could only be described as a rat's version of a bow.

I'm Caffiel. In days past, you knew of me as the sixth sigil.

He lifts his head from his bow so Corva can see into his strange red eyes.

And you are Durga. Harbinger of War.

4.13

Identity

War? Me? Corva searches the rat's face for any explanation, any answer that makes sense. But this rat, Caffiel, offers no hints in his expression. Of course, he's a rat. Why would she expect him to have any of the human mannerisms she could understand? Then again, why wouldn't she? She's having a telepathic conversation with a rodent. Expectations of normalcy should've gone out the window ages ago.

Caffiel raises himself from his bow, the whole time keeping his beady gaze fixed on her. He tilts his head as if perplexed.

Oh my, you don't know any of this. What has our dear Ezekiel been teaching you? Stubborn old man. Here you have the second sigil, the oldest of who's left of my kind, and he's done nothing to prepare you.

He casts a glance behind him at the three inert bodies lying on the barroom floor—the boy, the monkey, and Death.

Dear Thegn has always managed to kill you well before you've had any idea of who you are or what you can really do. Misplaced guilt, in my opinion. Also, frightfully boring. This could have been

281

really interesting! Granted, this time around has been more interesting than any of the others—it's so dreadfully dull when he finds you early. And he keeps doing it. There's no excitement in killing infants and toddlers in their sleep. This time, though, we couldn't find you for nearly two decades. I've had such high hopes. However, it looks like Ezekiel has managed to squander any chance of real entertainment.

Corva shifts her eyes over to Zeke's unconscious body, still lying at the base of the bar near Jack. *Zeke?*

Not to worry, child. He's still alive. I'm sure he'll remain that way for a good long while. Certainly longer than you. But time is our true enemy. The Umbrati have already crested the lip of the canyon. They are so hungry for our young friend here that they've sent their steel-faced demons to claw straight down the cliff wall. He lets out a small rat version of something like a sigh. **Whatever happened to simply taking a proper path? Their way has style, sure, but it's lost in their lack of finesse. This little alcove will be overrun within minutes. Less than ten would be my guess.**

The rat drops back to all fours and ambles toward Thegn, tracing along the pile of ash that was the scythe. **So if you'll excuse me, I'll just collect my fallen horseman here. The Karui have invested quite a bit in our little hunts. I doubt that the Umbrati will strike an equally favorable deal. I mean, it's been a century and a half, but I certainly—**

The large rat stands at Thegn's head, his face tightening. Is it concern? Confusion? It's difficult for Corva to tell; rats don't exactly have faces that lend themselves to showing a lot of expression.

What have you done?

Corva moves her gaze between the rat and the fallen Reaper, baffled. Is he talking about the subsonics, or did Jack really do it? Is the Old Beard reall—

No, he's not dead. Don't try to think too highly of yourself, child. In fact don't try to think at all. It's noisy in there. Ezekiel should have taught you to speak. I can hardly make sense of your

thoughts. You have, however, managed to present us with a pretty unexpected situation. What did you hit him with?

For a moment, Corva is pleased at the notion that she knows something this know-it-all rat doesn't. For a moment.

What was I thinking? I just got done saying that you can't think clearly enough to speak and then I go off and ask you a direct question. My apologies for assuming that you knew how to do anything.

Asshole.

That, I heard. The last hundred and fifty years have done nothing to improve your manners. Still, whatever it is that you've done, it's severed dear Thegn's telepathic connection with the Karui. I'm sure some part of him would thank you for this, but it definitely complicates our deal. No matter, though. We'll get it properly sorted. But first things first.

He tilts his head at her.

Although it's put you in quite the hilarious pose, this little sound trap certainly makes movement difficult for the big guy here. Could you kindly indicate where the control module is for it? No need to try to think of it, noisy-minded girl. Simply indicate the location with your eyes.

Corva hesitates, staring at Caffiel. Sure, she'd love to be free to move again, but the Old Beard would have his mobility back too. And trusting a rat? Especially one that has a clear alliance with Death? Yeah, the whole thing feels like a bad idea in general.

Come, child. You're causing an unnecessary delay. None of us wants to be here when the horde arrives. Certainly not like this.

Crap. He's right. Time is short. Besides, at least she's still conscious. Perhaps there's something she can do once she's able to move again. With a glance at Jack's utterly confused face, she points her eyes at the bar.

Thank you. With that, the albino rodent shuffles to the bar and claws his way over to the back of it. **Ah, here we go. Just need to pull these right here.**

The pulsing whir of the subsonics cut off and Corva immediately feels the tension leave her muscles. With effort, she pulls herself up to one knee. It feels like waking with her whole body numb. She looks over at Jack, who is already scrambling over to Zeke with large, awkward, almost drunken movements.

She turns toward Thegn, still inert on the floor. She needs a weapon. She reaches to a thigh pocket on her pants. She has one of those long carpenter nails from Cliff City in there. It's at least as long as her hand, plenty long enough to kill him when she shoves it through the temple of his wrinkled old head.

Pulling the nail, she ignores the numb tingling in her body and stands. She starts walking to Thegn, clumsily at first, but there's more control and assurance in her movements with each step she takes.

For once, her mind and her body agree on what she needs to do, and how she needs to do it. In her mind, she's already stabbed that dirty nail into his face six times. Her imagination is crisp, almost ultra-real. The nail is in her right hand, thumb resting on the nail head.

Another step. She's at a full sprint now.

She visualizes herself pouncing on the Old Beard's chest, her knees crunching on his shoulders, trapping him against the ground. Her left hand slams into the right side of his jaw, wrenching his head to the side, exposing her target. The nail plunges into the soft recess between his eye and his ear. There's a little resistance at first, but the nail does break through.

One more step.

She sees herself adjust her hand position, placing her palm on the flat top of the nail head, and shove it all the way through. She imagines a meaty sound and satisfactory crunch as the nail breaches the other side of his face and fastens his head to the wooden floor of the bar.

One last step. Striking distance. Her body tenses, ready to jump.

However, she never gets the chance to play out the scenario in her mind. The murk of reality interrupts her imagination. Caffiel is closer to Thegn, and faster than Corva expects. Before she's near enough to bring substance to her mental rehearsal, the large white rodent is at Thegn's shoulder. A gust of air blows through the bar, stopping Corva in her tracks. Instinctively, she raises her arm and buries her eyes into the back of her elbow, protecting them from the debris flying through the air.

As the dust settles, she peeks over her metal arm bracer and sees Death standing before her. His eyes are glazed over. Caffiel sits upon his shoulder, and an enormous pair of coal-black wings protrude from Death's back.

Corva shifts her weight to her rear leg, readying herself for round two. However, Thegn just stands there, his newly formed wings folding behind him, with no indication that he'll be forming his scythe again.

Don't worry yourself, child. He's not going to kill you right this moment. He's still unconscious from whatever it was you did to him. This youngster is essentially on autopilot. Only responds to a few commands. But it's a sight more than when he's—

Before Caffiel's thought finishes, Corva hurls the nail at Thegn. It's perfectly aimed at his throat, but it never gets there. Thegn's wings wrap around the front of his body, forming a dark, feathery shield. The nail is stopped, caught among the plumage. He swings his wings open again, dislodging the nail and hurling it away. It clangs into the wall, chipping a large dent in the stone surface.

I said he was unconscious, not vulnerable. But I admire your spirit. I think you actually *will* make this interesting. For me, at least. The youth has a tendency to be impatient, so he may get a bit testy when he discovers you're not yet dead. You won't be hard to find, though, especially since you now know who you are. Carnage will lie in your wake, wherever you go.

Corva's mind races. There are so many thoughts, so many questions, so many things to do in this very moment. *Can I really be War? That can't be possible, can it? War was supposed to have died along with Pestilence and Famine when the fight between the Umbrati and Karui began. What else can I use as a weapon? I know who I am … really? How is Zeke? If he's hurt, how do we fix him? Does a sigil need a vet? A doctor? A shaman? Also, what is a sigil? What's Jack going to do when he finds out I'm War? Shit! Where did he learn the Touch? Who else still knows that technique? What am I going to do about that?*

So noisy!

Caffiel's abuse of her inner voice and the knowledge that her mind is an open book—albeit a disorganized one—acts as a sand wall to her flood of thoughts. Instantly, she's refocused on the present. There's only one thought. One objective. Kill Death.

The wrecked bar is a veritable treasure trove of makeshift debris-based weapons. Broken chair legs, splintered tables, handfuls of screws and nails. They're all available and at the ready. They're weak, though, and easily blocked or redirected. She does, however, have one weapon that can't be blocked. The Touch.

Okay, so it's not really her weapon. It's Jack's. Only, how does she signal him to use it? She certainly doesn't have a telepathic link with him. She can't even reach Zeke. *Why do I keep finding myself in this position? Constantly out of reach of whomever I need to talk to. To explain what needs to be done. Even in Fareburne, I—*

So that's where you were hiding! That large collective of humans. They held out against the Karui and Umbrati so well. Of course, that whole colony got wiped out by your own kind. A cult of mages intent on killing off people before the hive or horde could take possession of them. Noble effort, that. Destined to fail, but noble nonetheless. To think that we somehow missed you when that cult sacked your township. What are the chances? It's lucky, really.

The rat adjusts its position in the same awkward manner as a person who's lost the knack of holding a proper conversation. Maybe he expects her to reply, but what is there to say, really? *Wow, what a coincidence! If I'd known you were looking for me, I would've raised my hand so you could have tried to kill me sooner.* Yeah. Not that.

Anyhow, thanks for that tidbit of information. It's been fun

seeing you go through such amusing mental gymnastics for the last few seconds—great focus by the way, very clear—but like I've been saying, we're short on time.

Caffiel tightens his grip on Thegn's shoulder and stares past Corva to the front of the bar. Thegn, eyes still glazed over, crouches with his wings spread open. Flapping the giant feathery things behind him, he makes a massive leap. As they launch toward Corva, she notices Thegn's hands reach to his sides. The glint of small knives show just before he throws them, one at her and one at Zeke, who is still being tended by Jack.

Quickly, she ducks clear of the knife thrown in her direction and grabs the closest thing she can find: the upper half of a broken barstool. Not missing a beat, she hurls the barstool to block the other knife before it reaches Zeke. Unfortunately, there's something else that's also perfectly in line with the broken barstool. Jack's head.

"Jack!"

"Wha—shit!"

Jack drops his head and body, narrowly ducking the largest part of the barstool as it deflects the knife from its path to Zeke. However, Jack can't dodge everything. One of the partially broken legs, dangling from the rest of the flung mess, clunks across the side of his head as the rest of the stool flies over him and clatters into the bar.

He lets out a yelp and rolls to his side, covering his ear with his hands.

Corva turns to see Caffiel and Thegn flying out the front of the bar. She can see Caffiel looking back at her.

Ah, well. It was worth a shot. Can't blame an old rat for trying. Be well, War-child. Do try to make our next meeting even more interesting.

And after that, Corva's inner voice is her own again.

289

5.1

MATH

"What in the world of living shits was that?" Jack stands up, vigorously rubbing the spot just over his ear where the piece of the barstool had smacked across his head. "Didja see ol' Wrinkles kickin' the shit outta me and decide you needed to get in on that action too? Holy hell."

He looks over to Corva. She's not paying any attention to him at all. Just staring out the front door. His missing front door. Jack takes a moment to look around the room. The only really clean and clear place is the empty path between where Thegn was standing and the gaping hole at the front of the bar where the door used to be. Everywhere else, well, it's not even worth the energy of tallying up the damage. His bar is wrecked. There's no way he'll be able to fix it without Harris finding out.

At this point, though, that's not even in the top three things that Jack has to worry about. Maybe not even in the top five. Death is in Bule. That itself brings its own bucket of trouble. There aren't many stories of what happens when Death comes to town. There's rarely anyone left alive to tell them. Jack's and Lyia's story is one of the few.

Lyia. What if Thegn finds out she's here and she also survived the mark? Granted, the old coot didn't seem to be in much of a hurry to finish off Jack. Maybe he'll overlook Lyia. Jack shakes his head to himself. That's not something he's willing to leave to chance. He's got to let her know. Death may not be here for them, but that doesn't mean he won't be back. He could just as easily come after them the way he's coming after Corva. Especially since Jack used the Touch on him.

Oh shit. The Touch. Corva. She saw him use it. She knows. She must know. He saw it in her eyes. The questions. The confusion. The betrayal. But he hadn't betrayed her, had he? It's not like he was there when the Fold took out her town. It's not like he'd done any of the attacking. He was just a kid back then. She couldn't hold him responsible for that, could she?

Guilt creeps in on the edges of Jack's thoughts. He should've told her that his people were the Shadowfold the first time she'd brought it up. But how do you do that? How do you share a horrible truth without losing an ally? Without losing a friend?

Friends. Is that what they are? They've had their laughs, but the bulk of their interactions had been filled with banter and insults. Or moments of terror when she was literally trying to kill him. Is that something friends do? But just today, she'd stopped herself. She controlled one of her fits and he'd been there to help. And she'd returned to the bar after running off. Returned to face Death when she didn't have to. They fought Death together. They'd even held their own against him. Granted, Corva did most of the work there. But Jack used the Touch to save her, to save them both. That's a thing a friend does, right?

Jack's arm is itchy and tingly under the chembraid. The gear is working, but his head still hurts, and not just from getting banged around. He chokes back a small wave of nausea. Now isn't the time to get overwhelmed. He turns away from the devastation of his bar and gives Corva his full attention. Jack has got to make sure they're on the same page. There's no way they're getting out of this unless they're working together.

Of course, there's the rub. She hasn't responded at all to anything Jack's said. She's still in a trance, staring at the empty entrance through the tossed chairs and shredded tables.

Jack softens the tone in his voice. "We're okay, you know, me n' Zeke. Far as I can tell, we ain't dead."

Corva slowly turns her head to him, her expression blank, but not in a dazed zombie kind of way. It's more like the look a person gets when she's trying to do the math on a split check where no one considered the cost of what they ate or drank.

"Hey! Corva! I'm talking to you. You in there?"

Her eyes snap back to the now. She's finally looking right at him. But only for a second.

"Oh no! Zeke!" She rushes by Jack and kneels at the small monkey's side.

Jack lets out a small sigh of relief. She doesn't hate him. Or, at least, she cares more about Zeke than she does about hating him. "Zeke's alright. Still breathin'. Don't seem like he's ready to wake up just yet. I think Wrinkles put a pretty heavy squeeze on him. Didn't seem like anything was broken when I checked. Was a bit rushed, though, what with all the shit flying around in my bar."

"You checked? How did you know how? Stuff like this has happened before?"

"Like this? Shit no. But he's a little monkey working a merc bar in a gray town. Everyone gets roughed up a bit. I'm surprised, though. Normally he's more wily. An old geezer like that wouldn't ever get the drop on 'em."

Corva keeps staring down at Zeke. "That 'old geezer' is Death. There's no one else in the world like him."

"You sure about that?" In his mind, Jack winces, regretting the words as they pass his lips.

She looks up at Jack. "What's that supposed to mean?"

He hesitates. "Nothing. Forget about it."

She narrows her eyes at him. He knows that look. She's not letting this go. Any attempt to talk his way out of it will just leave an awkward gap of trust. May as well rip the bandage off all at once.

"Fine. You really wanna know what that's supposed to mean? You just went head-to-head with the dude who's supposed to be frickin' Death. Then you spent a whole damn minute making lovey eyes at his damn rat. And when that rat got up on Wrinkles's shoulder, the old man's eyes were all blank like you get when you're close to Zeke. I got no clue what's goin' on, but workin' a bar has gotten me pretty good at math. I can put two n' two together."

Not really. He can do math, of course, but he's got no idea who Corva might be. But he does know that no one he's ever heard of has gone up against Death and lived, especially not one-on-one.

Yeah, he and Lyia survived when Death was part of the raid on the Fold. They've got the marks to prove it. But that's all they did. Survived. It's not like they ever really fought Death directly. Not like Corva just had.

Jack pauses to catch his breath and squat down next to her. He grimaces as he lowers himself. His chest hurts something fierce, and the itch from his new chembraid isn't helping. Gorm said the painkillers in his mix were a touch on the weak side, considering Jack's size, but they should still work unless Jack got hurt really badly. Maybe—no. He's fine. He can't focus on the pain. There are more important things to concentrate on right now.

Jack makes sure he's got Corva's attention, then asks, "So who the hell are you? Do you even know? I don't."

She turns away from him. "I don't know who I am. They seem to know who I *was*, though. And I guess—I guess it has to be true. Otherwise, how could I fight him and live?" Her body stiffens for a moment before rounding on him, eyes fresh with anger. "But I wasn't the one who stopped him, was I? Where did you learn the Touch?"

Shit.

He pauses for a moment, realizing something.

"Oh no. We've gotta get out of here. The Touch is straight-up soulmancy. The Goats n' Sheeps track that shit when they're close. You already said that Goats are on the way. Between me usin' the Touch and the imbued tech Wrinkles was sporting, Bule'll be crawlin' with foot soldiers in no time."

"They're already here. Caffiel said the Umbrati are coming straight down from the top of the canyon."

Jack tilts his head to better see her face. "Who the hell is Caffiel?"

"The rat." Corva stands up and grabs one of the go-bags, barely giving Jack enough time to process what she's just said. "Se liga, Jack. I think Zeke's hurt pretty bad. But we've got no time. We gotta go. Is there a doc in town or a vet or something where we can loot some gear to patch him up?"

Jack pushes all his new questions to the side and thinks for a second. A wide smile breaks across his face despite the pain in his ribs. "I got something even better."

5.2

LOWER

As they work their way through the narrow paths and alleyways of Bule, Corva looks over to Jack. He's obviously in a lot of pain, but he's keeping a good clip in his step despite it. He's hunched over, holding Zeke close to his chest. He insisted on carrying the little monkey. Said something about thinking she might drain the last bit of life from Zeke if he let her carry him. But with his injuries, having him carry Zeke and his own pack was really hurting their chances of getting out of town in time.

Of course, all the people darting back and forth along the path and the town siren blaring wasn't helping them move any faster, either. That said, although there are more folks running around than they saw in the last raid, there are a lot fewer than she would expect. A thought occurs to her.

"I'm not sure a siege cave is the best place to go, Jack. It's going to be crowded, maybe too crowded to get to any medkits fast enough."

Jack shakes his head. "This ain't Bule's first rodeo. We got a bunch of siege caves all over. Not just the one we went to last. At least six official ones and a handful of pockets that are nearly as secure. We ain't goin' to any of those, though. 'Sides, like you saw before, most of the caves in Upper are pretty shitty."

"You said it's close, right? Where exactly are we going?" She's only a few feet behind him, but she's got to yell to make sure he hears her.

"It is close. Just gotta get our way down to Lower Bule."

She grinds her teeth, frustration growing. *Kid can't stop talking most of the time and now he decides to keep a tight lip?* At least they're headed lower. With the Umbrati coming from the top, the lower into the canyon that they can get, the farther from the main action they'll be.

They reach the long stairway down to Lower Bule. It looks like a bunch of folks had the same idea. Hardly anyone is headed up the stairs. She looks around. There hasn't been any sign of Thegn or Caffiel since they left the bar. They've got to be close, though. They can't fly all the way out of town without being spotted and as long as he's semi-unconscious, the Old Beard is in no shape to fight off this much of the Umbrati horde.

If Zeke and Caffiel are to be believed, this will be the largest raid she's ever seen. She's seen up to a hundred Karui sweep a town. That place had a defense wall and a dozen or so strong soulmancers. It's hard to imagine that the Umbrati—or anyone, really—would send this large a force for just one man. *Is Thegn really that powerful? Would they send just as many for me if they learn I'm War?*

She shakes her head. She's not War. She can't be. Death is the last of the Four. The other three horseman—War among them—are dead. The histories say that they perished early, not long after the first wave of people were claimed, conscripted by the Karui or Umbrati. *Dying is final, isn't it?*

Corva realizes that in her distracted state, she's walked quite a bit ahead of Jack. She slows down to let him catch up.

Jack doesn't look at her. His attention appears to be on navigating his way down each step. Still, it's pretty obvious that his mind is swimming with questions, too. Corva catches him sending a sidelong glance at her. She can't read his expression, though. Suspicion?

Curiosity? Anger? He turns his head back toward the stairs, away from her.

His jaws flex, like he's silently testing his words before he speaks. "So you're a Whisperer too?"

"What"?

Jack's breathing is labored. Words come out between breaths as he steps down. "A Whisperer. You talk to animals."

"Wh—No. I don't." She looks at him as they walk. "Shouldn't you be focusing on *not* falling down these stairs?"

"Shit, please. I do these stairs all the time." He pauses, false bravado momentarily lowered. "'Sides, talkin' keeps my mind off all the parts of me that hurt."

He takes another step. "So you ain't a Whisperer, but you can talk to Zeke and that rat?"

"Not really. It's more like they talk to me. Or think to me. Or at me. Or something. At this point, I'm not sure that they're really animals." She looks away, catching a glimpse of the little group of steps where she collapsed after Zeke first spoke to her. "I'm not even sure what I am."

Jack keeps working his way down the stairs, a half step faster to get out of the way of a big burly guy, armed and armored to the hilt. It takes her a second to realize that it's Gorm, the guy Jack said was the swap shop owner and armorer for the Bule militia.

The brute yells over his shoulder as he passes, "Look alive or you're gonna look dead, Jackie-Boy! Put that braid you bought to some use!"

Uncharacteristically, Jack doesn't offer a response. He just scratches at his neck where his new braid shows and keeps moving.

Of course, with a guy *that* big and that heavily armed booking his way down to the lower end of town, whatever's behind him has got to be significant. "Jack, we might need to pick up the pace. There's—"

"Mercies."

Corva stares at him. "What?"

"That's what they called them. That's what *we* called them. Mercies."

"Jack, you're not—"

"When we sent mages into towns and killed everyone. They were called mercies. I mean, sure, I was only four or five when the Fold fell—not even old enough to seriously begin any training—so it's not like I knew all that much about it. But they were my people. I came from that."

Corva doesn't know how to respond. She's obviously not the only one with a lot on their mind. She keeps her mouth shut and lets him keep talking as they continue picking their way down the steps.

"You know what the weird thing is, though? When I close my eyes, it's not my people that I remember. I saw the Fold fall. I saw the raid. Only time the Sheeps and Goats attacked the same place together. Sounds like something pretty memorable, right? I lost everyone I knew —most everyone." He pauses after he corrects himself.

"Jack, I—"

"I mean, sure, I was really young at the time. How many people could I *really* know at that age, right? It's true. I don't even know most of their names. My own families' names are even a bit fuzzy at this point. But the faces I remember, the faces I think about when I close my eyes … they're not theirs. It's the faces of the people that got wiped out."

He stops and looks up to her. "Your people."

She stares back at him. "Is this really the best time to be talking about this? In case you haven't noticed, there's a raid arriving."

"Yes! This is exactly the best time. This won't work if we can't work together. We have to know we have each other's backs. That starts with laying everything on the table."

Corva takes her attention off Jack and looks at everything going on around them. "Okay. But can we do that some place where I'm not constantly afraid of being pushed off these steps?"

He pauses a beat before complying. No words. He turns and keeps working his way to the base of the stairs. Turning toward Lower Bule, he stumbles a bit and drops to one knee. He hunches over, holding Zeke closer to his chest. Corva steps closer to help him up, but he's back to his feet before she gets a chance.

"Jack, you think maybe I should carry Zeke? You don't want to drop him."

Jack stops in his tracks, and she immediately regrets saying anything. "Everything on the table. Until then, you watch yours. I'll watch mine."

He looks around and Corva follows his gaze. Surprisingly, they're in a pretty secluded spot. People are still running around, but Jack and Corva are more or less out of sight.

Jack goes on talking like he hadn't even stopped. "Ever since Old Man V started training me with that notebook he found, or traded for, or … however he got it. Ever since then, I've been seeing faces—not faces, more like shadows—of people. People I don't know. But I *do* know them."

"You're not making any sense."

He shakes his head. "It's from the Touch. They were killed with the Touch. That's how it works, ya know? You gotta see 'em to do it. Whole crowds of people looking like every one of them got shot in the head at the exact same time. It's their souls bein' ripped out. You know souls got a smell? Can't hardly detect it with just one person. Takes at least a room full of folks before you start to take notice. I'm not even sure how I know that. But sometimes I smell that smell at night when I see the not-faces. Works its way into my dreams. Makes me sick to my stomach every time."

He lifts his chin skyward, tears forming at the corners of his eyes. "Seems there's a weight that comes with using the Touch … even learning it. I wasn't there when Fareburne got taken out. I can't even say with any sureness that I'd be able to stop myself if I had been there. Everyone in the Fold had been so trained to think they were doing the right thing. The just thing."

Jack brings his attention back to Corva, his gray eyes locking on hers. He's still looking up since she's taller than him, but somehow, it feels like they're on an even level. "I don't know what I would've done then—what I could've done. But I know about the here and now. Those aren't my people anymore. *You're* my people now. And if you'll let me, I'll do everything I can to help you."

"I'm War," Corva blurts out the words before she even knows they're coming out.

Jack's mouth hangs open. It's hard to tell if it's because he was just interrupted or if it's slack-jawed surprise. Remarkably, he pulls it together pretty quickly. "Well, okay. Not quite what I was expecting, but okay."

A scream echoes across the canyon, bouncing off all the rock surfaces. The fact that it's impossible to tell where it originated makes it all the more ominous.

Jack's expression hardens. "Look, I know I said 'everything on the table' and I got a whole bucket of questions for you. But I think we're going to hafta count this as good enough. I'll be okay with you being one of the Four." He pauses. "I think. You gonna be okay with me and Lyia being from the Fold?"

Kid can get right to the point when he wants to, can't he? Corva has to wait a second. He just hit her with a whole bunch of information and she's got a slew of questions of her own. Pops of gunfire sound from somewhere in Upper Bule. Jack's right, though. Those extra details will have to wait.

She returns his fixed stare. "Yeah. I'll be okay. I think."

"Good." Jack puts on an awkward smile. "We gotta stash our packs. The next bit's gonna be a bit of a squeeze."

5.3

THEGN

Agreements falter. Plans fail. Nobody knew that better than their group. The terrestrial plane corrupted everything it touched. Everything. The light. Darkness. Prophesy. Nothing was safe. The team had tried to warn their patrons, but were ignored. They were sent first. The vanguard. A squad of four emissaries and twelve sigillary hosts, they were meant to share miraculous wonder. Conduits to other planes of existence. The sixteen of them were hardened for the effects of this plane and yet, even they still ultimately sowed the seeds of distrust, uncertainty, and fear.

Abundance fostered greed. Healing bred more resilient disease. Open communication only exposed the secrets and lies that hid the fragility of peace. Fucking telepathy. Better than any, that vanguard crew understood how this plane warped and bent the absolute into something indefinite, conditional. They experienced it. They're still experiencing it.

And yet, they were told to persist.

It was sheer arrogance to think that the terrestrial plane could be won in some thought game of judgment, let alone conformed by the victor. It's a realm defined by chaos. The moment the patrons set foot there, it was obvious that everything had changed. No amount of hardening could have prepared them for the terrestrial plane. They were too pure, and the plane was too chaotic. Light became the Karui. Darkness became the Umbrati. A smear of dirt is most noticeable on an empty canvas; it doesn't matter if that canvas is painted in white or black.

Durga was the first to notice. Even before Jörmaru's sacrifice, she understood that there was an obligation to protect. Not just the terrestrial plane or its people. It was about protecting a balance that had been ruined by their arrival. Without balance, chaos would spread.

She'd led the insurrection. It was a noble, futile attempt to stem the tide from those that sent that vanguard crew. She was their captain.

The mission changed. It was better. The right path. It was also impossible.

That's why Thegn had to kill her first.

5.4

Severed

Thegn shakes his head, slowly coming to. His whole body feels like it's vibrating out of phase with itself, like his skin is only just barely keeping his insides from the open air. He grunts and tries to figure out where he is. He's sitting upright. So that's something. Definitely not in the kid's bar anymore. Who lets a kid run a bar anyway?

He feels something move. Like a few sets of small needles in his left shoulder. It's dark enough that it's tough to make out details in this place, even for him. Thegn doesn't need to look, though. It's Caffiel. The albino rat continues to adjust his position to balance on Thegn's bony shoulder.

Welcome back. I didn't want to get in the way of you gathering your wits about you.

Thegn feels his face knit into a frown. *Such a strange feeling. It's like I'm remote-controlling my own body.* "I thought I told you to keep outta my head."

It's true, but since there's a bit of extra room in there, I didn't suppose you'd mind so much. Besides, there's a lot going on. We're going to need to be expedient about this.

"More room?" Thegn parses the rat's words, heard in his own voice. *At least it's not like the Karui, dumping full monologues of thought in an instant.* He rolls his shoulders and turns his head, cracking his neck. He feels a familiar residual burning sensation in his upper back. He'd used his wings recently.

You didn't notice? I thought that would have been the first thing. Your connection to the Karui hive has been severed.

Thegn straightens his back. He hadn't noticed, but it's certainly noticeable now. That barely perceptible but infuriatingly persistent buzzing in his brain that he's had for the last century and a half—it isn't there.

Do you know what your former captain hit you with?

"Durga? She never did anything to me. It was the other one."

The human boy? Really? What could he possibly have used on you?

"Not sure. Got an idea, though. Certainly complicates things a bit." He gets to his feet. "First though, bring me up to speed. Where are we?"

We're lower in the canyon. Below that town. Ancient cliff dwellings. It smells like the child and Ezekiel have been here before. Seems that the Umbrati have been getting better at tracking you. Without allowing Thegn any opportunity to protest, the rat rolls up to his haunches and reaches across Thegn's face, laying his paw on Thegn's forehead. **As I said, there's a need for expedience. You're going to hate this, but there's no faster way.**

5.5

Welcome to the Red Light

"Really, Jack? This was your great plan? Really?" Corva fumes, pacing around the small sub-basement. It's brighter here than the one under Jack's bar, and it's also much better maintained. The stone walls have been carved straight and smooth, nearly polished. A few unmarked boxes are stacked neatly along the far wall, covering a recess and the tunnel that they'd squirmed their way through. "The brothel?"

Still holding Zeke in his arms, almost cradling him, Jack hisses at Corva, "Hey! Keep it down. They don't like me here 'nuff as it is. Not gonna help us if we get nicked for your hollerin'."

"Why are we even here, Jack? We need to get out of here before the raid hits in full. Zeke needs to wake up and get better. Serving to your perverse whims isn't going to help that."

She pauses a beat to look him up and down. The kid is beat up pretty badly. There aren't really any marks or bruises on him that she can tell, a scratch or two, maybe. But all of the hits he took were on his chest and abdomen. He's breathing pretty heavily, and sweat is beaded up on his forehead. Squeezing their way through that tunnel took a lot out of him.

She rubs her thumb across his brow and shows him his own sweat before she resumes her pacing. "You're not doing so well, either. Are you even old enough to know what they do in a place like this?"

"Shut the hell up. I'm plenty old enough. 'Sides, do *you* even know what goes on in a place like this? When's the last time you've ever been in a red light?"

Corva stops moving. "Never."

In all her traveling since leaving Fareburne, she actually hadn't ever stepped foot in a single one. Avó had told her to steer clear of them. Red lights tended to be for mercs and merchants. Without any serious weapons or tech to trade, a young female like her would only be welcome there for one reason. And in some burgs, Corva could even be forced into service at such an establishment.

"Well it's more'n just *perversions* that they peddle here. With all your trampin' around, you ain't ever noticed how long it takes to recover when you visit a doc?"

"No. I—" Corva stops, her face slackening as she's hit with a revelation that hasn't ever occurred to her before. "I've never really been seriously hurt."

"You've never—really?"

"Really. Never. The fight in your bar with Tretch was probably the worst I've ever been."

"And you still killed damn near everyone that day." Jack chews on that thought for a bit. "Well anyway, docs in towns like Bule are quacks. And even the ones that ain't, their treatments take too damn long. Anyone who needs to get patched up proper goes to a red light. The 'happy ending' is just part of the regular service."

Corva scowls, not just from her own apparent ignorance, but also in disgust of the enthusiasm with which Jack spoke about that last bit. *Ugh.* She looks away from him, wishing for brain bleach. Stay on topic. "But still, that's for people. Zeke's not a person. What makes you think they can help him?"

"She helped you, didn't she? I'm startin' to think that you're about as much a person as Zeke is an animal."

"She?" Corva ignores Jack's insult, finally understanding who he's talking about, and why he's really here. "You mean that whore you were peeping back on the steps this morning? You're here for her?" She goes back to pacing around the room.

"Her name is Lyia. An' you still don't know a thing about me."

"If this is some kind of harebrained chivalry ploy in the middle of all the other things going on, I swear—"

"It ain't like that. She's a healer. I been busted up plenty of times since we got here. Between the old man and her, they kept me from dyin' more'n once. She even showed me how to do a little. Though I could probably use more practice. It ain't safe for me to heal myself."

Corva is reminded of the heavy bandage on her head he'd given her when she first arrived. "Wait, she's a healer? Like a soulmancy healer? How come she hasn't been picked up? Can't the Karui and Umbrati track that?"

"Sheeps an' Goats."

"Whatever. Point is, how's she not conscripted?"

"They can only sense fixins when they're near. Also, Lyia is Maddy Shard's special prize. Maddy's gone through a bunch of extra effort to insure her investment. Went so far as to carve out a barrier room for Lyia to work in. Charges a heap and sets up a barrel of hoops to give folks special access."

Corva scowls. "How the world does someone like you afford that kind of special access?"

"Damn you got a lotta questions. We're wastin' time. Goats're probably gettin' their start in Upper right now. I need you to head up n' get Lyia. Bring her down to help Zeke." He leans against the smooth wall of the sub-basement and slides to a seated position on the ground, knees up to his chest. The position seems to help him hold Zeke. "And me."

"I have to get her?"

"Oh come on, Corva! I ain't doin' so hot, like you said. An' they know my face here. As it stands, I wouldn't make it a few steps out that door up there 'fore someone spots me and kicks us out."

"How do you know she's even here? Wouldn't she be headed to a siege cave like everyone else."

"Like I said, Maddy spared no expense. This place has its own safe room. Lyia will be one of the last to go in it." He smiles, looking to the ground. "She's thoughtful. Likes to make sure everyone is okay ahead of herself."

"Alright. So where's this safe room so I can find her?"

"Three floors up. You'll know you're in the right place when the walls start lookin' like these. The safe room is dug right into the cliff wall."

Jack's eyes close and his shoulders slump down as he passes out.

She turns to the steps leading up and out of the sub-basement. "Right. Third floor. Find the only mage healer in the brothel. At least I know what she looks like."

"And Corva?" Jack's voice is weak behind her, like he's talking in his sleep.

"Yeah, Jack?"

"Probably best not to tell her about Wrinkles being here for you. She won't take that news as good as me."

"Yeah, Jack."

5.6

LYIA

"I said stay down!" Lyia swings her foot up at the chest of the crawling, pantsless mercenary. She feels his ribs crack across her instep and hears the wind knocked out of his lungs as he collapses to the ground. "Fuckwit."

She turns to the woman behind her. Dirty blond hair. Pouty lips. Large eyes set apart just a little bit too far. *Jess.* "You alright, Jess?"

"I had it under control."

Lyia looks Jess over. The woman barely has any clothes on at all. Every weapon she has for defense—a knife, a stun baton, and even the pair of escrima sticks that'd been stashed under the bed—lie inert on the other side of the room, cast aside and completely out of reach. "Yeah. Sure you did."

She steps over the downed merc, hardly taking notice of the fact that his robe is bunched up at his waist and his bare ass is shining up into the room. She picks up the stun baton and tosses it over to Jess. "Get on over to the safe room. Don't drop it this time."

Jess catches the baton, scowling. Wordless, she turns and stomps out the door.

Sighing, Lyia leans over and grabs the escrima sticks from the ground, one in each hand. *Better than nothing.* She looks over to the discarded knife, not too far away. Her face wrinkles in disgust as she kicks the handle. It clatters across the hardwood floor to a rest somewhere under the bed. She walks back toward the door, again stepping over the unconscious half-dressed mercenary.

Then she hears them. A new set of footsteps. Heavy. They're coming down the hall to this room's door.

"Broles, man! C'mon. Those damn steelplates will be on this side of town any minute. We gotta get—" The footsteps turn toward the open door and step through, revealing another merc. He's a bit shorter, but with a thicker, stocky build. Apparently he's the senior to the pantsless one, Broles. The short merc looks at Broles's embarrassingly prone position and then at Lyia. "You bitch!"

He drops the gear in his hands and rushes her before she can get a word out or her sticks up. Head down, his shoulder rams against her stomach and drives her toward the rear wall. They don't get far, though. Lyia's heel catches on Broles' hip, sending her and the short merc to the floor. He's on her in a second, knees pinning her shoulders to the ground. Grabbing a knot of her hair, he raises his other arm, ready to land a meaty fist into her face. He doesn't get the chance. Swinging at her elbow, she jabs the tip of one stick into his armpit.

That's the nice thing about pressure points. Even a weak hit, aimed just right, can be debilitating. The merc's arm drops to his side, completely out of his control.

Using both sticks, she swings at his back and bucks her hips. It's just enough to rock him forward. He has to catch his weight with his remaining good arm, which creates just enough space to wriggle out from under him.

She gets to her feet while he's still on his hands and knees. As she turns to face him, she sees him reach into his boot and pull a short ceramic dagger wrapped in paracord.

Shit.

Anyone who comes into the building is supposed to check in all of their gear, including weapons, removable cybernetics, chembraids, and even clothes. After bathing, patrons should only roam the interior with a complementary robe, always with an escort. Lyia suddenly realizes that this merc is fully dressed in his street gear. The stench trapped in his garments overwhelm any of the fresh scents that were applied in the bath. He must've geared up and then come back to retrieve his partner.

He turns to face her, knife hand forward. Emotion seems to have drained from his face. He's all business now.

Lyia loosens her shoulders. "Look, we don't have to do this. Take your buddy and get out before it's too late."

He sniffs out in a half laugh. "'S already too late. Whole town is 'bout to be run over. Madame already turned me away from the safe room. Said there's no space. Bitch."

He spits before continuing, "No way I get to a siege cave, even without dragging his naked ass with me." He looks at her like he's comparing choice cuts at a market. "May as well let them get me in the middle of a last hurrah."

Mercenary logic. Lyia can't help but roll her eyes. "Not happening."

She points her nose down at his partner, still unconscious and ass-up to the world. "How about you have a go at him. Looks like he's already primed for you."

"C'mon, girlie. I already told ya there's no space left in the safe room. You'd seriously rather become one of *them* than have one last big 'O'?"

Revolting. Even on a good day, she'd charge him double just to look at her. No one forces her to do anything she doesn't want. They haven't for a long time. No way she's letting it happen now. She tightens her grip on the escrima sticks. "No freebies. No exceptions."

"Fine. We'll do this the hard way." He lets out his annoying little sniffing laugh. "Besides, it's better for me when I know you don't want it."

He stomps toward her, rushing in, knife in hand. Heavy steps for such a little guy. One step. Two steps.

He's one step away from her and closing fast. A quick side-hop with a spin, and she dodges his charge entirely. It's almost too easy. Finishing her spin, she extends her arms, swinging both sticks at where she knows his head will be.

Whiff.

Shit. Short guy. Disappointment seeps onto Lyia's face as she realizes she misjudged the mercenary's height. His knife flashes at her. *Too fast.*

It slices both of her forearms, cutting deep. She screams in pain and drops the sticks, feeling the merc's blade make contact with bone as he follows through with his slice. She just barely manages to grab his wrist to stop him from redirecting the dagger toward her gut. Blood runs down her arms and on to his, covering them in red. It's hard to keep her grip.

She's so focused on the knife that she doesn't see his free hand come up to her throat. He grabs hold and starts to squeeze. She struggles to breathe while still trying to keep him from sinking his blade into her gut.

Then she hears it.

Footsteps, coming down the hall. They're lighter than his were, and faster. *The raid is in Lower Bule already?* The door alarm isn't ringing to signal a breach though. There's no time to know for sure. It couldn't be anyone else from the Red Light. Jess was the last one unaccounted for and there's no way that self-centered blond wench would backtrack from the safe room.

Gasping, she looks into the short merc's eyes. The emotionless look of business is gone, replaced with a sick, sadistic, yellow-toothed grin. His hand at her throat loosens for a moment, and then he immediately squeezes again. Lyia's eyes widen with the realization that this sick bastard is enjoying this, trying to take his time.

Fuck it. She lets go of his wrist with one hand and pushes it out to his chest, palm out, hovering just above his dirty shirt. Closing her eyes, she concentrates. She feels her palm warm and visualizes thousands of tendrils of energy emanating outward from its surface and into his chest cavity. Instantly, she knows everything there is to know about his body. His bum knee. His three herniated discs (now replaced). His increased adrenaline.

Her energy tendrils wrap themselves around his heart.

Lyia opens her eyes and looks into his. He's lost in his berserker frenzy, still grinning, still thinking he's in control. He hasn't even noticed that she's stopped struggling. That his hand at her throat has no strength at all. That she's not even using her other hand to keep his knife away from her.

She lifts her free hand and caresses the side of his face, smearing her blood into his poorly maintained facial hair. "Shh."

He barely has time to react to the feeling of his heart being crushed.

A second later, the short merc collapses to the floor, lifeless.

Scowling, Lyia spits on the dead mercenary and picks up his dagger. Holding the tip of the blade to her own throat, she looks to the door. If it's the Umbrati coming down the hall, they know she's there and they know she's a healing mage. No way she's going to give them the chance to conscript her.

The footsteps come closer to the doorway and Lyia braces herself, mentally preparing for what needs to be done.

She hears the feet slide and she sees a dark-skinned girl in dreadlocks swing around the doorframe and into the room. "I heard a scream and—whoa."

IN THE VOID

I wasn't lyin' when I told Corva about seeing the shadows of anyone who's been hit with the Touch. Mostly not lyin'. Thing is, it ain't usually this intense.

A sea of faces fills Jack's field of view. Only, they aren't exactly faces. It's more like a bright fog filled with vague shadows. But each shadow belongs—or, at least, belonged—to someone; Jack somehow knows this much. They're impressions of the folks they used to be, like handprints hastily forced into mud. Upset, unhappy handprints.

They crowd his vision, insistent. Each one vies for his attention like he's supposed to do something for them. This is new. In the past, he could see into the fog, silently observing the shadows mill about. He always felt like he was looking at them through a window. That window seemed to grow each time he'd train with Old Man V, but he always had the feeling of someone from the outside looking in.

One time he thought one of them had looked at him, but at the time Jack had dismissed that as a fluke, a trick of his mind. He never even mentioned that particular event to the old man or to Lyia. The old man used to say that "fixins have a price" and that people don't always know what the specific price is until they learn a particular soulmantic technique. Jack and the old man figured that if the price of learning the Touch was seeing a bunch of wandering souls every now and again, that was something he could handle.

But Jack's training of the Touch never got far enough along to him actually performing it on anything, or anyone. It was always about opening channels, visualizing targets, and connecting. They never got to the whole bit about forcing a soul out of its living host.

Just Jack's luck that the first time he tries the Touch, it's on Death himself.

And now? Now there's no window. Now the not-really-faces in this bright foggy emptiness are aware of him. They know he's there. And there's more of them. So many more. That sick smell of souls that he'd described to Corva nearly overwhelms his senses.

"What do you want?" Jack feels himself say the words, but he doesn't hear his own voice.

They seem to hear it, though. The reaction is instantaneous and frantic. Desperate. They press in on him harder, faster. There's still no sound, but he can feel their urgency. It's too much, though. They're all coming at the same time. If he could just get them one at a time, he might be able to understand. It's like trying to take a drink order during a busy night at the bar where everyone is so loud he can hardly even hear the music that's supposed to be blaring.

Out of habit, he makes to reach behind his ear and tune his audio filter kneak. It sometimes helps focus on the sound coming from a specific person during one of those busy nights at the bar. The thing is, he can't reach up. He doesn't have arms. In fact, as far as he can tell, there's not much "him" at all.

He can see and sense all the not-faces around him, but for himself, there's nothing. He's got a presence, that much is obvious by the fact that the not-faces see him. But he's got no substance. He's a void in the fog. A space where a person ought to be. But he can't move like a person. He can't talk like a person. He's just there.

Normally something like this would throw Jack into a panic. He'd be fighting back waves of nausea and thinking of places to hide. Not now, though. Although he's not calm, he's got this feeling of being where he's supposed to be. There's just a kind of mild anxiety from not quite knowing what he's supposed to do. An itch under his not-skin as he's surrounded by not-faces.

In some ways, it's even more like those nights in the bar. Everyone pressing him. Everyone wanting something from him. Everyone doing their own thing around him. And he's stuck there behind the bar all alone.

At least on those nights I get paid for my trouble.

The moment the thought forms in his mind, the not-faces react. If their behavior was insistent before, they've boiled to a frenzy. Their desperation increases, their shapes stretch. They push in on him, each one imploring him for his focus. Some even look like they're trying to offer him … something. It's so difficult to tell. If they would all just—

There's a voice behind him. A whisper where Jack's ear would be, but it's there. Actual sound. Raspy. Old. Powerful. "None of your people knew what to do here either. It's why they failed."

The not-faces all around Jack recoil at the sound. Their frenzy ebbs and is replaced with something else. Not fear. Disdain.

The whispering voice lets out a laugh that could be a cough. "Don't mind them. They're just pissed off because they ain't got voices."

If Jack were able to move he'd spin around, wide-eyed with surprise to check that his not-ears aren't playing tricks on him. But he can't. He can't even make sound on his own.

Old Man V? That you?

"How've you been, kiddo?"

OLD MAN V

Jack's mind reels with an onslaught of questions. *Why is Old Man V here? This plane is supposed to be for people who got hit by the Touch. And how come the old man can speak when none of the not-faces can? Hell, why can't Jack speak? Or move, for that matter? Why didn't the old man talk to him sooner? And why did the not-faces go all crazy a minute ago? Why don't they seem to like the old man? Why —*

"Whoa, whoa, kiddo. Slow it down. That brain of yours makes almost as much noise as all those other nuggets combined. Takes a lot of effort to filter that stuff down. If you want me to get what you're sayin', you've gotta be real clear with your thoughts. It's like thinkin' real loud."

Jack concentrates, fusing all of his thoughts into a single question. *WHY'D YOU HAFTA DIE?*

The not-faces all around Jack stop writhing in contempt at Vardin's voice. Their attention is all on Jack.

"Too loud! Too loud, kiddo." The old man's voice snorts his laughing cough. "I forgot how good your focus can be when you actually try. I—"

The old man's voice breaks, like he's distracted by something. His next words come out soft, softer than the raspy whisper he'd been using. "I know. *I know.* Let the kid get his damn bearings first."

The not-faces react to Vardin's words, almost thrashing at the sound like they're upset.

"Oh, cut it out!" The old man's voice pauses again, this time like he's trying to compose himself. "Sorry about that, Jack. The souls here are a bit sensitive about words like 'damn' and 'hell'—give it a rest!" The not-faces had gone into another flurry of movement as soon as Vardin mentioned the terms. "They're a buncha sensitive nuggets. You can say 'fuck' and 'shit' all you want, though. Doesn't bother them in the least."

Shitfuckers.

"Ha! Good volume that time. Well done. And I'm glad to see you're as foulmouthed as ever." Vardin lowers his voice like he's trying to tell a secret. "But let's not get in the habit of insulting them. I'm kinda stuck with them for eternity, so it's probably best not to make things any more uncomfortable than they already are."

As glad as Jack is to hear his old mentor's voice, it's still weird. Kind of unsettling. It doesn't help that he sounds like he's talking to himself when he's addressing the not-faces. And he still hasn't answered any of Jack's questions.

"Ah yes! Your question. Wait. What was it again?"

Why'd you have to die?

"Oh, Jack, you've seen enough death in your short life that you should already know that eventually we all die. No one is immortal, not in a way that's worth anything."

Jack can almost feel himself vibrate in frustration. *No. That's not what I mean.*

"Oh? What, then?"

Why did you die? It ain't like you were sick or anything. Did someone get to you? Poison you, maybe? Was it Harris? It was Harris, wasn't it?

The old man doesn't respond immediately. It's hard to tell if he's chewing on his thoughts or if he's just gone. Eventually, though, he does speak again. "Harris wants to take the bar, does he?"

Yes.

"Yeah, I can see how I kinda left you in a bit of a mess." Vardin lets out something that almost sounds like a sigh. "And no. As convenient as it would be for me to tell you that Harris killed me and give you the means of provin' it, that's not what happened. The truth is— well, the truth is quite a bit more embarrassing."

The not-faces pick up the pace in their movement. It's not like before, though. It's more like they're lining up to listen. Like they're eager to hear what he has to say.

Vardin seems to notice their change in behavior, too. "Yeah, yeah, sit down to hear your favorite story about how Old V fucked up. I swear, you nuggets are so predictable. Were you this easy to anticipate when you were alive? No wonder you're dead."

V.

"Right, kiddo. Sorry about that. Easy to get distracted here. In fact, I'm not even sure how long I've been here. There ain't exactly a calendar or even a wall to scratch lines for the passage of days. Makes it real simple to lose a sense of things."

Focus, old man. The question! Jack doesn't get it. Old Man V was always sharp as a tack, even as far into the gray as he'd gotten. It's really uncomfortable to hear his mind amble off in every which direction.

"Did it again, did I? What was—oh wait, I got it. You wanna know how I got here. Short version, I did it to myself."

What?

"Yeah. Well, think about it. You know how we started seeing this plane when we started training for the Touch? How we figured all these nuggets here are souls that got pushed out by the Shadowfold when they were still around?"

The not-faces all appear to contract as a single unit at the mention of the Shadowfold. Slowly, though, Jack is starting to put the pieces together, to make sense of what the old man is saying.

Wait. So you're saying that you put yourself here?

"It wasn't really on purpose, mind you. I was working my way through that training notebook ahead of you, like I do, tryin' to get you ready to attempt the real thing. Figured I'd try it on a rat or lizard. Not quite sure what I did wrong, but the whole thing ended up backfiring. Landed me here."

A sudden thought occurs to Jack. If he could, he'd be grinning right now. *You're here because you Touched yourself.*

"Well, yeah, I just got done saying—"

It takes a second to click before the old man understands what Jack is getting at. "Ha!"

The old man's laughter fills the space and goes on for quite a bit. Jack mentally laughs along with him while the not-faces all around them appear to heave a collective groan. Jack has no idea if the thought of laughing conveys like words do, but it doesn't matter. It's good to be able to talk to the old man again.

"Oh, kiddo. I do miss your perverse little mind."

So, wait. Is that why you can talk and no one else here can? Because you used the Touch on yourself?

"To be honest, I don't know. Could be that. It could just be you. Could also be just because you n' I have a connection. I wasn't even sure I was actually talking until you showed up. I've only heard one other voice on this plane and that ain't someone I'm inclined to hold a conversation with."

The old man's words hang in the air, meaningful. Jack knows exactly who he's talking about. *Thegn.*

"Yeah. Comes through every now and again. Normally moves around like he's wading through a dumpster. The last time was a bit different, though. Blasted through like—hold on. You jumped to his name right quick. What ain't you tellin' me?"

How do you think I got here?

"Well, you ain't dead. That much is obvious."

How can you tell?

"You're fixed in place. Think of yourself like a tree. You've still got roots in the material plane. The Touch cuts those roots. Sends the soul adrift on this plane, kinda like a seed in the wind."

Is that why you've been calling them nuggets?

"Yup. And because I think it bothers them. They don't like being reminded that they're the littlest kernels of who they used to be." The old man's voice does that snorting cough-laugh again. "Gotta amuse myself somehow."

The not-faces go back to their frenetic swirling in response to this.

But why aren't you floatin' all around? You've been outta my view this whole time.

"Hold on, Jack, now you're distracting me. Let's see, we said you're here, but you ain't dead—"

Death came to the bar and I used the Touch on him. The thought spills from Jack's mind, loud and fast. If he were able to talk, he would've just blurted it out.

"You *what*?"

The not-faces retract as a swarm, like a giant spiritual flinch. Their movement is jumpy, agitated. Jack doesn't pay them any mind.

Wrinkled old bastard was hurting Zeke and a friend of mine. And he was wrecking the bar. He's an annoying dick. No, a whole bag of dicks.

Vardin's voice doesn't respond immediately. When he does, it's quiet. Thoughtful. "He finally found Zeke, did he?"

Well, yeah, but no.

"What do you mean?"

Jack can almost feel himself squirm. *That's not why Wrinkles was at the bar. I mean, he did find Zeke—what in the world is so special about him, by the way?*

"Don't change the subject, Jack. This is important."

No, I'm serious. What's with everyone bein' all up on Zeke's junk? First, Corva has her fits when she's around him. Then ol' Wrinkles comes after Zeke like, like—

"Like they're mortal enemies."

Yeah. Like that. Jack pauses. It's so frustrating that he can't turn and face the old man, can't see him as he speaks. *How come you know all this?*

"There's a lot I never told you, kiddo. One of my greatest regrets. Zeke and I left you real unprepared for this world."

You could talk to Zeke, too?

"What? No. We just built our own little way of—hold up. Who can talk to Zeke? You?"

No. Corva. She's … well, she's—

A sudden sharp pain shoots across Jack's ribs and he feels himself move. Not much. Just a little. The odd thing, though, is that he can feel himself move on this plane, but the pain in his ribs isn't here. It's wherever his ribs are, wherever his body is.

"Jack? You okay?"

Yeah. I think so. I just moved a bit. But my ribs hurt and my chembraid itches. It's strange. He only just now realizes that he hasn't been feeling any pain from the beating he took back at the bar.

"Kiddo, that's not okay. Moving here means dying there. Did you get hurt?"

Yeah. Wrinkles got me an' Zeke pretty messed up. Shit, Zeke! He's hurt bad, V. Corva went to get Lyia, but I can't help if I'm stuck here. I've gotta get back to him. Jack stops as another sudden realization hits him. *How do I get back?*

"Not sure, little guy. My first time here was a one-way trip. You ain't dead yet, though. But from the sound of things, you ain't farin' much better than Zeke. You really need to be worried if you start moving here."

Moving?

"Yeah. Mobility. You start being able to move around here and you know you're dead."

Fuck V, I don't wanna be dead. Jack thinks he feels himself move again. Panicked thoughts start flooding his mind.

"Well just hold on, kiddo. Slow it down. You said your ribs hurt and—when did you get a chembraid? How old are you now?"

Now ain't the time for that, V.

"Right. Right. Don't think I'll forget about that, though. But yeah, you said your ribs hurt?"

Yes. Took some heavy hits.

"Use that. Pain lets you know you're still alive. Focus on it. Embrace it. See if you can follow it. Make it your own little path back to your body."

Follow the pain?

"Exactly. You've been here once. You can get here again after you get yourself patched up. It ain't like I'm goin' anywhere. We'll get to your questions. And maybe you can answer a few that I've got."

Jack turns his attention to the pain he's feeling. It's tough to do, though. His mind keeps going back to the idea that the more he can move, the closer he is to really being dead. It doesn't help that he's not overly fond of being hurt. Who *wants* to feel that?

"You come back from being this close to dying, kiddo, and you'll have a whole new appreciation for pain. Now focus."

Shit. Mind reading. Jack redoubles his efforts and concentrates. He tries to visualize the pain and its source, the same way Lyia taught him for doing healing work. A splotch of color, pulsing in time with a heartbeat. Mentally, he imagines wrapping a tendril around it and pulling. A little tug at first, like testing a rope before climbing. His hold is good, so he pulls harder.

In an instant, the not-faces dissolve away and his entire field of view is filled with that pulsing splotch of color. Agony burns its way across his mind. It hurts so much. He can feel that mental tendril slip a bit, the color shrink and fade. But he feels his face wince. The pulse on that splotch is his own. Air is filling his lungs and painfully pushing out. It's working!

It sucks, but it's working.

Jack redoubles his concentration on his splotch of pain and sends a second tendril to it. Just one more pull should do it.

5.9

DIE FREE

Corva looks around the room. Mostly clean, like the rest of this place. Smooth, nearly polished-looking walls, gleaming hardwood floors, and ornate trim work. A large bed with a thick mattress serves as the centerpiece to the room. One of the walls is covered with shelves, fully stocked in equal parts with alcohol and sex toys. Two guys are on the floor, one a bit older and substantially more clothed than the other.

The older one is—was—more obviously a merc, based on his clothes. He's also more obviously dead, his eyes open and lifelessly staring out into nothing. Strangely, though, there's no visible marks on him to indicate how he died. The younger one without pants is probably also a merc, judging from the tattoos all over his exposed legs. Hard to tell if he's dead, but he's unconscious enough that it's effectively the same thing at this point.

And she is in the room. Lyia.

The older, deader merc lies at her bare feet and she holds a short ceramic dagger to her own neck. Her forearms have a nasty gash across them that is still bleeding pretty heavily. Drops of her blood stain her gray slacks and her camisole is pulled up, exposing her finely sculpted abdomen. She's a bit more haggard looking than Corva remembers, but is definitely the same woman.

"Se liga—look. I don't know what's going on here, but I'm not with them. You're Lyia, right? Jack sent me."

Lyia lowers her knife ever so slightly. "I know who you are. You're the girl who wrecked Pinny's bar. Wait." She lowers her knife completely. "He sent you? From where?"

"Well, here, actually. He's stashed in the sub-basement with Zeke." Corva pauses a beat, frowning. "Pinny?"

Lyia is already next to Corva, passing her and headed into the hallway. "It's the name I call him. Is he okay?"

Corva turns and chases after her. "No, actually. Both of them got hurt pretty badly."

"What happened?" Lyia tosses the words over her shoulder as her long legs carry her forward at a faster pace than Corva might've expected.

"Long story." Corva, with nearly a whole head less height, needs to jog at just short of a full run in order to keep up.

"It ought to be. I haven't hardly seen Pin at all since his bar got trashed. Just the times I came to help clean you up. Usually he gets caught snooping or peeping around here every few days."

Corva lets the discussion fizzle as they round the corner to the echoing stairwell she'd used to get up to this floor. They work their way down the floors, Lyia skipping every other step, Corva skipping every three.

"Jack said that there's a special room or something where it's safe for you to do your healing thing. Is that where we're gonna take him and Zeke?"

"Afraid not. That room gets locked and hidden in the event of a raid. The missus doesn't even give me access when that happens." Lyia slows down as they reach the sub-basement door. "Besides, the cat's probably already out of the bag."

"Wait. I don't follow. What do you mean?" Corva grabs Lyia's arm, but she loosens her grip almost immediately, realizing that she's grabbed Lyia's arm right where the cut is—strike that, right where the cut is supposed to be. There's no deep gash there now. Just slowly drying blood and a slight warm feeling. She raises her head and looks up to Lyia's face.

"I think you understand."

"But why? Don't they—"

"Remember those two mercs back in the room? The older one. He got the opposite of healing."

Corva releases Lyia's arm, allowing her to open the door. "So if they can track you and we can't get into that barrier room, what's the plan?"

Lyia opens the door and bounds down the stairs. "Pinny! You down here?"

Corva leaps her way down the steps and puts herself square in front of Lyia. "You didn't answer me. I said, what's the plan?"

"The plan?" Lyia lifts her hand, staring at her own palm. "The plan is to die free."

SACRIFICE

"*What*?" Corva searches Lyia's face, not wanting to believe the words she's just heard. Lyia's expression is flat, almost calm in an unsettling kind of way. "You can't be serious."

"Absolutely serious. We're no match for the horde. And there's no way I, or anyone else I care about, is getting conscripted."

"But, your arm. You just healed it. Why would you do that if you're just going to kill yourself?"

Lyia checks her arm, apparently only now realizing that her cut is gone. She shrugs. "I've been able to use healing soulmancy since I was a child. Self-healing is a bit of a reflex. I actually have to consciously stop myself from doing that most of the time."

She makes to take the last couple of steps to the floor, but Corva stays in her way, blocking her route down.

"I can't believe you're saying this! I can't believe I let you down here! You're supposed to be a healer. You're supposed to make Jack and Zeke better! You want to kill them? Because you're afraid to fight?"

Lyia stares at Corva before responding, "I'm not afraid to fight. I'm afraid of what will happen when we lose, and we *will* lose. If you think otherwise, you're deluding yourself."

Again she tries to get by, but Corva doesn't budge.

"We don't have to fight if we can escape. That's what Jack and Zeke and I are doing. But we can't escape with them hurt like they are. Jack can't heal himself like you can."

A scowl flickers across Lyia's face. "He'd be able to if he practiced more. Jack is too young to be on the road on his own, especially with someone as hunted as—" Lyia stops and narrows her eyes at Corva. "You're the reason the raid is here, aren't you? You're the reason Jack is hurt! Why the fuck would I let him go with you? You don't know what we've been through."

She's right, of course. Corva drops her hands and hangs her head. Lyia takes that moment to shove by Corva, but Corva grabs Lyia's arm. "You'll do it because if anyone knows how to survive the road at that age, it's me. I've done it. And I had to do it because of *you*. The Shadowfold."

Lyia flinches at the name.

Corva continues, "That's right. You. I know where you come from. And unlike Jack, you're old enough to remember what your people did to countless townships. To my people. Don't you dare talk to me about what you've been through like I couldn't possibly understand."

Lyia looks back at her, eyes cold, but tears are collecting around them. "There's a reason they called what we did 'mercies.' You never had to witness a conscription. You never had to see the people you love become lost to the Karui and Umbrati, only to come after you again in a future raid. The Shadowfold gave your people the gift of freedom. If you can't see that, then no. You don't understand."

"So it's better for you to kill Jack before he even gets a chance to prove you wrong?"

"That's a risk I'm not willing—why am I even discussing this with you? This isn't a vote."

EPISODE FIVE: FIGHT OR FLIGHT

For a moment, they stand there as if stuck in place. Corva can't believe what she's hearing come out of this woman. It takes a beat for her to find her words. "No. No, no, no. We don't need you. We'll find another way." She calls out into the space of the basement, "Jack! You here? Your dream girlfriend isn't helping us. We've gotta go."

There's the sound of shuffling somewhere on the other side of the boxes hiding the tunnel they came in through. Corva can't see what's going on back there, but the change in Lyia's expression tells the story on its own. The corners of her mouth drop, lips quivering, and her eyes begin to well up.

"Pinny." Lyia takes a half step forward. "You know it's the right move."

Corva can hear Jack behind her. He makes a watery sniff between heavy breaths. His voice shakes. "You're for-real gonna kill me?"

Lyia drops to a kneel. "You don't want to be pulled into the horde, Pinny. It's worse than dying. It's losing everything. It's like reliving home every day. Forever."

Corva turns her body sideways, consciously making herself a smaller target. She turns her head and takes a quick glance at Jack. The kid is messed up. It's not just his injuries from the fight at the bar. If it's possible to see what it looks like to have a person's soul crushed, she imagines it would look just about like Jack does now. He's almost immaterial. His eyes and nose are red, wet, and puffy. His shoulders appear deflated. Cradling Zeke in his arms, he looks more like a child to her than he ever has before.

Jack's back straightens, like he's just listened to the surprise ending to a story only he can hear. His face lifts and his eyes tell a new story. One of clarity. Decisiveness. He raises Zeke up toward Lyia. "At least heal Zeke first. The Goats don't conscript animals. Zeke and Corva can still hide and get away."

Corva thinks she catches a sidelong glance from Jack as he says that last bit. She narrows her eyes, but gets no further hint from him to indicate whether she's seen what she thought she saw.

"Pin—"

"I'm sayin' okay. You're right. You n' me are no match for a swarm of them Goats. You make Zeke better and I'll stay with you here."

"Jack?"

He ignores Corva, walking right by her to Lyia and gently laying Zeke's unconscious body on the ground.

"Jack!"

He tilts his head down, hissing across his shoulder at her, "You need to shut your mouth. Zeke needs help. 'S all that matters right now. How about you watch the door?" He turns toward Lyia. "Please start."

There's no fight happening here. There's no sense in her even trying to stop anything. Jack has pretty much dissolved any defense she could've put up for him. Corva squares her shoulders and skulks over to the steps leading up to the door. On the way, she glares at Lyia. "Can you heal Zeke? Or are you only trained for humans?"

"Most of the people that come to this place are no better than animals. Zeke's got more humanity than most of them."

You've got no idea how right you are. Corva reaches the base of the steps and looks up to the door. "Alright. Do your thing."

Guide

Jack takes a step back as Lyia ties her hair with a bit of string. She reaches forward and hovers both of her hands a knuckle or so over Zeke's body. When she leans in, he can't help but look down the neckline of her shirt. It's a pretty form-fitting tank, so he doesn't see much, but—*Focus, moron!*

Jack blinks and wills himself to avert his eyes from her perfect breasts, forcing himself to look instead at her hands over Zeke and get his own heart rate under control. It doesn't feel good to lie to her, to make her think that he's ready to stay and die. He's not. He just got done not dying during his talk with whatever was left of Old Man V. Getting her to focus on healing Zeke is a pretty crap stalling tactic, but it's the last one he's got.

"How bad is it?"

No response.

He squats down so he can look up into her face. "Hey. Lyia?"

Her expression oscillates between wonder and confusion, her eyes focused somewhere in the distance. "Pin, I—I don't know. I can't make sense of it. There's more physiology in here than there ought to be for an animal Zeke's size. For any animal, really. It's like those nested dolls, except each time I open another layer, the doll inside is even bigger."

Lyia's hands start to shake, "I can't—I can't get out! It's like I'm being pulled in." She looks right at Jack, but it's like she can barely see him. "Pinny, just what in the world *is* Zeke?"

"No!" This isn't how it was supposed to happen. Jack stands and tries to push Lyia back, free of Zeke. She doesn't budge. It's like she's bolted in place. Beads of sweat build up on her arms. He runs around to her back to see if he can pull her off. No luck there either.

The sweat causes him to lose grip and he falls backward, landing rough. Pain radiates across his rib cage as he pulls himself to a seated position. He fires a glare over to Corva, who is looking at them, distracted from her duties of keeping watch. "Do something!"

"Like what?"

"I don't know! Anything. You're the one who's supposed to be connected to him. Guide her or some shit."

"Guide her? I hardly even know what Zeke is. You're the one that's supposed to have been practicing healing with her. I wouldn't even know where to start."

Lyia's right arm swings up, her palm facing toward Corva. The movement is so fast, it's almost mechanical. Judging from the look of distant terror in Lyia's face, it's also completely involuntary.

"Touch the palm." For that moment, Lyia's voice is smooth and even, though the cadence of the words isn't quite how she normally speaks. The second she finishes speaking, her mouth starts to quiver and tears start to stream from her eyes. "Shit, Pinny. That wasn't me. I didn't say that."

"Corv—" Whatever amount of insults or begging that Jack had in mind is cut short when he looks at Corva. Her expression is almost the opposite of Lyia's. There's surprise, but instead of being overcome with fear, she's engaged. Drawn closer.

"I know that way of speaking." She looks back at Jack. "It's Zeke." She takes a step closer, but is caught in a moment of hesitation.

"You can tell that from just three words?"

"Well, I—"

"Never mind. It doesn't matter. I believe you."

The expression on Corva's face morphs from surprise to gratitude, hitting a few unidentifiable looks along the way. "Thank you."

"You're quite welcome. Now do what he—she—shit. Do what they say!"

She stares at him and opens her mouth to respond.

"Fuckin' hell." Jack doesn't give her any time to form real words of protest. He stands. It hurts something awful, but he can't let that stop him. He stumbles over between Corva and Lyia. He places one hand in the small of Corva's back and grabs Lyia's wrist with his other hand. "We're all probably gonna die anyhow."

With that, he grits his teeth and shoves Corva, pulling her abdomen into Lyia's palm.

An instant later, everything has gone white.

SEARCH FROM THE AIR

Thegn circles in long arcs within the void of the canyon, catching updrafts to increase his altitude. The whole time, he keeps an eye trained on Bule through an imbued monocle. Caffiel rides on his back.

All these years with you and I'm still enamored with the thrill of flying.

"All these years with you and I still can't stand you in my head like this."

Temper, temper, young one. You need my help right now, and not for just these magnificent wings. He creeps up Thegn's back, placing his head by Thegn's ear. **Do you have any clue as to where our old friend went, or that she still exists?**

Thegn shakes his head. *Bastard rat, acting like he can whisper in my ear. You're still in my head, asshole. Don't act like you can actually speak!*

You're very good at fuzzing your thoughts. I only caught your last sentence.

"Yeah, fat lot of good it did me. Karui hive telepathy is completely different from what you're doin'. This at least feels like a real conversation, despite you bein' in my head. To hide anything from them, you basically have to think in code. The fuzzing technique you trained me with didn't hardly work at all. I tried to use it for the first ten years. Worked for long-term goals, but it's absolute shit for real time."

Fascinating! Caffiel's words boom in Thegn's inner voice, giving up on the mock whispering. **However, are you purposefully evading my question or are you really this easily distracted?**

"I know. I'm still looking. It seems like the Umbrati followed the residual energy from the boy's soulmancy trick out of the bar. He and Durga headed to the stairway between the upper part of the city and the lower. They've got some light resistance from the town's militia, but they're a paper wall."

So you've relegated it to a mere trick now, have you? That *boy* had you trapped and then put you on the flat of your back ... with a derivation of your own technique, no less. And that's not taking into account how the girl handled you. Durga's spirit hasn't even been fully awakened in her yet. You're out of practice.

Thegn casts a glance at the rat on his shoulder. "You're enjoying this, aren't you?"

Absolutely! This is the most excitement we've seen in at least fifty years.

Thegn thinks back to all the various skirmishes the two of them have been involved with over the last fifty years. "You have a very bizarre sense of what constitutes excitement."

I'm flying through the air on the wings of Death. You set the bar pretty high, youngster.

A snort is the most acknowledgment Thegn gives to Caffiel's comment. He goes back to surveying the town through his monocle. "For a horde unit this size, it looks like it's weighted heavily for fighting and capture."

Like they were specifically assembled to come after you.

"Could be. Probably. It's a new strategy from the horde, at least. In any case, I can't be sure, but it doesn't look like they were expecting much in the way of soulmancy. Not very many seekers. Probably aren't any in the group with enough nuance to tell the difference between energies. Probably."

Not nuanced enough to detect that imbued monocle you're using, either, or is that another "probably" thing?

Thegn scowls at Caffiel. "Probably."

So the child and the boy got to the stairs. It stands to reason that they were headed for the lower part of the city. Any sign of them down there?

"Too slow, old rat. Already looking. Traces down there are faint. Bunch of interference in that area for some reason. But maybe—"

Through the monocle, Thegn sees a sudden burst of color emanating from a single building, like it's on fire with soul energy. It's in the lower part of the town, not far from the base of the stairway connecting the upper and lower parts.

"Well, that's unexpected."

Out the Out Door

"Pinny! Pin!"

Jack wakes up to Lyia's voice and her face looking down on him. Internally, he forgives her for using her juvenile nickname for him. She's beautiful. Always has been. Her dark hair hangs in a loose and unkempt ponytail over her shoulder, almost pointing to the perfectly tanned and smooth skin on her outstretched arm. Her open palm hovers just over the surface of his chest. It's warm, inviting, almost pulsing.

Wait.

Open palm. Jack is fully alert now. *She was going to kill me. Kill us.* He bolts upright and pushes Lyia's hand off him. He scoots backward until his back is up against a wall. "Shitshitshit! Not yet! Not yet!"

"Pinny, wait." Lyia stands and reaches toward him.

He flails his arms out, repeatedly batting hers away. "I ain't ready to die yet!"

He never sees it coming. There's a loud smacking sound and the side of his face is suddenly hot, and in pain. He turns his head back forward and it's no longer Lyia in front of him.

"Hey, idiot! Snap out of it." Corva is nose-to-nose with Jack. Her hands are on the sides of his shoulders, squeezing so he can't move.

"She's gonna kill us, Corva! An' I'm never gonna get a chance to tell her I love her!" He continues to helplessly flap his arms around despite the fact that she's pinning his elbows to his waist.

"Hey!" Corva pushes him back into the wall behind him, almost knocking his wind out. "Stop and think for a minute. You're swinging around like a crazy man. Haven't you noticed that you can do that without hurting now?"

Jack slows and looks down, noticing himself for the first time since waking. She's right. His stomach and chest don't hurt at all. His face, however, is a different story. Corva loosens her grip and he reaches up to his jaw. "So you thought I needed a new source of pain? Ow."

Corva grins and backs up. "You were being stupid." She grabs his hand and helps him stand. She leans in, whispering at a volume that anyone in the room can still hear. "Also, I still say she's way too old for you."

A rush of blood races to Jack's face as he feels it redden all over. His ears are immediately hot; Lyia must've heard everything he said. Corva steps out from between them and he sees her, Lyia, smiling at him. It's not the smile that he wants to see, though. Not the one that says she feels the same. It's a knowing smile, an annoying smile. He turns his head away just as she's about to speak.

"Zeke is doing better, too."

Jack's eyes widen as he spins around, looking for his little fur-covered friend. All feelings of embarrassment evaporate from his mind. "Zeke!"

He looks at the spot on the ground where Lyia had started healing the little monkey, but he's not there. He looks back up to Lyia, ready to ask where Zeke is. And just like before, it's not her face he sees. This time, it's Zeke's little primate face, flying right toward him. Zeke lands on Jack's chest. He grabs Jack's shirt and climbs up and around his back to his shoulder. Wrapping his tail around the back of Jack's neck, Zeke swings around, planting his feet in Jack's chest so they can look at each other face-to-face. Zeke's little monkey face wrinkles into a frown.

Corva takes a step closer. "He's pretty pissed at you. Says he was sitting on Lyia's shoulder the whole time and you never even noticed."

Zeke's frown disappears as he tilts his head, amused. Jack's ears start warming up again.

"Shut up. Dick." He changes his focus back to Corva. "But wait. Why was she—" He turns to Lyia. "Why were you healing me? I thought your plan was for us to die here."

"I, well. I just—"

"She had a change of heart, Pinny. Cute name, by the way. But we'll need to talk about all of this later. We've gotta get. You feeling okay?"

"Yeah … 'cept for the sting you gave me on the side of my face. I think I'll manage." Jack lets Zeke swing back around to a perch on his shoulder. "What's the plan?"

Lyia tips her head up to the ceiling, pointing with her chin. "The Red Light's safe room. There should be enough space for us in there."

Jack eyes Lyia skeptically. "You think ol' Maddy Shard is gonna let me in? She ain't exactly my biggest fan."

"She'll let you in."

Corva interrupts. "Alright. Plan's made. Lyia, what floor's the room on?"

"The first basement. It's the floor above us."

"That stairwell we came down, is that the fastest way up?"

"It's the only way up."

"Cool. I'll take the lead." She points at Lyia. "You stay close to me so they'll know to open the door when we get there. Jack, you trail behind us, outta sight until they open the door. No reason to give the lady of the house an excuse to be inhospitable." Without waiting for a response, Corva turns and heads up the steps to the door leading out of the sub-basement.

Jack looks to Lyia and shrugs. "It's as good a plan as any. After you."

She nods and follows behind Corva.

Climbing the stairs, Jack looks up. *At least the view is good.* The curves of Lyia's hips swing left and right as she takes each step up to the door. His hypnosis is cut short when he feels a sharp chop to the back of his head. "Ow!"

Lyia stops and turns back toward Jack, concerned. "Pin, you okay? Did I miss an injury?"

Jack's face flushes as he looks to Zeke, who is sitting on his shoulder, arms crossed. "No. Zeke was hopping around. I think he's just excited to see me."

"Hey down there! Shut it," Corva's hushed hiss turns everyone's attention to the door.

Jack looks to Zeke, mumbling, "Not cool, Zeke."

The little monkey simply stares back at him for a moment, like a disappointed parent, then turns his attention back upward to Corva as she silently eases the door open and peeks into the stairwell.

Almost immediately, she pulls the door shut and looks back down at Lyia. "You said that's the only way up?"

"Yeah, what's the matter?"

"Safe room isn't an option. That floor is crawling with grunts. Probably trying to break their way in to that room." She slides past them and bounds to the base of the stairs. "We don't have much time before their seekers sniff out the healing soulmancy you did and find their way down here. What've we got for weapons?"

They rush down the stairs. Lyia points at the boxes close to the wall. "Not much. Those boxes just have bottles of Pin's cornshine."

Corva turns to Jack. "You gotta light?"

Realizing what she wants to do, Jack's face drops. "Oh, dude, no. That's like five or six batches. That's a lotta damn work you're askin' to blaze up."

"You got paid for it, didn't you?"

"Yeah, course I did. That ain't the point. You're askin' me to burn art here."

"Oh, for fuck's sake." Lyia rushes over to Jack, reaches in his pocket, and pulls out his lighter. "You can make more. Besides," she walks over to the crates, shaking the lighter above her head, "I told you that you shouldn't be smoking anyway."

"Well, but, but what about the fire? Maddy ain't gonna like us burnin' down her business … 'specially with her in it."

Lyia looks back at Jack. "Maddy has a fire suppression system. Actually"—she hands the lighter over to Corva—"what good is this going to do? The fire might be big, but it won't last long. Best it'll do is have us go out in a literal blaze of glory."

Corva frowns at her. "What? No. For a healer, you're uncomfortably interested in dying. Break open a few more of these boxes." She tears the top off of one of the boxes, revealing the bottles of Jack's custom distillation packed between corn husks and bundles of long grass. She nods her head at the tiny tunnel she and Jack squeezed through to get in. "We go back the way we came. The fire will cover our tracks."

"Then what?" Lyia narrows her eyes, matching Corva's frown. "We'll be out in the open then."

"Better than dying down here." Corva rips open another box.

Lyia turns to Jack. "Pin?"

Jack looks from Lyia to Corva, and back to Lyia again. He can feel Zeke adjust on his shoulder.

"Shit." He steps up to the boxes and starts opening one. "But gimme my light back. If anyone's gonna burn my work, it's gonna be me."

Hardly pausing in her breakdown of the boxes, Corva tosses the lighter over. It sails a bit too high for Jack to reach, but Zeke leaps up and catches it, landing back on Jack's shoulder. Begrudgingly, Lyia steps in to help open more boxes.

As he opens another box, Jack continues talking. "Siege caves are no good. Even if they open the door for us, that only helps with the raid." He looks at Corva. "We still have Wrinkles to deal with."

Lyia's voice pipes up, "Alright, I'm going to guess you're not talking about getting old. Is this another one of your silly names, Pinny?"

"Oh, yeah." Jack pulls a bottle from his box and pops it open. They haven't told Lyia anything about Thegn. As he pours the contents of the bottle over the pile of open boxes he remembers Old Man V's reaction to hearing about their encounter with Death. Not exactly positive. "I'll explain when we're outta here."

Skepticism paints itself all over Lyia's face. "It sounds like there's going to be a lot of explaining later. Don't think I haven't noticed that leech rope you've got now."

There's no time for Jack to respond to Lyia's comment about his chembraid. The door at the top of the sub-basement swings open and a foot from one of the Umbrati grunts steps into view. Jack drops the bottle he'd been emptying and grabs two others along with a handful of the corn husk packing material. "Go!"

The girls make faces in protest, but Jack points at the hole in the wall. "Get goin'! I got this. You make sure it's safe where we get out."

Corva nods and grabs Lyia's wrist to lead her to the wall.

Jack walks over to the base of the stairs and hands the mass of corn husks to Zeke. "They better move fast. It's gonna get pretty hot in here. Squeezin' through is hard enough. Tryin' to do it while bein' cooked is gonna suck."

At the bottom of the stairs, he stops and looks up at the Umbrati grunt. It's a hideous thing, barely resembling the person it once was. Its skin has no shine, just a dead grayish green. It stands on two legs, but its arms are longer than normal arms, almost reaching the ground. Short talons extend from nails at each fingertip. Torn remnants of whatever this former person was wearing hang from its body. It has no eyes. There's a palm-length metal spike jammed in one eye socket. The other orbital is covered with scar tissue where it looks like the eye was clawed out. There's a steel plate riveted on the thing's face where its mouth is supposed to be. It sniffs the air and turns its head to better listen down into the room. The whole time, it makes a grunting sound, like it's constantly trying to clear its throat.

Not wasting any more time, Jack throws one of the bottles up toward the doorway. The grunt easily dodges the bottle, allowing it to shatter on the wall in the stairwell behind it. Jack's cornshine rolls down the wall and puddles on the floor around broken shards of glass as well as the grunt's feet.

Not waiting to see the grunt's reaction, Jack kneels down and opens his second bottle. "Zeke! Husks."

He takes the packing material from Zeke and jams as much of it into the top of the bottle as he can. Pulling out his lighter, he looks back up. The grunt is already almost on top of him and there's a second one showing in the doorway. Zeke jumps free of Jack's shoulder just as the closest grunt reaches out with a single arm. The thing's hand spreads across Jack's entire chest and pushes forward, pinning him to the ground.

Jack struggles to move but with every buck and twist, it feels like the grunt locks him tighter to the ground. He flips the spark on his lighter and holds the flame to the grunt's arm. There's a sick smell of searing flesh, but the grunt doesn't give any indication that it's in pain. It just lifts its other arm, ready to strike. Jack exhales and relaxes. *At least it's just death.*

He doesn't even get the chance to fully complete the thought before he sees Zeke bolt by his head. The little monkey shoots up along the grunt's arm and leaps at its face, using both of his paws to grab hold of the spike stuck in its eye socket. With a lot less effort than should be necessary for a little creature Zeke's size, he extracts the spike in a single tug. Zeke wastes no energy in his fluid movements. He uses the momentum from that tug to spin around to the back of the grunt's head, stabbing the spike into the base of its skull.

Jack feels the muscles in the grunt's hand stiffen and then immediately slacken the moment he hears a pop from Zeke pulling the spike's head to the side, breaking the grunt's neck and severing its spinal column. Off-balance, the corpse of the thing releases its grip and slumps over sideways. Zeke leaps free and lands lightly on Jack's chest as the grunt's body hits the ground.

There's no time for Jack to act surprised. Zeke points to the bottle of cornshine in Jack's hand and then points at the second grunt, now fully visible in the doorway at the top of the stairs. Jack nods and squirms up to his feet as quickly as he can. Zeke climbs back to his shoulder perch. Pulling the lighter, Jack sparks a new flame and ignites the length of packing husks protruding from the bottle's top.

Jack pauses a moment. *This would be a perfect time to say something cool.* He looks up the stairs and sees the second grunt about to jump its way down. *Nope.* "No time."

He hurls his flaming makeshift cornshine grenade up past the second grunt and through the doorway where the alcohol from the first bottle has formed a nice puddle. The flaming bottle shatters against the wall with a satisfying crash followed by a bassy *whoomp* as the entire doorway—including the second grunt—bursts into flame.

"That should hold 'em for a second." Jack turns away and heads to the tunnel opening. Both Corva and Lyia have already wiggled their way in. Zeke jumps from his shoulder and dives into the tunnel as Jack dashes around the pile, opening bottles and lighting bits of packing material. He pockets his lighter and grabs one of the boxes that hasn't quite caught on fire. As he backs his way into the tunnel, he pulls the box over the tunnel opening. *With any luck, the charred bits from this will cover our way out.*

Backward, he squirms away from Maddy Shard's Red Light, mostly the same way he's done many times in the past.

5.14

Through Lower Bule

Corva hands Jack's backpack to Lyia. "Hold on to this. We'll need to book as soon as he's through." She makes a quick assessment of Lyia's clothes. The woman is basically just wearing bed clothes, nothing particularly well-suited for traveling. She doesn't even have shoes on. "If you're sticking with us, we'll have to find a way to get you some travel clothes and gear on the way."

Lyia takes the bag from Corva, but doesn't do anything with it. She just holds it. "Wait, what? 'On the way'? On the way where?"

Slinging the straps of her own backpack on her shoulders, Corva wonders just how much she should be sharing about her situation. Advice from Avó echoes in her mind. *Tread slowly.* "The bar's trashed. Again. And it's not really safe here for Jack anymore. For either of us, really." She walks over to the tunnel exit, waiting for Jack to come out.

"Is someone after Jack?" Lyia walks after her, bag still in her hands.

"Not Jack."

"After you?" Corva watches as Lyia tries to make sense of the cryptic answers she's getting.

"Not exactly. It's … complicated. You gathered that much when you healed Zeke. Put the bag on."

Lyia drops the bag and grabs Corva's arm. "No. You need to tell me what's—"

"Did you guys see that?" Jack's excited face pokes out of the tunnel. He worms his way out of the hole, talking the whole time. "It was totally sweet. That grunt was a giant ball of fire. Boom! And Zeke!" He turns his head over to Zeke, who is patiently standing and waiting for Jack to get out. "Oh man, Zeke. You little flippy, jumpy badass! He did some real damage to that first one." Jack pulls himself out and slaps the dirt and dust from his clothes. "With any luck, we slowed them from followin' us at least. Bought us some time. Oh, hey, my bag. Thanks!" He grabs his pack from the ground near Lyia and pulls the straps over his shoulders. "We ready? We just gotta make it over to the—"

Jack's voice trails off as he finally looks up and sees the stand-off between Corva and Lyia. "What's going on?"

"Girlie here says that you guys are skipping town. This raid is here because of her, isn't it?"

Jack takes the briefest of moments to glance over at Corva before answering, "Nah. They ain't after her. Well, they weren't, anyway." He shakes his head. "But that ain't important right now. Right now we gotta get safe. We can explain the rest then."

Lyia takes a step forward. "Where's safe? We just torched the Red Light. You've nixed the siege caves for some unknown reason. What else is there?"

Jack turns toward the far end of Lower Bule. "We'll go to Slim's. He's got a bunch of tech for protection and his building is dug right into the cliff wall. There's even a way to get down to Cliff City from there if we need some shielding for doing fixins. Though that way is a bit, um, me-sized." Corva watches Jack's eyes work their way up Lyia's profile. "Might be a bit of a tight fit for you."

Now it's Corva's turn to be surprised. "Slim's place? That crazy guy who made your stupid psionic paranizers or whatever? That's your plan?"

Jack's eyes narrow. "Subsonic paralyzers. They sure as shit saved your hide earlier. And yes. Slim's is a safe place for Lyia and a good route for us getting out of here."

Corva is about to continue her argument, but she's interrupted by Lyia. "So you are leaving? I don't believe it. You fought so hard to keep that bar. Jackspin, you need to tell me what's going on, right now. If I'm going to risk living, I need to know why."

Jackspin? That's his full name?

The kid looks at Corva with a half-hearted shrug and then turns to address Lyia. "Alright, I'll give you the short version, but it's gonna raise more questions we ain't got time for and I ain't sure I've actually got the answers to. You gotta promise me that you'll hold your new questions until we're safe."

Lyia, still looking confused, gives her own shrug. "Yeah. Fine."

That's all the prompting Jack needs. Words spill out of his mouth like a waterfall. "The horde ain't here for Corva. I figure that they're here after the ol' wrinkly fuck who showed at my bar with imbued tech. He was after Corva. Turns out, he's Death. But I call him Wrinkles."

With that, Jack starts walking down the narrow alley between buildings, away from the tunnel that leads to the Red Light. Zeke jumps up to a perch on his shoulder.

"Death?" Lyia swings her face toward Corva. "Like Death, Death? You're being hunted by the last of the Four?"

Inwardly, Corva groans. *Jack. Você é idiota. What dumb thing are you going to say next?* Deciding it's best not to answer at this point, she starts following Jack.

Lyia walks past Corva and grabs Jack by the arm to stop him. "And you let her stay at your bar? Are you stupid? Why is he after her?"

"Hey, I didn't know. You didn't either when you helped me patch her up. 'Sides, it's cool now. I knocked him out with—" Apparently Jack is having trouble telling Lyia that he knows how to use the Touch. "Well, I knocked him out."

Smooth. Moron.

"Anyhow, point is he ran off. We're clear of that for now." He shrugs, strangely aloof, and continues his hike down the path. "In any case, between what we did back at Maddy's and the fact that now that we're out in the open, the Goats're after all of us. We need to gitfo, like, now. 'Specially before any of 'em see us."

Lyia, still sorting through everything Jack's said, looks back to Corva. Not sure what exactly she could say or do at this point, Corva merely claps her hands together once like she's closing a book and then walks after Jack. She hears Lyia's footsteps trail close behind them. A little farther back, she thinks she can hear the Umbrati grunts working their way through the lower burg. As she catches up to Jack, she looks over to Zeke, still sitting on his shoulder.

The monkey points his face toward Jack. **You need to tell him to pick up the pace. Grunts from the horde will track the residual energy of soulmancy. Both he and Lyia used it, so our little group here is a lighthouse in the night.**

She's not sure what a lighthouse is, but she gets the point. She turns her attention to Jack. "Hey Jack, how far away is Slim's? We need to get to it pretty quick."

"It ain't far. Normally it don't take but a few minutes. However—" He takes a turn that doubles back the way they came, but down a different alley. "We've gotta take a few detours to get there."

Jack then takes a few more turns that zigzag their way between buildings and puts them in a direction that Corva *thinks* is perpendicular to the direction they should be going. A few steps in, he grabs a ladder that looks like it leads up to a terrace created by a series of adjoining buildings.

Corva exchanges a look with Zeke before she decides she's had enough. She grabs his hand before he starts climbing up the ladder. "Listen to me. The horde is going to track us all. There was a whole lot of soul energy used in that basement."

He stops and looks back at her. "You think I don't know that? I ain't totally stupid. Why do you think we're takin' so many turns and doublin' back on our route? Gotta let some of that juice wear off a bit. Otherwise, we're gonna lead the Goats right to Slim's place and anywhere we go after." He jerks his hand away and resumes his climb.

Corva stops, surprised and momentarily impressed with Jack's forethought. *Zeke hadn't even thought of that.* She lets Lyia up the ladder ahead of her.

Climbing the ladder, Lyia calls up to Jack, "How do you know how fast the trail dissipates?"

Reaching the top, he turns around and reaches out to help her up the last couple rungs. "I don't. But even if it doesn't wear away completely, takin' a crazy path like this will hopefully slow 'em down a bit ... so long as they don't sniff us out first. So keep your head on a swivel." When Corva gets all the way up to the terrace, he turns and keeps going, now at a light jog.

From this place up on the terrace, Corva tries to look out over Lower Bule and see what kind of progress the raid party has made in following them. The Red Light isn't all that far away. A little, barely perceptible wisp of smoke curls in the air nearby. It's kind of eerie how quiet Bule is. Normally at this time of day, it's a bustling little town with mercs and travelers weaving through the paths and stairs, stopping in various shops to do business, get some R and R, and restock for the next leg of whatever their trip is.

Now it's different. There's still movement in the paths and alleys, but the flow is distinctly away from the stairs connecting to Upper Bule. Aside from the three of them, the only people not following that pattern are a handful of folks that look like they're in Harris's militia. They're either standing in place, guiding folks to the nearest siege cave, or they're running against the flow, armed to hold back the raiding horde.

They're not going to have it easy. Upper Bule looks to be completely overrun. The Umbrati swarmed that section of town and now teams of grunts pour their way down and over the steps between Upper and Lower Bule. It's a terrifying sight, but there's hardly any sound. Every now and again, she thinks she can hear the creepy throat-clearing noise that the grunts make, but it's tough to tell if that's just her mind being paranoid.

She turns to catch up to Jack and Lyia, allowing herself a moment to look out into the canyon. It's an impressive view. In a different context, this place could almost be beautiful. Then, just as she's about to return her full attention to the other two, she catches a glimpse of something in her periphery. She turns to get a better view, but finds herself looking into the sun. Raising her arm to shield her eyes, she thinks she can *just* make out a dark shape cutting in front of it.

"Corva! C'mon. We have a lead, but them grunts move faster than—shit!"

Corva turns just in time to see a pair of Umbrati grunts blocking Jack and Lyia's way across the rooftops. She rushes up to their side. "Where did they come from?"

"I dunno. I don't think they were followin' from the Red Light. Maybe they were a search group starting on this side of town." He looks to his side. "Shit, there's more."

Two more grunts climb up to the rooftop on their side. Corva looks back toward the ladder that they came up just as one more pair of grunts crest the edge of the building there. "And behind us."

The trio turns, defensively putting their backs up against one another.

Lyia looks over her shoulder and down at Corva. "Doesn't matter now, anyway. It's six to three. We're done."

Zeke hops from Jack's shoulder to Corva's. **It's six to four. Do you trust me?**

Corva glances over to Zeke. "Yeah. Well enough, I guess."

"What?" Confusion knits across Lyia's face.

Jack interrupts, "Oh yeah. That's one more thing we need to talk about when bringing you up to speed later. Apparently Corva here can talk to Zeke."

Corva ignores Jack's statement and the continued escalation of Lyia's perplexity. Instead, she focuses on the words coming through her own inner voice, words coming from the little monkey on her shoulder.

Nodding in understanding, she closes her eyes. "We're not done. But you guys probably won't like this very much."

5.15

REMOTE CONTROL

"What is that s'posed to mean?"

Jack barely gets the words out before he feels himself sliding his backpack off and rushing headlong toward the two Umbrati grunts closest to him. Like the one that Zeke took out back at the Red Light, these two have the same extended arms and pale green-gray skin. But they're not uniform. They each still wear whatever clothing they were wearing when brought into the horde. Well, what remains of that clothing at least. The tattered scraps that remain aren't covering very much.

Also, their faces are certainly unique from one another. Jack had heard all the stories from the nomads and mercs who came through his bar. Apparently grunts are given a choice as to the specific technique they use for removing their own eyes. Further, they fabricate their own faceplates before they're riveted on.

As for the two he's currently running toward—weaponless and without any control over himself, by the way—one of them apparently stitched its own eyes shut with some kind of thread, poorly. At the end of its right arm, this grunt has a large spiked ball where its hand is supposed to be. As for the other grunt, it's difficult to tell what it did to its eyes. That grunt's entire face is almost totally covered with a steel plate. There's just a single vertical cut starting at the top and going about halfway down, allowing just enough room for its nose to stick out.

Jack tries to stop himself from rushing the grunts, but his body doesn't respond to him at all. He wants to turn his head, or even his eyes, to see what Lyia and Corva are doing, but he can't.

Is this some Goat thing I never heard of? Do they mind control you to capture you?

His vision is focused solely on the two grunts ahead of him. He feels his hands curl open and close, squeezing into fists and then relaxing back to open hands, like they're testing themselves out for the first time. His shoulders roll forward as he feels himself tuck his head down, protecting his neck.

Wait. Am I gonna fight them?

When he gets within a step or two of the grunts, his body jukes to the right so the two monstrosities are no longer facing him side-by-side, but instead now the eye-stitched grunt is standing in front of the one with a nosehole in its faceplate. Stitches swings down at Jack with its spiked-ball arm. At the same time, Nosehole steps out of line, trying to square up to Jack and cut off his path.

Jack's body dodges the spiked ball by continuing his move to the right. He expects to hear the ball collide with the ground where he just was, but in the corner of his eye, he sees that Stitches has redirected its spiked-ball arm, mid-swing, right at Jack's head. *Shit!*

Jack feels his body bend at the waist, slipping under the ball arm. His hands reach up to the arm and give it a push, adding enough momentum to its swing to bury the spiked ball right in Nosehole's chest. Thick blood bursts around the ball as if it'd just crushed a bag full of dark red paint.

Before he can fully register what he's done, Jack's palms come together, elbows high, and he steps farther into Stitches, slamming the point of his left elbow into the grunt's ribs. He can hear a pop and feels at least one of those ribs snap.

Stitches leans over from the strike, wordlessly grunting right near Jack's ears. Jack's hands reach up, burying fingertips on either side of the grunt's neck.

No way. No way!

Jack's fingers push deeper and deeper. He's not sure if he's grabbing muscle or the thing's throat, but it's a lot softer than he expects. His nails start penetrating skin and he feels a bit of blood trickle along the back of his hand. Then, suddenly, his thumbs jam right into the center of Stitches' throat and Jack feels himself pull downward with as much force as his little body can muster. Whatever it is that Jack's got gripped in his hands comes down with him, torn right from the grunt's neck. It's still connected, just torn and stretched like a bad loop in a knit scarf. All the same, blood sprays all over the back of Jack's head.

Jack tries to make sense of what just happened as his feet pull the rest of him away. Behind him, he can hear Stitches slacken and collapse. The grunt's carcass knocks over Nosehole's equally limp body. Jack's body doesn't move after that. He just stands there. It's not that he really wants to move at this point. He just can't, not even his eyes.

A moment later, he feels his weight shift to a standing position he's more accustomed to. He's not sure why, but he thinks he somehow has control over himself again. *Fingers, toes.*

He looks down at his hands. They're covered in blood. Bits of flesh and meat are still caught under his nails. The longer he looks at them, the more it seems that they start to shake. They won't stop shaking. He reaches up to the back of his head and feels around. He can't tell how much of the blood he feels was already there and how much he's just smearing around from his hand.

He turns to look at the two dead grunts and tries to piece together how exactly he did that. Was it even him? It felt like he did it, but there was an overwhelming feeling of being a passenger in his own body.

Seeing the Umbrati corpses in front of him, he remembers that they aren't the only ones that had surrounded them. He spins to look back where he came from, searching for signs of Lyia and Corva. He sees Lyia near two of her own grunts. They lay on the dirty rooftop, completely inert. She's bent over on her hands and knees. It looks like she's convulsing.

"Lyia!"

Jack runs to her side, sliding to a stop when he realizes that she's not convulsing. Not really, anyway. Her body is shaking, but it's because she's vomiting, almost uncontrollably. Aside from that, she appears to be relatively unharmed, certainly faring better than the dispatched grunts on the ground next to her.

It seems that somehow the two grunts managed to get their hands shoved into each other's faces. One has a hand plunged into the other's temple, buried all the way to the last knuckles. The other has a hand jammed upward through the bottom of its chin. It lays with its face toward Jack, empty eye sockets staring into space.

Swallowing back his own immediate gag reflex at the sight, Jack waits for a moment between heaves and puts his hand on Lyia's shoulder. "Hey. Are you okay?"

Lyia looks at Jack's blood-covered hand on her shoulder and flinches. She appears to contain a scream, but at the same time she pulls herself away from his grip, leaving a smear of blood on her shirt and arm.

Realizing that he probably looks like a nightmare soaked in grunt blood, Jack hastily wipes his hands on his pants, trying to get them as clean as possible. He squats down to look at her eye to eye. "Hey. Hey!" He grabs her by the shoulders. "It's me. You're okay. Take a breath."

Recognition spreads over Lyia's face as she pulls free of him again and sits upright. "What the fuck was that?"

It's Corva's voice that sounds behind them. "I told you guys that you probably weren't going to like it."

Jack and Lyia spin to see Corva walking toward them, Zeke seated on her shoulder. It looks like she never even took her pack off. Jack peeks past her at the last pair of grunts in the team that had them surrounded. They lie on the rooftop in what looks like a disorganized pile of surplus body parts. There's not a mark on her. Not even blood from her opponents.

She tosses Jack's bag at the ground in front of him. "Here. Let's get rolling." She looks back and forth between the completely slack-jawed expressions on Jack and Lyia's faces. "Look, I'll explain as best as I can along the way, but we can't stay here. We've gotta keep moving."

Jack doesn't move. "Wait. That was you? You did that to us?"

"It was Zeke's idea. I didn't even know I could do that. But yeah. It was me. Now come on."

"Or what? You'll just make us?" Lyia's voice cuts through the air, almost shrill.

Corva rushes a couple steps forward and gets right in Lyia's face. "Look here, sua puta. I'm sorry for saving you. I'm also tired of saving you. Tired of you being an ungrateful little bitch … especially now that I know where you're from. You're welcome to stay up here and die if you want. Seems to be the only solution you ever come up with. Me? I'm living." She stands back up and looks over to Jack. "And you're coming with me."

Caught in the middle of picking up his pack, Jack looks up at Corva. "I—I am?"

"You're the only one who knows the way down to Cliff City from Slim's place. Zeke says even he doesn't know the way you're talking about. Also says he won't leave without you."

Jack straightens, bag in hand. "Well, I ain't goin' nowhere without Lyia. So—" He feels a hand on his shoulder.

"It's okay, Pin. She's right. We can't stay up here." Lyia looks over to Corva. "I don't know what you are. I don't care. If you talk to me like that again, though, I'll end you."

"Lyia, no." Standing between Lyia and Corva, Jack can feel the tension mounting between the two.

"No, that's fine. I'm alright with that." Corva turns to leave. "Now let's go."

Jack jogs up to Corva while Lyia follows behind them. "Right. Slim's building is right over there. We can drop in through the roof. I'll grab what we need. Then on to Cliff City."

"Right. What in the world are you getting from him, anyway?"

They barely take three more steps in the direction of Slim's building before a large dark form drops from the sky, blocking their path. The figure stands from his landing position, regarding the group. The hood of his cloak shadows most of his bearded face, but it's not hard to guess at who this is. The black wings, the giant scythe held in a bloody hand, and the albino rat peeking over his back give it away.

Thegn is back.

Jack's chin drops to his chest and his shoulders slump as he lets out an exasperated sigh. "Really?"

Thegn's attention is entirely on Corva. "I was almost worried that those things were going to dispatch you before I could."

His giant wings fold behind him as he takes a step forward. "Now we can do this properly."

FILM
SEASON ONE
J.J. VEGA
EPISODE SIX:
FAILURE TO GITFO

Episode Six: Failure to Gitfo

Contents

DEATH FROM ABOVE

Jack edges his foot backward. No way he wants to throw down with—or, more accurately, get thrown down by—Thegn again. And neither should Corva. She came out on top last time, but last time Thegn didn't have wings. With the open space out here and hundreds of grunts from the Umbrati horde spilling down into Lower Bule, the odds are more stacked against them than before.

Looking at her posture, though, Jack isn't so sure that Corva realizes this. He shifts his attention to her shoulder, where Zeke crouches. The monkey is holding on like he's bracing himself.

Corva turns her head and looks back to Jack and Lyia. Her voice is only a step above a whisper. "The second he steps clear, you two run by him as fast as you can."

He catches Lyia giving a single silent nod in affirmation.

Jack looks back to Corva. "But—"

He stops himself, interrupted by the sight of Thegn looming right over them. *Wasn't he just on the other end of this rooftop?* Smiling through the rot and decay in his teeth, Thegn swings his scythe at

Corva. She takes a step forward and grabs the shaft of the scythe with both of her hands, stopping it with a hard snap.

The moment her grip sets, the smile on the old man's face widens. Jack flinches at the sight. It's almost unnatural how wide it is. It distracts Jack so much that he almost doesn't notice Thegn's wings stretching open.

From Corva's shoulder, Zeke gets a fraction of a second to gesture with his head that Jack and Lyia should go now. A moment later, Thegn shoots upward with Corva still holding onto the scythe. Jack lifts his backpack to block the dust and sand kicked up by the force of those enormous wings beating the air. He looks up and catches a view of their silhouettes as they get smaller and smaller.

Turning his head back down, he sees Lyia already ten steps in front of him, bolting to Slim's rooftop at a full sprint.

Jack hesitates, but resists the urge to look back skyward to see what's happening. *Shit. Can't help her like this anyhow.* He slings his go-bag over his shoulder and chases after Lyia.

6.2

Corva

"Don't pass out yet, little girl. You still need to tell me where your stash is."

It was the first active burg Corva had found since escaping Fareburne and she'd royally messed up.

She thought she was ready. She'd done everything Avó had told her to. Her bag was stowed just outside of town. She'd pulled out just enough seed to trade for food and supplies. Any markings that said where she was from were hidden. Still, it wasn't enough. Corva didn't know anything about haggling. About looking people in the eye. About how showing the slightest hint of weakness would paint a target on you. She was not at all ready.

But there she was, pressed against a wall and held off the ground by her throat. A scruffy street kid had his forearm pressed against her while his buddies egged him on. Even now, she can still smell his nasty breath. Feel the grime that covered his skin. Hear his raspy voice push across his chapped lips. He was only a handful of years older than Corva, just into his teens. But at that age, a few years makes all the difference. They were all bigger than her. Stronger. Faster.

They'd caught Corva's scent the moment she'd stepped foot into town. Knew she was an outsider. Knew she was alone. That was before Corva had figured out that she had to make up a story about how she got to a town and why she didn't have anyone with her. "Mamãe is hurt and Papai sent me to town to get her food and medicine." "Our caravan is headed north and they let me come in and trade for provisions; they're watching from over there to make sure I do it right." Or sometimes she'd try to blend in with a group as they came into town.

This was before all of that, though. They pegged Corva as a mark and came after her the moment she made her first trade in the bazaar. Dragged her to an alley, took everything she had on her, and wanted more.

Her clothes were torn. Her nose bloody. Corva had tried to fight back, to resist, but the girl had never been much of a fighter. Running, evasion, hiding; those had always been her strongest skills. But those skills were worthless here. She was trapped. Outmatched, outnumbered, and out of options. Even if Corva told those kids what they wanted, they were going to beat her down for their own enjoyment, perhaps even worse. She could see it in their eyes. There were gangs like this back in Fareburne, but she'd always been shielded from them. Protected by Avó.

But the old woman wasn't with Corva anymore.

Blood from Corva's nose trickled down to her mouth. She could taste it. Salty. Metallic. Warm. Breathing was hard with that boy's arm against her neck. Tears blurred her vision as she tried to look at him.

Corva tried to speak, but there wasn't enough air. Choking sounds came out instead of words.

"What's that?" The kid grinned, toothy and malicious. He reduced the pressure on Corva's throat enough to let her slide down the wall, but only enough that her toes touched the ground. Only enough to let her talk.

The words came out strained. Hardly a whisper. "Outside of town. Half a klick. South entrance."

He pressed his arm against her harder. "You think we're stupid? You came in from the east."

With his free hand, he delivered a punch to her stomach. Punishment. It didn't matter that she was telling the truth. That she'd been extra careful and skirted the edge of town to come in from a different direction than the one she'd traveled from. It didn't matter at all. They didn't want to believe. Corva gasped for air, and spit and blood flew out of her mouth. It landed on his face.

One of the kid's friends piped up, "Aw, gross, Puck! She spit on you! You gonna take that dis?"

"Fuck no!"

Helpless, Corva looked up at the kid holding her, the one named Puck. Corva still couldn't breathe, couldn't speak. Couldn't even apologize or explain it wasn't on purpose. Tears streamed down her cheeks as she looked at the faces of each kid in the gang, pleading with her eyes to show some mercy, to let her go.

They responded with jeers and laughter.

Puck took the pressure off Corva's throat, but before her heels could fully touch the ground, he swept his leg and kicked her feet out from beneath her. She fell to the ground sideways and landed with a thud. Coughing and sputtering, she tried to get back to her feet.

Out of the corner of her eye, Corva saw a foot swinging at her head. Reflexively, she pulled her arms in to block, to shield her face and protect herself from any more pain. And it worked! The foot connected with her forearms. It hurt awfully bad, but it was better than taking a boot in the jaw. She should've known better. She should've stayed down.

A stab of pain cut across her body as a different foot connected with her ribs. Could've been delivered by Puck. Could've been anyone. It didn't really matter. It was the first of many, and it had to be from all of them. The kicks just came too fast. No rhythm or pattern. Just fury piled on top of anger.

Somewhere in the distance there was a voice. A woman. Corva didn't know if the voice was muffled by the sound of her sobs or the thumping of feet against her body, but it was soft. But Corva heard the woman clearly. It was only one word. "Pathetic."

Corva wanted to look up, to see where the woman was. To ask her what her problem was. To find out why she couldn't help. But Corva couldn't. The kicks kept coming. Even with her arms over her head, dirt and dust flew into Corva's eyes, stinging them shut.

Her eyes were closed, but she could see lights flash every time a kick landed. Even still, she could feel darkness encroaching. She was becoming delirious. She was about to pass out. The laughter and insults from the gang beating her faded away. Corva was even becoming deaf to her own sobbing. She heard nothing. She felt nothing. She was nothing. This was the end of her.

Then the woman spoke again.

"Fine."

Corva can't remember what happened after that. She just knows that she didn't die. She woke in a daze. Groggy. But not really hurting, not like she should've been. She looked at her hands. They were covered in blood, a lot more blood than what would be generated by the cuts and scrapes on her arms. Corva reached for her face, her head. More blood. She was covered in the stuff. *Just how long did they beat me?* In a panic, she started running her hands all over her body. If she was bleeding that much, she needed to find the source and stop it. Prevent herself from losing any more before it was too late.

Corva had some cuts and scrapes and a couple tender spots, but there was no open wound gushing blood. No lacerated artery spraying the walls of the alleyway. She braced her hand against the ground to try to stand. But the ground was wet, just as blood covered as she was. Her hand slipped and she fell over into something that wasn't the ground. Something that squished.

It was then that she noticed them. Or what was left of them. It was a tangle of limbs. Wet. Cold. Lifeless.

Episode Six: Failure to Gitfo

Corva screamed and scrambled back to the alley wall, slipping and flopping like a freshly caught fish. She hugged the wall as if it could somehow protect her, as if that sloppy mass of bodies would somehow come to life and come after her. They wouldn't. She knew that much. Not just from looking at them. She knew in her core that they would never come back.

And in a corner of her mind, Corva heard the woman's voice again. Soft. Distant. Fading into nothingness as if she were never there.

"You're welcome."

376

Let Go

Concentrate!

Corva forces her eyes open against the air rushing by her. Even before she gets them all the way open, she can hear the Old Beard's raspy laugh. She sees him looking down at her. The rat, Caffiel, peeks over Thegn's shoulder at her. She can feel Zeke clinging to her back, his paws clenched to the shoulder strap of her pack as well as her shirt.

"Still haven't broken your sigil, it seems. Pathetic. You used to control legions."

Corva hazards a glance below them. At this distance below her dangling feet, Bule looks more like a child's diorama than a functional canyonside town. Umbrati grunts spread over Upper Bule like a swarm of ants. A mass of them work their way through Lower Bule, following Jack's disorganized path and converging on the rooftop Thegn had just pulled her from.

The sheer number of Umbrati in the town is disturbing enough, but the accuracy of their tracking feeds a feeling of despair in the pit of her stomach. There are pockets of resistance here and there. Gunfire echoes across the canyon as Bule's militia tries to hold back the wave and protect the siege caves. Most of those pockets look like they're getting overwhelmed, though. *No way Jack and Lyia can outrun that. Definitely can't fight them off.*

Thegn lifts his scythe, pulling Corva closer to the putrid folds of skin in his face. "Your friend, the kid with my mark, I'm really hoping he stays alive a bit longer. I have a whole bunch of questions for him and it would be an incredible waste if the horde got to him first. They don't hold soulmancers in quite the same esteem as the hive. Probably will just turn him into a seeker."

Let go of the scythe.

"What?" She feels Zeke's grip tighten, but looking up at Caffiel, she can't tell which one is speaking to her in her mind.

"I see your manners haven't improved, either." Thegn doesn't give her the chance to explain that she wasn't talking to him. He spins them into a short dive.

Corva's feet start to swing forward from the shift in momentum, pulling the rest of her body right into his knee as his wings beat downward, swooping them back into an ascent. The blow forces the air from her lungs and spit from her mouth. It feels like everything in her chest has been crushed against the back of her teeth. Her left hand loses its grip on the scythe. Below her, the ground spins as they spiral farther upward.

Corva! Let go. You can't win up here. Not yet.

Her eyes widen. *It's Zeke.* Immediately, she lets go with her remaining hand and allows herself to fall.

Little monkey, you better tell me how exactly I'm supposed to land.

6.4

What's the Plan?

Jack catches up with Lyia at the rooftop entrance to Slim's building.

She turns to him. "Where to from here?"

"Slim's place is on the top floor, so we just need to go one level down." He slips the second strap of his pack on so it more comfortably fits at the center of his back.

"Not Slim's! I know where that is. I want to know about the place that you're planning on hiding out. This 'Cliff City' you keep talking about. Where's that?"

He doesn't answer. Instead, he looks at his hands. The blood he wasn't able to wipe off has already started drying and staining his skin with brown spots. "We gotta get to Slim."

"Forget Slim! We've gotta get out of here! Wait." Lyia stops and her brows knit together in a scowl at Jack. "Slim's there?"

"I'm sure he is. You know he's never left his shop for a raid. 'Sides, if he weren't there, we'd never be able to get in. Dude's place is locked down good n' tight." Jack swings open the rooftop entrance door. "Now c'mon. Let's go."

He turns back to Lyia, catching a moment of hesitation in her step before finally stepping through the entrance. Before closing the door behind them, Jack takes a quick moment to search the sky. It's tough to tell where Corva and that old bearded bag of skin have gone off to. However, there's an unmistakable sound of Umbrati foot soldiers and their distinctive throat-clearing coughs. A lot of them. And they're close.

GROUNDWARD

Air screams past Corva's ears as she plummets back to the ground. She splays out her arms and legs, trying to slow down and control her descent.

No. Pull back in. You need to dive faster.

Is he trying to get me killed? She looks to her shoulder, but can't see Zeke. She knows he's there, though. She can feel his little forepaws gripping on with all the strength they can muster. She tries to yell out at him, ask him why, but the wind either tears the words from her mouth or shoves them back into her face each time she tries. *No use. How in the world am I going to talk to him?*

To her side, she catches sight of a thin black bar shoot by her. *The scythe!* She reaches out to grab it, not wanting Thegn to have an angle to take a swipe at her with it.

Don't touch it! It'll pull him here!

It's too late. The moment she grabs the scythe, Thegn is right there, his broken grin showing through the loose skin flapping on his face. He wraps his long, spindly fingers around her hand and clamps down so she can't let go again. A network of callouses grate the back of her hand like coarse sand. She tries to pull free, but he's locked in.

Thegn's wings beat down, driving them upward again. As her body swings downward, he raises his knee again, trying to deliver another blow to her ribs.

This time, though, she bends her elbows, pulling her body up and preventing it from swinging as low as it had previously. Now, rather than connecting with her ribs again, the top of Thegn's knee only finds the point of her elbow. She can feel the muscles and connective tissue above his knee split at the point of impact. Thegn doesn't make a sound, though. Not one that she can hear, at least. She chances a moment to look up at his face.

He's still looking at her. Still smiling.

He changes direction again, spinning hard toward one side while twisting his scythe the opposite way. Corva is caught off guard, and she pays for it by receiving a knee to her kidney and an elbow across the side of her head, just above the temple. Her vision blurs and gets dark around the edges. Her arms straighten and she feels her grip slacken on the scythe.

She shakes her head and blinks, struggling to avoid blacking out.

Corva, you've got to free your hand. We've got to get back to the ground.

Her head swims, but she reactively nods to Zeke's words in her mind. Thegn's hold of her hand on his scythe tightens as he changes direction again. This time, though, she manages to swing her body with the turn, adding enough momentum for her to swing her legs around and plant her feet flat on his chest.

She pushes with her legs as hard as she can, kicking Thegn upward and freeing her hand from his grip. Roughly aiming her body toward Bule, she straightens her legs, points her toes, and brings her arms tightly against her sides. Wind screams by and the air beats her face, forcing tears to her eyes as she bullets groundward. She feels a tug on her dreadlocks. Four small paws climb from behind her shoulder to the back of her head. One of them reaches around and touches her on the forehead.

Corva flinches, remembering how utterly incapacitated Zeke had left her the last time he put his paw on her forehead.

Don't.

Zeke spreads the fingers of his paw, flattening his palm against the center of her brow. She feels a warm sensation tingle its way over the surface of her skin, despite the coolness of the air rushing by.

Close your eyes.

6.6

SLIM

"Slim, man! Let us in! It's me." Jack beats on the reinforced door to Slim's place. Actually, calling it a mere "place" doesn't quite do it justice. Slim's building is nestled down in the corner of Lower Bule, one of the only buildings that has two of its sides touching the canyon walls. In fact, Slim had expanded his available space by digging away at the rock. At this point, a greater percentage of his floorspace is burrowed into the cliff than within the building. With the heavy reinforced door at the entrance, it's probably the most secure location in all of Bule, second only to the siege caves.

Of course, none of it does Jack any good if he's on the wrong side of that door.

Jack stops hammering on the door with the bottoms of his hands and kicks it in frustration. He steps over to the comm box and jams his thumb on the talk button. "Dammit, Slim. I know you're in there. We're mid-raid here. You just gonna sit in there an' let me get got?"

"Pin. He's not here. We should just get going."

Jack turns his head back to Lyia. "Naw. He's here. He's just—"

There's a scratching sound on the comm box, like the person on the other end suddenly made the decision to take up juggling radio gear as a hobby. "Lee—Lyia? Is that you, babe?"

Jack looks at the comm box and pulls his thumb from the talk button, frowning. He eyes Lyia. "Babe?"

Lyia doesn't respond, doesn't even really look at him. There's no chance to prod further, though. A heavy *chunk* sounds on the other side of Slim's door before it slowly cracks open. Through the breach, a wiry tendril sticks through and regards Jack and Lyia through the glass hemisphere at its tip.

Jack puts his hand over the lens and shoves his way in through the door. "Cut it out, Slim. You know it's us."

The tendril retracts to its coiled base mounted over the door. The room is dark. The sliver of light from the partially open front door is the small room's only illumination. Jack's shin collides with the corner of some large block of something. "Fffffuuuh! What in the world is that?"

At the back of the room, a door slides open. Bright light pours around the silhouette of a tall, lanky figure. "You could be hostages, coerced into getting me to open my door."

"For shit's sake, man. Just fix the vid on your comm box." Jack steps to the side to allow Lyia to come in. "Then you wouldn't hafta be so damn paranoid." He peeks back through the open doorway into the hallway before slapping the door close button on the wall. The moment the door reseals itself shut, lights glow up throughout, brightening the whole place.

"Fixed cameras can be tricked. Besides, my neighbors steal any decent gear I set outside my door." Slim steps through from his back room, tapping a sequence with grease-stained fingers across a tattoo on his forearm.

As Slim works his tat, Jack spins around the room, watching an array of small red lights on the wall blink to green. A length of dark wire twists a haphazard route across the wall connecting each of the little lights. Tiny scorch marks pepper the wall's surface along the wire. "You were gonna use your room incinerator? On us? Really?"

"Can't be too careful. Especially since I didn't even know there was a raid. Was, um, engrossed with something in the back." Slim finishes tapping and proceeds to rub the palm of his hand across the top of his shaven head. He raises his eyes, darkened by the signature bags of someone who hasn't slept in a couple days, and smiles at Lyia. It's the warm, open-mouthed kind of smile that a person gives to someone they care about, but haven't seen in a while. Or at least that's how Jack sees it.

Slim takes two long steps into the room and wraps his arms around Lyia. "It's been too long, Lee. No matter. You're safe now."

Jack clears his throat as Slim completes his hug, allowing Lyia to take a step back. Keeping his arms on her shoulders, he turns to Jack. "Damn, boy. You two look like a shit that took a shit. And is that a chembraid? When'd you get that?"

"Been a shit morning." Jack can feel the grunt's blood on his head drying, caking. The chembraid still itches where it's mounted on his skin. But there's no time for feeling uncomfortable. "You about finished with my pieces of kit?"

"Well, yeah. Both things. Ain't tested 'em yet, though. The one set was a right sombitch to get sorted out. Never woulda thought there'd be two layers of traps on—"

"Good. I need 'em. Now."

"Wait." Slim trades a look with Lyia before giving his full attention to Jack. "I thought you said there was a raid goin' on. You're not headed back out there, are ya? And with untested gear? You're not making any sense."

Jack stares at Slim's hand, still sitting on Lyia's shoulder. *Yeah. There's a lot not makin' sense right now.* He turns his face to Slim. "And we're gonna need some cave gear. Rope an' some lights, mostly."

"Dude. What's going on?" Slim takes a step over to Jack and squats down so they're eye to eye. A thick odor wafts down with the movement. Whatever's been occupying Slim's time has also prevented him from bathing. No wonder Lyia took a step back.

But Jack won't let himself be distracted by a bit of stink. There are bigger things in need of attention. "We've still got two out there."

Slim lets out a low whistle. "Who? Your new bar girl?"

"An' Zeke."

The words hang in the air awkwardly as Jack catches Slim exchange glances with Lyia. Slim leans forward and puts his lanky hand on Jack's shoulder. "Look, man. Zeke is clever. He knows how to hide out during things like this. I'm sure they're going to be fine."

Disagreeing, Jack shakes his head. He can't even get the words out.

Lyia steps forward, addressing Slim. "It's too late for hiding. For them, anyway." She turns to face Jack. "Pinny. I know Zeke means a lot to you, but there's nothing you can do. You *just* got healed. Both you and Zeke. He and that girl—"

"Corva."

"Yeah, Corva. They're done. Death took them. Death, Pinny! And even if he hadn't, Bule's overrun with the horde. If those two are smart, they've already killed themselves."

Slim bolts upright and takes a step to the side so he can see both Jack and Lyia. "Whoa, whoa. What the hell kinda raid is this? Death is here? Like the guy, Death?"

Ignoring Slim, Jack stares at Lyia. "How can you say that? After what you seen? I can't even—ah!" Jack starts pacing. Frustrated, he runs his hands through his hair, inadvertently clearing out some of the crusted blood. It half drips, half sprinkles on Slim's floor. "You know they ain't goin' down so easy."

He pauses, noticing the continued confusion in Slim's face. "It's a long damn story. I don't even know all of it. I ain't askin' for help. I just want the kit I already paid you for."

"And the stuff for caving." Slim crosses his arms in front of him, his "ready to do business, but not a fan of this deal" pose.

"Yeah. That, too. We're taking that crevice you tapped into during your last expansion of this place, but we'll probably still need the gear after that. So I'll hafta tab that one. Just have it ready for when I come back with them."

"Then you better not die."

"In that case, best hope your work holds up." Jack turns back to Lyia, scowling. "You wanna stay safe, *babe*? Then stay here. I got employees to take care of."

New Memories

"You can open them now."

Corva opens her eyes and is immediately confused. An old woman stands before her. Corva blinks in disbelief. "Avó?"

The old woman tilts her head in exactly a way that Corva doesn't remember her ever doing. It's more curious, more feral, more—

"Zeke?"

Avó's face widens to an almost unnatural grin. "You figured it out faster than I expected you would."

"Yeah, well, I'm a quick study." Corva takes a moment to take in her surroundings. They're back in Fareburne, just as it was getting destroyed. They're in a storage cellar. Avó has a small bag of seeds in her hand. "What is this? How are you in Avó's body?"

"I'm not. Not really. We're in a memory. And a pretty important one to you, it would seem. You need to think of a different memory. One that matters less to you. Otherwise, you'll remember this one wrong later."

"How?"

"Just close your eyes and think of it."

With a skeptical frown, Corva shuts her eyes. When they reopen, they're back at Jack's bar. It's nighttime. Jack just got done introducing himself.

Jack's head tilts in the same way Avó's did. "A first introduction? Ouch. This would probably hurt Jack's feelings. How about something even less significant? Maybe something more mundane?"

"Fine." Corva closes her eyes again and then reopens them. She's staring at her reflection in a mirror, a bathroom by the looks of it. She's much younger. Eight years old. Her eyes are swollen and bloodshot. Dried tears streak through the dirt on her face. She's got a toothbrush in her hand. This is one of the first places she crashed after escaping the raid.

Her reflection tilts its head and looks back at her. "It's a start."

"So what're we doing here? What's going on?"

"I need to get a lot of information to you and there isn't a lot of time. We're still angled to be a lawn dart in the center of Bule."

"What's a lawn dart?"

Corva's reflection pauses, closing its eyes as if it were frustrated by her question. "It's an old reference. No matter. We're still falling from the sky and if you don't learn a few things very quickly, you're going to die in a really ugly way … either from the fall or from what happens after."

Corva looks at her reflection; its mannerisms and expressions are completely unrecognizable as hers. "How much do I have to learn?"

"Multiple lifetimes."

Corva's hands start shaking. She reaches up and slams both hands on either side of the mirror. "What? We're seconds from smashing into the ground. How am I supposed to—"

Her reflection holds its hand up. "Time works a little differently in your memories. We can work through memories much faster than action in the conscious world. So calm down. Yes, time is still ticking forward and we can't stay here forever. There isn't enough time to give you all that you need to know. But I can try to give you the abridged version."

Calming a bit, Corva pulls her arms back down to her sides. "Alright. Abridge me."

Her reflection sighs. "That's not what—never mind." The reflection refocuses and looks Corva in the eye. "For the last one hundred and fifty years, people have called Thegn the 'Last of the Four.' This isn't entirely true. The rest of the Four live on. With each generation, the three of you are born anew. And each time, Death hunts for your reborn selves and kills you before—"

"Wait. 'You'? What do you mean?"

"Corva, you are the reborn manifestation of War. You've carried a number of names across cultures throughout millennia, often without those cultures knowing your true nature." The reflection shakes its head, almost nostalgically. "Most of them refused to believe that you're female." It stops, suddenly serious again. "Thegn knows you as Durga."

"Yeah. He and his rat have said as much. They also said something about 'breaking' you."

The reflection looks down and curses under its breath. "Caffiel. Little instigator." Regaining composure, Corva's reflection keeps its head down. "Thegn and Caffiel have a distorted perspective on how this works."

"This?"

"Caffiel and I are sigils. Seals. Locks, if you will. There are—were— twelve of us. We were meant to be the reservoirs of power and knowledge for the Four. Until now, Thegn has never been able to find any of us."

"He's got the rat."

"Caffiel doesn't count. He never left Thegn's side. And as far as I know, this is the first time that one of you other three have come in contact with a sigil before Thegn has found you."

"That's why I get stronger and faster when you're near me?"

"If I will it to be, yes. And it doesn't stop with strength and speed."

Corva's eyes widen. "Like on the rooftop! What was that? Mind control?"

Her reflection laughs bitterly and looks back up to Corva. "No. Not mind control. That's not possible. What I had you do was an advanced technique. More like puppetry. And your mastery of it is pretty weak. You're going to need to start with something simpler in your training."

"Training?"

"Why do you think we're here? The ground is getting closer and I need to get you caught up on a lot in this very short time we have."

Feeling her well of panic growing again at the thought of smashing into the ground, Corva takes a deep breath and leans in toward the mirror. "What's the catch?"

The reflection smiles. It's not her smile. It doesn't even feel like a natural smile that a normal person would make. Unnatural as it is, it's still somewhat reassuring. "We're going to have to override some of your memories. When we're done, you're going to remember those moments wrong. Instead of remembering what happened, you'll remember a training lesson in that time or place. It isn't the most ideal way to do this, but we don't have a lot of choice." Corva's reflection pauses, giving her a second to wrap her brain around the concept. "I'm going to need you to queue up another memory or two. This mirror thing isn't bad for talking, but—"

"I'm already ahead of you." Corva closes her eyes. When she opens them, she's still only eight years old, but she's having trouble breathing. The dirty face of a kid named Puck leers at her while his forearm presses against her throat. She feels herself smile. *This could be fun.*

Eyes on the Ground

"We don't have time for this! Zeke and Corva need help. You n' me both know there ain't no one else in this town who'll bring it." Jack wipes his head one last time with a now-bloodsoaked towel from Slim before adding it to a pile of bloody towels. He pulls the straps on his pack tighter and tries to make his way to Slim's door, again.

Lyia continues to step in his way. She puts her hand—now also clean of blood—on his chest, lightly pushing him back. "Exactly what kind of help do you think you're going to provide? Remember Death took them into the sky. You've got nothing for that. And even if they escape Death, there's still a legion of grunts swarming the town." She looks over her shoulder to the door. "They're probably already covering all of Lower Bule by now. Let Harris and the militia handle giving any help. If it's even possible."

Jack feels his neck and ears warm up more and more each time Lyia blocks his path. He tries to sidestep her, but is blocked yet again. "Hairless? Talk about having nothing to bring to the table! We saw Gorm running ahead of us to get down here to Lower Bule. They've probably already given up on Upper. If they're not overrun, they're huddled up in one of the siege caves. Seriously"—he makes another attempt to get to Slim's door—"we just gotta give Zeke n' Corva enough space for an exit. You ain't seen 'em. You don't know what they can do!"

"Really?" Lyia's eyes start to well up. Her hands appear to be shaking uncontrollably. "I don't know what they can do? Really? I just got shoved into the passenger seat of my own body by that girl. Who is this Corva girl, Jack? What she did, that wasn't soulmancy. She—she had me face off with two grunts. Made me kill them with my bare hands. Made—"

Her words trail off as her eyes lose focus on Jack and jump around the room, but on places in space that are either too close or too far away to be any specific thing there. It looks like she's recalling a nightmare, recreating the scene in her mind, looking through her current surroundings and instead seeing the rooftop.

"Their own hands." Slim's interruption is low, but it's enough to get both Jack's and Lyia's attention.

"What?" Brought back from her waking nightmare of a memory, Lyia spins to face Slim.

Slim smiles a meek kind of smile. It's the kind of look a person gives when they out themselves for something they assume people will figure out eventually. He clears his throat and speaks a bit more loudly. "I said, technically, you killed them with their own hands."

Lyia squints, narrowing her eyes at Slim. "How did—you weren't there. How'd you know what happened?"

Jack alternates looking between Lyia and Slim. There's something being said here between their words, but he can't quite put his finger on it. He already knew that Slim used to visit Lyia at the Red Light every now and again, but this is something different. He's seen this particular brand of unspoken conversation before at the bar. This is the same kind of secret language reserved for people with a long history between them. Commitment. Friendship. Partnership. If the "babe" thing wasn't a giveaway before, it's pretty obvious now. Jack bites on the inside of his cheek to keep himself from talking, not that he'd have the words to say what he's feeling now anyway. All the same, he feels his heart lower in his chest.

Slim reaches up and rubs the top of his head, almost nervous. He keeps his lopsided smirk but avoids eye contact with Lyia. "I, um—I saw it happen."

"I thought you said that you didn't even know that a raid was happening." Jack frowns at Slim.

"Heh. Yeah. About that." The lanky tech runs his hand over his scalp, leaving it resting on the back of his head.

His back straightens as Lyia takes a step in.

"How?" She says it slow, almost like a parent ramping up to an eventual scolding of her child.

"Heh. C'mon babe. It's an insurance thing. Part of the biz. I told you it was baked into the original design."

"Motherfuck, Slim! You said you weren't peddling that shit anymore!"

A few seconds ago, Jack would have said that he had a complete understanding of the situation. Now, he's completely lost. He raises his hands and steps between the two. "Hold up. Someone wanna bring me up to speed?"

"Asshole here is peeping for profit!"

Slim takes a step back. "What? No! It's not like that, babe. I'm not doing that anymore." He turns to address Jack. "Short version: I've got a backdoor in every playback kneak I make. Gives me real-time access to the media streams of anyone within range of my receiver."

Jack reaches up and touches his own playback kneak, still plugged into the array behind his ear. "You can see what I see?" He looks to Lyia. "What she sees?"

"Yeah. He can. And he records it. And pushes it through the satmesh to anyone willing to pay for a peep."

"I told you I'm not doin' that anymore. But—"

"Then why didn't you destroy your receiver like you said you would?"

"I was." Slim takes a step closer to Lyia and holds her by her shoulders so he can look at her face. "But I got to thinking. When a raid comes through—like now—this tech would be damn useful for knowing what's going on outside."

Jack scowls. This is starting to sound familiar. "You got to thinking? Don't you mean Harris got you thinking? How many nits did he pay you?"

Slim turns his attention away from Lyia momentarily to respond to Jack. "I won't deny that the pay was a good incentive to keep me from focusing on other projects. But the thinking was absolutely all on my end. Harris just found out about the gen one version of this tech and asked how hard it would be to expand it for covering the whole town. I told him it wouldn't be too hard. I just needed to get a wider range than my first receiver had."

"You made *more* receivers?" Lyia's voice is shrill. "So, what? You're going to peep on the whole damn town?"

"Actually a meshnet of receivers. But yeah. I made more. It's for security, though. With this, I can—"

Lyia yanks away, turning to the side. "Holy hell, Slim. Unbe-fucking-lievable. I can't believe that—"

"How wide is your range now?"

Lyia and Slim stop and stare at Jack. Impatient, he looks to Slim. "I said, how wide is your range?"

Slim hesitates, but Jack can see that he's holding back his smirk. The skinny tech is proud of himself. "At this point? 'Bout two-thirds of Lower Bule."

"Son of a—"

Jack snaps his head to Lyia, glaring. "Look. You two can finish your little spat n' have your reconciliation fuck—or whatever ya wanna call it—after I'm out. Meantime, it could be handy to have eyes out there 'fore I take my happy ass back on the roof." Confident that his point's been made, he turns back to Slim. "Show me."

"Yeah, kid. Sure." Slim leads Jack through the threshold to his expanded back room and approaches a standing terminal at the center of a mismatched array of screens and monitors. "No telling what we'll see, though. Can't imagine that there are too many people out there. Most should be in the caves."

"I'll take what I can get."

Slim pauses a second to exchange looks with Lyia, still standing back in the smaller "main" room. Jack tries to guess at what exactly those looks mean, but quickly loses interest. He assumes it's some variation of "you cool?" and "whatever" and turns his attention to the sequence of commands Slim is punching into the terminal. A moment later, each of the various screens flash on with different images of varying quality.

"Alright, so you're looking through the eyes of every person within range of my meshnet. Folks closest to our location are on the screens closest to the terminal. Folks farther away are on the far screens, roughly in the direction they're at."

Jack looks at the cluster of screens and is immediately drawn to two of them right near the terminal. He points. "This me n' Lyia?"

"Shit. Yeah. Meant to filter you guys out." He scans across the assorted screens. "But from the look of it, I don't think I'll need to. Most of these are just different views of the same thing."

Jack looks over the screens himself. Sure enough, the majority of them are different angles on the same cavernous dark room packed with people, mostly standing. "This the siege cave over by Cress's place?"

"Looks to be."

"Right on. Then we'll skip them an' stick with this little handful of folks close-by." Jack leans forward, placing his weight on his elbows. "Gotta say, this is pretty cool. Kinda fucked up that you saw us facin' down them grunts an' you didn't toss any help our way. But the tech is pretty sweet."

He points to another screen near the terminal. The image on it is a bit fuzzier than the rest, but it appears to be looking at a strange, almost upward angle. Buildings flank the sides of the view, framing a few wispy clouds in an otherwise clear blue sky. Every few seconds, he can see the shadow of an Umbrati grunt pass across the view. "Where's this one? An' why ain't it movin'?"

Slim frowns. "Huh. That's new." He taps a few keys on the terminal and a pair of speakers hum to life. "You hear that?"

"Yeah. You brought up the audio from the kneak. So what?"

"No, no. I mean—yes—I did bring up the audio. But there should be a different sound there. Playback kneaks pull audio from within the ear. We should be hearing this person's heartbeat. It ain't there."

"This is a dead person's view?"

"Apparently."

"Any chance we know who it is?"

"Maybe. Would need to cross-ref the kneak's serial against my sales log. Didn't actually know it worked on a dead person. Better make a note." Slim raises his tattooed arm in front of his face and uses his opposite arm's forefinger to make a series of writing-like gestures on a blank space in the center of his lanky forearm. "Dead woman, actually. You remember Tessy?"

Lyia gasps in recognition while Jack can only give a blank look. "Who's Tessy?"

Slim faces Jack. "Ran the bakery on this side of town. You had a name for her. I think you called her 'Birthmark.'"

"Oh yeah! Great loafs at that place. That thing on her face was weird, though." He notices Lyia give him a disapproving look. "What? It was all over the side of her head. The name fit. But we're getting distracted." He points at the screen with video from Birthm—Tessy's playback. "Where's that at?"

The thin tech stops and inspects the screen. "See the corner of that building on the left inside the view area?"

Jack squints and gets his face closer to the display. "Yeah."

"I think that's the roof you were on when you guys got surrounded by those grunts." Slim glances over at Lyia before asking his next question in a low whisper, "By the way, what in the world happened back there? I didn't know either of you could fight like that."

"We can't." Jack feels a light shudder go up his spine. The sight of his fingers pushing in on that grunt's neck crowds out any other thought. He makes fists and relaxes his fingers. His hands are starting to feel sore. Suddenly, something in the dead woman's vid gets his attention. He pushes his finger right on the center of the screen. "What's that?"

Exasperation leaks from Slim in the form of a sigh. "I told you, it's right near—"

"No! This thing here in the view. What's that?"

Slim pushes Jack's hand out of the way and picks up the little screen. "Hard to see with your hand covering the thing. Yeesh." He pulls the screen close to his face. "You mean this thing?" He points to a pair of small dark dots in the sky. "It could be bad pixels or dying connections to the optical nerve. No, wait. Can't be that. Those dots are moving. I think something's falling from the sky. And pretty fast, too."

"Corva."

6.9

Back to the Present

Unfortunately, I think that this is all we have time for. Zeke's words through Corva's inner voice reverberates in her mind. He jumps off of Corva's shoulder, landing in front of her. The smell of sweetgrass permeates the air. Unexploded bundles of winged dynamite litter the ground all around them.

"Time to pick another memory?" Corva places her hands on her knees and catches her breath. Sweat steams off her skin in the cool evening air.

No. Time to face Thegn. Or the ground. He takes a moment to soak in his surroundings. **I've got to say, though, this last memory was a masterful choice. I had no idea that this would work in the memory of a dream.** He returns his gaze to Corva. **Or that you had dreams with me in them.**

Corva, still a bit out of breath, keeps one hand on her knee, but uses the other to point at the little monkey. "I figured you'd appreciate the familiar digs. Shame you can't speak normally, though, and you've gotta do the mind talking thing."

403

I probably could speak as you do. But remember that these are still memories. Probably best to stick with reality.

"Yeah, because talking to myself through a mirror is totally realistic."

Point taken.

Corva reaches down and pokes one of the dynamite creatures. She'd started calling them "Dynaflights" in her mind. This one under her finger is a variation with wings like those of a bat. "Any clue about what these are?"

Zeke looks at the one she's prodding, then the assorted others around them. **No idea. This is your dream.**

"Damn. I was hoping that this was one of her—Durga's— memories. I think that I sometimes get those as dreams. This was one of the first I had and the one I'm least sure about. Thought you might know a thing or two about it."

It still could be a memory of hers. I couldn't say for sure, though. These explosive little creatures certainly aren't anything I've encountered before.

Corva straightens and rolls her shoulders back. She twists her head to the side a bit, just enough to feel a little pop in her neck. "Alright. Let's do this thing."

Very well. Open your eyes.

6.10

Slowing the Descent

Corva opens her eyes and is immediately greeted with the feeling of air slapping against her face as she plummets headfirst through the sky. Zeke's hand is no longer on her forehead, though he remains perched on the back of her head, clinging to dreadlocks as they flap behind her. The ground is a lot closer now than when she closed her eyes. That was only a few meager seconds ago, but the time spent in her memories felt like half a lifetime.

She tucks her chin so she can look to the sky above her feet. Thegn is still back there, chasing after her in his own dive. She turns her head back toward the ground. *Getting close. Scary close.*

Remember, Corva, you want to aim for Bule.

She nods and then opens her arms and legs, spreading her body out as much as possible to slow her descent. As expected, she sees the blade of Thegn's scythe shoot by and then swing toward her. Like before, she catches the shaft with both hands, and the Old Beard is immediately upon them.

He grins his broken grin and despite the roar of the air rushing past them, she can still hear his voice. "Thought you'da learned from the first two times!"

He looks up and his wings beat downward. Corva feels her body start to change direction as they begin their ascent. *Now!*

Corva uses the momentum of her lower body to swing her legs up and plant her feet on the scythe's shaft, right between each of her hands.

The gate is open. You have my flow. Zeke's words push through her mind. Insistent.

With a single nod of acknowledgment, she takes a deep breath and grits her teeth. This is going to hurt.

The bones and muscles in her upper back pop and move under her skin. New bone, new muscle, new connective tissue—they manifest and push against the skin just above her shoulder blades. Sharp pain sears across her back. It's exactly like she remembers. Her skin grows, tearing and stretching as it wraps around a second pair of arms as they extend from her back in a fraction of a second, ripping holes through her shirt. The straps of her pack strain against the space taken up by her new set of arms. Corva's back is soaked in blood. The pain is almost unbearable; she screams through her clenched teeth and her vision blurs as water streams from her eyes.

Before Thegn is able to lift his wings from the giant flap downward that began their ascent, Corva reaches out with her freshly formed arms. She claws her new fingers into his wings, gripping them with as much force as she can muster. Corva and Thegn start to fall together. It's a controlled, gliding descent. She glances over her shoulder to ensure that they're still aimed toward Bule. Turning her head back, she sees him look down at her.

His face is a slow progression of emotions. Recognition transforms into realization. For the briefest of moments, Corva thinks she can see a wave of fear run over him, but it's quickly replaced—if it was there at all—with pure anger. The wrinkles on his aged face fold over themselves as he struggles in vain to free his wings from her grasp.

Corva looks up at Thegn and smiles.

6.11

Interlopers

Thegn tries to wrench his wings free, but the grip from the damn girl's new hands is just too tight. Her elbows are locked, so trying to open or close his wings to shake free is no good. He looks down and gives a yank on his scythe. Nope. That's stuck in a pinch between her feet and her lower hands.

Smiling, she gives a push with her feet, leveraging herself so she can control the angle of his wings. He checks their trajectory. *Bitch is treating me like a damn hang glider. Got us on a straight line back to that canyon town.*

He can see the dark swarms on the pathways and rooftops of the burg. The Umbrati horde is there among the fires and muzzle flashes, disregarding the town's defenses. Waiting for him.

He feels tiny paws clinching the fabric around his shoulder. **Oh my. She's got you in quite the state, doesn't she?**

"Caffiel. Almost prefer the hive to your smart ass." The words hiss through his teeth and he enjoys the momentary look of confusion in the girl's face before she realizes he isn't addressing her. No matter. He wants the rat to hear that. Besides—

Thegn takes advantage of her moment of distraction and tries again to yank free. He pulls both at his wings and at his scythe. No dice. He rolls his eyes and lets out an exasperated sigh. *For fuck's sake.*

He releases the scythe and it immediately turns to ash, vaporizing right out of her grasp. With nothing holding her in place, her feet shoot forward and her lower arms flail backward. Her upper hands never lose their grip, though. Instead, she pulls with them, swinging her legs and planting her feet right in the center of Thegn's chest.

But his hands are free now. Thegn rolls his bony fingers into fists. He takes a swing at her midsection and connects hard with her ribs. However, she doesn't crumple at the force of his blow like so many other people would.

She doesn't let go, either.

Instead, she clamps down with the lower arm closest to where he hit, trapping his hand in place. Then her other lower arm shoots forward and she wraps her fingers around his neck. He grabs her wrist with his remaining free hand, but it's all he can do to keep her from squeezing and crushing his trachea.

Despite all of this, he finds himself smiling. He looks down her arm and into her face. "It's been too long, Durga."

There's a flicker of recognition, but it disappears just as quickly. She pulls herself closer to him, her green eyes blazing through her dark mask of a face, their foreheads nearly touching. There's a sweetness in her breath that he can barely smell with the wind whipping around them. "The name, is Corva!"

She leans back, upside down with her face toward Bule, and pulls down on his wings. Her feet wedge against his chest and she straightens their course.

Episode Six: Failure to Gitfo

They're very close now. Thegn can see individual grunts crawling over each other, turning their steel-plated faces up to the sky. He can here the cacophony of that grotesque throat-clearing noise they make.

It's liquid-sounding and guttural, like the whole mass of them is dry heaving.

Disgusted, Thegn leans into the glide, trying to speed up their descent. *Let's see if a game of chicken with the ground will loosen her up.*

You may want to have a look to your left.

Thegn turns his head to see what it is that the rat's referring to. Sure enough, two groups of Umbrati grunts are working their way to a small cleared-off rooftop. The first team is carrying an enormous crate made of a fine wire mesh. It's impossible to see the contents of the crate, but with its darkness and increasingly pervasive buzzing, Thegn knows exactly what's in there.

"Shit. If it isn't one thing—"

412

6.12

Watching the Fall

"What is that? What've them Goats brought out?" Jack paces from side to side, cycling through each of the available screens in Slim's workshop. Squinting and scowling, he tries to get a better angle on the strange box the grunts just brought out. "And why the shit won't these people sit still long enough to get a good view of it?"

"Easy, little man. Remember that these are people who didn't make it to the siege caves. They're damn scared of getting pinched." Slim's back is to Jack; he inserts a metal rod into a pipe while he speaks over his shoulder. Jack looks over at him. The guy had suddenly gotten very obsessed with something on his workbench not long after showing the basics of how his surveillance array works.

Lyia stands in the main room of Slim's place, eyeing the door. "You think this thing will hold? I've never seen a raid with this many in the horde."

Slim responds without looking up. "It'll hold fine, unless the whole horde is specifically gunning for you." He thumb-points over his shoulder toward Jack. "Looking at the vid, though, I'd say this group's focused on someone else."

"Ol' Wrinkles ain't gonna go down easy." Jack peeks around the doorway at Lyia. She'd gotten curious enough to look at what was going on outside through the surveillance monitors, but once she caught sight of the sheer number of grunts hunting through Bule, she got really interested in ensuring that Slim's door is adequately fortified. Jack gives himself a moment to trace the curves of her body—again. She's been acting unusually fatalistic in this raid, but he still finds himself envisioning the details of her body hidden beneath her clothes.

Shaking his head to clear his mind, he returns focus to the surveillance screens. "Any chance we could get one of these folks on radio so we can tell 'em where to look?"

"Yeah, that'll go over great." Slim turns to Jack and mimes picking up an imaginary radio, putting it to the side of his face. "'So, I'm spying on you through your playback kneak. Any chance you could take a step to the right so I can see better?' I'm sure they'd be instantly cooperative."

Jack feels his shoulders drop. "Yeah. I guess they wouldn't take too kindly to bein' told that." He goes back to studying the images on each screen. "Still, what's in those boxes?"

Slim puts down the gadgets he was fiddling with and takes a couple long strides over to the bank of monitors. "You said that's Death out there, right? You gotta figure that the Umbrati tracked him here. With numbers like these, my guess is that they're looking to catch and conscript him."

"Still doesn't tell me what's in the box."

"Well, you see any wings on those grunts? The Old Beard's got air superiority goin' on. I'm thinking that whatever's in that box is supposed to help get him out of the sky."

"Makes sense. What would you use?"

Slim smiles. "I got an idea or two on how I'd do it. But, first, how about you?"

Jack frowns. "I know what you're doin'. You sure as shit pick a weird time to do a quiz."

"Humor me. You're not stepping out there any time soon. May as well test your skills while you wait."

Jack scratches the side of his face, still scowling. However, he complies. "Hrm. Well, the biggest thing is gettin' him down. Then ya gotta keep 'em there. Were it me, I'd just try to hit him surface-to-ground."

"For capture?"

"Shit. Um. Nets? A surface-to-air net launcher."

Slim strokes the stubble on his chin. "Not bad. Not a bad call at all. But ol' Death looks pretty agile up there." He points at one of the screens where someone is looking up at Thegn and Corva gliding across the sky. "Even with your friend hanging off him like that. And you can't always count on some crazy chick to be there and drag him down like that."

"Yeah? Then what would you do?"

"Me? It ain't likely that this is what's in the box, but I might try some explosive nanodrones. Can't hardly see 'em. They'd fly up and latch on his wings before they go boom. Blow just enough to get him down without killing him. Then blow the rest once he's on the ground to keep him there."

Jack nods approvingly. *Gotta give the guy credit. He's definitely got some slick ideas.* He pauses, allowing an idea of his own to slowly coalesce. "How many of them drones you think it'd take?"

"Hard to guess. Dude looks pretty tough. Probably more'n I've got on hand."

"And just how many is that?" Jack's stupid grin broadens.

"I've got a few. What're you thinkin', little man?"

Leap of Faith

Corva tilts her head back to check their course. Her hands—all four of them—ache from

gripping for so long. *Just a little bit closer.*

She's planning on jumping as soon as they get close enough to the ground. That said, she's not quite sure what to do from there. First priority is getting to terra firma. Then she can't let Thegn take her skyward like this again; he'd find a way to block this glider setup she'd lucked into. The problem, though, is that she just doesn't have the tools to keep him from escaping to the sky.

And then there's the Umbrati to consider. There's just too many for her to take on by herself. Also, whatever they've got in that mesh cage can't be good for anyone. It's definitely gotten Thegn's attention. Ever since they brought it out, he's been trying to angle away.

She feels a tug on her hair and a paw at her shoulder. **It's almost time to jump free.**

Corva nods in reply and squeezes tighter on Thegn's wings. Then she pushes with her feet and jerks herself backward with as much strength as she can, stealing control of their descent. They're angled for a rooftop in Lower Bule, not far from where Thegn initially grabbed her. There's still a fair amount of altitude between that rooftop and where they're gliding, but she thinks back to her newly overridden memories of training with Zeke. *I can make it.*

Now, Corva! Now!

She pulls in as close to Thegn as she can—only marginally closer than she can bear. Releasing his throat, she bends her arm to land an elbow solidly on his cheek. The moment he lets go of her wrist, she lets go of his wings and his arm, then kicks off his chest as hard as she can.

Descending quickly, she twists in the air so she's facing the ground more comfortably.

If you're planning on rolling when you hit that roof, please remember that you've got a passenger back here ... and a bag full of who-knows-what.

Corva shakes her head slowly. *Zeke, Zeke, Zeke. All this time we've been together and you still don't trust me.* Using her upper arms, she reaches back and pulls the little monkey off the back of her head and cradles him close to her chest.

Spreading out her lower arms, she gets just enough air resistance to swing her legs beneath her. An instant later, her feet make contact with the rooftop. Cracks spider out as the stone and concrete surface buckles from her impact. Her knees bend and her lower arms slap the rough, sandy slab. More cracks. The rooftop feels less like a solid chunk of rock and more like individual pieces of a puzzle sliding apart from one another.

"Damn shoddy—"

The rooftop gives way below Corva's feet. As she falls, a cloud of dust blots out the sky above her and Zeke.

6.14

DEATH AND THE PLAGUE

"Stupid girl." Thegn watches a small squad of grunts plunge into the hazy fog hanging over the rubble, ready to attack. He smiles when he sees one fly back out sideways before smacking against a wall. There's no way that roof collapse would end her, especially now that she's reached this state.

The smile fades and he puts on a grim face. She still has to die. As much as he enjoys seeing her work, it's a problem that she's started to wield Durga's powers. The world can't know she exists. It's bad enough that he let her existence slip to the Karui. Death delivering death is the only way to ensure she's safe for another generation.

Thegn glides right, searching for an updraft to help carry him skyward. He needs a moment to regroup. He tests his wings by flexing them with half a flap. They're pretty sore from where she'd been clinging to them.

You must admit that she got you pretty well.

"Is this idle babbling of yours going to become a regular thing? Because I could do without it."

419

We can discuss the renegotiation of our arrangement later. For now, you have greater concerns. Caffiel gives a tug on Thegn's left shoulder. **This side.**

"That's my hood, old rodent! Not a set of damn reins. Mind your place."

Respect your elders, young one! Just have a look. It appears that our green-skinned friends have released phase one.

Thegn turns his head just in time to see the small group of Umbrati open a panel on the mesh cage. The buzzing from the cage becomes exponentially louder as a cloud of darkness bursts from the open panel and up into the sky.

"Fucking locusts? Really? You think they would've learned their lesson the last time they tried to use those foul bugs."

Maybe they appreciate the irony of attacking Death with a plague.

Snorting in disgust, Thegn flaps his wings and redirects himself on a straight course with the oncoming cloud of insects. "May as well finish them all. Drive the point home right from the start."

Pulling his wings tight, he dives right into the pitch-black cloud of insects. From within the deafening buzz at the center of the plague, Thegn twists his body and extends his wings. A gale of wind launches from his spinning motion like a wall of air. There's enough force to explosively crush and scatter all of the insects from their tight grouping. A mist of vaporized locust juices replaces the swarm of actual bugs that had surrounded him. He can feel the thick goop of their guts dripping all over him.

Thegn can't help but grin. "Too easy."

Don't be so sure. Do you smell that?

Thegn sniffs. The goopy guts feel a bit thicker than he remembers, but he can't really—

"Shit!" The word comes out impulsively, and echoes across his mind again when he sees the flaming arrow flying right at him.

Load Me Up

"Holy—! Wow!" Jack reactively ducks when he sees the explosion on the screens of the surveillance array. He turns to Slim. "Did you see that?"

Slim leans in. He'd given up fiddling at his workbench to watch the fight unfold on the screens. "Yeah. Saw it. Not as elegant as nanobots, but it looks like they had the same basic idea. I'm guessing each of those bugs carried some kind of incendiary payload."

"Incendiary?" Jack scrunches his nose, tasting the word for the first time.

"Flammable."

Jack's eyes widen. "They can do that?"

"Sure thing. Probably something similar to those fuel sacs in that flamethrower chick you told me about. But with the bugs, they probably engineered them in, rather than doin' surgery on each one."

"Badass." Jack watches a dark form fall toward Bule from the smokey fireball in the sky. "You think they killed him?"

Slim squints, as if that would somehow let him see the screen in front of him more clearly. "Kill the last of the Four? Not likely. They're here to capture. 'Sides—" He taps on the screen where they saw Thegn falling. The old man's wings, still on fire, spread open just in time to allow him to land with at least a modicum of grace on an empty rooftop in Lower Bule. "Looks like that guy's a pretty tough old bird."

"Damn. Was hopin' he bit it." Jack scans the other screens in front of him. "We got any eyes on that spot Corva landed?"

Slim is already turned back to his workbench, assembling some other gadget. "Sorry, man. She kicked up quite a mean puff of dirt. I think anyone we had hiding near there has long since bugged out."

Jack doesn't respond. He just keeps looking from one screen to another, hoping to catch any sight, any sign of Zeke or Corva.

Slim clears his throat. "Yeah, but, um, the good news is that she dropped back in just two buildings away. It's just on the other side of where you guys faced off with those grunts on the way here."

That's all Jack needs to hear. He steps away from the surveillance array and heads back into the main room. Snagging his go-bag, he notices the disapproving scowl from Lyia, still standing vigil at the heavy entrance door.

"Fine." He turns away from Lyia and looks at Slim. "You got a way to get in touch with Harris an' his crew?"

Slim raises his head from his work and swivels to face Jack. "Maybe. I got a line to his private comm. So long as his gear is still active, I should be able to reach him. But why—"

Jack strides into the workshop and drops his go-bag on Slim's workbench.

"Good. Do that. Then load me up. I don't care how ready you aren't."

Beginning of the End

On the rooftop, Thegn gives his wings a mighty flap, extinguishing any of the remaining flames on and around him. They hurt something awful. He brings them around to get a better look. It's just about what he thinks. Most of the feathers have burned away. What were once shiny and glorious wings are now simply a pair of charred appendages sticking from his back. Disappointed, he slowly shakes his head and rolls his shoulders. He feels the bone and muscles in his back shift under his skin as his wings detach and puff into ash.

Twisting his head to one side, he cracks his neck. The sick smells of singed hair and the burns in his cloak overwhelm his nose. Even with his mouth closed, he can taste the foul stench.

Well, young one. It looks like they did, in fact, learn a thing or two since last time.

Thegn scans the rooftop. He can hear the grunts from the horde on their way up. "Oh shut up, rodent. You didn't see it coming either. Now keep a tight hold. This isn't over."

Yes. Regarding that …

Thegn swivels his head to look at his shoulder. It doesn't look good. What was once a coat of meticulously well-maintained clean white fur on the albino rat is now a mess of darkly singed fur and darker charred skin.

Caffiel sees Thegn's reaction and shows his teeth in his closest approximation of a smile. **Looks that good, huh?**

Thegn returns to looking straight ahead. The blood seeping from his burns has already started finding its way to his right hand, shaping itself into his scythe. The dust is settling at the partially demolished building where the girl and the monkey crashed. He can just make out her silhouette standing at the center of the destruction.

There's a long pause, but he finally responds to the rat. "You've seen better days. Will you recover?"

Caffiel shifts his weight on Thegn's shoulder, whimpering a bit. **Difficult to tell. This body isn't much more resilient than its terrestrial counterpart. You're cut off from the Karui, so your backup—and a healing technician—isn't likely to arrive any time soon.**

"Options?" From the corner of his eye, he can see that his scythe is almost fully reformed.

Although I can keep the gate open, I doubt you have the energy to rebuild your wings. We can't do this fight on the ground with the Umbrati here. Although she's likely weakened as well, it would be a long slog and she's already at risk of getting discovered.

The rat pulls itself a bit forward, as if whispering in Thegn's ear.

Even without wings, it's possible that you and I may still be able to escape, but that leaves the girl alive. She'd have to kill off what's left of the horde's raid party to guarantee that word doesn't get back. To be completely sure, she'd need to end the whole town. Do you trust she can do that?

"Not on her own." Thegn sees her silhouette falter and drop to a knee. The shapes of her recently formed upper arms dissolve into the thin dusty haze. A monkey-shaped outline of the second sigil rests on her shoulder. Around them both, individual grunts begin to crest the rooftops. The din of hissing and growling floods his ears.

Well then, young one, it seems that your options are pretty sparse. I think you know what needs to be done.

Thegn regards the rat. "What's this now?" He catches a meaningful nod from Caffiel, as if the rodent is giving him permission. Slowly, it dawns on him what's being suggested. "The sacrifice? No. No, we're not in *that* tough a spot."

It will give you more than you need to—

"Not an option!"

Thegn slams the butt of his scythe down with enough force to crack the rooftop at his feet. An uncomfortable silence settles between them. The scratching sound of grunts climbing the sides of the building he's standing on gets louder as they ascend closer to him. He never got that chance to regroup. This is the most he's had to exert himself in nearly a decade. If he could just find a second or two to think; the other three were always better at improvisation.

Finally, Caffiel sounds in Thegn's mind. **Well, if you have a plan, you're going to need to execute it soon.**

Thegn sighs, readying himself. "I have a plan. But I'll need some time to prepare. Think you can handle that?"

Absolutely. Take as much time as you need.

Mark of Death

Oh no. Corva can feel Zeke's entire body stiffen. He's on her back again, but she can feel his paws dig into her shoulder through her go-bag's straps. An overwhelming sense of dread—Zeke's dread—floods the back of her mind. She leans forward, her knee digging into the debris of the rooftop.

"What? Are you hurt?"

Zeke shudders. **This is bad. Really bad.**

"Well, could you worry without moving so much? You're not making it any easier to get out of this hole." She tries to reach up with her second pair of arms and realizes they're no longer there. All that remains of them are some smudges of ash and blood along a pair of tears in her shirt. They must have puffed away when they fell. Her concentration lapsed and her new arms were no more.

With some effort, though, she's able to push herself up to more stable footing on the roof. Standing, she lets out a heavy breath, half in celebration of not dying, half in surprise—also of not dying.

Zeke's attention is somewhere else entirely. **We're out of reach of the closest militia station. And you don't have any comms on you.**

"What are you talking about, Zeke? You're not making any sense." To Corva's right, she hears the first Umbrati grunt begin to scramble amongst the rubble near where she stands. *So much for having time to celebrate.*

She sidesteps the charging grunt. As it brushes by, she reaches out across its face. The moment her fingertips find the edge of the steel plate on its face, she grips down and yanks toward herself. There's a cracking snap in the grunt's neck as its head twists completely backward.

Watching the grunt's collapsed body skid to a stop in front of her, she sees the little monkey's hand break her peripheral vision, pointing through their fog of dust at a rough form on another rooftop in front of them. **He's there. He must be desperate.**

"Who?"

Another grunt scrambles over the edge of the roof behind them. It carries a heavy club on its back. A steel plate covers its entire face.

Thegn. Thegn is desperate.

"Good! That means he's scared. We can beat him and he knows it." The dust around them starts to settle and Corva gets a clearer view of Thegn as he lowers himself to rest on his knees. The rat on his shoulder looks to be gently swaying from side to side.

Corva notices the club-carrying grunt. It's reaching over the edge of the rooftop to help pull another one up. If she's not careful, there's going to be a whole swarm of them. She gets an idea. It'll be hard to concentrate while still talking to Zeke, but she thinks she can do it.

You don't understand. Zeke's arm pulls back out of view and Corva gets the feeling that he's buried his face in his palms. **I'd hoped that our training would've awakened more of your latent memories. It seems that's not the case.**

She feels his hand reach out and pull her chin to the right so she can see him on her shoulder. His face is right up close to hers; it's almost startling. Something has really gotten to him. It shows in his eyes. Their vertical slitting always made him look a little strange, a little difficult to read. But now, now it's clear. Zeke is worried. **He—Thegn is going to *mark* Bule.**

"What does that mean?" As she says this, her attention shifts fully to the club grunt. She can see what it sees. Well, it's not seeing, exactly. For one, that steel plate is covering its eyes. But all of its other senses are amplified. It can sense the world around it. And so can she. It's almost better than seeing. She has total control. Halfway through pulling its comrade to the roof, the grunt reaches up and grabs the heavy club off its back, swinging with full force at the other's head, flattening it against the grunt's own shoulders. Corva can't help but smile a little.

Having fun?

"Hey, I'm buying you time to explain what's going on. Don't change the subject." She has the heavy club grunt pace at the roof's edge, periodically swinging at any other grunt close enough to climb over.

Zeke gives his little monkey version of a sigh. **Alright. You know that streak of white in Jack's hair?** He waits for her to nod slowly. **Do you remember how he said he got it?**

Corva works her way to the edge of the roof, keeping an eye on Thegn. He just seems to be sitting on his knees, not doing anything. *But wait, Zeke just asked a question.* Something about Jack's hair. That white streak. "Yeah, he said he got it when he and Lyia escaped the Shadowfold. Said it was Death's Mark—oh."

It suddenly dawns on her what's going on. "He's going to kill everyone in town?"

Exactly that. Did Jack ever tell you how the Shadowfold was defeated?

"He didn't have to. Everyone knows that. It was the only time the Karui and Umbrati worked together to take out a common enemy." *WHAM.* Another grunt gets a club to the head.

Not quite. It wasn't the only time. But more importantly, it wasn't the joint attack that got them. The Shadowfold was

actually weathering the siege successfully. **No. It ultimately took Thegn's ability to defeat them. He marked everyone in their compound. Anyone who carried his mark was killed.**

"Except for Jack and Lyia. How'd they get out of it?" *Thunk!*

That part is unclear. Jack doesn't seem to remember and Lyia hasn't told anyone who's asked.

"So you're saying we need to take him out before he gets those marks on everyone? I can handle that."

No!

But it's too late. Corva is already moving. She feels Zeke's grip tighten on her pack's straps to avoid falling off. It only takes a few fast steps and a couple long jumps for her to leap to the rooftop Thegn is kneeling upon.

Right when she lands, though, she can tell that something is wrong. Something is off. It's a familiar feeling, a comfortable one. She's calm, relaxed. It's the perfect time to lie down and sleep for a few hours. Maybe even the rest of the day.

CORVA! Zeke screeches through her mind like a million steel pipes dragging across a tin roof. Immediately, Corva snaps out of her daze and leaps back the way she came, landing just one rooftop away from Thegn's position.

"What was that?"

Your impulsiveness will be the end of you if you're not careful.

Concentrating, Corva checks her connection to the club grunt. It's still good. She wills the thing to come to her current rooftop. "You didn't answer my question, Zeke. What was that? Am I marked?"

No. I'm surprised you don't recognize it. You were caught in the exact same trap earlier today. It was Caffiel.

"The rat?" Corva paces her rooftop, staring at Thegn as her club grunt works its way over, smashing the heads of other grunts along the way.

Zeke sighs. **Yes, the rat. Besides amplifying the capabilities of the horseman we bond to, we sigils each have an innate ability befitting our disposition. Caffiel can selectively reduce inhibitions and sedate unwitting targets.**

"He's the sleepytime sigil?"

That's a rather reductive way to put it. But yes. He's manifested a fog of influence around Thegn. If you would've gotten any closer, you'd collapse and I wouldn't be able to reach you at all. We can't attack Thegn head-on. We can't stop him from making his marks. We have to go. Now.

Corva thinks for a moment as her grunt finally clambers over the edge of her rooftop. "Hey Zeke, what's you're special sigil ability?"

You should hope that you never learn. Now let's get Jack and get out of here.

"Why? If we can just get through that fog thing, we can beat him. I know we can." Another grunt works its way to the rooftop in front of Corva. This one has a set of curved blades running along the length of its forearms, a sharpened tip at each end.

This town is lost. We need to make sure we don't go with it.

"I can't do that, Zeke." Corva drops to a knee and picks up a large chunk of rock. "I can't watch another town fall like Fareburne. Like my home. And—I can't believe I'm saying this—I don't think Jack would be too excited about seeing another place fall like the Shadowfold did. Now is where we finally stop the Old Beard."

She scrunches her face, ducking a swing from the arm-blade grunt. Using the chunk of rock, she smashes the inside of the grunt's forward knee. Unable to hold its own weight, the grunt collapses. Still holding the rock, Corva stands and swings upward, smashing the rock against the grunt's lower jaw. The force of the blow straightens the grunt's back, lifting its head above hers. In that moment, a heavy club swings above Corva and collides with the head of the arm-bladed grunt. A mist of blood puffs from the point of impact.

Face still scrunched, she keeps her eyes locked on Thegn, not bothering to watch the club grunt return to the edge of the roof behind her and resume its task of keeping more from climbing up.

Zeke shifts his weight, grabbing a dreadlock and swinging himself around the front of her face. **The risk is too great. I've made a promise. Jack must live and I need you to help ensure that.**

"What makes him so important?"

Nothing. For a fraction of a second, it seems like Zeke is hesitating, like he's wrestling with sharing something more. But the expression is gone so fast that Corva thinks she could've imagined it. **I just have promises to keep. Besides, he took you in. Helped heal you up. In his own way, he even helped you figure out who you really are. Surely that counts for something.**

"Yeah, and I took him—and you, I'll add—to his suicidal friend to heal up. That makes us even." But as she says the words, her fists relax. The kid did stick out his neck for her more than once, despite trying to sell her out that first day. Her shoulders lower. "Fine. How much time do you think we've got?"

The Umbrati are likely to swarm his roof. There's a chance they'll break his concentration and slow him down a bit, but they won't get through Caffiel's fog. I think it's best to hope that Jack and Lyia have already made it down to Cliff City through whatever route Jack knows about in Slim's place.

"What about everyone else in Bule?"

She follows the little monkey's gaze as he looks around. Most windows and doorways are dark and vacant, abandoned by the crowds holed up in the siege caves. With the exception of the grunts in the horde, Bule already feels empty and desolate. Zeke doesn't turn back to her. He keeps looking around as he resumes his position on her shoulder. **The world's a horrible place.**

Corva stands somewhat in shock, still processing, when she starts to feel a buzzing, burning feeling in her nose and ear canal. That feeling is immediately replaced with a pain unlike any she's ever felt before. It's sharp, like a balloon covered with spikes was just inflated inside her skull. Muffling a scream with her hand, she drops to her knees. She pulls her hand from her mouth. It's covered in blood. She tastes it as it leaks over her lips and in the corners of her mouth. "What—What just happened?"

Corva! Are you okay?

She doesn't respond. Something else is different. She spins just in time to see the heavy club grunt collapse. What used to be its head is now a meaty stump. All that's left is its lower jaw. The steel plate that used to cover its face swings from the side, hinged by a single remaining rivet. A little bit farther behind her she hears a voice.

"Yeah-ha! Nanobots!"

Corva spits a small puddle of blood that'd drained into her mouth. "Jack. Idiota. Your timing is horrible."

JACK ATTACK

"Did you see that shit? Boom! Totally sweet! Ol' Clubby McDumbface there just dropped like nothing." Jack sprints across the top of a couple smaller buildings as he makes his way to Corva's rooftop.

His pack is heavy and awkward, swinging side to side with each step, ensuring that he's never really got full control over where he's going. Jack doesn't care, though. The juice from his chembraid sings in his veins. He's feeling great. He's already made quick work of nearly a dozen grunts since he got back on the roof. There's a clear path of dispatched Umbrati foot soldiers between him and Corva.

Slim's voice, conveyed compliments of a comm kneak, scratches loudly in Jack's head. "Yeah, kid, he fell just like all the ones you're running by right now. Don't get cocky." There's a small burst of static at the tail end of Slim's comment. "And get your finger outta your ear. It won't help you hear any better and it's gummin' up my audio stream from you."

Realizing that his finger is, in fact, stuffed in his ear, he removes it. "Right. But about that one grunt, Clubby. He was the first one where them nanos exploded. All these others, we just used 'em to do some brain-scramblin' by bouncin' 'round in their skulls."

"Which is the right way to do it. I gave you a good-sized swarm of nanobots, but not infinite. You've only got but so many. There aren't enough to blow up every grunt in this raid party."

Jack skids to a stop at the edge of Corva's rooftop. "Oh c'mon, Slim. Clubby was on Corva's roof with a bat. It was just a few steps away. Worth a few nanos to get the quick kill there." He gauges the distance in the gap between rooftops. He can see more grunts in the alley below. Some are starting to scale the building wall and make their way to the top. "You think I can clear this?"

"Distance looks a bit long for you, little guy, even with the rocket fuel in that chembraid. Plus, you've got that sack on your back loaded up pretty good. Check your left. There should be a gangway across to the other roof. Go that way. See if it ain't damaged."

Nodding in affirmation, Jack makes his way to the gangway. He jams his finger back in his left ear. "This cheap-ass comm kneak of yours sure is buzzy. Makes my ears tickle."

"That's because it ain't exactly a comm kneak. I had to cobble parts from an old radio and a VR kneak."

Jack stops just short of the gangway. A sickened chill runs over his skin. "Aw, gross, man! Don't tell me it was one of your perv scenes. Not cool, man. This thing is stuck in my head. Who wore it last?"

"Relax, kid. I sterilized it. You're fine. Now pull your friggin' finger out so I can hear around you." There's a pause as Slim stops talking and waits for Jack to comply. "Thanks. Now, that gangway looks pretty beat to shit, but I think you should be able to cross it. Go ahead and set your controller kneak to 'passthrough.' I'll remote the nanobots and keep your path clear so you can concentrate on getting to the other side."

Jack reaches up and finds the needle-shaped device sticking out among the small grouping behind his left ear. It's the tallest of the set, so his fingers find it pretty easily. He grimaces.

"I don't even wanna touch this thing. Shoulda made it controlled with a neurolink." Pinching the top, he twists it clockwise. "You should be good to go."

Edging up to the narrow gangway, Jack peers over the edge of the roof. At three stories from the alley below, it's not that far down, but a drop would hurt pretty bad. It'd certainly make him easy pickings for the grunts down there. His mind flashes to the image of his fingers tearing out that one grunt's throat. He shudders, but not from the brutality of the act. It's that those were his fingers, his hands. But it wasn't him. *What was that shit? Could I do that again? On my own? Could I even get close enough?*

He shakes his head, clearing the thought and focusing his attention on the gangway. It's a narrow steel thing, not too long. Shouldn't take more than three to four steps to cross it. Lightweight pipes form a simple railing on one side. He can see through the honeycomb mesh that serves as the walkway, barely as wide as his two feet together. A few grunts climbing up near the gangway suddenly lose their grip and drop down, flopping across the grunts on the alley floor. Slim's doing his job clearing the way.

Another blast of static in his head. "You gonna stand there starin', kid, or are you gonna get moving?"

Jack blinks. "Right."

He grabs the rail and gingerly steps up on the gangway, testing his weight. It feels pretty solid. No creaks or squeaks. Tightening his grip on the rail, he holds his breath and bends his knees to bounce a bit. Still no sounds or vibrations that might indicate the gangway's readiness to plummet to the ground below. Reassured that the crossing is safe, Jack gives a single nod to himself. With his hand still on the rail, he turns and runs across to Corva's roof.

Two steps away from the end of the gangway, he hears it. His foot makes contact with the mesh walkway, and then there's the loud metallic pop of a bolt head snapping off and shooting across the gap.

Feeling the little metal bridge give way beneath him, Jack takes a leap at Corva's roof. His upper body clears the edge just fine, but he feels his shins smack against the roof's edge.

"Kid! Jack! You alright?"

"Yeah. I'm good. Giving the painkillers in my braid a helluva workout today, though." Jack looks back to the gangway and the corner of the roof he tripped over. The thing didn't fall completely. It's wedged between the two buildings at an ugly angle, held in place mostly by the light railing caught on the edge of the rooftop. "That bridge ain't alright, though."

Slowly, he gets up. The pain in his shins throbs. *That's gonna leave a mark.* His pants haven't been torn, but he can feel the heat pulsing from where his legs hit the roof. On the upside, it doesn't feel like anything is broken. So at least there's that.

Slapping dust and little bits of rock from his chest and shoulder, he turns back in the direction of Corva. He doesn't have to look very hard. She's right there up in his face.

"You witless shit!" Blood drains from her nose, smearing past her mouth to one side, clearing a slightly more clean area where she's otherwise covered in dirt and grime. It looks like the back of her shirt is in tatters. It's possible that the straps of her backpack and Zeke's weight on her shoulder are the only things keeping it from falling off.

"Holy hell, girlie. You look horrible."

"Yeah. No thanks to you." She reaches up and uses her forefinger and thumb to wipe away a bit more of the blood from her nose. "And I told you to stop calling me 'girlie.' Pinny."

He frowns. "There's only one person allowed to call me that, an' you ain't her." Jack winces to himself as the words leave his mouth. Lyia is back at Slim's. It's likely that she's hearing all of this.

"Good. Remember that when you start trying to give me names."

"Sure. Whatever, Corva. Besides, what're you talkin' about, 'no thanks to me'? I just helped save your ass by poppin' the top on Clubby over there." Jack points his thumb over to the collapsed body of the grunt with the heavy club.

"Yeah. That one was mine. He was keeping the roof clear."

"Oh." Jack is quiet for a moment while it sinks in. "Oh! Like with Lyia an' me before? You can do that with them, too?"

"Yeah. Apparently." She spits a bit of excess blood.

"Shit. I didn't know." A thought occurs to him. "Wait … then why didn't you just control those three grunts last time, instead of controlling me an' Lyia?"

"I didn't know I could control them. You and Lyia are more familiar to me. Zeke thought that would make it easier since I'd never done it before."

There's a scratchy buzz in Jack's head. "Hey kid, this little chat of yours is nice n' all, but you need to get outta there. The whole reason we let you go was so you could get Zeke and the girl, then bug out. I've been holding off the climbers with the nanobots, but there's a lot of them grunts. Can't keep this up forever."

"Yeah. Gotcha." Jack directs his attention to Thegn on the other roof. Something's not right. The old codger is just kneeling there with his head down. Maybe he's mumbling something. Jack watches as the old coot extends his scythe and easily cuts down a pair of grunts clambering onto his rooftop.

Jack's curiosity gets the better of him. He pokes Corva on the arm and points at Thegn. "Hey, what's ol' Wrinkles up to, anyway? You gotta plan for the ancient fuck?"

"Actually . . ." She looks to Zeke on her shoulder before turning back to Jack. "We were hoping you were already in Cliff City. Our next move was to meet you there. We were just about to get out of here."

"Good. Everyone's on the same sheet of music." Jack pauses for a moment as a thought occurs to him. "Wait, why are you so interested in ducking out? You've been doing pretty good standing toe-to-toe with the old dude. What's goin' on?"

"He's—the fight's done. We need to get moving."

"Oh c'mon! That ain't an answer! I saw how you handled him. He's tough for an old man, but you were able to get him to the ground. Now he's just sittin' there, starin' at the rooftop. I'm guessin' you can probably take 'em. 'Specially with the kit I brought you. It's totally sweet. Just—"

Corva grabs his arm, interrupting. "Look. We can talk about this after. There's no time. We need—"

"No, *you* look. I'm tired hearing 'later' and 'when you're ready.' I'm ready now. I deserve—"

"Jack! He's going to kill everyone here! He's going to put his mark on everyone in Bule. You want to be around for that all over again?"

For the first time in a long time, Jack has no words.

IGNORANCE IS BLISS

He never told anyone, but Jack remembers everything.

"Why do I have to be quiet, Lee-Lee?"

Lee-Lee. That's what Jack used to call Lyia when he was a kid. It took him forever to figure out how to make that "y" sound in her name.

"Hush, Pinny. Hush and pay attention." Lyia's face was set. A serious icing on a cake made of terror.

Jack had no idea what was going on at the time. She had to explain it to him later. All he knew was that something bad was happening. They had to get out and Jack had to keep his yap shut. He sucked at both of those. But it was to be expected. He was five.

The siege on the Shadowfold's compound was sudden, but it wasn't like it was unexpected. The Fold had put a mean dent in the number of new recruits for both the Karui and the Umbrati. Of course, they did it by killing folks before they could be conscripted. "Mercies," they called them. Jack was part of the "they." He might have been a little kid, but Jack was for-sure in the Shadowfold. He'd already started his training in soulmancy.

In any case, the Shadowfold had a pretty shitty solution to the whole conscription thing, but their body count wasn't a fraction of what had been taken by the Karui and Umbrati. It wasn't just their raids. Cities and mountains had been flattened for just being in the way during the huge battles they'd have. And as ugly of a solution as it was, the Fold's approach was actually working. Fewer reports of raids. Battles reduced to skirmishes. The hope was that without a steady stream of new blood in the ranks on each side, the war could simply peter out. That it would go back to a time where although there was still fighting, it took place in the shadows, out of view for most people. At the very least, most folks might be able to return to dying on their own terms. They could avoid getting their souls dragged into a never-ending fight for the rest of forever.

But, again, none of that was on Jack's mind at the time. He'd been in lessons that morning. The Fold's compound had been under siege for about a week, attacked in alternating waves by raids from the Karui and then the Umbrati. The Shadowfold had supplies, though, and their perimeter was strong. They could've held out for months. So they kept to their regular routines like nothing was different. For Jack, that meant a morning of beginner magecraft drills. The folks in the Fold always liked to give fancy names to things. Magecraft was just their word for soulmancy.

An alarm had gone off during the morning lessons, but they'd been going like that for a few days. Jack and most of the children in his class had just gotten used to it. Still, they were all pretty restless. The teacher lady—she liked cats, so Jack remembered her as Teacher Meow—had told them to ignore the alarm and focus on imbuing their sets of glass beads. It wasn't five minutes after that when Lyia busted in, fifteen years old and all out of breath. She had a look of panic in her eyes that Jack had never seen before.

"Crows."

She said it like it was supposed to mean something. It didn't to Jack, but it did to the teacher. She'd leapt to her feet in an instant and hissed, "Scatter!"

That was something the children did understand. Every kid in the class—there were about ten of them—dropped what they were doing and shot for their designated hiding places. Jack was the youngest, so his spot was the smallest; a little Jack-sized lean-to gap under a stack of portable shielding walls.

Lyia didn't have a pre-arranged spot in the room, so she managed as best as she could. She grabbed one of the portable walls from Jack's stack and crouched beneath it. She pulled a knife from her boot and held it, reversed grip. Jack called out to her in a five-year-old not-really-whisper.

"Hi Lee-Lee!"

She flinched at the sound of Jack's voice. It's unlikely that she even knew Jack was under the stack next to her. That's when she told him to be quiet.

"But what's going on, Lee-Lee? You look scared."

"They think the Karui have activated the last of the Four. Now hush, Pin. Seriously."

And Jack did hush. For at least a whole minute. But it was boring to just sit there with nothing to do. Waiting for some unknown scary thing to happen. Jack could hear some of the other kids from my class starting to fidget in their spots. Even Lyia had to adjust herself from a crouch to a kneel.

Jack couldn't help himself. He had more questions. "How do they know it's him? How do they know it's Death?"

He could tell Lyia was agitated, but she still tried to give him a reassuring smile. She didn't answer, though. And, really, she didn't have to. The answer came on its own when they heard a pecking at the window.

At first it was just one set of pecks. A clacking, like someone throwing pebbles at the room. Then it got louder, and there were more of them. A lot more. There was so much tapping and pecking. It was like thunder that wouldn't stop. Jack couldn't hear anything else. He could've shouted at the top of his lungs and Lyia wouldn't have heard him, even though he was close enough to almost touch her.

The rumble of pecks gave way to loud caws and a rackety flapping of wings as the windows shattered, salting the room with shards of glass.

Jack couldn't see much from his hiding spot, but it sounded like the crows were everywhere. Their shadows oozed over every surface in sight. Everything they touched seemed to lose color and look sadder. Jack saw Lyia cower and try to make herself small. Her knuckles turned white from how tightly she gripped her knife.

That was the first time in Jack's life that he was ever really scared. Like, truly, I-don't-wanna-die scared. There were certainly times before that. Kids get scared all the time. But that's the first time Jack really remembers. He froze. He couldn't move even if he'd wanted to. He could feel his pulse thumping in his ears, and his stomach did cartwheels in his belly.

Jack has never gotten used to that feeling.

One of the crows hopped into the space between Jack and Lyia. He could tell it wasn't a normal crow. Its eyes were the wrong color. And it moved strangely. It didn't have the jerky twitch movements of a bird. It was smooth, almost casual, in how it looked around. But it was most certainly searching. Hunting.

The thing caught sight of Jack, and he could feel a searing, scorching pain at the top of his head, just at his hairline. He screamed and grabbed his head. His vision blurred. It could've been from the pain or the tears that were welling up. It didn't matter; he just started bucking around in his hiding spot, like a panicked baby cow. Jack didn't know it then, but that's when he received Death's Mark.

A second later, the pain was gone. Jack stopped moving and looked across the gap at Lyia. The bird was still between them, but it wasn't moving anymore. Lyia had taken care of it. She'd stabbed the tip of her knife right through that creepy bird's head. She let go of the knife immediately like it burned, leaving it buried in the crow.

The two of them stared at each other for a moment, not sure whether they were saved or screwed. A long stretch of Lyia's hair looked like it'd turned white. Jack had no idea at the time that a bit of his had done the same. In any case, their moment didn't last long.

A bloodcurdling scream cut through the din of feathers and cackles. It was Teacher Meow. Her hidey-hole was at the center of the room, not far from Jack. He chanced a peek out from his spot despite Lyia shaking her head that he shouldn't. Jack didn't particularly like putting his head that close to the dead crow between them, but he just had to see what was going on.

He was better off not knowing.

Teacher Meow was right there. It's likely that she'd lost her nerve and had stepped out to try and escape. But she wasn't alone. Standing in front of her was the Reaper. Death. Old Wrinkles himself. Of course, Jack didn't know it was Wrinkles back then. He never saw the Reaper's face. The hood of his big black cloak was drawn up and the rest of the thing was flapping everywhere, surrounded by the beating wings of flying crows all around. All Jack could see was a hint of his wiry beard sticking out.

Teacher Meow didn't even try to put up a fight. She turned in Jack's direction and bolted for the door. It was no use. Death's scythe was already out. She didn't make it two steps. Faster than fast, there was a blur near her neck and it was over. Her legs kept moving, but there was no control, no direction. Her momentum carried her body crashing into Jack's and Lyia's hiding spot. Their lean-tos held, but Teacher Meow's additional weight, small as she was, trapped them in place. Her body slumped down over the gap between Jack and Lyia, shrouding them in her frail shadow.

They weren't in complete darkness, though. Light leaked through at the top as the teacher's head rolled forward. But it didn't stop where it should've. It kept going and dropped right off her neck. The mass of it bounced off the stabbed crow's carcass and thumped to a stop.

Her eyes were still open, staring at Jack. A terrified look of shock was frozen on her face.

It took a bit for Jack's brain to register what had just happened. He caught himself staring back at his teacher's stock-still face, wondering when she was going to blink. Things didn't really sink in until Jack looked up to Lyia, thinking that maybe she had an answer.

She didn't.

Lyia's hands were clapped over her mouth. She shook like she was an ice cube holding back a scream. Tears flooded the bottoms of her eyes. It was at that point that Jack noticed the blood. It'd sprayed out from Teacher Meow's neck and splattered against the wall. But it didn't stay there. There was so much. The blood slid down the wall, into and on their lean-tos. It dripped all around them, forming a pool around the crow and Teacher Meow's head.

It's amazing how sometimes a person's senses don't always notice things at the same time. Jack was suddenly hit with the nastiest stink. He hadn't learned yet that most people end up shitting themselves when they die. This was a hell of a way to learn that. Jack felt so sick. He mirrored Lyia, clamping his hands over his mouth. *Thanks for the lesson, Teacher Meow.*

Jack and Lyia exchanged a look. That may have been the moment where everything started going wrong. Jack was pretty sure her look meant something like, "There's no way we can stay here," while his own look said, "Sure we can."

The worst of it was that it didn't stop there. Teacher Meow was just the first. From where Jack and Lyia were, they couldn't see what was going on in the room. But they could hear. The roar of the crows had gone away and was replaced by the crying and screaming of Jack's classmates. There were more thumps on their lean-tos. It seemed that the Reaper had decided that Jack's stack of shielding was the best place for piling up bodies.

Jack looked up at the gap in front of Teacher Meow's neck where her head should've been just in time to see the head of one of his classmates land in the space. Orris was his name. His bushy little head nearly blotted out the rest of what little light Jack and Lyia had left. But Jack could still see Orris's eyes staring down at him. Tear-filled. Confused. His mouth gaped soundlessly. It was like he kept silently asking, "Why?" Why was he and everyone else dead while Jack somehow was still alive?

Jack has no idea why the Reaper never found Lyia and him. Maybe it was the shielding walls they were under. Maybe it was the mound of bodies over them. Maybe Death is just a lazy old fuck. Who knows? The only thing that's certain is that it got very quiet after that.

No crows. No screams. No thumping of bodies. Just the steady drip into the growing puddle of blood between Jack and Lyia. They stayed there, trembling scared, for longer than either of them will ever know.

But it was after they finally crawled our way out, clawing through bodies and blood and filth, that they really started to understand the size of things. The stink of death was everywhere. The Reaper had killed the whole Shadowfold compound, their whole town. How was he able to do that so fast?

There were corpses everywhere they looked. Steam raised off them, forming a muggy evening fog over the whole place. A miasma of souls. That's actually where Jack learned that word. Miasma. Even the sound of it seeps out of your mouth like it doesn't want to be there. Lyia taught it to him. She'd tried healing half a dozen folks that hadn't fully died yet, but it was no use. They were gone. Everyone.

Gone.

It's something Jack will never forget.

6.20

Never Again

"Jack!"

Lyia's voice crackles in Jack's brain, snapping him out of his daze.

"Pin!"

He starts to reach up to his ear, but stops short, remembering that he's hearing her by comm kneak and not an ear wig. "I hear you, Lyia. Didn't know you were listening in on Slim's comm."

"Pinny. You can't stop him. You've got to get out—"

Jack feels the heat starting to emanate from his neck and work its way up behind his ears. Memories flash in his mind. Blood pooling under his teacher's head. That kid Orris. Jack starts to pace. "You know what I'm thinkin', do you?"

He feels Corva's hand rest on his shoulder for an instant. She doesn't say anything, but he jerks away, continuing to speak with Lyia over the comm. "I remember everything that happened back at the Fold. You were there! You watched them go, just like me. How can you tell me to stand by and let the same damn thing play out? Corva says the kill zone is all of Bule. All of Bule, Lee. We've heard this song before."

He stops in the middle of his pacing and talking. Corva's hands are on both of his shoulders now, reaching from behind him. She tries to push down. He resists, but only for a moment. He feels her foot kick behind his knee, forcing him to collapse down to a kneel. She gives him an additional shove and he finds himself on all fours. There's the breeze of something sailing over his back.

Rolling to his side, he looks back. "Hey! What the—"

The last words of that sentence don't make their way out. They clog the back of his throat as he realizes that the breeze over his back was a large axe blade swinging at him. The grunt that was wielding that axe isn't holding it in its hands any longer, though. Somehow, in the time it took Jack to roll from his hands and knees to his side, Corva managed to remove the axe from the grunt's hands and bury its blade deep in the back of the creature's skull.

The long-armed grunt wavers a bit in front of Jack; its steel-covered face seems to point blankly at him. Without warning, the mass of the thing lurches forward, a result of Corva kicking it in the back and prying the axe loose.

Jack scrambles backward, clearing himself of the landing zone for the grunt's carcass. "Shit, Corva!"

"Pay attention."

He looks around and realizes that all his pacing while talking to Lyia had brought him close to the rooftop's edge. Also, there are more grunts making their way up and over the edge. Corva connects the blade of her newly acquired axe to the neck of a nearby grunt. Two other grunts on the far side of the roof also collapse, but not from Corva. Using the visual overlay from the control kneak, Jack can see blips from the small pack of nanobots leaving the heads of those grunts. Slim's handiwork.

"Lyia, put Slim on."

"I'm here, kid. Sound's piped through the main. Both of us can hear and talk to you."

"What's going on, man? You're s'posed to be keepin' things clear."

"Cut me some slack, kid. I'm all friggin' *Space Invaders* here. Fuckers know where you guys are and they just keep comin'."

There's a series of metallic pops and a loud screeching sound over the edge of the roof where Jack had crossed. He turns just in time to see the last bit of the metal gangway twist off of both buildings and crash to the alley below. In its place, he sees the spindly fingers from the grunts that tore it down. They claw at the edge of the roof, trying to find any decent kind of grip.

"Shit." Jack squats down, swinging his heavy pack off his shoulders to the ground in front of him.

"What are you doing?" Corva's voice is sharp, insistent.

"Yeah, kid. Now ain't the time for a picnic."

"Will everyone just shut the fuck up a sec? Our only clear way off this rooftop just got torn down. I guarantee that the roof access is locked tight. So even if we wanted to make a run for it—an' I ain't so sure we should—we're in for a helluva fight. Every bit of gear is gonna help." He digs in his bag, shoving items to the sides, then looks up to Corva. "I got somethin' for ya."

Jack drags a long, roughly cylindrical item wrapped in cloth from the bag and offers it up to her. Corva grabs the bundle, a quizzical look on her face. Zeke switches his perch to her other shoulder so he can see better. Unrolling the bundle, both Corva's and Zeke's eyes widen. Jack smiles as she realizes that she's holding the two explodey batons from her first fight at his bar.

"Slim told me that disarming an' re-encoding the biometrics was a right sumbitch."

Dropping the cloth, she holds a baton in each hand and gives them a bit of a test swing. "They work?"

There's a crackle in Jack's brain. "Do they work? Jack, this chick is insulting my art. You best—"

"Yeah, they work. We already bound 'em to your bio. Check the strike surface. Gel's already coating. That means they're activated. They recognize you."

Jack closes up his bag and slings it back over his shoulder. "Jus' don't go blowin' any more holes in the ground, yeah?"

She smiles. It's warm and genuine, the kind of face he imagines that a friend might make. It actually takes him off guard for a moment. Then her expression changes, like an idea just came to her. She looks at the roof access door. "Hey, Jack. Holes in the ground are off-limits, but what about holes in roofs?"

He follows her gaze to the door. "Yeah. Thought of that. This building is Spitz' place. Bit of a storehouse. One floor. High ceiling. Helluva fall if you boom too big. Besides, didn't you just fall through a roof? You wanna do that again?"

Corva and Zeke exchange a look. Zeke nods, disappointed. Corva gives the access door one more plaintive look before turning back to Jack. "Yeah. Okay."

Jack stares at her for a moment while his ears fill with the sounds of grunting and scratching from the horde still trying to make their way onto the roof. They don't have time to argue about this. "Look. Let's call it a backup plan. Okay?"

Corva gives a slight tip of her head. It's not much of an affirmation, but it's enough.

Rubbing his hands together, Jack refocuses on the task at hand. "Alright. You watch my back. I got a bit of business to handle with ol' Wrinkles."

He runs up to the building edge closest to Thegn and brings his hand up to his left ear. "Hey, Slim. You still got summa them nanos for me to play with?"

Slim's voice crackles in Jack's head. "Yeah, kid. But hey, maybe you should—"

"Thanks." With that, Jack twists the tip of the nanobot control kneak, disabling the passthrough to Slim and giving himself control of them once more. *Where are you little fuckers?*

His mind tingles with the added awareness of each nanobot in the swarm. Despite knowing that there are at least three Umbrati grunts an arm length or two from reaching the top edge of the roof where he stands, Jack allows himself to close his eyes. For a moment, he sees a brief wisp of a not-face filling the darkness, its mouth opening and closing silently.

Jack shakes the vision from his mind and focuses on reacclimating himself to the nanodrones. Slim did well; most of the nanobots remain unexploded and generally undamaged. They're split into two minor swarms, one on each side of the building. Using the controls afforded by the kneak, he reunites the swarms and brings the full collection of nanobots forward to his current position. Another voice scratches in his mind.

"Jack. Pinny. What are you doing? We've gotta get away from here. We can hide like before—"

Lyia.

Somber, Jack shakes his head. Of course, they can't see him do that. His eyes are still closed. He speaks out loud; at least Slim and Lyia can hear him. "Sorry, Lee. I can't stand by while another town dies—gets killed. Not when I'm here and I might be able to do something about it. Ya'll need to keep your mouths shut for a spell. I'm gonna need to concentrate."

He opens his eyes and looks up toward Thegn's roof, expecting to see that old sack of loose skin kneeling there, not looking at anything. Instead, his entire view is filled with the hideous steel-plated face of yet another grunt.

Jack flinches. The nanobots aren't going to get to his position in time to protect him. He looks at the grunt's throat, wondering if he can strike out and attack like when he was being controlled by Corva's weird power.

He edges a foot to the side, preparing to do a quick sidestep. The grunt lunges forward. He slips to the grunt's side, but there's another problem; he's too close to the edge of the rooftop. While dodging the grunt, Jack's shin slams into the low wall that wraps the roof. Right in the same spot he hit before. It hurts horribly, and he's on the verge of careening over the edge and into the ally below. The thought briefly runs through his mind that the swarm of grunts choking that confined space would break his fall. *Great, I'll live just long enough to feel myself being torn apart.*

Jack feels his weight threaten to drag him over the edge. His feet lift off the rooftop. His arms flail out, grabbing at nothing, and his stomach tightens as his mouth fills with saliva. Inexplicably, he smiles. He can't help it. The thought is too amusing. His last act in the world is going to be to vomit all over a crowd of Umbrati as he plummets to his death.

Just as he feels his feet start to clear the roof's low wall, he's stopped midair. He's not falling anymore. Long, spindly fingers wrap his shoulder to the back of his neck, gripping him tightly. His body twists a bit from its own inertia, allowing him to see the blank, covered face of the grunt he just dodged. For a moment, they stare at one another. Well, Jack stares at the grunt. Without eyes, it's difficult to tell where exactly the grunt might be looking. Stranger still, it isn't making any of its typical hissing or grunting sounds.

In a single mechanical move, barely shifting its weight at all, the grunt hurls Jack back on the rooftop. The second it lets go, Jack hears the grunt resume its familiar sick throat-clearing noise. It only lasts a blink, though. The guttural sounds of the grunt are cut short, replaced by a small boom muffled by something wet and meaty. Jack rolls over in time to see Corva's follow-through with her new batons, right where the grunt's head used to be.

"Pay attention, Jack!"

He watches as Corva takes a second swing at the body of the now-headless grunt, caving in its chest and sending it over the edge and into the alley. Still riding her shoulder, Zeke looks down on Jack. The expression on the monkey's face seems like it reflects a certain amount of pity.

Corva bounces on her toes, keeping her body turned sideways so both Jack and Thegn are in her field of view. "So, you're not listening to anyone with more sense than you. Big surprise."

"You heard me?"

"Yeah. Subtlety really isn't your thing."

Jack opens his mouth to argue, but Corva interrupts before he gets any words out. "Look, I get it. I really do. You don't want to see another town get wiped out. Neither do I. I had the same argument with Zeke. He says the smart move is to run. But he also says you always have a plan. I trust that. We trust that."

Jack feels himself smile involuntarily.

"However," Corva's voice is enough to push the smile away. "Your plan won't work unless you let us in on it."

Corva takes a swing at the wall just as another grunt's hand reaches over its lip. As the wall crumbles and the grunt's hand disappears, she steps between Jack and the roof's edge; between Jack and Thegn. "So what's your plan?"

456

EPISODE SEVEN:
MEMORY AND SACRIFICE

Episode Seven: Memory and Sacrifice

Contents

7.1

Plans

"Jack. That's a stupid plan."

Corva watches Jack sigh in frustration. Why did she even bother asking him what his plan would be? She redirects her attention, putting her focus on keeping the roof clear. She has two grunts roaming the perimeter knocking back any new ones that want to crest over the edge. In her mind's eye, she can sense the world around them and control their limbs as if they are her own. It takes some effort, but not nearly as much as she would've thought.

As far as anyone else can tell, though, she's just standing there, glaring at Jack. *Yeah, like anyone else would be crazy enough to be out here and see this.*

"What's so stupid about it?" Jack kneels at his pack and starts rummaging in it some more. Apparently he's not deterred by her criticism of his plan and there's something else that he thinks is useful in that bag of his.

For a moment, Corva wonders what kind of madness Jack has packed in her bag. And how much damage that stuff has taken in her last few minutes of falling through the sky and partially caving in a rooftop.

"Jack. Jack!" Despite her efforts to get his attention, Jack ignores her and continues burying himself in his pack.

Enough of this. She puts both batons in a single hand so she can grab his shoulder with her free one and pull his attention to her. "Stop that! What are you looking for now? *Para*! It's a stupid plan because it's not even a plan, even by your standards. You want us to play the part of blunt instrument here. Brute force." Corva forces Jack to face her. It's easy given the small size of his frame. "You're not built for brute force."

Jack rips away from Corva's grip, but keeps his face pointed at her. Defiant. "I don't need muscles, I've got—"

"You've got what?" It takes everything in her to resist laughing at his naivety. "You've got tech? Magic? This is Death. He's been defeating the best of those weapons for over a century. You think you've got something he hasn't seen?"

Finally, Jack looks away. Starts digging in his bag again. He's still scowling, but his shoulders have dropped, more like he's pouting. "It's not magic."

"Magic, fixins … whatever you call it. The Old Beard has seen it and beat it."

"The Touch worked on him pretty good."

Corva grabs Jack's chin and directs his attention across to the other rooftop. Thegn is still sitting there with that rat on his shoulder, untouchable. "Yeah. How'd that work out?"

He jerks his face out of her hands. "It was my first time really usin' it! I just need to get close enough. I'll finish him right this time."

"Take a good look over there. Look at him! Look at Death." Corva points at the Old Beard with the two batons in one hand.

Moodily, Jack complies.

Corva continues, "Have you noticed that none of these grunts can get near him? He's just sitting there, but do you see bodies piled up around him? Kind of a perfect ring. Anyone, grunt or otherwise, collapses if they so much as step on that rooftop. Even me. I was there. That rat of his can put anyone to sleep if they get too close. I was only able to get away because of Zeke. Even the grunts have gotten the message and aren't trying to get closer. There's no way you can get close enough to use the Touch."

Jack stares across at Thegn and Caffiel, but his face is different. He's still wearing a scowl, but he's not pouting. It's something else.

There's no time for this.

Zeke adjusts his position on her shoulder. **Give him a chance.**

Now you want to stay and fight? Make up your mind, Zeke!

Don't discount the boy entirely. The situation is different now compared to when I thought he and Lyia had made it down to Cliff City. At this point, I'm not sure that they'd be safe even there. So we have to improvise. If there's anything Jack's good at, it's adjusting in the moment. Otherwise, he would've died years ago.

There's no reasoning with either of you! She turns her head away from the monkey and settles her view on Thegn. She locks her mind on her grunt puppets, still diligently keeping their rooftop clear. Although their proportions are all messed up, there's a certain rhythm in their movement. It's too much to call it graceful, but there's an easiness there. An almost pure lack of resistance. She thinks. They act. Natural extensions of herself, just like when she had extra arms. Comfortable. It's as easy as breathing.

Finally, Jack speaks up.

"When you say that rat puts everyone to sleep, do you mean actual sleep, or do you mean that as a fanciful way of saying 'dead'?"

Corva checks with Zeke on her shoulder.

It's the former. Though I suppose if Caffiel concentrated, he could put someone in a coma.

She looks back to Jack. "Zeke says it's just sleep, but it's probably not a good idea to test it out."

"And you're sure it's the rat doing that?"

Corva faces Jack. "Yeah. Caffiel. The sleepytime sigil."

Jack tilts his head. "What's a sig—never mind. Doesn't matter. New plan."

She crosses her arms and waits for him to explain himself. Jack doesn't seem to notice. Apparently his next harebrained idea has him fully engrossed.

He crosses the rooftop so he's at the edge closest to Thegn's building and puts one foot on the low wall there. Corva maneuvers her grunts to keep the area around her and Jack clear.

Jack points in the direction of the other rooftop. "We start by taking out the rat. Slim, you still there?"

He pauses a beat, apparently waiting for Slim to respond on the other side of his comms.

It's not a long pause, because almost immediately, Jack nods. The tinkerer apparently has been listening to them this whole time. "Good. I'm gonna need you to pilot your nanobots again. Break up the swarm into as many smaller groups as you can control. Position them around that rooftop. When I give the go-ahead, you get that rat. My guess is that the little pink-eyed bastard's nighty-night mojo only works on things that are alive. Tech should get by without a prob."

Another pause. The reply on the other end is more than a simple yes or no. Finally Jack responds, "We'll have to risk it. Even if the tech can't get through, hopefully it's enough of a distraction for the rest of this."

He reaches up and twists one of the kneaks behind his ear before turning to regard Corva. "Now you. I'm gonna need your help gettin' me close once Slim takes out the rodent."

Corva feels her face crinkle. "What kind of help?"

Jack takes a deep breath and tilts his head in the direction of the nearest grunt under Corva's control. "That kind of help. I need you to get me close to ol' Wrinkles."

"How close?"

Jack reaches out his arm and extends two fingers, just like he had in the bar when he used the Touch on Thegn. "About that close."

It takes a second for the full scope of Jack's plan to sink in for Corva. If her surprise shows in her face, Jack isn't reacting to it. He just lowers his arm and stares at her. Corva collects herself and narrows her eyes at him. "I didn't get the impression that you liked it the last time I controlled you."

"I *don't* like it. But you can make me move in a way that I never thought I could. You saw me when I tried getting here. Damn near dropped my own ass in the alley. Can't afford me fuckin' this up."

"What if your buddy Slim can't get to the rat? I'm not sure I can control you if you're unconscious."

"I'd love to have some way to test that out, but there's no time." Jack stands up and stretches. It would seem that whatever he was after in his pack isn't important anymore. "We're just gonna have to hope for the best."

Zeke adjusts his position on her shoulder. **There's a pretty large margin for error, but it's not a bad approach. The Touch is powerful. Even if it doesn't kill Thegn, it's already incapacitated him once.**

Jack groans and makes a face. "Oh c'mon. Not you, too! The vid wasn't reliable. There aren't very many folks about, and we couldn't control where any of them was looking."

Corva pokes Jack in the chest. "Zeke was complimenting you, *idiota.*"

"I wasn't talkin' to you. Or to Zeke. Can't hear his monkey ass anyway. I got Slim an' Lyia on comms in my head. They're doubtin' me, too. Askin' why I just didn't use the Touch through Slim's surveillance rig."

"You can do that?"

"Yeah. In theory. Lyia would know better. But Old Man V said that's how the Fold was so effective in their mercies. They'd cruise in with a small swarm of drones. Each mage had a vid screen with live footage from a few of them drones. Most of a town would be cleared that way. Then they'd go in and do cleanup for anyone they missed."

"Can't you see vid from those nanobots or whatever?"

"Kinda, but the playback goes right through the kneak an' it overlays what I see. I gotta be able to touch something in order to, you know, use the Touch."

"But then why d—"

"I'm tired of always hiding! Tired of being afraid. I'm not gonna hide while my town gets torn apart and the folks I care about get hurt. Again." Jack's face is painted with a mix of frustration and impatience.

Corva sighs and refrains from sharing all her doubts. Instead, she packs it all into making one point, the only one that matters. "I don't know the Touch. I can control your body, but I can only make you do things I know how to do. Even if I can get your body close enough …"

She lets the end of the sentence hang in the air between them.

"I know. You're going to need to drop control once you get me there. If I'm awake, I'll probably only have a couple seconds before Wrinkles ends my day." Jack holds up his hand, brandishing two fingers. "Just get these two fingers on him. I'll handle the rest."

Corva.

"Já deu, Zeke! I get it." She turns her attention to the little monkey on her shoulder. Only, he's not looking at her. His face is pointed across the alley, toward the other rooftop. Toward Thegn. "What is it?"

Whatever you two choose to do, you need to do it now. Zeke's paws dig into Corva's shoulder through her pack's straps. **He's starting.**

Before those words echo across her mind, Corva is already following Zeke's gaze to watch Thegn. The old man leans forward, and for a moment, he appears to be levitating, like there's a swell of energy pushing up from under him. It's enough to raise him from his seated position so he can place his feet beneath himself in a high squat. The rat scurries down Thegn's arm to a new post at Death's feet.

Thegn doesn't lift his head at all. For a moment, a subtle shudder seems to work its way over his whole body.

Half a breath later, Thegn's back bursts open, erupting with feathery darkness. Crows. An unspeakable, unimaginable number of crows spew from an enormous gash in Thegn's back. The entire view before Corva, Jack, and Zeke is filled with the dark swarm of Death. It's a living cloud of feathered shadows. Ominous. Sinister. And deafeningly loud.

Corva looks to Jack. His slack-jawed expression of surprise mirrors how she feels. He says something. Screams it. She can't hear him at all. It doesn't matter. His meaning is clear.

"We're screwed."

466

AVOID. A VOID.

Fuck, this hurts. Thegn clenches his teeth. His bony fingers ball into fists. It doesn't matter how many times he's done this before. There's no getting used to it. The pain is nearly indescribable. It's not just the gaping wound torn across his back. It isn't even the thousands of black birds bursting out from that laceration. That's not exactly a picnic, but the pain is more than that. More existential.

Imagine being a balloon constantly getting inflated. There's a million holes punched into the surface. The tears threaten the integrity of the surface, so they must be patched. Continuously patched. But there's simply no possible way to contain the sheer volume of air that keeps coming. So more holes need to be punched. And then patched. And punched again. All the while, the air keeps coming.

Regardless, it still has to be done. It's necessary. Issuing death at this scale should never be comfortable, no matter how noble the intentions.

I can sense your distress. Caffiel turns from his post at Thegn's feet and trains his pink slitted eyes on the old man's face. **You look unwell.**

Thegn speaks back through gritted teeth. "You figure that out all by yourself? Real insight you've got, rat."

Don't get indignant with me, youngster. I only mean to say that it's been quite some time since you've had to exert yourself this much. A skirmish with another horseman—even one who's not fully awakened. That is no small matter. And then releasing your crows on top of that. Are you sure you haven't reached your limit?

"I'll manage."

See that you do. I have no desire to roam the land like my brothers and sisters. My present circumstances with you are particularly favorable in comparison. Rodents don't get nearly the same kind of pleasant treatment as other fauna.

Thegn can't help but let a tight-lipped smile seep through the pain. "What? You don't think anyone would let you tend a bar?"

The rat turns away in disgust. **Don't speak of my elder brother. Ezekiel is such a disappointment. So much wasted potential.**

Thegn tilts his head quizzically. In all the years that they've been together, Caffiel rarely ever referenced any of the other sigils. Of course, for the majority of that time Thegn was under the employ of the Karui. Between their monopolization of mental communication and his general hatred of telepathy, it's not like they had many in-depth discussions. Still, a hundred and fifty-some years is a long time to hold in feelings this strong. Thegn understands this better than most.

Speaking of my sibling ... Caffiel's attention is locked across to another rooftop, the one upon which Durga's host is standing with that bartender kid and the second sigil. **It appears that Ezekiel is concocting a plan with his cohorts. Are you sure you want to proceed?**

"The Umbrati have swarmed the township. There's no telling how many of them, or how many of the people here, have seen Durga in her new form." Thegn can feel his pulse in his face, a rhythmic agony. "This has to happen. It's bad enough that the Karui know about her.

Think of the mayhem if both sides, as well as all humanity, knows that she lives, let alone any of the other horsemen."

I believe that the phrase is supposed to be "two birds with one stone," not "two stones with a few thousand birds."

"That's cute, rat."

Isn't it? I'm rather proud of myself. Popular idioms are so fleeting and difficult to keep track of. Caffiel returns his attention to Thegn, his rodent face almost sympathetic. **Still, your reasoning is sound. Lack of choice is so very distasteful. However, you may want to proceed at a faster rate. It seems that they've started to muster their resolve. It would be quite nice if I were able to dip into my brother's mind and get a sense of their strategy. Alas, I can't.**

"Doesn't matter what they try. It's too late."

The piercing pain eases a little as the last of his crows, his surrogates, exits his back. Thegn feels his back slowly attempt to heal and reassemble itself. He lifts Caffiel and places the rat on his shoulder perch where he belongs. Then, stiff and tender, he lifts himself to his full height.

I still dislike traveling the Void with you. The dead can be so …

"Sad?"

Clingy.

Thegn shakes his head. "You'll just have to exercise tolerance. They're about to get some new neighbors."

He reaches behind his back to let the blood there collect in his hand and reform as his scythe.

Going straight for her?

"No." Thegn rolls his shoulders. "First, we clear the field."

And with that, he and Caffiel disappear from view.

7.3

BOOM

"What happened? Where'd he go?" Lyia leans over Slim's shoulder; panic creeps its way up her back. She knows what this is. Knows what's coming. The crows are here. She's been through this before. It can't be happening again, though. Not here.

"I—I don't know. Can't see him on anyone's playback. The nanobots can't see him, either. Dude's just … gone. All those birds are still around, but he's not anywhere." Slim shifts in his seat and looks up at her. There's a bit of a spark in his eye, a playfulness despite his stern squint. "You think maybe he just gave up and went away?"

She scowls. Sure, Slim knows that they're not out of danger, but he's got no idea what's coming. He hasn't been through this like she and Jack have. Hasn't seen the piles of bodies from the decimation of a whole town. Hasn't felt the burn of Death's Mark.

It's not a time for jokes.

Lyia grabs the sides of Slim's face and turns him back to the array of monitors. "Don't look at me. Look at those screens. Find out where he went. How can he even do that?"

471

"Shit, Lee, I dunno. He's fuckin' Death. He's got a scythe made of his own blood and up until a few minutes ago, he was flying. I'm pretty sure he can do a lot of things we can't."

"Well, then tell me where the crows are going."

"Where they're going? They're not moving like a flock, Lee. I don't think these are normal birds. They're spreading out. They're going everywhere."

Her heart sinks. "They're not normal birds. They're emissaries of Death. Where they go, he follows. They mark. He reaps."

Slim cocks his head like he wants to look at her, but he can't tear his gaze from the images on his monitors. "So this is it? Bule is doomed?"

She lets the question roll in her mind. The day had started so normal. Even the alert of a coming raid wasn't all that out of the ordinary. Since then, though, the day has been an unending series of emotional ups and downs. It's like her spirit has been dragged on the footpaths that weave along the canyon walls.

On the screens, she sees Jack. Deflated, but not defeated. There's still hope there. After all that kid has been through, all he's seen, somehow he still manages to hope. To think there's a way out. But not this time. Not by himself, at least. An idea hits her.

"He needs help."

Slim finally peels his gaze off his screens and looks at Lyia. "Who needs help? Death? This isn't a good time for you to have a whole conversation in your head and then talk to me like I heard it."

"Jack, asshole. Jack needs help."

"We are helping. We're his eyes and ears. Tiny, explosive eyes and ears."

"That's not enough. We need to be his voice."

"What are you talking about?"

Lyia grabs a stool and pulls next to Slim. "We've got to work fast. Once the crows start finding people, it won't be long before Death shows up to collect them."

"Dammit, Lee! I can't help you if I don't know what you're trying to do."

She grits her teeth as memories of past arguments flood her mind. This is exactly why they were no good together. Slim could never just be along for the ride. He had to know every little detail; he still does. It isn't enough to share physical space for him, he's got to be all up in her headspace too. But …

She stares at the terminal and array of monitors in front of her. He *doesn't* know what she's trying to do. She closes her eyes and lets out a breath. It's more infuriating when he's right.

Opening her eyes, she turns to face Slim. "I'm going to say a bunch of things right now. There's no time, so you're going to let me say these things and you're not going to interrupt. Ah—"

Slim opens his mouth to say something, but Lyia stops him with a glare before he gets going. "No questions."

She pauses for half a beat to ensure he's compliant before continuing. "Good. Here's what's going to happen. We need to get word to Harris. Hiding isn't going to work this time. Those birds go everywhere. There's no getting away from them. And they're like portals or beacons that tell Death where to go. But the birds can be killed. I killed one with Jack when Death came to us."

Slim nods. "Killing the crows shuts the doors. I get it."

"I thought I said no interruptions." Lyia scowls.

But Slim has already turned back to his terminal. "Do you want to argue about that or do you want to get this done?" After a few quick jabs at the keys, he continues. "After Jack asked, I checked. Harris's gear is off. I've got no comms to him and as far as I can tell, he's out of range of my 'eyes and ears' hack with the playback kneaks. How do you want to get in touch with him?"

"What about your little nano-whatevers?"

"The nanobots? Yeah, I guess they're not doing Jack much good now. I could get them over to Harris's siege cave. But then what? They're too small to see and I designed them to be no louder than a mosquito buzzing."

"They blow up, though."

"You want me to set off an explosion inside a cave full of people?"

"Do you have a better idea?"

Now it's Slim's turn to scowl. "No. Not yet, at least. Lemme get the bots over there. I might have an idea, but I'll have to work on it while the bots make their way." He points to one of his monitors. "I'll leave this bot with Jack so we can see him. Tell me if Jack turns his comms back on so we can tell him what we're doing."

Lyia focuses on the image of Jack on the screen. She's never seen him this dispirited. That isn't right. That needs to be fixed.

"I need two bots." Lyia looks over to Slim, who is already focused on his task of reaching out to Harris. He's so absorbed, he doesn't seem to hear her. She smacks the back of his head. "Hey!"

"Ow! What did you—"

"Save it. I need another bot."

"What for?"

"For Jack."

"Why? We already have the one looking at him. If you need a different angle—"

"I need to blow it up next to his head."

"You what?"

"Look at him! That's not Jack. Not the one we know. No matter how many times life has handed him a raw deal, he always has another angle, another plan, another idea on how to turn a mess in his favor."

Slim can't help but grin. "Most of those schemes never pan out."

"But that never stops him, does it? It's one of the truly admirable things about the kid."

"Youthful naivety. He'll grow out of it. Get jaded and bitter like the rest of us."

"I thought the same thing. But now? Seeing him in this moment where that spark of his is missing? No. It's a critical part of him. A core of who he is. I can't let him lose that. Especially now."

Slim raises an eyebrow. "And your solution is to detonate an explosion in his face."

Lyia shrugs with a weak smile. "Pinny has never been good with subtlety. We just need to get his attention. Snap him out of this, this—"

"Funk. I get it. A slap to the head is sometimes exactly what's necessary to get the brain going." Slim rubs the back of his own head where Lyia had smacked him.

She winces. "Yeah, sorry about that."

"Nope. It kinda proved your point." Slim eyes are alight with the old mischief that drew her toward him years ago. "Let's get Jack's attention with a little boom."

7.4

Should've Expected

"What the fuck, Slim!" Jack enables his comm kneak while rubbing the side of his head. His ears are still ringing from the unmistakable loud pop of a nanobot being set off right next to him. He looks over to Corva and Zeke, concern knitted across their faces. "I'm okay. You just keep an eye out for Wrinkles."

"Sorry little boss." Slim's voice crackles through the comm. "We needed to tell you some—"

"We needed your attention, Pinny." Lyia's voice interrupts Slim through the scratchy sound of the kneak. "You and I both know what happens next. There's not much time. Slim and I are taking the nanobots so we can warn Harris and the rest of the town. We'll leave one with you so we can track where you are. You and Zeke need to figure out how to stop this."

Jack sees Zeke point out across the rooftops. He tracks the same direction and catches a glimpse of a dark scythe cutting through a pocket of Umbrati grunts. Then, just as quickly, it disappears. "Yeah. Stop Death. That's the perfect job for a monkey and a pair of kids." He

477

catches Corva raising her eyebrows at him. "What? Don't act like you're all that much older than I am."

Lyia breaks in again over the comm, "You and I are the only ones in this town who've seen Death attack a town, let alone survived it. The two of us are the ones with the best chance of stopping him."

"The four of us, actually." Jack still hasn't taken his eyes off Corva and Zeke. Corva is still keeping the roof clear, working with her grunt puppets. Zeke keeps a vigil watching across the rest of Bule, pointing out brief sightings of Thegn taking out another group of grunts. It's not clear if he's gotten to any of the siege caves, but there's a chance he hasn't. The Reaper seems to be working in a slowly shrinking ring, with their happy little trio at the center. That gives them some time, but not much.

"What's that?" Lyia's voice sounds confused.

But Jack's mind is already on a roll. Maybe it was the blast from that nanobot by his head or seeing that Corva and Zeke haven't given up, but a new plan is starting to form. He's talking to himself as much as he is to Lyia. "The four of us. We're the best possible team for taking on Wrinkles. Zeke an' Corva have tangled with the ol' fuck before. Maybe even did better than just survivin'. We need a way to get ahead of him, though."

"I don't understand, Jack. Slim, he's not making sense on your comm kneaks. Can you get that bot to track his face better? Maybe I can read his—"

Then it hits him. "Tracking!"

"What?" The question comes from everyone at the same time. Lyia and Slim on the comms. Corva in front of him. Even Zeke stops and points a look of confusion at Jack.

"Corva! Zeke looks like he's doing more than guessin' at where Wrinkles is gonna show next. Can he see the spiritual plane? Is that what he's doing?"

Corva looks at Zeke and then back to Jack. "He says yes, but how do you—"

"I've been there. Old Man V said Death passes through there sometimes. That's gotta be how he's popping from one crow to the next."

"Jackspin." Lyia's voice scratches over the comm kneak. "You're talking crazy. What's going on?"

"I'm still fuzzy on a lot of the details myself, but that's okay. You go get Harris an' everyone up to speed. Tell 'em that their best bet is to get away from town. At least push away from where we are. Some of them caves have deeper cuts in the back. Gotta squeeze a bit to get through, but it should be enough to get them from the crows. Anyone still in a building is gonna hafta make a run for it, though. You'll hafta signal 'em to go once I get started."

"Jack." The hesitant voice is Corva's this time. Jack notices that although Corva's grunts are still diligently working, her attention— her's and Zeke's, actually—is on him. They still have that look of concern etched into each of their faces. However, instead of worrying about something that exploded next to his head, it's clear that their apprehension is related to what's going on *inside* his head.

He lets out a sigh. "Alright. Everything on the table. But this is what we're doing. You're all going to hear things you don't like. There's no time for debate. Unless you have ideas on how to make this plan work better, I don't want to hear it."

It takes a moment, but he gets slow nods from Corva and Zeke. Slim's voice scrapes across the comms. "Lee's on board, little boss. She's just a little tongue-tied."

Jack shakes his head. "I need to hear her say it."

"Say what you need to, Pin. I reserve the right to tell you how much I dislike it after your plan works."

"I can handle that." An enormous grin stretches its way across Jack's face and then immediately dissolves as he starts getting into what he has to say next. "Alright. Here's the deal. Lyia, you should know by now that Wrinkles came here for Corva. She's a survivor from Fareburne. Yeah, that Fareburne. But that's not why Wrinkles is after her. You can also probably tell that her little puppet trick isn't a fixin. Ol' Wrinkles ain't exactly the last of the Four. I don't know how it works, but Corva here, she's War. And Zeke can apparently talk to her because he's some kinda amplifier. My guess is that Wrinkles's rat is the same. And—"

He hesitates. This one is the hardest to share with Lyia.

"And I know how to use the Touch. Old Man V was trainin' me from a Fold text he'd traded for a long time back. V died before we finished, but I figured out the rest, I think. I used it on Wrinkles. And when I was half dead in the basement of the Red Light, I was able to talk to Old Man V on the spiritual plane."

Jack waits a beat before continuing. It's a weird feeling. This is the first time he's laid out everything he knows about a given situation. In the past, it's always been more to his advantage if everyone else only sees their part and he's the only one who can see the whole board, the only one who knows all the angles. It's easy to tilt things in his favor when he's the fulcrum that everything balances on. This isn't the time for that, though. He doesn't need the better part of a deal. He needs a team—no, he needs *friends*. Friends that trust him.

No one has said anything yet. Could be that they're each stuck in their own stunned silence after finding out something they didn't know before. Doesn't matter. It's time to get to the actual plan.

He continues, "Okay. Now that everyone knows what's up—as best as we can tell—here's what's gonna happen. Lyia, you n' Slim go ahead and find Harris. Tell him everything."

"Everything?" Lyia's voice echoes Jack's own concerns about that idea.

"Yeah. Everything. Ol' Hairless is a self-serving dick, but he's smart and he likes this town. With half the picture of what's goin' on, he might think he has a play of some sort. Knowin' everything, he'll see his choices are either to help out or to bug out. It'll be tough, getting him to believe you, but you'll hafta figure that part out."

Jack turns his attention to Zeke and Corva. "Now you two. Corva, how many of them grunts can you control?"

"I've had up to three."

"Damn. That ain't much. Can you do more?"

"Merda, Jack, I don't know. I'm still figuring this out. Zeke says I can, but I've never tried. How many do you need?"

"A lot more. As many as you can get. And you're wrong. If you're War, then you've definitely done this before. You just gotta remember how."

Corva stares at Jack, unconvinced. "Assuming I can control more grunts, what am I supposed to do with them?"

"Get in Death's way. Slow him down. Buy some time. Work with Zeke to figure out where Wrinkles is going and make things harder for him." Jack digs into his pack and pulls out a few sealed cylinders. He hands them to Zeke. "I ain't entirely sure how, but these might help. Imbued beads. Originally packed them to trade while on the roam, but I think we're gonna need every toy we can get."

Corva watches as Zeke unscrews the cap on one of the cylinders and extracts a single bead, glowing a soft blue. "How do they work?"

"Zeke knows, but rule of thumb is, 'blue adds energy, orange takes away.' You can use the blue ones on yourself as a kind of booster, but I don't recommend it unless it's a last resort. Side effects."

"What kind of side effects?"

Jack shrugs. "Everything from explosive diarrhea to spontaneous combustion."

Zeke puts the bead back and scowls at Jack. Corva gives a slow wary nod without removing her gaze from the cylinders. "Yeah. Last resort." She turns her attention back to Jack. "What about you? What's your part in this?"

Jack takes a deep breath. "I'm gonna try to blink myself into the spiritual plane. Try to track after Wrinkles there. Slow him down in my own way. Together, we might just buy enough time for everyone to get away safely."

It takes a second for it all to sink in. Corva is the first one to piece it together. "Your plan doesn't involve us surviving, does it?"

Jack's hand goes to the back of his head and rubs, almost embarrassed-like. "It would sure be nice to have a chance of living through this, that's for sure. Thing is, I don't think we can do what needs to be done if we're lookin' for a way out while we do it."

He looks hard into Corva's eyes. "You don't hafta play along with this if you don't wanna. He's after you. You don't owe this town nothing. I wouldn't think any less of you if you dropped everything now and got yourself to safety. None of you, really." He jerks his head in the direction of Slim's building. "But I'm doin' this. I'm not gonna stand around and watch another burg turn into an instant ghost town. Maybe the folks here are assholes. Or maybe they think they've been carrying weight for me because I ain't fully grown. Either way, I don't care. I have a chance to stop this, or slow it at least, and I'm gonna feel like dirt if I live without trying."

Zeke is the first one to respond. The little monkey hops off Corva's shoulder and scurries over to climb up to Jack's. Jack feels Zeke's tiny paw come to a rest on the side of his head; warmth radiates from the spot.

Corva looks from Jack to Zeke and back to Jack. "He says he's proud of you. Says Vardin would be, too. Zeke will do everything he can to help you. I will too. I'm not going anywhere. I run now and Thegn is just going to follow me. And he'll destroy every small town and gray haven where he finds me. War might be somewhere in my head, but these are my hands. I'm responsible for the blood that gets on them."

"Slim and I are in, too, Pinny." Lyia's voice flows over the scratchy signal on Jack's comm kneak. "I will always have your back."

"Besides," Slim's voice butts in with a lightness that makes it obvious that he's smiling, "if you're gone, I won't have anyone to knowingly guinea pig my—ow!"

"Don't listen to him, Pinny." Lyia comes back on the line. "Slim wouldn't recognize a tender moment if it slapped him in the face."

"You call that tender? You got me right on my ear!"

The banter relaxes Jack. Reassures him. He can't help but grin. These are his people. There's no one else in the world he'd rather have next to him, no matter the odds. He looks around at Bule's dingy brown skyline, if it could be called that, and regains a feeling of seriousness.

"Alright. We're all in, then. Let's do this."

Untouchable

Jack watches the path of one of Thegn's crows as it arcs across the sky toward one of the far buildings in Bule. There's just one problem with this whole plan of his. Him. Jack. He's got no idea how he's going to blink himself over to the spiritual plane. The last time he was there—the last time? That was just an hour or so ago. It's hard to believe how much has happened in such a short stretch of time.

He traces the path of another crow. This one is a little bit closer. Regardless of how recently any of this happened, the last time he was on the spiritual plane, he was nearly dead himself after a combination of abuse at the hands of Thegn and pure exhaustion from using the Touch. How did the mages in the Shadowfold manage to go through a full mercy of a town without collapsing after the first couple of people they used the Touch on?

He hears Corva's foot crunch on the rough gravel of the rooftop as she takes a step closer to him. He turns his attention to her. She's got a weak, knowing smile.

"You don't know how to get there, do you?"

Jack shakes his head. "I've got ideas, but none of 'em sound too pleasant."

"Need me to kick your ass a bit?" Corva's smile has broadened. It's kind, not the cruel, half-crazed show of teeth that she usually wears while fighting. She's trying to lighten the mood. Trying to help.

He snorts out a short laugh. "I'll let you know if it comes to that." He lets his head follow yet another crow. There doesn't seem to be any clear pattern that shows where they're going. Nothing that could help him predict their movement. He needs a change of topic. "How it coming on getting control of more grunts?"

"Easier than I thought. I'm up in the twenties now. Got most of the ones that are surrounding this building. Nearly ready to start trying to get in Thegn's way. I'm going to need his help with that, though." Corva tilts her head toward Zeke, still sitting on Jack's shoulder.

Jack nods and lifts his arm toward Corva, forming a bridge for the monkey to travel across. As Zeke clambers over to his roost on her should, Corva raises her chin like an idea has just struck her. "You told me you could see the dead when you closed your eyes. Can you still? If that's the case, aren't you able to see the spiritual plane like Zeke can? Maybe that's your route in."

Is it that simple? Why hadn't I thought of that? He closes his eyes. The not-faces are still there. And that stench of souls. He'd gotten used to it. Gotten used to them. He'd taken them for granted, an ever-present annoyance, like specks on a dirty window when trying to see through it. Jack opens his eyes, astonished. There's Corva and Zeke.

He closes his eyes. Not-faces.

Open eyes. Corva and Zeke.

Jack changes his focus and finds one of the flying crows before closing his eyes. There! A white dot creating a rip of light in the distance. Actually, there are a lot of those dots moving in all manner of directions. Jack has to concentrate to see them through the wall of not-faces feverishly trying to fill his view. It's like they know he's recognized them again. "I can see the crows on the spiritual plane. But it's damn hard."

He opens and closes his eyes quickly, trying to burn in the afterimage of their surroundings. "I can't quite get a bead on where they're going without opening my eyes, though. And I can't really see ol' Wrinkles there; too much noise."

He tries covering one eye while opening the other. That kind of works. "It's tough as shit to focus on what you can't see. How does Zeke do it?"

"Zeke says he's had a lot more practice than you … and that his eyes are better for this kind of thing." Corva puts herself directly in front of Jack so he can't see around her. "Zeke also says you're getting distracted. His job is to track Thegn by watching the crows. Your job is to see how to get on the spiritual plane, preferably without dying."

Jack stops his experiments at trying to see the spiritual plane and the regular world. He puts attention back on Corva and Zeke. He wants to argue, wants to be indignant. But they're right. He lets his shoulders sag. "I don't know what I'm doing! I barely know how to use the Touch here. How am I supposed to know how to do anything on a totally different plane of existence?"

Zeke's eyes suddenly widen and he slaps Corva on her shoulder excitedly.

"Ow! Why'd you—" Corva's voice trails off as she looks at Zeke, listening. This must've been what it was like to watch Jack have his conversation on comms with Lyia and Slim.

It only takes a few seconds for impatience to get the better of Jack. "What? What's he saying?"

"Zeke says he can see you on the spiritual plane. A kind of shadow of you, at least. He's asking if you can see yourself."

Curious, Jack closes his eyes. He wasn't able to sense any of himself when he was on the spiritual plane before; he hadn't even considered trying here. He raises his hands in front of his face to check if he can see them. "Holy shit."

They're right there. His hands. Well, sort of his hands. It's more like a void in front of the not-faces, but a void that's in the shape of his hands.

"You can see them, can't you?" Excitement raises Corva's voice.

"Yeah. I can. But what does that mean? How does that help?"

"Can you touch any of the spirits?"

Jack opens his eyes. "You want me to use the Touch on them?"

Corva's face wrinkles in a combination of horror and confusion. "What? No! That's not what I meant. Zeke was asking if you could grab them, move them around. That kind of thing. Not 'the Touch' touching. Right?" She looks over at Zeke, whose face is strangely impassive.

But Jack isn't paying attention. His mind is already on a roll. It's like something clicked and now everything makes sense. He closes his eyes to confirm. The not-faces are moving faster than ever before, almost vibrating. This is why they've wanted his attention. He reopens his eyes. "I think I know how it works."

Corva returns her attention to Jack. "What do you mean?"

"The Touch. I know how it works. Like, for-real how it works. The Touch doesn't kill people, not really. It—It pushes souls out of their bodies; kinda detaches them. Yeah, their body does eventually die, but their spirit isn't dead. Death never collected them. That's the difference between Death's Mark and the Touch. Death's Mark is a full cleaning. The Touch is like soaping up the dishes and never rinsing them off."

"Jack, you're not making sense."

Corva's words are enough to give Jack a moment of pause, but not enough to stop him. "Lyia would get it." He pauses a beat to see if Lyia is listening. Nothing. She's either focusing on her own task, or she's just got nothing to add to this. Hopefully it's the former. "The point is that those not-faces—the souls of folks hit with the Touch—are just wandering about. Their bodies are dead, but the spirits have nowhere to go."

Corva's face is uneasy. "I don't think that's what Zeke—"

"It totally is! I need to do the Touch, just in reverse, kind of."

"Do what?"

"Look, I don't know all the details, but I *know* this is the way in."

"But how do you get back out once you're there?" It's clear from Corva's expression that she's not at all a fan of how the conversation has turned.

"I'll just hafta figure that out on the fly, too. But I know this is going to work. I can't explain how, but it will. Maybe Zeke can explain later. In the meantime, I'm doing this. You just focus on your part of the plan. Track where Wrinkles is going. Put a bunch of grunts in his way. And I'll slow him down from my side, too. This can still work."

"I thought you said there was too much noise to see Thegn."

"Too much noise when trying to see all this stuff at the same time." Jack waves an arm, indicating everything around them. "Without that, it should be much easier."

"Should be?"

"You said you were on board, whatever the plan. You're just going to have to trust me. I trust you." Jack closes his eyes and reaches out to the closest not-face. He sees the dark void shaped like his hand move into position. The not-face doesn't move away. He extends two fingers. There's a tingling sensation at the tips, right where they contact the side of the not-face. Unlike all the other not-faces, it's not moving. It's just holding position right in front of him. Waiting.

Jack snaps his eyes open. "Shit! I almost forgot."

He squats down to his go-bag and withdraws a long fixed-blade knife with a forward curve.

"What do you need that for?" Corva's voice is tense, filled with impatience.

Jack stands back up, but he doesn't take his eyes off the knife. "Last time I was there, I had a tough time getting back. The only thing that helped me find my body was when Old Man V told me to follow my pain." He vaguely indicates a couple different places on his body. "I've got some scrapes and it's not like I'm feelin' great, but I think I need something more specific."

"I could just punch you in the mouth."

Jack smiles at Corva. "Yeah. No. Probably best if it's something I can control. Thing is"—he looks down at himself—"where to cut so it hurts, but won't get in the way of moving?"

Lyia's voice sounds over the comms. "Outside of your thigh. Outer part of your forearm. If you'd been practicing your healing, I'd suggest the webbing between your fingers, but it's too easy to accidentally cut all the way through. That's hard to fix quickly. Hell, if you'd been practicing, you'd know how to create pain without cutting yourself at all."

She answered that a bit too quickly for comfort. She was listening. Jack shakes the additional questions—along with Lyia's chiding for not practicing—from his head and focuses on the task at hand. And, looking at his hand, she's right. He doesn't have enough practice with healing to fix things if he does that wrong. His thigh would work, but his pants are in the way. Forearm it is.

He takes the knife and runs it across the top of his forearm, fast and smooth. At first, he doesn't feel anything, the benefit of a sharp blade. But as the blood starts flowing, he starts to feel the pain set in, sharp and stinging. Almost automatically, he swaps the knife between hands so he can put pressure on his new cut. That makes it hurt more. This will work.

"Okay. Now I'm ready." Jack closes his eyes. That same not-face is still there, like it's been waiting. He reaches out again and extends his two fingers. Again, his fingertips tingle. This is it. He concentrates on performing the Touch, like Vardin had taught him, like he'd done on Thegn.

For a moment, nothing seems to happen.

Then suddenly, Jack feels a harsh, twisting feeling deep inside him, a tornado spinning deeper than he could describe by pointing to any part of his body. Likewise, the not-face that he's touching appears to spin in an opposite direction, but focused around the tips of his fingers. Almost involuntarily, he feels his other arm come up and his hand flatten on his chest. It's like a path abruptly opened up. One tornado travels along it one way while the other comes the other. As they pass each other, there's a small whisper. At least, Jack thinks it's a whisper. It sounds like one. He doesn't recognize the voice at first, but the words are unmistakable.

"You did alright, kiddo."

An instant later, the feeling of spinning tornadoes is gone and Jack is in a familiar place. Bright. Surrounded by not-faces. And he has no eyes to open back up.

Houseguest

Corva watches Jack go slack as his outstretched arm drops to his side. His body wavers a bit, like someone sleepwalking. She's sure he's going to collapse at any moment—well, not him. Jack's not going to collapse. He's gone. It's just his body that's left here. She can stop him from falling, though. She just needs to reach a tendril to him and keep control of his body for safekeeping.

But just as she's about to take control, she sees Jack's eyes flutter and his jaw work its way in circles, like a goat chewing. He stops when he notices her looking at him. He smiles, but it's not Jack's smile, and it's not at her. "Hello, old friend."

This isn't Jack. Not at all. His mannerisms are all wrong. Even his voice isn't quite the same. It's rougher, older.

Something has gone wrong. Somehow, Jack has screwed up and now there's someone else in his body. Immediately, Corva reaches out with a mental tendril and completes the process of controlling his body. She feels Jack, or whomever it is in his body, try to resist her control. He can't, but he's putting up an awfully good fight.

Wait, Corva.

She cuts an eye over to Zeke. "What? That's not Jack. We need to keep his body safe."

I know. Zeke hops off her shoulder and scampers up to Jack's feet. He looks up at the boy's face. **Could it be? Could it really be you?**

"Be who?"

Vardin.

"Vardin? The old guy Jack always talks about?"

The moment Corva says the name, Jack's body stops resisting her control. It's difficult to describe the sensation, but there's a flicker of recognition in that act of compliance. Like whoever is in Jack's body is responding to the name.

Free him.

Corva looks at Zeke. The monkey's attention is entirely on Jack's face.

"Are you sure? We don't know—"

Free him, Corva. I know an old friend when I see him. Zeke's thoughts in her mind are forceful, insistent. She gets the impression that in this moment, if he could control her with his thoughts, he would.

Scowling, she complies with the monkey's request and relinquishes control of Jack's body. She squeezes the handles of her batons in frustration. "Fine. But I still need you over here to point out the next place Thegn is going to show up."

She's been getting better with the number of individuals she can control; the whole block surrounding the building they're on is full of grunts under her command. They're position is pretty well protected. But projecting control at a distance is still a challenge for her, and she still hasn't managed to get full control over anyone before Thegn appears to dispatch them. And that's with Zeke's guidance to give her a couple of seconds of lead time.

Unfortunately, Zeke isn't coming back to her. His attention is still entirely on this Vardin guy possessing Jack's body. "Zeke! Did you hear me? I need your help."

"Give an old man and his dear friend a moment for a reunion." Vardin kneels Jack and reaches out to Zeke. He comes down too hard, though, and slams Jack's knee into the rooftop. Grimacing, he grabs the knee and rubs it. "Yow! Jack's still a little guy, is he? Gonna take a sec to get my bearings in his skin." His hand goes up to scratch at part of the chembraid that's wrapped around Jack's arm. "Ah—and he did get a chembraid. He's right, this thing is itchy."

"Where's Jack?" Corva takes a step forward, trying to appear intimidating. However, what's she going to do? Hurting Jack's body isn't going to hurt this spirit.

"You must be the girl that Jack was tellin' me about. You're War, right?" He smiles at her surprise. "You n' me both know Jack's a talker. Our kiddo has jumped over to the spiritual plane. He chose a pretty clever way to do it. Clever and dangerous. It's a good thing I made sure he swapped with me, made me a bit of a houseguest in his body. Otherwise, who knows which of those poor nuggets he'd have gotten in his body."

Vardin jerks his hands up to his head. "Whoa, whoa! Too loud, Lyia. It's good to hear your voice, though." He looks at Corva, whispering. "Jack fancies her. I always thought she was a bit too overbearing, though."

His face stretches in mock surprise. "Oops. She heard that."

Vardin's expression changes, though, at the sound of a chirp from Zeke. He focuses his attention back on the monkey. "You're right, Zeke. Time is short. I'll get to the point."

Vardin reaches out his hand and lets Zeke climb up into it. "Wow, is Jack really this weak, or did you put on a pound or two?" He smiles and raises the spitting, indignant little monkey to his shoulder before stepping closer to Corva.

He looks at her with Jack's cool gray eyes; they've never looked this focused or perceptive. "Pretty soon, kiddo is going to figure out how to use those crows to move himself around. I'll disappear from here and he'll show up wherever that crow is. Knowing Jack, he won't've thought ahead enough to know what to do when he gets there. His first thought is probably gonna be to sneak attack Death with the Touch. I'd talk him out of that if I were you. Too risky."

"How am I going to tell him any of this if he's not here?" Corva's words come out sounding a lot more whiny than she intends.

Vardin shakes Jack's head at her and taps his finger on the comm kneak behind Jack's ear. "Not you, young horseman. Them. You've got your own job to tend to."

Corva can't seem to relax the scowl on her face. "Yeah. I know. We're slowing Thegn down whenever he shows. That's why I need Zeke to—"

"Yes, but that's not all you and Zeke need to do. You need a way for Jack to get back here, right? That means you need to catch one of those crows without killing it. Then bring it here. That way Jack has a route back when he's done."

Corva pauses. She hadn't thought about how Jack was going to get back. Neither had Jack, obviously. "Okay. But won't that also lead Thegn back here?"

"It might. You were planning on fighting Death anyway, weren't you? Least this way, you'll know where he's coming."

Thegn more likely has a "last crow" of his own that's near here. We can capture that one and secure the area around it.

Corva nods at Zeke in acknowledgment. Vardin notices.

"I see ol' Zeke is already ahead of me, like always." Vardin smiles and extends his arm so Zeke can travel back to Corva's shoulder. "Alright then. I'll leave that to you."

He turns as if he's going to leave. The knife that Jack used to cut himself dances in his hand as he flips it through a series of different grips.

"Wait." Corva grabs his shoulder. "Where are you going?"

He speaks over his shoulder as he walks away. "I've got to protect Jack's body when he's not in it. I'm going to need some practice with it."

Corva moves one of her rooftop grunts in his way. "I can't let you go off into the unknown. You could get Jack killed."

She feels Zeke's paw on the side of her head. **You underestimate him.**

Corva glances over to Zeke. "No I don't! I've controlled Jack's body, too. I know its limits."

"Fine." Vardin's voice hardens and, through her grunt, she senses him bounce on his toes. "I'll practice here."

It takes less than two seconds for Vardin to step around the grunt and climb up its back. The knife in his hand moves the whole time, playing from one grip to the next, slicing with every transition. It's not that he's all that fast; his movements are just incredibly efficient. The grunt is already on its knees, incapable of standing, by the time Vardin drives the blade's tip into the base of its head. Corva barely has enough time to relinquish control of the creature so she doesn't get hurt by that killing strike.

The grunt slumps forward and lands facedown as Vardin hops lightly to the ground in front of it. He stumbles a bit, but manages to recover without falling. He smiles at Corva. "Still getting used to the kiddo's proportions, but I think I can manage. He's got a springyness that I haven't had in a long time."

Corva lets out a sigh. "Okay. So you know how to handle yourself."

"I've been around the block a few times. I ain't no horseman, though." Vardin squints at her. "Your name's Corva, right?"

"Yes. Did Jack tell you that, too?"

"Yup. But ever since he brought up your name, I had this one nugget hounding me, trying to get my attention, asking me to get a message out. A message to you."

"To me?"

"Yeah. I thought it was weird, too." Vardin wipes his knife clean on Jack's pants. "Most nuggets' thoughts are too jumbled to even know who or where they are. This one, though, was real clear on you. On your name, specifically."

"My name?"

"That's right. At first it was just repeating your name over and over again. Incredibly bothersome." Vardin stops what he's doing and locks eyes with Corva. "But then it started getting a sense of self. A memory of who it was. That's when it gave me the message. It said to tell you that your name wasn't just a gift, but that you earned it."

"Avó?"

Vardin smiles. "Good. I'm glad it made sense to you. For myself, I couldn't figure out what it meant." He pauses, and it almost seems like he flickers, kind of like he's a bad video projection. "Ooh. It looks like the kid might've figured things out. You two be sure to catch that crow."

A moment later, Jack's body—and Vardin with it—is gone.

VIBRATION

Lyia notices that Slim is staring at the same screen she is, the one showing an image from the lone nanobot that they left with Jack.

Slim cuts a glance at Lyia. "Do you have any idea what just happened there?"

"Yeah."

In truth, she's pretty sure that her understanding of the whole situation falls on the lower side of a scale between "no clue" and "barely getting it."

Slim turns to face her full-on. "Well can you explain it to me? I'm feeling awfully stupid here."

Lyia's eyebrow lifts. "Oh? I would've thought that's familiar territory for you."

"Asshole." Slim's grin is a reminder of those moments when the two of them worked well as a couple. There just wasn't enough of those moments.

She shakes her head. "Jack's following through on his part of the plan. Fortunately, he's got a friend on the spiritual plane who will look out for him. Now we have to focus on our part of it."

Lyia points to the other set of screens where the rest of the nanobot swarm is on its way to the closest siege cave. "Have you figured out how we're going to actually talk to the people in there? How are we even going to get in?"

Slim swivels back around in his chair to look at those screens as well, but then he stops and spins back toward her. "I can't let it go yet. Did you see how he moved? I forgot how spry that old guy was. With him in a younger body like Jack's, it's downright scary. Do you think—"

He pauses.

"What?" Lyia knows where his mind went. He has to say it out loud, though. He needs to hear how wrong it is. "Do I think what?"

"I … I just wonder if we might have better chances if Vardin stays in Jack's body."

The sound of her hand slapping Slim's face registers before she realizes what she's done. The look on his face, though, is a lot less surprised than what she's feeling. He knows he had that coming. However, she's never lashed out like that before. Not with him. A corrective smack to the back of his head is one thing. A full-on slap to the face is something else entirely.

Lyia regains her composure and scowls. "I don't want to hear you talk like that again. Vardin is dead. Jack isn't." She feels her face relax for a moment before knitting in worry as she sees crows collecting on Slim's screens. "Not yet, at least."

Slim has his back to her again, focusing on his terminals. "I've got a few ideas on how to talk to the folks in the caves."

Back to business. "Yeah? Let's go with the fastest one."

"There are trade-offs, Lee. Always trade-offs." Slim doesn't turn to face her. His nose is in his screens, fingers clickity-clacking on an ancient keyboard. "The fast way damages the caves and gives us a pretty limited way of communicating—think about it like a complicated game of charades. The other way is—"

"Aren't there comm links in each of the caves? Can't we just call them on those?"

Slim's head drops. "I'm getting there! The links in the caves are hardline only, buried deep, and the caves are exclusively wired to each other. They're not connected to the town's comm network."

"Well that's stupid. Why would—"

"It's a security measure. Not as easy to compromise."

Lyia throws up her arms, frustrated. "So what do we do? Jack's counting on us to get these people safe."

Slim finally swivels around to face her again. His face is red, and not just on the side of the face where she slapped him. "I'm getting there. If you'd just—you know what? Just sit." He points to a dusty chair a few steps away. "Sit right there." He grabs an orb mic and tosses it to her. "And hold this."

Lyia catches the grapefruit-sized microphone and flumps down in the chair. "I just—"

"Ah-ah." Slim holds up a single finger before turning his back on her and refocusing on his terminal. "Now's the time when you listen. I have an idea. It's a bit of a longshot, but it's our best shot."

He points to the monitors displaying some of the views from the nanobots on the way to the siege cave. Only, now that they're closer, they're not headed to the entry door.

As if guessing her thoughts, Slim explains, "The main door is sealed pretty tightly. Too tight to get in, even with the nanobots. But, we can work our way through the air handling system. It's a maze, but I helped design it, so …"

Slim's voice drifts off as his focus shifts to the task at hand. Lyia watches the nanobots route their way up to the vents for the air handler and navigate the dark labyrinth of ducts, filters, and pipework. They sit in silence like that for a bit. Slim clacking at his keyboard. Lyia tracking the progress of the bots.

It's unbearable.

Reaching the end of her limit—really, any reasonable person's limit—Lyia breaks through the dead air. "You still haven't answered my question. How are we going to talk to them once we're there?"

As she speaks, the images from the nanobots appear to violently shake and shudder.

"Shit!" Slim's arm bolts to a knob on a different console and adjusts it.

"What? What? Are we too late? Is Death already there?" The images continue to quake as she speaks, but the movement is quite a bit less harsh now compared to moments ago.

Slim continues to dial down the adjustment knob. "Will you shut up for a tic so I can lower the gain? You're rattling the whole ventilation system."

I did that?

Slim returns his attention to his terminal. "It's my fault, really. I handed you a hot mic." He swivels to face her, smiling. The overall redness in his face is gone, but the mark from her hand is still pretty clear. "You can talk normally now. Plus, on the upside, I think you've proven that it works. Let's just hope we haven't freaked out the people in the cave."

None of this makes any sense to Lyia. "What works? What did I do? Slim, you better start explaining things, or I'm going to shove this thing right up your—" She stares at the orb mic that she's brandishing at him and suddenly everything clicks. "Oh."

Slim's grin widens. "Yeah! You get it. I hacked together a tweak on the nanobots' control function so they vibrate in time with input from that mic. Basically made the swarm a floating speaker. The code is rushed and ugly as hell, but you've just shown that it does actually work. And now—" He points to the screens showing the view as the nanobots emerge from the ductwork into the siege caves. "Now we should be able to talk to them."

It's a depressing scene. Time spent in the siege caves is never pleasant. With the frequency and duration of raids in Bule, a lot of care was put into making the caves reasonably comfortable places to stay for an extended period of time. The area is well-lit with plenty of cushioned spaces to sit or lie down. There's a modest little kitchen stocked with decent food and a small command center with a few screens to check on the town and keep in touch with the other siege caves.

However, no amount of comfort can overcome the natural fear and anxiety of having to go there in the first place. The people in the cave are showing all the signs of angsty tension. A few of them are pacing. The ones that are sitting or trying to sleep are just as restless, fidgeting. A few periodically cast apprehensive glances at the solid steel entry door, but no one is actually near the door. Another clump of people crowds around the screens at the command center, trying to get some sense of what's going on. They've got no clue.

Lyia catches a glimpse of a distinctive balding head among the pack of people at the command center. "Harris. You were right, Slim. He is in this one."

Slim has already spun back to his terminal, clacking away. "Okay. I've pulled one bot out of the swarm so you can see." Without looking, he points to the screen closest to Lyia while readjusting the gain control knob on his other console. "Your mic is hot. Try not to make him jump out of his skin. The bots don't have mics of their own, so you're not going to be able to hear him respond … or hear how you sound, for that matter. So we're limited, but it's better than hand signals."

Lyia nods in affirmation and immediately realizes the futility of doing so, since Slim still isn't looking at her. No matter, though. He knows she gets it. With her eyes riveted to the screen showing the image of Bule's militia leader, she raises the orb mic to her mouth. "Harris."

Nothing.

Slim dials up the gain. "Try again."

"Harris." Lyia says the name a little louder, projecting like she's speaking to a crowd of people.

Still, nothing. There's no indication at all that he's heard her.

"Why can't he hear me? Is it working?"

Slim turns his head and Lyia follows his gaze up to the shaky images from the other bots. He grunts. "Yeah, little guys are rattling up a storm. They just can't move enough air to be heard. I was worried this might—ooh!"

Hit with a sudden burst of inspiration, Slim twists back to his keyboard. "Just need a flat surface that vibrates well."

"Where are you going to find that?" Lyia looks at the images from within the siege cave. As comfortable as they were made to be, the walls were left unfinished as natural rock, none of it flat.

Slim tilts his head at the same screens, now showing the view of the bots approaching the steel entry door to the siege cave. "There. Gimme a sec to get the bots positioned and in firm contact with the door." *Clackity-clackity-clack.* "Okay. Give it a shot. No one is near the door, though, so you'll probably have to be pretty loud for them to hear."

Lyia takes a deep breath and shouts into the mic, "Harris!"

The reaction from the people in the cave is immediate. Sitters are now on their feet. Pacers stand still. All heads swing to face the door.

Slim looks over his shoulder at Lyia and they share a brief smile. She pulls the mic closer to her. "Alright. We don't have a lot of time and I can't hear you talk. So no discussion. You just listen."

7.8

SPIRITUAL

This is fucking worthless. Jack feels like he's been on the spiritual plane for ages, and it's the same crap scenario as last time. Tons of not-faces crowding his view. No ability to move or make any kind of sound. He can't even blink to get a break from the intense brightness of the place. And since Old Man V did the switcheroo with him, he's got no guidance on how to do anything here.

At least he's figured out how Thegn is moving around. Vardin was right about the crows being a kind of portal. From here, they're a kind of vaguely colored splotch. But they're different from the not-faces. They don't move and they're more vibrant, the opposite of shadows. It's difficult to tell how exactly he knows that those splotches belong to crows, but he's certain of it. If he could just see how Thegn uses them, maybe he could do the same thing.

"Welcome back, kiddo."

Jack's mind spins with questions. Hadn't he swapped places with Old Man V? Why is he back? Did something happen to Jack's body? Is Jack dead? Why is it that he still can't see the old man like he can see the not-faces?

The not-faces around Jack writhe and swarm as the questions continue to cycle in his mind.

"Still having trouble with that focusing thing, are you?"

That's right. Last time he was here, he had to separate his thoughts. Think them one at a time. *What are you doing here, V?*

"Sorry kiddo, I haven't done shit. I'm back here because of something you did. And I've got your body in tow. So, whatever you're doing, you best finish it. Meat an' bones don't last here very long."

Something I did? I wasn't doing anything. Can't do anything. That's what's been pissing me off since I got back here. I can see the portals. Jack points his attention at the most recent one he was focused on. If he had arms or a head or even eyes, he'd point at it. *I just got no way of—*

"Whoa kiddo. That. That right there."

What?

"Whatever it was you were just doing. That was the pull that got me here with your skin sack. Keep doing that."

Keep doing that, you say. I was being pissed off because I can't even point at one of those crow portals. Like, say, that one over there.

The instant he puts his whole attention on a portal, he feels a hard pull and his whole world looks like it twists around him, spinning and whirling in a blur of colors and pain.

Somewhere in the distance he can hear Vardin's voice. "That. You figured it out."

A moment later, he's solid. He can move. He hurts all over, his chembraid itches, and his stomach—

Jack drops to his knees and vomits on the floor. He's got no time to find a bucket or a hole; the best he can do is clinch his eyes shut and vaguely aim the acid and bile away from himself. The not-faces still crowd his view when his eyes are closed. Internally, he can't help but be amused. Do they know that if they were really that close to his face, he'd be puking all over them? Granted, not much comes out. He hasn't really eaten since this morning's training with Corva—was that really just earlier today?

Finished, he opens his eyes and tries to take stock. He's still got a knife in his hand. There's more blood on it than he remembers. Somehow he knows, though, that this new blood isn't his. The floor he's on is clean—well, with the exception of the mess he just made—but it's old, cracked. It looks like it's taken a few decades worth of use. He lifts his head to see more of the room he's in. *Where am I?*

There's no voice answering him. No Vardin. The old barman must still be on the spiritual plane.

An indignant squawk sounds in front of Jack. He looks up and sees the back of a large crow, fluttering its wings and preening its tail feathers. The crow's wrong-colored eyes meet Jack's and immediately Jack feels that unbearable searing feeling at his hairline, the same as the first time he saw one of these crows all those years ago.

Jack reacts without thinking. He grabs his head with his free hand as if trying to staunch a wound there. At the same time, he lashes out at the bird with his knife. He doesn't really expect to connect to anything. He just wants the pain to stop.

But he does connect.

It's not a pretty cut and not a killing blow. The blade is lodged in the side of the crow, through its wing. The thing is making an awful racket. Jack tries to pull the knife out, but it's stuck. The bird moves with the blade. The pain in his forehead is more intense than ever. He's got to make it stop.

He lifts the knife with the bird still attached and slams it to the ground. He can feel the blade's edge sink deeper into the crow. It's still cackling, but the squawks are less angry now, more desperate. Pleading.

Jack's head still feels like it's on fire.

He beats the ground with the knife-bird again. This time, he feels the blade strike the ground, hears the crow let out its last feeble cry. Then it's done. The knife is free. The bird is quiet. The pain in Jack's head is reduced to a manageable dull ache.

Jack gets to his feet and manages to tear his focus away from the bloody wreckage of the crow's carcass. Thegn is nowhere to be seen. Is it possible? Did Jack really beat the old bastard here?

He scans the room and finally gets a sense of where he's at. It's a shop in Lower Bule not far from the Red Light. Not a place that Jack has been to much; they make something that he doesn't care a lot about. Maybe blankets?

The old cow that runs the place—Lotte, that's her name—is kind of a bitch, but Jack's never had any problems with her. Not directly. She'd always directed the same stink-eyed glare at him that most folks in this town did. It was always something. He was too young, too small, too weak to be of use to anyone. A burden on the town. And even when he'd gotten older and could do more, they still looked at him like that. He'd given up on trying to prove himself to them until Old Man V died. Then they had a new reason to glower at him. Why should he be the one to run the most lucrative business in town, instead of being sold with it?

Jack shakes the thoughts from his head. *Where did that come from?*

If there's a crow here, then there needs to be a body, either breathing or bleeding. Jack doesn't have time for hide-and-seek, though. He clears his throat before speaking to the room, loud. "I don't know who's here, but you mighta noticed that this ain't your typical raid. Death is here. The last of the Four. He's clearing the town. It won't do to hole up and wait for it to pass."

There's a shuffling sound to his left, deeper in the shop. Jack whirls around, raising his knife for protection. It's Lotte. Her face is a mixed mask of fear and curiosity. A trail of white hair starts above her forehead and smears back, just like on him. She holds a knife of her own, though it's smaller than Jack's.

"Jackie? That you?"

Jack scowls. It's annoying how many people think that's his name. "Did you hear what I just said? Also, it's not 'Jackie.' It's Jack."

The woman nods thoughtlessly, but her attention isn't on him. She's staring at the dead crow in a pool of blood and vomit at Jack's feet. "It's true?"

"Yeah. Your best bet is to get out of here. As far as you can, but at least get out of Lower Bule. You got comms?"

Lotte nods, finally meeting Jack's eyes.

Jack grunts. "Good. Spread the word. Get out. We'll slow down the old wrinkly bastard as best as we can."

"We?"

But it's too late; Jack isn't paying attention to her. His eyes are closed and he's already looking at the not-faces. He's almost able to tell them apart now. But he's looking for one specific one, the most familiar one. Vardin's spirit.

There he is.

Jack reaches out like before and goes through the process of performing the Touch. The void of his hand on the spirit plane does the same. A moment later, he feels the twisted feeling of swapping places with the old man along his arm.

As before, he hears a voice, Vardin's voice. "Looks like you've got a strategy, kiddo."

A strategy. Right.

But the doubt in Jack's mind is starting to ebb away. This might actually work.

THIS IS NEW

"Something strange is going on." Thegn runs his scythe through another pack of Umbrati. It's actually pretty impressive how large this party is. Not just this particular group, but the whole contingent.

They do seem pretty intent on securing you. And have you noticed that their ability to fight has gotten better recently? You don't think she's controlling them, do you? Caffiel crawls across Thegn's back from one shoulder to the next, presumably to get a better view.

"Oh, the girl is absolutely controlling them. Or trying to. She's nowhere near Durga's full strength. But I'm not talking about that." Thegn extends his hand and his crow hops up into it. The old Reaper inspects the bird, checking its eyes and feathers before ultimately letting it flutter back down to the ground. "The last few conduits that I'd planned to take weren't there."

That's not unexpected, though. You lose a small collection of birds every time you work at this scale.

Thegn shakes his head. "No. This is happening at a faster rate than usual."

Caffiel peeks his head into Thegn's view. **I know it goes against your sense of order, but try one out of sequence.**

It's not a bad suggestion, though it grates on Thegn all the same for exactly the reason that Caffiel says. There's an order to things. A way they ought to be done. To subvert that natural order is to subvert reality itself. The consequences for that run the full spectrum from mild to severe. But there are always consequences.

Also, Caffiel is still encroaching on Thegn's vision. The rat's expression is playful, but sincere. Thegn grinds his teeth. "Fine. If only to get that smug rodent version of a grin off your face."

With his scythe, Thegn collects the crow. There's no squawk or cry of surprise from the bird, merely silent acceptance that its job is complete as it dissolves in a cloud of ash and dust. Before the last speck drifts to the ground, Thegn relaxes his face and slides to the spiritual plane.

It's a bleak place despite its intense brightness, a kind of purgatory brimming with a sea of lost souls that he didn't collect. It's not that it's unpleasant. It's just filled with a pervasive dullness, despite the forlorn undulations of the spirits here. They always have this hopeful insistence that there's something he could do about their situation. There isn't. There's an order to things and this is the consequence of not adhering to that order.

Thegn wades through the radiant void, concentrating on finding the next conduit, the next echo of a crow. Caffiel tags along, his energy latched onto Thegn's, just like sitting on his shoulder on the terrestrial plane. However, at least here, Thegn doesn't have the rat's voice in his head. At least here, it's quiet.

"I know you're tired, but you're doin' great, kiddo. Which one is next?"

The voice catches Thegn completely off guard. *What fresh bullshit is this?*

"Oh shit. Whichever you're picking, do it now. I think your old friend with the beard and hood finally found you."

The shadowy souls in the bright fog jitter with a bizarre mixture of excitement and disappointment as a pocket of energy spins toward one of Thegn's conduits. It's the same feeling as being unable to hold on to a squirming live fish. And just as quickly, the spiritual plane is quiet again. No sound. Just brilliant silence.

Thegn can feel Caffiel absolutely buzzing. *You must be getting a real kick out of this.*

The rat is going to be unbearably talkative when they get back to the terrestrial plane. Unfortunately, that's exactly where Thegn has to go. He has to give chase. He has to break the sequence, his sequence. Thegn has to follow that pocket of energy—that person—through his conduit. The wrong conduit. *What a bother.*

Thegn peers through the conduit to see what awaits him. However, everything is a blur. It's not the stable, controlled view of the scene that he's used to. He's going to have to slide blind. Annoyed, the Reaper uses the conduit and slides back to the terrestrial plane. The dazzling empty void is replaced with a world of brown and red, filled with noise.

Oh, this is more than I could've hoped for. How wonderful!

Not even a second in and you're already talking. Thegn thinks the words, but his attention has already moved to the scene around him.

It's absolute chaos.

He's in an alley that perhaps normally serves as an open-air market. Trinkets, gear, and food line a string of covered tables. Or they would, if they weren't flying through the air. A trio of Umbrati grunts are laying waste to the scene, flipping the tables or smashing through them as they chase something—no, someone who's obviously trying to get away from them.

Almost without thinking about it, Thegn extends his scythe and slices through two of the Umbrati with a single pass. The third grunt, one of the hulkingly obese variations of the creatures, leans over a table, trying to attack the space behind it.

There he is.

Jack. That bartender kid. He clambers under the table and rolls between the grunt's legs. Under one arm, he's got one of Thegn's crows, cawing and vainly trying to free itself. In Jack's other hand, he holds a kukri-style blade, shining and blood-soaked. The kid is looking pretty rough, covered in cuts, scrapes, and bruises. And although his eyes are active and alert, they're darkened and deep-set. Tired. Jack glances over his shoulder at the grunt he just evaded, but gets distracted when he notices the remains of the two severed grunts, still crumbling to the ground in separate parts.

Caffiel paws at Thegn's shoulder in anticipation of the moment.

Thegn sighs. *Fine. Just this once.*

He leaves his scythe extended so it's just within Jack's field of vision. It doesn't take long for the kid to recognize it, tracing the length of the snath up Thegn's arm and resting on his face.

Jack's eyes widen as he realizes the predicament that he's in. "Fuckfuckfuckfuck!"

It's almost enough to make Thegn smile. "It's you. Clever boy."

The flush of panic in Jack's face is replaced with defiance. "Yeah. Me. You probably shoulda killed me when you had the chance." Now it's Jack's turn to smile. "The second chance, actually."

Thegn can feel his own expression darken. "It's still early."

The remaining Umbrati grunt isn't waiting for them to finish their conversation. It's recognized Thegn's presence and is ambling toward him, reverting to its primary mission. It steps past Jack as if he's not even there. These larger grunts may be more powerful, but they're slower, clumsier. Thegn easily sidesteps the creature as it approaches.

Jack, realizing his fortune, flashes his smirk up at Thegn. "These portals of yours are a pain in the ass. How do you know what's waiting for you on the other side?"

He's following the conduits blindly? Thegn evades another charge from the bulky grunt.

It seems so. I was unsure about this youngster when we first met. But he has gotten more interesting the longer we let him live, hasn't he?

Thegn casts a sideways scowl at Caffiel. The last thing he needs is the rat's self-amused side commentary.

Jack's smile dissolves in disappointment, like he'd actually expected Thegn to answer. He shrugs. "Fine. The system I've got seems to be working anyway."

Using his knife, Jack dispatches the crow in his arms. It's not a well-practiced stroke; in fact, it's graceless and ham-fisted. All the same, though, the crow lets out a throaty caw and bleeds out. Jack probes Thegn's face for any kind of reaction, but gets none.

"Damn. Was hoping that it would at least hurt you a little."

Thegn says nothing, but keeps his attention on Jack while sidestepping another charge from the large grunt.

Jack takes Thegn's minor moment of distraction as an opportunity to close his eyes and reach out, but there's nothing in front of him. Thegn feels that same squirming fish feeling from earlier, and immediately the child's composure completely changes. He drops the crow's carcass and stares at Thegn as if seeing him for the first time.

"So you're Death, huh? We've never met formally, but I've seen you around, strolling through the nuggets on the spiritual side of things." The kid bows. "The name is Vardin."

Thegn dodges as the fat grunt charges from behind him, allowing the grunt to continue toward the child.

The kid—or whoever this Vardin person is—recognizes the threat coming to him, but doesn't shrink or flinch in the least. "Oh, this won't do." With more agility than Jack's ever shown the possibility of having, the kid slips to the side of the grunt while keeping his leg extended. The grunt trips over the outstretched leg and falls forward, right into the waiting curved edge of Jack's knife.

Vardin finishes the movement by withdrawing the knife, slicing it across the rest of the grunt's throat. Shaking his head, he looks up at Thegn, smiling as if they were having a casual conversation in a park. "Spent the last ten years of my life cleaning up after that boy. Guess the work of raisin' a kid is never done."

Jack's body starts to flicker. "Oh. Looks like that's my cue. Now that we've met, I hope we'll be able to talk again after all this calms down. In the meantime, my boy's got a few more of these portals to take out."

Vardin half waves, half salutes at Thegn and then completely disappears.

Thegn stands there, flat-footed, eyes fixed on the space where Jack's body had been. The kid is gone. All that's left are the corpses of Umbrati grunts and one of his crows, still bleeding out across the shattered tables and knickknacks in the alley.

Oh, I do so love surprises. At least we know why your conduits have been disappearing. It seems we have a race on our hands now.

Thegn grunts. "Fucking annoying. The kid doesn't even know how much he's fucking everything up."

Caffiel adjust his position so Thegn can see his face. **You knew this was coming. Your arrangement was never going to hold forever. This child is at least making things amusing, especially for a human. Can we keep him?**

"Shut up, rat."

ON THE VERGE

Corva grimaces and wipes a bit of blood from her nose. "I think Thegn's caught on that I'm controlling the grunts he sees when he comes through."

What gives you that impression? Zeke scans the horizon from a pipe sticking out from their rooftop, trying to track the movement of both Jack and Thegn through the spiritual plane.

"I don't know. Kind of a gut feeling." Corva pauses to think about it. "Like, early on, his focus was on efficiency. He'd show up, clear the space, and then slip away. Now? He's still fast, but he's hitting harder. Like he wants to hurt *and* kill."

It's possible that he's just getting frustrated. In any case, don't speculate too much on what's going on in that man's head. Just focus on expanding your reach. Zeke points in the direction of the stairway to Upper Bule. **Over there!**

"Thegn or Jack?" They've gotten themselves a pretty decent system. If it's Jack, protect him and give him time to destroy the crow. If it's Thegn, get in his way by fighting and slowing him down.

Thegn.

Of course, while the system is good, the follow-through isn't always the best. Corva sees where he's pointing and mentally reaches out to control whomever is over there. But the control she has is thin, wavering. She doesn't even really have time to tell if they're grunts or humans before Thegn cuts through them. "Nem fodendo!"

Zeke glances back at her. **What?**

Corva bends forward and places her hands on her knees, tired. Exhausted. She shakes her head. "Thegn isn't the only one frustrated. It seems the farther I reach out, the less control I have. These ones—" She waves her arm around at the collection of grunts around the rooftop, each one raising an arm in a kind of wave as her hand points at them. The closest one, holding one of Thegn's crows, gestures by lifting the bird in the air. "I can control them completely. The farther away they get, though, the more it's like trying to push on a rope ... a floppy rope."

The monkey turns away and returns to his task of tracking the spiritual plane. **It has nothing to do with distance. You're micromanaging.**

"How do you mean?"

Zeke lets out an audible sigh and turns to face Corva full-on. **You're shackled by the amount of control you think you need.**

Corva tilts her head. "Zeke, that doesn't make any sense at all."

Think about your control like a glass of water. The more control you take, the more of that water you use. You've got full control over the grunts here, but there's a limit to the number you can control that way.

"So, what? I take less control and I have greater numbers?"

In essence, yes.

"I can't do that. They'd tear us apart."

Episode Seven: Memory and Sacrifice

Zeke hops down from the pipe to Corva's shoulder and then crawls along her lifted arm so he can perch there as if she's a falconer and he's a falcon. He looks deep in her eyes. **You're too focused on you. Focus on them.**

Corva's face wrinkles in protest, but Zeke continues before she gets to say anything. **Durga—War—used to control hundreds of thousands of people. Not because her control was absolute, but because she understood people. Cared about them, even.**

"Não fode. War? Compassionate?"

Zeke shrugs. **If you understand people, you know what they want. If you know what they want, you can use that to control them with far less effort than you would otherwise need.**

Suddenly, Zeke's attention snaps to the grunt holding the crow. **Incoming!**

Corva spins to face the crow, ready. "Thegn or Jack?"

The question is answered for her as Jack appears in front of them. Unlike the flickering and blinking that happened when he left them, his arrival is more fluid, almost like he's being poured out of the crow into their space on the rooftop.

Once fully materialized, Jack scans the area wildly, like a squirrel thrown into a crate. A beat-up squirrel with a long, bloody knife. It only takes him a moment to realize that he's back with Corva and Zeke. His shoulders relax and he collapses to his knees, breathing heavily.

"Jack!" Corva lets Zeke jump from her arm as they both run over to him. She kneels as she reaches him and puts a hand on his shoulder. "Are you okay?"

Jack lifts his face to meet hers. He's not doing great. His eyes are sunken and dark, and he's covered in cuts and blood. The side of his face is swollen in an unnatural mix of purple and red. His clothes are tattered, dirty rags.

And yet, he's smiling. "Ol' Wrinkles is pissed."

"Yeah, I bet."

With Corva's help, Jack pulls himself back to his feet. He's favoring his left side a bit, but he manages to stand all the same. He winces while looking at her. "You look like shit."

Corva smiles back. "You're not looking so great yourself, bar boy."

"Yeah … Lyia's gonna cuss me out for not practicin' enough with self-healing." He covers his ear as if suddenly hearing a loud noise. "Hi Lyia."

Jack focuses back on Corva. "Everything go okay here? Seemed like you were doing alright slowing down the old dude."

Corva trades a quick look with Zeke. "We managed. How'd your part go?"

Jack grabs at his side and limps around the rooftop, looking at all the grunts under Corva's control. "Looks like you did better than manage. I got back here sooner than I wanted to—got no idea what's waiting on the other side of any portal—but I think I maybe took out half of 'em. Got a lot of folks from town to bug out, too. The last few were already on the way, though. I don't know if it's from what I was doing or 'cause of Lyia and Slim, but word is spreadin' pretty fast."

He pauses, listening to a conversation that Corva can't hear. He shakes his head. "No, you can't do that. There's no time. Look, I can do it myself."

Jack places both hands on his rib cage on the side of his body that he's been favoring. There's no glow or anything, but Corva can tell he's using soulmancy. Every Umbrati grunt under her control perks up, and even if they aren't looking at Jack, their attention is absolutely in his direction.

But the sense she feels through them flutters and goes away almost as quickly as it appears.

Jack falters and his hand drops from his side. "Dammit, Lee, I've got this! Slim, you gotta stop—Fuck!"

Tell Jack it doesn't matter. We have incoming.

Corva looks at Zeke. "Here?"

Episode Seven: Memory and Sacrifice

Jack notices Corva's sudden change in demeanor. "What's up?"

The answer comes in the form of a throaty cawing sound. All heads turn to face the crow being held by Corva's grunt.

Death is coming.

522

CAVALRY

Jack tries to tell Corva to crush the crow. Smash it out of existence. But it's too late.

Thegn materializes before them as a kind of spinning assembly of ash and blood. It takes less than a second and he's there, towering in height, seething in anger. Caffiel crouches on the Reaper's shoulder, all pretense of amusement wiped from the rat's face.

"You've ruined everything." Thegn points his scythe at Jack and growls the words more than he speaks them. "Your people always have."

"My people?" Jack readies himself. There isn't a single part of him that doesn't hurt and he's got no idea how he'd ever defend against any kind of direct attack from the wrinkled old Reaper. But none of that matters. The longer he can keep the old man talking, the more time people have to get out of town. At the very least, Jack is determined to make sure he sees Thegn's attack coming, whatever it is.

Thegn stops pointing and squares his shoulders, lifting himself to his full height. Haughty. His wiry body shows through the torn and tattered holes in his cloak. "Yeah. Your people. Mages, wizards, witches, tinkers, Shadowfold … whatever you call yourselves. There's a natural order to things. A balance. You're agents of chaos. You fuck it up. All you've ever done is make things worse."

A lull is starting to fog over Jack's mind, but he can't contain himself. He can't let that comment stand. "Balance? How exactly is killing off whole towns of people balanced?"

Thegn glowers. His lined and worn face doubles up in a menacing mask of furrows and rotten teeth. "I don't need to explain myself to you boy. Shouldn't need to. How many outposts like this did *your* people destroy? Fucking hypocrite. There are bigger things at play here than the fates of a few thousand people." He nods at Corva, also standing at the ready, but her face is tired. Unfocused. Bits of spit fly from Thegn's mouth as he speaks. "No one can know you exist. No one."

The haze on Jack's mind grows heavier. It would be so nice to lie down and sleep right now. Jack feels his shoulders slacken. But no, he can't let this argument go. "Hypocrite? I was fucking four. I didn't do any of that shit. But at least they had a reason. What's yours? Keeping a secret? Making sure you're still the last of the Four? Selfish fuck. You got no right."

"Selfish? You have no idea what I sacrificed! Everything I cared for. Everything I loved. All for the fragile balance *you* currently enjoy." The Reaper walks closer to Jack. He's only a few steps away. The white rat paces from one of Thegn's shoulders to the other.

Jack can no longer stand. He drops to a knee. A quick glance around shows that nearly everyone else on the rooftop—Corva, her grunts, even Zeke—has done the same. Some have even collapsed entirely.

With effort, he raises his head to look at Thegn's face. "You call this balance?"

Thegn is nearly close enough to touch. He speaks at just over a whisper. "What do you care? I've heard the people here talk about you. Even this girl hosting Durga's spirit." He points his scythe in her direction, slowly extending its blade. "You're as much a nuisance to them as you are to me. They hate you."

If Jack could reach up right now, he'd punch Thegn in his wrinkled old vulture face. Smack that rat in the mouth, too. But Jack can't do any of that; he's so tired. Nonetheless, he manages to keep his chin lifted and stare Death in the face. "Doesn't matter. I stopped you. *We* stopped you. Took out your crows before you could get everyone. Half the town is probably outta your reach by now. And they'll have vid of everything that's happened. Ain't that right, Slim?"

"Well, kinda, kid." Slim's voice on the scratchy comms is sheepish. Almost embarrassed.

"What?" The surprise is enough to momentarily clear some of the fog from Jack's mind. He speaks through his teeth while still staring at the spectrum of expressions flitting over Thegn's face. "Tell me you've been recording; that you're gonna push to the satmesh."

"Oh yeah ... that bit's covered, kid. Streaming it out live. His secret is out. And so is yours." Despite the rough, crackly nature of Slim's voice through the comm kneak, the news allows Jack to relax. Who cares if anyone knows he was from the Shadowfold? He'll be dead soon anyway. However, it's the next thing from Slim that rankles his anxiety. "It's the other thing you said about folks gettin' away. That ... that isn't exactly true."

Confused and groggy, Jack can't piece together what Slim means. He just knows he doesn't like it. All he wants to do is lie down and sleep. He doesn't even have the energy to ask Slim to explain himself.

Somewhere in the blurry haze of Jack's perception, he hears a deep thud and feels a gust of air rush over his head. It's actually enough force to push him facedown onto the ground. Indignant, Jack jumps to his feet. *Who's the asshole that knocked me over?* Just as quickly, he realizes that the fog has lifted from his mind, as well as the others on the rooftop.

Still, who did that?

"Hey, Jackie-Boy. You didn't think we were gonna stand by and let you save our asses, did you?" An air cannon slings from the shoulder of a man with a familiar balding head and annoying toothy grin.

The rasp of Slim's voice sounds over the comm. "Sorry, kid. Lyia changed the plan on us a bit."

Alternating waves of anger, panic, and relief wash over Jack as he sees small crowds of people clustering on the rooftops surrounding him. Not just the militia, but folks from all over Bule are here. Maybe half the town. Some are armed, but a lot are just standing there, hands balled into fists, ready to fight as the sun starts to set across the canyon. Each of them now carries the same signature streak of white in their hairline that he does.

And right there behind him, standing with one foot on a roof's edge with a rebuilt version of his air cannon, is Harris. *Fucking Harris.*

Despite himself, Jack finds himself smiling back.

Putting a Bow on It

Laughter.

That's what Jack hears behind him. The maddened cackle of Death echoes across the canyon, loud but mirthless. Jack turns away from Harris and sees Thegn pushing himself to his feet. The blast from Harris's air cannon was enough to knock him down, but it doesn't look like it hurt him all that much. At least it stopped Caffiel from doing his sleepytime thing. The rat is still on Thegn's shoulder, shaking his head clear.

The old Reaper's nasty, crooked teeth show behind his beard. It's a sneer, more like a wolf baring its teeth than any kind of smile. A cloud of crows collects above them, cawing and screeching as they blot out the last remnants of the weak sunset.

Jack hears Corva's voice yelling over the din, "I thought you said you got half of his crows!"

"I did! There were a fuckin' lot of them!" Jack doesn't take his eyes off Thegn. What are they going to do? The wrinkled old coot isn't going down easily.

Thegn stops laughing as one of the crows lands on the blade of his scythe. All at once, all the crows above them stop making any sound. An eerie silence settles and Thegn speaks easily over the hushed flutter of wings. "At least you've collected everyone in a single spot. Like they're gift wrapped with a nice little bow. This will go much faster now."

In the distance, Jack can hear the unsettling throat-clearing noises of all the remaining Umbrati grunts in town converging on their position. In a matter of seconds, everyone really will be in one place.

An idea starts to form. Jack has no clue how to pull it off, but he has to know Thegn's play first. Whatever it is, it's probably going to involve that rat trying to pull his sandman mojo on everyone at once. That's the first thing they need to stop. Jack touches the red ultrasonic kneak behind his ear and starts murmuring a short message to Zeke. Hopefully the monkey hears him and can make sense of the message. Maybe Slim hears him, too. Maybe.

Thegn notices. "Mumbling is rude, boy."

Jack straightens his back and tries to stand like he's casual. Everything hurts. The painkillers from his chembraid can only do so much. But he needs just a bit more time. Just a few seconds. "I'm just tryin' to figure your play, Wrinkles. We got the numbers, but that didn't matter before. Maybe it don't matter now, either. But before, you weren't fightin' us direct. Before, we weren't fightin' back."

The response from Death is cold and slow. "Oh, I think I'll manage."

A spike extends from Thegn's scythe and skewers the crow sitting upon it. Only, the bird doesn't react. It doesn't even bleed. It just stares forward with its beady little red eyes.

Suddenly, he hears Corva yelp in pain. He turns and sees her holding her head. Her attention is on the grunt that's holding the crow that both he and Thegn used to get back here. Jack follows her gaze and sees the problem. The other half of Thegn's spike is coming out of that crow, impaling the grunt through its head.

Episode Seven: Memory and Sacrifice

The grunt wavers for a moment before crumpling to the ground. The crow in its hands and the spike through its head disintegrate in a puff of ash.

As if on cue, all the crows circling in the sky above them restart their cacophony of squawks and cackles, taunting. All at once, the mob of Bule townsfolk comes to the realization of what's about to rain down upon them from the swarm of crows.

It's now or never.

"Zeke! Now!"

In a single fluid motion with his tail and hands, Zeke uncaps the cylinder Jack gave him earlier, extracts an orange bead, and hurls it at Thegn's head.

The reaper dodges easily with a simple shift of his head, but the bead wasn't intended for him. It zips by Thegn's head and hits Caffiel the rat, broadside. The rat loses grip on Thegn's shoulder and drops to the ground, stunned but still moving.

It's a signal for everyone to act.

Corva and Zeke charge Thegn with Zeke leaping off at the last moment to engage with Caffiel. Thegn sends dozens of spikes from his scythe through the crow sitting on it. They detach and zing as a hail of black arrows from the cloud of crows and ash. Jack turns to Harris and points to the sky. "Aim for the crows!"

Harris nods in understanding as a few people around him fall prey to Thegn's spikes. He shoulders his air cannon and fires it at the sky. All of the other Bule townsfolk with weapons follow his lead and do likewise. A few without weapons grab rocks or chunks of stone and throw them up at the birds.

The spikes are far more accurate than the people are, and the crows more evasive. Harris and the mob hardly have any cover or protection at all. Worse, because she's focused all of her effort on fighting Thegn, Corva seems to be losing her control over the grunts surrounding their rooftop and crowding the alleys below.

First things first. *Gotta help the folks.*

Jack puts his attention on Thegn. He's struggling with Corva, but still holding his own. The crow that was sitting on his scythe circles around as Thegn and Corva fight. Every chance he gets, Thegn sends out another volley of spikes through the bird.

"Slim! Where are your nanobots?" Jack grips the handle on his knife, useless in his hands when everyone else has so much more skill being up close and personal.

Slim's voice crackles in response on the comm kneak. "I'd sent a chunk of them up to that swarm of crows. Why?"

A small string of explosions lights up the dusk sky.

"That's fine, but I need you to focus on that crow right there." Jack points to the one circling over Thegn and Corva's fight. "Take that one out and then stop any others from gettin' close."

"Roger, kid." A blast detonates right next to the crow. The bird falters, but still manages to avoid the majority of its force. Slim curses. "Slippery little rot-eater. Don't worry about me, Jack. I've got this. Go find Lyia."

"Shit. Lyia." Jack had forgotten that she said she was coming out to heal him just before Thegn showed up. He scans the skyline for some sign of her. *Please be okay. Please be okay.*

There she is. Same rooftop as Harris. She's tending to one of the people who'd been speared by one of Thegn's spikes. It's great that she's okay, but there's no way he can get over there to her. The bridge between rooftops is still gone and the horde of grunts is growing larger. Corva's rooftop grunts are starting to struggle to hold them back. He has to stay here. But what is there for him to do?

He can't help keep the grunts back. Even one-on-one with a grunt, he's hardly a match without Corva's help. He looks at the fight between Corva and Thegn, a fight between War and Death. They're moving so quickly, he can barely track them. An explosion arcs above them as one of Slim's nanobots finally catches its crow.

"Gotcha!" Slim's celebration is short-lived though, as another crow swoops in to take the previous one's place. Immediately, Thegn looses another volley of spikes. "Dammit!"

Episode Seven: Memory and Sacrifice

Near Corva's and Thegn's feet, another epic brawl is happening between Zeke and Caffiel. The monkey and rat are a spinning flurry of teeth, claws, and fur, with neither one quite getting a full advantage over the other.

Everyone needs help, but Jack can't help them all. He tightens his grip on his useless knife and feels the collective pain of all his injuries weigh down upon him at the same time. He can hardly help himself.

He casts his eyes downward, and that's when he sees it. The cylinder he gave to Zeke, opened and lying on the ground. A single blue bead has rolled out and sits there, leaned up against the cylinder.

He kneels down and picks up the bead. All the sound and commotion around him seems to have fallen away, muffled and distant. In truth, Jack has never used one of these beads on himself. Too often, he's seen what happens when people do that. He wasn't lying when he told Corva about the consequences.

"Side effects." He hears himself murmur the words, but they sound removed and far-off.

Jack made this bead, put a lot of work into it. There's a tiny little bit of his essence living in that glowing blue capsule. There's a chance that nothing could happen at all. Just energy going home. Of course, there's just as much of a chance of him bursting into flames. He looks up to see how the fight is going. It all seems like it's in slow motion. He imagines the folks he cares about—Zeke, Corva, Slim, Lyia, even Old Man V—stopping whatever it is they're doing to give him a thumbs-up or thumbs-down.

That's not what's happening, though. They're all caught in their individual challenges, trying against all hope to hold their own. And here he is, staring at a little blue bead like there's even a choice.

Reality slams back into full speed as Jack tosses the bead in his mouth and swallows. Having nothing happen wouldn't help at all, about as much as him spontaneously combusting. So Jack finds himself hoping for the lesser of the potential side effects. "Come on, explosive diarrhea!"

The effect is immediate. The first thing Jack notices is his pain, or more specifically, the lack of it. His ribs, his face, his arms, even the itch from his chembraid—all that discomfort is gone, replaced with a soothing tingle that starts in his gut and pushes out to each of his extremities.

The sensation could stop there and Jack would be pretty pleased with the results. At the very least, he wouldn't be hurting anymore. He could jump into any of his friends' fights with renewed vigor and strength. The thing is, however, that it isn't stopping. It's like that bead dropped on a door inside Jack and blew it wide open.

What was a soothing trickle of energy transforms into an avalanche. Jack can't contain it, can't control it. His hands open involuntarily, and he hears his knife clinking to the ground.

Somewhere deep in the back of Jack's mind, he hears a voice. Vardin's voice, maybe? Whoever it is, they're old. Doesn't really matter though. There's a voice in Jack's head and it's talking to him. *Give up on control. Direct it, Jack.*

Jack nods and then immediately feels stupid. How's a voice in his head going to know he's nodding?

Focus, Jack!

Jack shakes the distraction from his mind and pulls himself back to the moment. Whoever the voice is, it's right. There's no point in trying to control this. A renewed pain erupts across the surface of his skin. It feels like he's burning from the inside out. He feels each of the connection points of his chembraid spark and singe. The matrix of kneaks burns behind his ear. Control is futile. Guiding this energy is his only option.

It takes a lot of effort, but Jack manages to put his attention skyward, to the throng of crows swarming in the sky. Thegn's spikes still pelt down with startling precision, almost always finding a target.

Jack feels his body rotate to face the swarm, like he's levitating a hair's distance off the rooftop. He notices that one of the spikes has directed itself toward him. It soars at him, almost faster than he can perceive. By the time he knows it's coming, there's already a hole in his chest. That doesn't seem to matter, though. The gate is already open and Jack has already told the avalanche where to go.

An immense glowing light erupts from Jack and fires up at the cloud of crows. Jack's ears ring with the rush of thousands of voices screaming at the same time. Not a single bird escapes the rush of shadows in the flood of light and energy. Each crow vaporizes in turn, and a haze of ash snows upon Bule.

As Jack feels himself collapse, he's vaguely aware of shouting all around him. Sounds of explosions and gunfire echo in alleyways. The softest of touches as he's caught. The faintest light of stars in the sky.

And then the world is bright and empty again.

"Ya done good, kiddo."

Not Yet

V? That you? The bright, glowing fog of the spiritual plane floods Jack's view.

"That's right."

Vardin is still just a voice, and the sound is softer than Jack remembers. There's no shadow or anything to go with that voice. In fact, there don't seem to be any shadows or spirits at all. *Something's different.*

"You noticed, didja? Never saw them nuggets that excited."

Jack finds his sense of awareness coming back to him, like he's just now remembering everything that happened a few seconds ago. At least, he thinks it was only a few seconds ago.

Am I dead?

"I think, kiddo, that's up to you. You put on an awfully good show out there. You've done more in your short time than most folks will ever do with theirs. No one would think less of you if you called it a day."

I have a choice?

"Sure you do. But only one. We only ever have one choice, Jack. It's the same choice no matter what we do. And we make that choice over and over again. Every time we pull air in our lungs. Every time our hearts beat."

Why are you still here?

"To be honest … I ain't for long. I just needed one last word with ya, whatever you choose."

I can't just stay here with you?

"Heh heh." The old man's voice croaks with laughter. "This place was never meant for permanent storage. More like a holding warehouse, as best as I can figure. So no. Stickin' around isn't an option. Not for either of us."

What about the others? Corva, Zeke, Lyia … everyone?

"All I know is that they ain't here, but that don't mean they didn't come through. But there's only one way to know for certain."

The choice.

"Yeah. And really, it comes down to one question."

What's that?

"Are you done?"

Jack knows the answer, but doesn't think it out loud. It's a more difficult question than it ought to be. Both possible answers to the question are short, but neither is really easy. Each one pulls a planet of gravity along with it.

Vardin already knows Jack's answer, too. Jack isn't sure how, but he knows the old man's presence is fading.

"I'm proud of you, kiddo."

7.14

ESTABLISHMENT

Jack's eyes bolt open with a start, and he immediately tries to sit up.

Big mistake.

Pain radiates across his chest as he feels multiple sets of hands press down upon him. Everything is blurry. There's so much noise. It's impossible to focus on anything. The whole world hurts.

"Shh. Shh. Rest now, Pin. You're through the worst of it."

As Jack lets himself drift off into a deep, restful sleep, he hears another familiar voice. "He *is* through the worst of it, then?"

"Yes."

* * *

The next time Jack wakes up, he moves a lot slower. There's no need, though. The majority of the pain he'd felt has all but faded away. All that remains are flittering traces of it, particularly in and around his chest and head.

He sits up and finds that he has no trouble focusing his vision. He's on the cot in the bar's sub-basement. Corva is in there with him, packing a go-bag. Or, by the looks of things, re-packing a bag that she's emptied and reorganized a few dozen times.

"How long have I been out?" Jack's voice is croaky, frog-like. Like he spent a full day shouting at the top of his lungs. His breath tastes terrible.

His words must've caught Corva by surprise because for half a beat, she jumps and stares at him like he was a statue that suddenly moved. It doesn't last long, though. She's back to stuffing the go-bag. Composure regained. "Good. You're awake."

"Corva. Corva!" It's the second time of Jack saying her name that ultimately stops her. "What's going on? What happened? Are you leaving?"

She finally looks back at his face, the green in her eyes glistening. She's been upset. "Short version?"

"Short is good." Jack swings his legs to the floor. Stiff. "I'll ask questions when things get confusing."

Corva raises an eyebrow, her expression oozing skepticism. "You'll have questions pretty quickly."

"Asshole."

She grins back at Jack. Momentarily, her guard is down and her all-business façade fades away. Just as quickly, though, the smile melts back into seriousness. "Okay. Short version. Whatever it is you did took out all of Thegn's crows and knocked him down a peg or two. You also burned out or surprised enough of the Umbrati raid party to send them trucking."

"Is Thegn—did I kill Death?" Jack knows it's too much to hope for, but he has to ask.

Corva shakes her head and resumes packing, but not really. She's just lifting up bits of gear and putting them back down. "Not even close. But he's on the run. Wanted by both the Umbrati and the Karui. Just like me."

Something is wrong. Corva's holding something back. "What aren't you telling me?"

Jack tries to stand, but falters. Corva is right there to catch him. "Easy there. You burned out a lot of your own tech, too. Slim's been in and out of here trying to patch it, but it's been slow. He's not sure he can fix all of it."

The glistening in Corva's eyes has graduated to full-on tears. "He's got Zeke, Jack. Somehow in all the commotion at the end, Thegn got away. Slithered off like a coward. But he took Zeke with him."

"What? Where'd they go?" Jack tears away from her and starts pacing the room.

"We don't know for sure, but we've got a few leads, thanks to that one."

"What one?"

Jack turns to Corva and follows her gaze to the darkest corner of the room where, perched up on his rear haunches, sits an abnormally large rat.

"You!" Rage bubbles up from somewhere deep inside Jack as he stomps over to Caffiel. He grips the rat by the scruff of his neck and raises the fist of his other hand. "Where's my friend, you shit-eating rodent?"

"Whoa whoa whoa!" Corva steps between Jack and Caffiel. "Put him down, Jack."

"Why?" The word hisses through Jack's teeth.

"Caffiel has been extraordinarily cooperative since Thegn abandoned him here. So put him down." She glances over her shoulder at the rat, who stares at her in indignation. "And you be quiet. You're not helping."

Jack drops the rat and resumes his pacing of the room. "I gotta go talk to … to—"

He pauses. Who does he have to talk to? Zeke's the one he spoke with the most, though admittedly the conversations were pretty one-sided. Old Man V is gone for good now. Lyia is—

"Where's Lyia?" Jack starts to make for the ladder to get up to the bar, but is stopped by Corva's hand on his shoulder.

"Lyia is fine. You'll talk to her in a bit. She and Slim are working with Harris to rebuild Bule. You can try to convince her to come along, but she seemed pretty firm in her decision."

Jack swivels around to face Corva again. "Come along?"

Corva points her head at the foot of the cot where a second go-bag sits. Jack's go-bag. "It's been a pain waiting for you to wake up. Thegn already has a three-day head start. I was giving you until tomorrow to wake up, then I was leaving without you. Lyia said you'd—hey, what are you doing?"

Jack has already picked up his bag and slung it onto his back. Two more steps and he's back at the ladder, face-to-face with Corva. "You coming?"

A flash of excitement shimmers across Corva's face before being replaced with resolve and determination.

"Absolutely."

542

Author's Note

Yay! You made it to the end of Season One! Or, maybe you skipped ahead to the end because you thought this last bit of text would be interesting. That's a bit weird, but you do you.

In any case, thank you for arriving here at the end of the text. This story has been a long time coming and I've been working on it, on and off for ... well, let's just leave it at "long time." Jack, Corva, Zeke, and Thegn have been kicking around in my head for a while and I'm super stoked to have been able to share them with you.

So what next?

Well, I'm working on *Fulcrum: Season Two*. Our friends in this story have some unfinished business to attend to and they want to get to it soon. So Season Two is absolutely coming. If you want to get updates on my progress (and perhaps a couple other updates), head on over to jjvega.com and add yourself to my mailing list. That's the best way to stay in the loop with what's coming next.

As a closing thought, there is one thing that I'd very much appreciate you doing. Where ever you purchased this book, please make it a point to leave a review. Reviews are helpful to other readers and they go a long way toward helping other readers discover books like this one. I don't have a gigantic marketing team for this book; it's just me. So reviews are one of the best ways to bump up the book's visibility.

So yeah, thank you. You're a beautiful, fantastic person, and I can't easily express how much I appreciate you taking the time to read my words.

Take care.

-Jason

Acknowledgements

Oh wow ... I've got so many people to thank. *Fulcrum* wouldn't exist at all without the care, attention, expertise, and patience of a whole bevy of people. First and foremost, I've got to thank my family. They've tolerated hours and hours of me with my head in this story. Heather played the part of sounding board for every plot idea and marketing scheme while we drove down the road. Ender and Zane managed to stay asleep despite the loud clackity-clack of my keyboard at all hours of the day. By their existence, I'm motivated. By their tolerance, I have permission to do this crazy writing thing.

A big thank you needs to go out to Mic Mell of Eleven Coaching. Without his continued encouragement, advice, and occasional mental ass-kicking, I'd probably still be talking about "when I finish *Fulcrum* one day" rather than having it done and available for you to actually read.

I also need to give a special thanks to Courtney Andersson of Elevation Editorial. It takes a special kind of editor to agree to edit a story like this one, and Courtney is exactly that. She took everything I threw at her and helped me mold it into the story that it is now.

Books are judged by their covers, no matter how many times people say to do otherwise. Thanks to the immense skill and talent of Zoe Badini, *Fulcrum* has phenomenal cover art that's dynamic and engaging.

I need to make a special thank-you to Dalai Felinto. It's thanks to his help that Corva's Brazilian Portuguese makes any sense at all.

As I said in the Author Note, this story has been banging around as multiple drafts for a long time. So, I've accosted many a friend and writing group with early versions of the story. The list of critque partners and beta readers is extensive, but I'll do my best to get everyone listed (in alphabetical order): Bassam Kurdali, Beth Carey,

Bob Holcomb, Colleen Diamond, Diane van Gumster, Grace Green, Greg Zaal, John Oakes, Leiza Wyrick Lewis, Lisa Mistry, Mandy Ackley, Mary Helen Witten, Sue Horner, ThomasJ Sullivant, Warren Belfield, and W.H. van Gumster. And I'm sure I've forgotten at least a dozen other people who've been subjected to my ramblings on this story. Thank you all. Seriously. This wouldn't be what it is without you.

My last bit of thanks (finally!) goes to the developers of every open source application that was used to get this story from implausible idea to published story. Inkscape, GIMP, Hugo, Krita, LibreOffice, Mercurial, Pandoc, phpList, Scribus, Sigil, SC-IM, Vim, and VYM. Sometimes the choice to use open source tools can make certain steps in the production process a bit ... trying. But the fact that it's possible represents an incredible amount of freedom that can't be overstated. Thank you, developers for continuing to make these tools available.

J.J. Vega is what happens when your name is Jason J. van Gumster and you try to sound out the initials of that name. Then you turn those sounds into an alter ego for writing exciting adventure stories in a dark and unhappy future. Okay, maybe *you* don't do that, but that's exactly who J.J. Vega is. He lives in someone else's brain, mixing and matching the disparate concepts that float around in there until they coalesce into a story worth committing to words and sentences. It's an odd life, with exposure to the world limited to the wee hours of the morning when most folks are asleep. However, if he does his job right, you'll be awake, too, unable to stop reading the words that were written at that same hour.